Eva comes from a family of storytellers and has been writing her own stories since she could hold a pencil. Growing up in a multicultural neighbourhood in Melbourne, Eva developed her wanderlust and a passion for culture and language. She travelled the world, living in Britain before coming home to Australia to study Anthropology. Wanderlust got the better of her again, so Eva packed up and headed to Papua New Guinea to live and work where she was completely in her element. Eva's passion for the Australian country is born of her large extended family, which is spread out across the land. She volunteers at the local primary schools, teaching writing and working with children to incite a love of books and reading. Eva's books explore relationships, culture, our roles in changing society, love and loss. She loves finding connections with readers over shared experiences.

Also by Eva Scott

Meet Me In Bendigo

First Published 2020
Second Australian Paperback Edition 2021
ISBN 9781867225379

Lonely in Longreach
© 2020 by Eva Scott
Australian Copyright 2020
New Zealand Copyright 2020

This is a work of fiction. Names, characters, places, and incidents are either the product of the author's imagination or are used fictitiously, and any resemblance to actual persons, living or dead, business establishments, events, or locales is entirely coincidental.

Published by
Mira
An imprint of Harlequin Enterprises (Australia) Pty Limited (ABN 47 001 180 918), a subsidiary of HarperCollins Publishers Australia Pty Limited (ABN 36 009 913 517)
Level 13, 201 Elizabeth St
SYDNEY NSW 2000
AUSTRALIA

* and TM (apart from those relating to FSC*) are trademarks of Harlequin Enterprises (Australia) Pty Limited or its corporate affiliates. Trademarks indicated with * are registered in Australia, New Zealand and in other countries.

A catalogue record for this book is available from the National Library of Australia
www.librariesaustralia.nla.gov.au

Printed and bound in Australia by McPherson's Printing Group

Lonely in Longreach

by

Eva Scott

mira

In loving memory of Nora.

CHAPTER ONE

The dry grass crackled like cellophane underfoot as Sam Costello and his son Levi made their way across what passed for the lawn of the Longreach Remembrance Garden. The lively yellow daisies Sam carried seemed to wilt during the short walk from the car. Michelle had loved daisies. She always said their sunny vibe made her feel as if everything would work out okay, even when it became clear it wouldn't.

The trees near the entrance to the cemetery huddled together as if for comfort, drooping in the relentless sun, their leaves limp and lifeless in the still air. The sky arced overhead in a vault of deepest blue without a cloud in sight giving Sam the impression he lived in one of those snow globes, one where someone had swapped out the snow for dust.

Brown, rocky patches made up most of the grounds, testimony to the lack of rain. Drought made water a precious

commodity, not to be wasted on keeping the cemetery green. It wasn't as if the people buried there noticed one way or another.

They picked their way across the barren soil, skirting remembrance plaques and gravestones of the people who had braved this hard, wild country before them. Had their lives been as challenging as his? Had they buried wives, watched their stock die and tried to raise grumpy teenage boys alone? Had they been as clueless as him?

Sam took off his akubra hat and wiped away the bead of sweat heading south on his forehead with the back of his hand. His shirt stuck to his back and he no longer noticed the flies pestering him, automatically waving them away with one hand. The relentless heat made him weary, adding weight to every one of his thirty-eight years.

Levi, at fifteen, seemed impervious to the weather. He wore a t-shirt, frayed at the seams, and a baseball cap that had seen better days. Sam had wanted him to change into something more suitable for the visit to his mother's grave. The fight had proved more than it's worth and Sam had given in, grateful Levi had agreed to come at all.

Levi kicked at what was left of the grass as he slouched across towards the headstone, his hands shoved deep in his pockets and his eyes down. His reluctance oozed out of the pores of his skin, creating the miasma of defiance he'd carried with him all morning.

Sam knew his days having Levi by his side were numbered. Hanging out with your old man got downright embarrassing at about this age, if he remembered right. That's how Sam had felt about his father. No reason to think it would be any different with his son.

Sam sighed and turned down the row where Michelle was buried.

The last seven years had taken their toll, not only on Sam but on the tombstones around them. Weeds pushed their way up through graves once well-tended, loved ones having moved on or simply stopped coming. The relentless sun, wind and rain had worn away the inscriptions on the older stones, the ones dating back to the nineteenth century when people had first come to Longreach to farm.

Michelle's grave at least looked like someone cared. A modest slab of marble with the inscription outlined in gold, the best he could afford at the time. He made sure to keep it neat, bringing fresh flowers as often as he could. Even so, he came less and less. Time had a way of warping the best of intentions.

He didn't know if Levi came at all—he was afraid to ask.

He bent down and removed the dead flowers, the remains of his last offerings. He stepped back, holding the dead in one hand and the living in the other. They stood side by side in silence, father and son, both staring at Michelle's headstone, as if anything had changed since their last visit. A breeze moved across the lawn setting the leaves of a eucalypt tree rustling like a whisper on the wind.

Michelle Marie Costello.
Beloved wife and mother. Sorely missed and never forgotten.
Survived by her husband Sam and son Levi.
1981–2012

Survived was a strong word.

No matter how many times Sam read the inscription it still had the power to deliver a jolt to his heart. An unnecessary reminder that she was gone. He managed to get through

some days without thinking of her at all until the evening when it would be just him and Levi. Then he noticed her absence, as he watched their son, head bent over his homework at the kitchen table. In the way Levi had of flicking his fringe back off his face with a toss of his head, a mirror image of Michelle. Or in those moments when he realised Levi had outgrown his current crop of clothes—things his mother would have noticed long before a trip to the shops became a necessity.

Sam passed the fresh flowers he carried to Levi, who took them without a word. What he would give to know what went on in that boy's head. Levi stepped forward, all gangly arms and legs like a newborn colt, and placed the flowers on his mother's grave without ceremony.

He took off his hat and swept his long, sandy-coloured fringe back with one hand. Sam couldn't be sure if the gesture was one of respect or a simple response to the heat. The boy needed a haircut. Why hadn't he noticed that before now? He made a mental note to take him to the barber in town.

The afternoon filled with the seasonal song of cicadas giving it everything they had like tiny rock gods performing a final encore.

'You know, Dad … I don't think I remember Mum like I used to.' Levi spoke matter-of-factly, his eyes on his mother's gravestone, while daggers plunged into Sam's heart at every word.

Sam swallowed hard, pushing down the lump in his throat so he could speak.

'How do you mean?' He already knew the answer. He had the same problem, although he preferred not to look at it head on.

Beside him Levi shrugged. 'Dunno. When I think of her it's kind of blurry, like I can't see her face properly or something.'

Sam nodded slowly, weighing up his response. There'd been a time when he thought Michelle's face was indelible, carved into his memory so he'd never forget even the tiniest detail. Seven years on, he relied on the photo beside his bed to keep her in focus.

He sighed. 'Time does that to memories.'

He sounded lame and cliched. What else could he say? He wanted to beg Levi to try harder, to not let his mother fade away, to keep her vibrant and alive forever. Sam knew he asked the impossible, especially as Levi had only been eight when she passed.

'Yeah, that's what Maddie says too.' Levi kicked at a stone and sent it scuttling off, scaring a small lizard sunning itself two headstones down the row.

Sam smiled. Maddie had become the font of all knowledge lately. The kids had been best friends since kindergarten, growing even closer when Michelle died as Levi sought comfort and stability. He wondered if Levi's interest in the dirt-bike riding tom-boy would shift as adolescence took hold.

'In this case, she's right,' he said.

'She also said it's about time you started dating again.' Seemingly emboldened by Sam's agreement, Levi turned the conversation in a direction he hadn't seen coming.

'Oh, she did now?' Where the hell was this going?

'Yeah, like it's been way too long and you're not getting any younger.'

'Gee, thanks.' Nothing like a teenage kid to put it all in perspective for you.

'Well, you're not *that* old but if you wait much longer you might find it hard. Competition and all. We *do* live in a small town a million miles from nowhere. I mean, you don't even have a dog anymore.'

'I'll take that on board.' Sam brushed a fly away and crossed his arms, hoping to signal an end to the conversation. His son made him sound a bit pathetic, especially with the jab about the dog. Kevin, their much-loved black and tan kelpie, had passed on two years ago and Sam hadn't found the heart to replace him. There was only so much loss a man could take.

'I won't be around forever, you know,' Levi persisted as he placed his hat back on his head. 'I hate the idea of you rattling around in that house on your own.'

'You thinking of moving out?' Sam turned to face Levi, eyebrows raised.

'Not right away. When I finish school me and Maddie will go to university and then what will you do?' Levi squinted up at the tree above them as if looking for something in its branches. The little boy he'd been shimmered for a moment in the bright sunshine before fading as if he'd never been.

Flashes of Levi's first day of school, Levi catching his first fish in the Thomson River, learning to ride his first dirt bike, a thing so dinky it looked like it could fit on Sam's key chain, ran through Sam's mind. All gone in a flash, to be replaced by this man-child that, on some days, Sam didn't recognise.

'So, a bit of forward planning is what you're advocating here?'

'Yes,' said Levi, the relief in his voice evident. Sam repressed the urge to chuckle, reminded of his frustration with his own father at that age. *Finally, the old man got it.*

This kid could carve up his heart one minute and have him in hysterics the next.

'All I'm saying is you should consider it.'

'The moving out bit?' Sam wanted to make him work for it.

'No,' Levi sighed, 'the dating thing.'

'Okay,' Sam conceded. 'I promise to consider the dating thing on one condition.'

'What's that?' Levi returned his gaze to Sam, his wariness showing in the way he frowned, drawing his brows together until a furrow formed between them. In that moment, he reminded Sam so much of Michelle, he couldn't draw breath.

'That you clean your room and do a load of laundry when we get home.'

'Dad,' Levi groaned, 'you're not taking this seriously. Maddie says single men don't live as long as married men. You're shortening your life, even as we speak.'

Sam reached out and knocked Levi's cap off his head in a playful move, designed to break the tension. He knew what was really going on here.

'Far be it for me to doubt the wisdom of Miss Maddison McRae. I will think about it, okay? Either way, I'm sure I will live a long life, with or without a girlfriend.'

'Okay,' muttered Levi, bending to pick up his hat.

'Come on.' Sam put his arm around his son's shoulders. 'Let's go home and get something to eat.'

'Can I go over to Maddie's? I said I'd go dirt-bike riding with her this afternoon.'

Once upon a time they'd have visited Michelle and then eaten a special lunch together before spending the afternoon

on the couch watching movies. Levi had outgrown the tradition it would seem. Sam's heart weighed heavy in his chest. If only he could keep Levi suspended in time. Not forever, only for a little bit longer.

'Okay,' he said, giving in. 'Only after you've tidied your room and put your laundry on to wash.'

'Come on, Dad. That's eating into valuable riding time. Can't I do it later?'

'What did I just say?'

They continued to argue all the way to the car, their banter tried and tested. Sam had the sense he'd not only left Michelle behind today, but that a part of Levi's childhood had separated and would remain with her, gone forever.

Maddie lay on her bed with her legs stretched up the wall, pondering her poster of Liam Newson, the handsomest actor on her favourite soap, *Getaway Bay*, as she waited for Levi to arrive.

She twirled a long strand of hair and chewed absently on the end as she stared into the greenest eyes God ever gave a man. The way his t-shirt clung to his muscular shoulders—and those arms—gave her fluttery feelings she didn't have a name for. Like Liam generated his own magnetic field and she'd become caught up in it, powerless against his charm.

The relentless dry heat caused the poster to curl up at the edges, robbing the putty adhesive of its grip. The paper had crinkled and the print worn where Maddie had smoothed it flat time and again. She needed another poster, one to sit on the opposite wall so she could see Liam from anywhere in the room.

She'd read a passage in one of her mother's motivational books that you should meditate on your goal for a part of every day. Maddie set the timer on her phone for fifteen minutes and spent them staring as hard as she could at Liam's image, summoning him into her life.

The fact he'd grown up in Longreach only added to her certainty. He'd graduated high school the year before Maddie had started, so they'd never got to meet. If they had, things would be easier. He'd *know*, as well as she did, that they were made for each other.

They were destined to be together, she'd known that from the very first time she'd seen him walk on in an episode of *Getaway Bay*. Her heart had literally stopped in her chest and she'd died, right there on the couch, although no one in her family was savvy enough to notice the gargantuan event taking place right before their eyes. What could you expect, right? Her parents, too old for love, were only concerned with boring town gossip. As if anything ever went on in this place.

No way was she growing up to be them. As soon as she could, she'd apply for university in Sydney. Didn't matter what she studied. Maybe marketing or public relations. Whatever. The point was to get as close to Liam as possible. If a boy from Longreach could make his dreams come true, then so could she.

She'd move to Bondi Beach because that's where he lived. Fate would take care of the details. All she knew was that she had to get to Sydney and let Fate guide her to Liam. He would take one look at her and get struck by lightning too. That's how Fate worked. She imagined Fate as a cool chick with long red hair, wearing a black leather jacket.

According to her mother's book, to make her dreams a reality she had to visualise every detail. Of course, Levi would be with her and they could work to afford the rent while they studied. She could get a job making coffee or something. Levi would love Bondi. Neither of them had ever seen the sea and, as they'd done everything together all their lives, it seemed appropriate they'd have this adventure together too.

The easiest way to get to meet Liam might be through his sister, Alexis, who was in her final year at Maddie's school. The year twelve formal was her in with Alexis, if only Maddie could swing an invite. Then later, when Maddie moved to Sydney, Alexis could introduce her to Liam. The plan could work. She just had to get herself to Sydney.

Her thoughts wandered to Levi and his dad. Levi agreed in principle to Maddie's plan for them, happy to apply for university in Sydney when they reached year twelve, though she was pretty sure he didn't know about her main motivation. There was one giant snag: his reluctance to leave his dad all on his own. He knew he couldn't stay in Longreach forever yet he got all vague about anything more than what university he might apply to in the future. At that point, he'd change the subject. He might think he was being clever, but Maddie had his number. She knew what was going on.

Poor Mr C had lost the love of his life. She knew how he must feel. Imagine if she finally won Liam's heart, only to lose him! Mr C did okay but you could see the damage on him. He needed a girlfriend, someone to distract him and help him get over Mrs C. Someone to make it alright for Levi to leave him and start a life of his own.

The timer on her phone buzzed.

Maddie slipped her ear buds on, selecting her favourite playlist on her iPhone. She did her best thinking when listening to music. She needed to think now, find some way of matching Mr C with the right woman. If there'd been anyone in town suitable he would have found them by now. Fate would have brought them together. Maddie would have to act as Fate's handmaiden, a role she relished.

Wasn't it she who brought together Mr Ozzie, the PE teacher, and Miss Carmichael, the art teacher, last year? A skilful pairing if she did say so herself. It had been *super* obvious they'd be a good match. She'd dropped a few hints, engineered a few accidental meetings. Hadn't been that hard. And look where they were today—happy and in love. All down to her.

Of course, her triumphs had to include the matches she'd made among her friends. Six successful hook-ups so far. She had a talent for this stuff. Mr C might prove to be her biggest challenge, only because he wasn't interested in anyone. No sparks flying anywhere. Which meant she'd have to be clever and think outside of the box. Without Levi there was no way she could afford to live in Bondi, so her whole future happiness with the man of her dreams depended on Levi coming with her.

Nothing could get in the way of her becoming Mrs Liam Newson. Nothing.

She closed her eyes and let the music carry her away.

The afternoon sun slanted in through the kitchen window, highlighting the dust motes' joyful and defiant dance. Why

were dust motes always so damned happy? He needed a cleaner. If he could afford a cleaner. Which he couldn't.

Sam sat at the Tasmanian oak table, scarred with generations of use, and poured two fingers of malt whisky into a glass. He took a moment to hold the glass to the light, enjoying the way the sunlight turned the liquid bright amber, taking pleasure in the small things that remained the same even when all else changed.

As soon as they'd got home Levi had grabbed what passed for a sandwich—two bits of bread with some ham wedged between—and disappeared to change. Probably keen to get away from the tragic air of depression Sam emanated annually, beginning the first week of September and lasting far longer than it should. Couldn't blame the boy. If Sam could get away from himself, he would too.

He stretched out his long legs and settled into the chair. The kitchen carried the debris of breakfast, crumbs littering the bench, dishes in the sink. He'd get to them eventually. Some of those dust motes, done with their dancing, had settled on surfaces. The wide hardwood floorboards, polished a honey colour from generations of Costello feet sliding across them, needed a sweep and a mop. He'd get to that too. Levi could help when he got home. For now, Sam needed to stop and just be.

'Here's to you.' He toasted the picture of Michelle hanging on the wall next to Levi's baby photo and one of their wedding day with the two of them looking like they'd burst with happiness at the future before them.

You couldn't tell by looking at the photo, but Michelle's dress had been dip-dyed pink to imitate Gwen Stefani's famous Dior gown. They'd got married the same year and

Michelle had been a huge fan of No Doubt. He'd kept her CD collection. They'd been packed away somewhere he couldn't see them every day and be reminded of the way she used to dance around the lounge room to *Hey Baby* when she was pregnant with Levi.

Her mother had kept the wedding dress.

Sam threw back the shot, wincing as it burned all the way down.

Silence fell thick and heavy, the whisky taking him down deep to rest within it.

Levi had left for Maddie's an hour ago, his dirt bike sounding like a swarm of angry mosquitoes as he buzzed away in a cloud of palpable relief, heading for the neighbouring farm. He wouldn't be back until dusk.

A long, empty afternoon stretched out before him.

'What do you think?' he asked Michelle. 'Is Miss Maddie right? Should I start dating again?'.

She smiled at him as she always did, her fair hair falling across the sweep of her cheek, a sprinkle of freckles across her nose, caught in a moment of contentment he liked to think he'd contributed to. Him and Levi.

He tried to recall the sound of her voice, the way she laughed. The memories became more and more elusive with every passing year no matter how much he tried to hang on. On the other hand, the sense of emptiness, the space she'd left, only grew more defined with time. The whole thing seemed entirely unfair.

In the absence of an answer, the silence thickened and spread until it went for miles in every direction of his life. He was alone. Levi had a point. When he left to begin his own life, Sam would be living with memories and ghosts.

The prospect made him shiver and he reached for the bottle to pour another drink.

He stopped. Another drink on an empty stomach could only be a bad idea. He needed a feed and some company instead of sitting around feeling sorry for himself.

Sam pushed the chair back. He left the bottle and glass on the table. Might need them later. Plucking his hat from the hook by the back door, he grabbed his car keys. He let the door slam behind him as he went, trapping the ghosts inside.

Saturday afternoon at the Longreach Royal Arms had a reassuring timeless rhythm.

Sam pushed open the heavy dark wooden doors to be met with a blast of air-conditioning and the sound of male laughter, accompanied by the clink of billiard balls. The lingering smell of roast lamb and stale beer, the old pub's signature scent, enveloped him like a hug.

He moved into the bar with the confidence of someone who knew they'd be welcomed. And he was.

'Look who the cat dragged in,' bellowed a bearded, rotund man known as Big Mike.

'Nearly forgotten what you look like it's been so long since we saw you,' said a smaller man as he pocketed the eight ball with a flourish. Craig had been skinny since high school. No matter how much he ate he always looked slightly starved. He embraced Sam, slapping him heartily on the back. What he lacked in size, he made up for with power. Sam staggered under the force of his welcome.

'Good to see you too,' he said. 'Am I too late for a feed?' he asked Sharon, landlady extraordinaire, and keeper of the town's gossip.

'Scraping in by the skin of your teeth, you are,' she replied as she wiped the bar down with a damp rag. 'I'm sure I can find something for you if you'd like a couple of slices of lamb and some veg.'

'As long as you have mint sauce, I'm good to go.' Already he felt more cheerful, as if someone had thrown a switch and a light had gone on inside the darkest part of him.

'What have you been doing with yourself?' Big Mike hoisted himself up on a stool by the bar, his billiard game momentarily forgotten.

'Bit of this and that. Working around the farm, you know the sort of thing.' Sam shrugged. His uncomplicated life, full of farm tasks and Levi-related activities, left no time for interesting hobbies or anything resembling a social life.

'Yeah, me too.' Craig joined them, hitching up his jeans, having no hips at all to catch their downward slide. 'Saturday arvos here at the pub is what passes for fun these days.'

'You mean it's the only time your wife will let you out on your own.' Big Mike laughed. 'And only because you're in my tender care.'

'I'm not sure that's how she puts it,' said Craig. 'Another beer, Sharon, when you have a moment. Can I get you anything?' he asked Sam.

'Whatever you're having will be fine,' Sam said. The creeping loneliness began to recede as if he'd taken medicine for it. He began to wonder if he'd imagined its intensity.

'How's Levi?' asked Big Mike.

'Good for a fifteen-year-old who thinks he knows everything.' Sam occupied the last stool, resting his elbows on the counter. Sharon had renovated the place in recent times and he took the panels of corrugated iron around the bar and on the wall as her nod to modernity. Outback style.

She deposited a plate piled high with roast lamb and oven baked vegetables, accompanied by an ice-cold beer to wash it down.

'Thank you,' he said as he speared a crispy potato, his mouth watering in anticipation. His potatoes never turned out this way.

Big Mike nodded in sympathy. 'Try living with a houseful of teenage girls. Not only do they know everything, they know everything you do is wrong. Hence me being here. Get some peace and quiet. Top up my testosterone levels.'

'How's Wendy?' Sam asked after Big Mike's wife. They'd all gone to high school together and Big Mike had never stood a chance.

'You know Wendy. Would have made an excellent army general.'

'And Veronica?' Craig's wife had been a good friend to Michelle.

'Taking to quilting like it's crack. Driving me nuts. Every surface in the house has a piece of half-finished quilting draped over it.' Craig took a swig of his beer and sighed with satisfaction. 'Can't complain though. Better than the scrapbooking phase. Talk about a challenging time.'

'Remember that phase. Nightmare,' said Big Mike.

The three men sat and nodded together, remembering Veronica and her scrapbooking mania—glue, glitter and little stickers had infiltrated every part of the house and stuck

to visitors in very odd places. All the chairs in the place had contained a work in progress and woe betide anyone who sat on one by accident. It had been a trying time.

Sam ate his meal meditatively while he listened to the boys talk. He'd known them all his life. They'd been through everything together—school, first loves, heartbreak, losing parents, birth of children and, of course, Michelle's illness and death.

'Veronica said the other day we ought to get you over for dinner,' said Craig.

'Sounds good,' said Sam. Veronica married the right man. She held a legendary status in the community for the quality of her cooking. A lesser man would have ballooned in size, but not Craig. As nothing stuck to his ribs, he could enjoy his wife's delectable food to both their hearts' content.

'In the interests of full disclosure, I feel compelled to let you know she's wanting to set you up with her cousin.' Craig lowered his voice and looked around the bar as if someone might overhear and report his indiscretion.

'Really? What's she like?' asked Big Mike with enthusiasm. Sam and Craig turned to look at him. 'I'm only curious,' he said quickly. 'I'm a happily married man.'

'Funny you should mention dating,' said Sam. He finished the last bit of his lunch and stacked his knife and fork on the plate, his stomach pleasantly full. 'Levi reckons I ought to get out there and find someone. Says I've been single long enough. Or at least Maddie says that.'

'Well, I hate to publicly agree with a teenage girl, but she's right,' said Big Mike. 'Michelle was one of a kind, we all know that, but it's time to get back in the saddle. You should be capitalising on that show. What's it called?' Big

Mike snapped his fingers as if to capture the name from out of thin air. 'That's it: *Farmer Goes a Courting*. You're a farmer, time to get courting.'

'Don't tell me you watch reality television?' Sam snorted into his beer. 'You've got two chances of getting me on that show, Buckley's and none.'

'You can't replace Michelle,' said Craig, placing his hand on Sam's shoulder. 'We all loved her too and she wouldn't have wanted to see you this way.'

What way? He was the same old Sam, maybe a little slower and a little sadder, but the same. How did they see him?

'All crumpled up and folded in on yourself,' said Craig as if he'd read his mind. 'Like one of Veronica's scrapbook projects.'

'And let's not forget you haven't been laid in seven years,' said Big Mike, as he scratched his rather majestic beer belly.

'How do you know? I might have been.' Sam bristled for reasons he couldn't identify. Call it a response to small town mentality. Everyone knew your business, or at least thought they did. He might have snuck out of town for a rendezvous somewhere. Not likely, but possible.

'Come on, mate,' said Big Mike. 'We'd have known if you had.'

'Or at least our wives would have,' chortled Craig, sending both men off into gales of laughter.

Sam took their ribbing in good humour. They were right. He hadn't been laid since Michelle died. The very thought of sleeping with another woman made him feel as if he were committing adultery. Even he couldn't deny that seemed ridiculous after so many years. And Craig had a point.

Michelle had made him promise he wouldn't wallow too long after she died. Only she hadn't said how long was too long.

'There's a cute new teacher at the high school. On her country service,' said Big Mike. 'Might be a goer.' He nudged Sam in the ribs and wiggled his eyebrows. 'I could get one of my girls to check out her availability, like an undercover operation or something.'

'A love spy,' said Craig. 'What your daughters can't find out I'm sure Veronica will know. She's up to her armpits with the P&C.'

Sam shook the uncomfortable image of Veronica's armpits out of his head. He picked up his beer and sipped at it thoughtfully. Maybe Levi had a point and it was time he got back out there again. Wouldn't hurt to consider his options. He hadn't been on a date for over a decade. A harmless outing with Veronica's cousin or the new high school teacher might be what he needed.

CHAPTER TWO

'Do they know I'm vegan?' Greg struggled to carry his over-night bag as well as the two shopping bags filled with gifts for Sarah's extended family. It wasn't a lack of strength that caused him problems. Quite the opposite. He had become so muscle-bound he had to have his clothes custom-made to fit.

'Don't worry, I told Mum.' Sarah held open the gate to the Lewis family home as she juggled her own bags. Greg crab-stepped through, banging the presents on the post as he went. 'Careful!' she said.

Greg stopped and looked mournfully at Sarah. 'I want to make a good impression.' There was something tragic about this big, beautiful man laden with shopping bags and expectations that tugged at her heart.

She smiled and leaned in to kiss him gently on his lips. 'I know,' she said. 'What's not to love, right? It will all be fine.' She spoke with more confidence than she felt.

The gate slammed shut behind them and Sarah turned to survey the house. The elegant Victorian home, with its wide sweeping veranda and manicured gardens, looked the picture of serenity and civilisation. Immaculately clipped hedges lined the perimeter. Her mother always said: everything has a place and everything in its place—sheer perfection. If it had been an Airbnb you'd booked for the weekend, you'd have been delighted when you pulled up out the front.

Sarah knew better. Woe betide anyone fooled by the exterior. Chaos lay within. The minute that front door opened they would be sucked into the vortex of madness that was her family.

'Have you said anything about … you know?' Greg spoke *sotto voce*, not realising the walls had ears. When they'd been kids, her and her brother, Hayden, had suspected their mother had the house bugged. She knew *everything* in a spooky CIA kind of way.

Sarah noticed a curtain twitch at the enormous picture window beside the door. No sneaking up to this establishment.

'Not a thing. I wanted it to be a surprise.' She picked up the brass knocker and let it fall against the door. The bang echoed through the house. Her mother hated that knocker which only made Sarah and Hayden want to use it more.

The door flung open immediately, as if there had been someone stationed on the other side, waiting.

'Sarah!' Her mother appeared in a crisp floral dress, her hair perfect in an Iron-Lady sort of way. Eleanor Lewis had been a devotee of the hot roller and Elnett Satin hairspray since the 1970s when she'd borrowed her mother's. She'd never looked back, swapping the loose cheerleader curls of

the seventies for the big bouffant of the eighties with perfect ease. And there she'd stayed for the past thirty years. Hayden called it her security hair.

'Mum!' Sarah put her bags down to accept a hug. 'Is everyone here?'

'Of course they are, dear. No one would miss meeting your man.' Eleanor stepped back and looked over Sarah's shoulder. 'Is this him?' As if Sarah may have swapped Greg out for someone else on the way over.

'Mum. Let me introduce you to Greg.' Sarah stood aside and made a grand sweeping gesture. 'Greg, this is my mother.'

Greg had abandoned his bags and wiped his hands on his shorts before holding one out. 'Pleased to meet you, Mrs Lewis.'

'Oh, do call me Eleanor.' Sarah's mother touched her dark, structured hair with one hand while taking Greg's with the other. 'Goodness, you are strong,' Eleanor simpered, patting Greg's biceps while Sarah tried to control the urge to roll her eyes.

'Come inside, the two of you. Everyone is dying to meet you, Greg,' Eleanor called over her shoulder as she led them inside.

He dutifully followed her mother while Sarah brought the bags in off the front veranda and shut the door. She heard the dining room erupt into cries of greeting as the family devoured poor Greg whole. He had no idea what he was getting himself into.

She sighed and followed, already regretting her decision to introduce him to everyone all at once. What had she been thinking? The last boyfriend she'd done that to had

never called her again. With good reason. She wouldn't have called her either. The poor man had been subjected to a long and drawn out description of Grandpa's recent bowel surgery, a subject the family all had an opinion on. Nothing was sacred.

Eleanor had cycled through the introductions by the time Sarah entered the room. The family looked at Greg expectantly, as if he was there to do a PowerPoint presentation on how to manage their retirement fund. The poor man looked like a deer caught in headlights as he stood in the formal dining room, taking in the heavy damask curtains, the framed portraits of Lewis ancestors and the ridiculous crystal chandelier her mother had insisted hanging over the table. Total overkill.

Everyone was already seated, claiming their spots well ahead of lunch. Competition for food could be fierce and the Lewis family had honed their skills over generations. A clan lunch wasn't just a family gathering, it was a sport.

She took him by the arm and led him to an empty chair between her brother and her aunt. Possibly the safest place for him.

'Hey, sis.' Hayden kissed her on the cheek as Greg sat down. 'Alright?' He cocked an eyebrow and gave a nod in Eleanor's direction, who was too busy placing the gravy in exactly the right position on the table to notice. His dark hair tumbled across his forehead in a way designed to send their mother batty.

'Alright,' she said, screwing up her nose in their ancient childhood semaphore for *not really*.

'Ah,' he said, his sherry eyes filling with empathy. If anyone at the table had her back, it would be Hayden. Three

years her junior, he'd scandalised the family by doing whatever he pleased with his life and not following the sensible path laid out for him by generations of Lewises before him. She could count on him.

With Greg settled, taking up more than his allocated share of the table with his broad shoulders, Sarah skipped around to the other side of the table to sit between Uncle Lance and Grandma.

'What a nice-looking man,' Grandma said, patting her hand. 'Very beef biscuit.'

'I think you mean beef cake, Grandma,' said Hayden. 'Would you like some water, Greg?' He began to pour a glass without waiting for an answer.

'Cake, biscuits—he looks yummy all the same,' sniffed Grandma as she unfolded her linen napkin with a snap.

'Can't say stuff like that anymore, Mum,' said Sarah's father, Adam. 'Not politically correct. Anyone want a Scotch before lunch?' He stood up, empty glass in hand.

'No one wants a Scotch before lunch, Adam. Please sit down,' said Eleanor as she delivered a basket of warm rolls to the table. Her husband dutifully obeyed, compensating himself with a roll instead, slicing it open carefully with his butter knife.

'I once knew a Scotsman with muscles like yours,' said Grandpa. His bushy white eyebrows dominated his face like two aged caterpillars squaring up for a fight.

'Dad said Scotch not Scots,' said Hayden. He winked at Sarah.

'What difference does it make? Muscles are muscles.' Grandpa grabbed a roll and broke it open with vigour.

'I like mussels when they're done in a cream sauce,' said Aunt Lily with a dreamy far-away look in her eyes. Her hair, a scaled down version of her sister's, trembled with the power of the memory. 'We had them that time, Lance, where were we?'

'Venice. We were in Venice,' said Uncle Lance. 'Bet Greg here doesn't eat cream.' He patted his own stomach to emphasise the point, his preference for the good life evident beneath his slightly too-small shirt.

'I'm lactose intolerant,' said Greg. 'I can't eat dairy.'

'Really?' said Eleanor. 'What a shame. We've got a lovely pavlova for dessert. Loads of cream. Are you sure you won't have some?'

'I'm actually vegan,' said Greg in the humble-brag way of his. Sarah felt a prickle of annoyance. Why did he always feel the need to tell everyone?

'Is that so?' said Grandpa, through a mouthful of bread roll. 'Pavlova has loads of fruit on it. They count as vegetables.'

'I think it's the cream that's the issue,' said Hayden. 'Animal product *and* full of lactose.'

'No cheese or anything?' asked Aunt Lily, a look of horror on her face.

'What's life without cheese, hey, Greg?' Uncle Lance winked as if he thought Greg might be hiding a secret cheese addiction.

'Well—' Greg began as if he intended to answer the question.

'Surely you can manage a bit of pavlova without the cream,' said Eleanor.

'Pavlova is made from eggs and sugar,' Hayden pointed out.

'Of course it is,' said Grandma crossly, 'otherwise it wouldn't be a pavlova. Everyone knows that.'

'Vegans don't eat eggs,' said Hayden. He met Sarah's eyes and grinned.

The beginning of a headache set up in the base of her skull. Her brother could enjoy himself less at her expense. The food wasn't even on the table and they were slicing Greg up.

'I don't eat sugar either.' Greg smiled uncertainly before flexing one impressive bicep. 'Body is a temple, and all that.'

'A temple?' Grandpa said. 'Did the boy say he's religious?' He looked around the table for confirmation.

'Not unless he worships at the gym,' snorted Adam. 'I miss those days. When I was a young man I had a physique rather like yours ...'

Eleanor returned from the kitchen and placed some steamed green beans on the table. She snapped the tea towel she carried at her husband's shoulder. 'You did not, Adam Lewis. You were flat out carrying me over the threshold when we got married.'

'In my defence I was nursing a football injury at the time,' said Adam, flushing red. 'Did my cruciate ligament, left knee. Excruciating.' He leaned in a little and put his hand up to cover his mouth. 'And someone wasn't exactly svelte, if you know what I mean.'

'I heard that,' Eleanor called from the kitchen.

'I've had a knee replacement,' said Grandpa. 'Not a big deal. Don't know what you're on about.'

'I bet Greg has nice knees,' said Grandma.

'Yes, show us your knees then, Greg,' said Uncle Lance, proceeding to laugh overly loud at his own joke.

Greg looked at Sarah with fear in his eyes, unsure what he was supposed to do next.

'I say we take a good look at Greg's knees *after* lunch.' Hayden jumped in to save the day. 'In fact, I propose a sexiest knee competition.'

'Should have got the surgeon to give me a knee lift while he was at it,' said Grandpa.

'Can you do that?' asked Aunt Lily. 'Is that a thing? My knees are getting a little saggy. No one told me knees did that as you get older.'

'They can lift anything these days,' said Grandma. 'Breast lift, tummy tuck, arse—'

'Even Elle McPherson has saggy knees,' said Aunt Lily.

'LAMB!' roared Eleanor, causing everyone to duck as she entered the room carrying a silver carving tray with an enormous leg of lamb upon it, placing it on the table like a prize.

'Would you like some lamb, Greg?' she asked as she rolled up her sleeves and took up the carving knife like she meant business.

'I'm a vegan,' Greg said weakly.

'Lambs eat vegetables and you eat the lamb. That's the order of things,' said Grandpa. 'I'll have his lamb.' He shoved his empty plate in Eleanor's direction.

'Don't worry,' said Hayden quietly as the table erupted into cries for more meat and requests for the gravy or various vegetables. 'Have my potatoes. They're delicious.' He shovelled them over to Greg's plate and Sarah gave him a grateful smile.

This was going to be a very long afternoon.

✉

'Here you are.' Sarah found Hayden sitting outside on an upturned ceramic flowerpot against the garden shed smoking what looked and smelled suspiciously like a joint.

He held it out to her. 'Want some?'

She sighed and pulled up a flowerpot of her own. 'What I wouldn't give. If Greg smells it on me I'll get lectured all the way home about how the body ...'

'... is a temple,' they finished together.

'I can't get through a family lunch without one,' Hayden said, and he took another toke, blowing the smoke out in a long lazy string. They watched it disperse against the clear blue sky in companionable silence.

'What gives with Greg? The whole body-builder-vegan vibe doesn't seem like your kind of thing.' Hayden stretched out his long legs and settled his back against the potting shed.

Sarah sighed. 'He read how Chris Hemsworth trained for the last Thor movie on an entirely vegan diet.' She leaned back against the shed, the warmth of the sun on her upturned face. 'Thought he'd try it.'

'Quite the trendsetter.'

'I shouldn't have brought him. I told Mother Greg's vegan and she goes and makes lamb and pavlova.' Sarah laughed despite the sinking feeling in her stomach this whole visit had been a tactical error on her behalf.

'What did you expect? You've got generations of sensible, conservative accountants and quantity surveyors, all born and bred in the twentieth century and you ...'

'Bring a lactose-intolerant, sugar-free, gluten-free body-building vegan to dinner.'

'Didn't know about the gluten thing,' said Hayden. 'A man of many facets.'

She nudged him. 'Be kind. He's a lovely guy really. Very sweet and thoughtful.'

'And with excellent knees.'

'Yes, well, winning the inaugural Lewis Sexiest Knee contest is bound to boost his confidence. I can't believe you suggested it.' Sarah shook her head.

'What was I supposed to do? I had to throw the drowning man a lifeline. Just as well he went on to win. Put us all to shame.' Hayden threw the butt on the ground and scrunched it out underfoot. 'Do you think Aunt Lily will *really* go and have her knees lifted?'

'Anything is possible.' Sarah rested her elbows on her knees and put her chin in her hand, admiring her mother's perfectly cultivated lawn bordered by beds of pink and white impatiens. 'How are you?'

Hayden shrugged. 'Well enough, I suppose. I'm happy, if that's what you mean.'

'That will do me fine.' The black sheep of the family, her brother caused her more worry than either of them would like.

'And you?' His tone, while light, suggested he suspected the truth.

'I feel as if I'm stuck at a bit of a crossroad,' she said.

'Ah! The dreaded mid-life crisis.'

'Steady on, I'm only thirty-five.' When had thirty-five become the new forty?

'And unmarried.' He looked sideways at her.

'Don't you start with that misogynist rubbish. Did you know a bloke at work actually asked what's wrong with me because I'm over thirty and unmarried? The cheek.' Sarah blew out a lungful of air as if she could be rid of the insult so easily.

'Barbarian. Bet he was older.'

'Yes, he was. How did you know?'

'Such a baby boomer thing to say. Is that what drove you into the arms of Beef Biscuit?'

Sarah laughed. 'You make him sound like a dog snack.'

'If the leash fits.' He shrugged. 'I'm not sure I get the attraction.'

'Can I ask some advice?' Sarah leaned all the way forward, hunched over as if what she had to say needed to be physically squeezed out of her. Something had been casting long shadows from the edge of her consciousness for weeks and it had finally begun to come into focus.

'Hold on a minute.' Hayden held up his hand to stop her speaking. 'You're confused about my role as a brother. Advice comes from *older* brothers. I am the *younger* brother, therefore I am only good for practical jokes, rude comments about relatives and recreational drugs.'

She shoved him playfully. 'Come on, I'm serious.'

'So is she.' He nodded towards Eleanor striding purposefully across the lawn towards them. Hayden kicked the butt of his joint into the grass.

'Darlings, *what* are you doing out here? Greg says he's got something important to tell us and you must come inside at once, so he can do so.'

They both stood up.

'Don't tell me.' Hayden brushed down his jeans. He looked from his mother to Sarah. 'He's reconsidering his vegan status.'

'How can a grown man go about not eating meat and cheese?' Eleanor shook her head, her hair moving as one. 'Did you know he doesn't eat pasta either? So new age. Come

along, dears.' She linked her arms with each of her children and dragged them with her back towards the house, carrying them on a cloud of Red Door perfume.

'This had better be good,' Hayden said to Sarah behind their mother's back.

'Brace yourself, it's going to be completely underwhelming.'

CHAPTER THREE

'Did you talk to your dad?' Maddie McRae sat curled up on her bed watching a movie she'd downloaded on her laptop. Her fair hair, damp from the shower, curled softly around her face. She wore a black and red oversized flannel shirt and a pair of shorts.

They'd spent the afternoon riding their trail bikes over makeshift jumps and dusty tracks laid out in a back paddock of the McRae farm. They'd come back so dirty Mrs McRae had made Levi change into some of Mr McRae's old clothes before she'd let him in the house.

'Exactly like you said.' Levi sat on the corner of the bed balancing a plate of newly baked chocolate chip cookies on his knee. His stomach growled. The ham sandwich he'd made at home barely sustained him on the ride over to Maddie's, let alone during the afternoon riding session.

Guilt tugged at him over abandoning his dad and not having lunch with him like they did every year since his mum died. Levi couldn't stand to see his dad sad when he could do nothing about it. Being with him only made Levi sadder and the way he saw it, no point the two of them being miserable.

'And?' Maddie held out her hand for a cookie without taking her eyes off the screen. Her bedroom sat completely at odds with the girl he knew. Pink throw cushions, lacy bedspread, a dresser filled with makeup he never saw her wear and an enormous poster of some floppy-haired boy band next to one of that Newson guy who was now on some TV show he could never remember the name of. That side of her remained a mystery to him.

'Who knows?' Levi replied through a mouthful of cookie. They were *so* good. Still warm from the oven, the little chocolatey bits were all melty. 'Every year it's the same thing. He gets depressed the day before we go to the cemetery. We go to the cemetery and he gets all sad and emotional. The rest of the week is a total blast because he's back to depressed again.'

'We need to help him.'

'How exactly? We're, like, fifteen, living in the middle of nowhere. Don't know if you noticed, but there's not that many eligible old people around here.' He licked the chocolate off his fingers and contemplated a second cookie.

'It doesn't have to be someone from around here.' Maddie sat up straight and hooked her fair hair behind her ears. 'Look at this,' she said as she rewound the movie she'd been watching.

'What's this?' He never paid attention to anything Maddie watched. Mostly she was into *Keeping Up with the Kardashians*, totally pointless from his perspective. All those enormous, rubbery lips scared him, gave him nightmares about being chased by puffer fish.

'It's an old movie Mum loves from when she was a little girl. She made me watch it with her and I think it might have the solution to our problem.' She squinted at the screen.

'I keep telling you, you need glasses,' he said, earning a pillow in the head for his concern. 'Hey! Mind the cookies.'

'Pay attention,' she said as she patted the space next to her on the bed.

Levi scooted up, careful to sit far enough apart so they didn't come into contact by accident. Lately he'd been feeling odd around Maddie whenever they touched, all fizzy and weird, a little like the time he'd put his tongue on the end of a brand-new 9-volt battery.

'This is *Sleepless in Seattle*. It's, like, really old from back in the days when they didn't have mobile phones or the internet or anything.'

'Analogue,' he said sagely. 'Can you imagine living like that?' Levi shook his head. 'Primitive, man.'

'I know, right? Anyways … watch this bit.' Maddie pushed play and forced Levi to sit through a chunk of romantic rubbish he barely understood. A widower—got that. A little boy wanting his dad to be happy—totally got that. The bit about the woman and the radio show confused him. Who'd travel across the country for someone they hadn't even *seen*?

'What do you think?' Finally, she pushed pause and turned to him, all lit up like she'd discovered electricity or something.

'I dunno,' he mumbled, afraid whatever he said would be the wrong thing. Girls could be tricky.

She smacked him over the head with a pillow sporting a kitten wearing a crown.

'Okay, okay.' He held his hands up to ward off the blows. 'Did you clock those desktops? They were, like, *huge*. And the screen display, what was with that? How did those people cope?'

'Pay attention, would you. It's all about the story. The boy in the movie goes on the radio and tells everyone his dad needs a girlfriend and then women from all over the country write in. The boy picks his favourite and writes back. The girl thinks the letters are from the dad—blah blah blah— and the dad finally meets the girl and falls in love with her. Ta dah! HEA.'

Levi blinked. 'What is a HEA?'

'Happy ever after of course. Everyone knows that.'

'Okay, you're saying we need to go on the radio and advertise for someone for Dad.' Levi picked up another cookie and ate it as he mulled over the idea. 'Not sure local radio has much impact.'

'No, dummy.' She wacked him with the pillow again. 'I'm saying we set up an account with an online dating site and see who responds. Then we pick someone we like and write back.'

'I did *not* get that.' Levi shook his head. Somehow Maddie seemed to always be four steps ahead of him.

'The way I see it,' she said, jumping off the bed in her excitement, 'is the whole *Farmer Goes a Courting* TV show

is huge, right?' He nodded. 'Your dad is a farmer and they're trending right now. We get a hot photo of him and write up a profile. I reckon we'll get plenty of ladies wanting a piece of that action.'

'It's totally weird when you talk about my dad that way.'

'Sorry, I mean he's not that bad looking for an old dude. Can you get a photo of him?' She sat back down on the bed. 'Hey, you ate the last cookie.'

Levi shrugged. 'You snooze, you lose. What kind of photo? Please don't say one where he's half naked or something.'

Maddie laughed, and the sound made Levi tingle in a way that was not entirely uncomfortable.

'No, a regular picture is fine. Make sure his face can be seen clearly and he looks hot.'

'How do I tell if my dad looks hot? He's my dad.' The whole thing seemed like a bad idea, likely to end in humili-ation and pain—probably his.

'Come on, I'll help you. We can go over to your place and tell him we're doing a photographic project on … men of the land. Or making a calendar for next year for charity or something. I dunno, we'll work it out. Either way we'll get a photo good enough to put up online. Then we can work on his profile.'

Levi hunched his shoulders against the trouble he could feel coming his way.

'Besides, you can't go to university in Sydney or some-where and leave him by himself all depressed and stuff. What do you reckon?'

She had a point. Even though they didn't graduate for two more years, they'd planned a future where they both went to university on the coast, as far away from this town

as possible. How could he go and have fun if he knew his dad was moping about all alone with a broken heart? What if the depression really took a hold on him and something bad happened? Maddie was right. They needed to hook his dad up with something solid before they could go anywhere.

Despite the logic of it all, a little voice in the back of his head told him not to do this. Yet when Maddie looked at him that way with her cheeks all flushed and her eyes sparkling he couldn't manage a no. 'Sure, why not,' he heard himself say. 'What can go wrong?'

Sam lay on his bed, drowsy from a big feed and a few too many beers. Coming home to an empty house had reinforced his sense of loneliness, something an afternoon at the pub with his friends had managed to assuage temporarily. Now it was back with a vengeance.

He'd had another couple of beers sitting on the veranda as the wind made little dust eddies in the field, watching the sky for the rain that never came and trying not to think of Michelle.

Scraps of clouds skittered across the sky, trailing their reflections in the rows of solar panels standing to attention in the field nearest the house. Sam watched them evaporate in the hot air, his thoughts disappearing with them. The solar array comforted him in a weird way, like they watched over him and Levi, standing guard against an uncertain future. The merino sheep liked to laze in the shade of the solar panels and a handful regarded him now. One in particular looked down its long nose with what appeared to be judgement, like

it knew he'd been drinking and thoroughly disapproved. He resisted the childish urge to poke his tongue out at it.

By late afternoon, he realised too late that he'd overdone it. The weekend had become a reminder of pain and struggle, of how far he *hadn't* come since Michelle died. The silence coiled around him like thick, heavy ropes, corralling his life to one of work and parental duties. He had no joy, little laughter and zero sex.

Now he stared at the bedroom ceiling with narrow eyes, sensing himself drifting, the lines blurring between reality and dream. The overhead fan turned in lazy circles, hypnotic in its slightly wobbly motion. The dusky green walls gave the room a sense of calm, as though he were in a forest under a canopy of trees, rather than perched on the edge of the outback.

Sam kicked his boots off, hearing each one hit the floor with a thump. He'd lie here for a bit and listen to the old farmhouse settle under the afternoon sun. Just until Levi got home from the McRaes' place.

'You should sleep.' He often heard her voice before he drifted off. The one true memory he had left.

'I'm okay,' he muttered. 'Stay with me.' He patted the empty side of the bed, even though he knew he was alone, yearning to feel the warmth of her next to him.

'I'm worried about you,' she said softly, her voice sending a thousand tiny electric currents through his body. 'I don't like to see you this sad.'

'Can't help it.' People always acted like he had some control over his misery. He'd turn it off if he could, but he was powerless against it.

'You could go out and have some fun for a start. Might help.' He thought he could feel the touch of her fingers trailing along the length of his arm. 'Why not go on a date?'

'You been talking to Big Mike and Craig?' Seemed like his love life, or lack thereof, was the topic of the day.

She laughed, warm and throaty, causing a shaft of longing to pierce his heart. 'They've got a point. You should be loved by someone who can take care of you like I would take care of you. I told you not to wallow for long.'

'Yes, you did.' He nodded, the back of his head rubbing against the pillow. 'You neglected to say how long I *could* wallow, so I've kept going. It's my hobby.'

'That's the most ridiculous thing I've ever heard you say.' Michelle never did take any of his bullshit. 'I want you to pull yourself together and go out and find love. It's not right that a man of your quality should lock himself away.'

'But I love you.'

'And I love you. I'll always be here, you know that. But you need to move on with your life and let me go.'

'Don't want to.' He sounded like a stubborn three-year-old. Lord knew, he *felt* like a stubborn toddler as tears welled behind his closed eyes.

'You need to do it for Levi as much as yourself. How do you think he feels seeing his dad lost and alone?'

Guilt clutched Sam's stomach. Michelle had a point. Levi deserved better from him. He'd been locked in his pain for so long he didn't know if he could find the way out. They had a good relationship, him and his boy, although he hadn't exactly been a stellar example of how to be happy in this world. Neutral had been the best he could muster over the last few years.

'Try, for me,' she said as if she could read his thoughts. Of course, she could, she was a ghost, or a figment of his imagination. Or something. 'Try and sleep now.' Before he let sleep claim him, he could swear he felt the sensation of her kiss featherlight against his cheek.

'Okay,' he managed before he drifted off.

CHAPTER FOUR

'Hurry up, it's about to start,' Fiona, Sarah's best friend and flatmate, called from their well-worn purple velvet couch. 'Have I told you how happy I am they've brought this show back.' She snuggled into the overstuffed cushions with an enormous bowl of popcorn balanced on her lap.

'How do I look?' Sarah slid across the polished floorboards of the lounge room in her pink fluffy bed socks.

'OMG!' Fiona choked on a fistful of popcorn, coughing so hard her face turned an alarming shade of red.

'Are you okay?' Sarah passed her a glass of wine as Fiona struggled to gain her composure. She took a decent slug of sauvignon blanc.

'That's your mother's wedding dress? Eleanor prim-and-proper-is-my-middle-name Lewis?' Tears streamed down Fiona's face and her voice sounded like she'd come down with instant laryngitis. Sarah couldn't be sure it was the

result of nearly choking, or at the sight of her mother's wedding dress.

She did a little twirl; the tulle skirt spun out around her hips like a limp tutu. 'Greg nearly had a fit when he saw it yesterday.'

'Because you were only announcing your intent to *think* about getting married and the wedding dress made it all too real? Or does he have an aversion to eighties high fashion?' Fiona took another gulp of wine to settle her throat. 'Did he see it as parental pressure?'

'No, none of the above. Whatever mothball stuff Mum had used to store the dress gave Greg hives.' Sarah flopped on the couch not bothering to change. This could be the only time she would ever wear the dress and she wanted to enjoy every minute of it.

'You're kidding.' Fiona laughed. 'I can see it now.' She leaned in a little closer and wrinkled up her nose. 'I can smell it now.'

'Stop laughing,' Sarah said. 'It was a horrible end to a very trying day. He came up in big red itchy welts all over his neck and face.' She grabbed a cushion and hugged it to her, trying to buffer herself from the memory. 'We had to leave early.'

Fiona snorted. 'I don't think it had anything to do with a reaction to the mothballs.'

'What else could it be?' Sarah curled her feet up underneath her and settled in, reaching for a handful of popcorn.

'The only committed relationship that man wants is with his medications and supplements.'

'He's very sweet when he's not obsessing about his health.' She focused on the television, not wanting to have this conversation. It always led to the same place.

'All I'm saying is, you could do better.' Fiona grabbed the remote control and turned the volume up. 'And you know it.'

Sarah fingered the skirt of the wedding dress. A classic eighties design, its strapless bodice made of creamy taffeta gave way to ruffles of white tulle ending mid-thigh. Not to her personal taste. But her mother had been so keen on her taking the dress that she couldn't stand to break her heart. That and the fact her mother had a Madonna-inspired past had proven too good to resist.

The long drive from Newcastle back to Sydney last night had been awkward with Greg brooding in the passenger seat, scratching in silence, eyes straight ahead.

His announcement of his intent to eventually ask Sarah to marry him had landed like a lead balloon. Her family had looked at him in stony silence as if he'd gathered them together under false pretences. They'd expected an announcement, not a sneak preview of an announcement. He, in turn, couldn't understand their disappointment.

The first episode of the revived series *Farmer Goes a Courting* began to roll and Fiona topped up their wine glasses, offering Sarah more popcorn. She took another handful, taking pleasure in the crunchy salty sensation, as she got lost in the show.

Six good-looking rural bachelors seeking love helped to lessen the pain of the lunch with her family. As she watched the contestants she couldn't help comparing them to Greg. No way were these guys vegan, sugar-free, gluten-free, dairy-free … fun-free. Even though she lived in the city, she'd always felt she had the soul of a country girl. Her dad's family had come from a tiny town in rural New South Wales, so maybe it was in her DNA.

She blew out a big breath and leaned over to get more popcorn.

'I love Sunday nights. I think number two is my pick,' said Fiona, eyes glued to the screen. 'What is it about a farmer that gets me?'

'Those bodies honed by hard, outside work?'

'Big, calloused hands …' sighed Fiona. 'Those thighs.'

'The ability to fix anything,' said Sarah.

'Capable.'

'Robust. Strong. Dependable. Authentic.'

Fiona turned to look at her. 'Sounds like a shopping list to me.'

'What?' Sarah laughed nervously and shook her head. 'Oh, no. I'm perfectly happy.'

'Really?' Fiona raised her eyebrows. 'She says as she sits here in her mother's retro wedding dress watching a dating show while her almost-fiancé is off somewhere making love to a bottle of anti-histamine.'

'He's very sensitive,' Sarah protested. 'And it's sensible to go slowly and think carefully about getting married. We both want to be sure it's the right thing to do.'

'Yes, because you've been together two years and it's way too soon to think about an actual commitment, let alone living together.'

'Fiona!' Sarah pretended an outrage she didn't feel. Only loyalty to Greg made her try.

'Come on, you're telling me you wouldn't trade Greg for one of these hunky farmers in a heartbeat? All that fresh country air? Those muscular arms and great butts?'

'And no parking issues. Here, I don't want to go anywhere in case I've nowhere to park when I get back.' Sarah

let her friend's comment slide. She needed time to process the uncomfortable truth underneath it first.

'Randwick has become ridiculous. Sydney is crammed to the gills with people. What we need is a sea change. Maybe we should apply to go on the show?'

Sarah looked at her, startled. '*Farmer Goes a Courting*? I'm not good-looking enough for that show. I'd be off in episode one. Besides, I'm almost nearly-engaged.'

Fiona laughed. 'You are *so* funny. Not good-looking enough? Have you looked in the mirror lately? And I reckon you could take those other girls. I know what you're like, competitive as hell once you get going. As for almost nearly-engaged … if he likes it, he should put a ring on it.'

'Gee, thanks for the advice, Beyoncé.' She launched a piece of popcorn at her friend who caught it and popped it in her mouth.

'Now stop distracting me while the show is on,' Fiona said as she chewed.

Sarah lost herself in the show as she fantasised about a life outdoors on the land with a man like that. She held no illusions about the hard graft required. The thought of getting up early in the morning to the sound of bird song and silence, no traffic roaring away in the background, seemed like heaven. No crowds, no public transport, no jostling and hustling every day. Just good, pure, honest hard work and down-to-earth people. It certainly held an appeal.

'You know what we should do?' Fiona suddenly sat up, depositing her popcorn bowl on the coffee table. 'We should look up some rural dating sites, see what kind of farmers are out there looking for love.'

'I don't know about that.' Sarah snapped out of her fantasy.

'Why not?' Fiona fetched her laptop from the kitchen bench where it had been recharging. 'No harm in looking, is there?'

'I don't suppose so.' Nerves fluttered in Sarah's stomach as if looking at a dating site constituted infidelity.

'Looking at a dating site over your flatmate's shoulder does not count as cheating,' said Fiona, reading her mind. She sat on the couch and powered up her laptop. 'Let's see what we have.'

She rapidly typed some keywords into the search engine. 'OutbackSingles.com. Just what we're looking for.'

Sarah's curiosity overcame her caution and she moved a little closer to get a better look.

'I am a woman looking for a man aged thirty to forty-five. What?' Fiona stopped as Sarah dug her elbow into her ribs.

'Thirty? Don't you think that's a bit on the young side?'

'Five years younger is totally acceptable. It allows for the ones who like older women. Now are we willing to relocate or travel?' Fiona hesitated, looking at Sarah as if it were a serious question.

'I guess.' Sarah shrugged. Hadn't she been fantasising about getting out of the rat race?

'Yes.' Fiona typed. 'Occupation, journalist.'

'Hey, why don't you put in your occupation?' Suddenly, the whole enterprise began to feel a little close to home.

'Because I'm happy dating my inner-city hipster with a man-bun and commitment issues. It's *you* who longs for the open range and a salt-of-the-earth type who smells of hay and lord knows what else. We should have been swapped at birth, you and me. I'm country born and bred but love the city and you're the other way around.' Fiona kept her

focus on the screen, carefully typing in answers with her long manicured nails.

'Newcastle isn't exactly full of sophisticated urbanites.'

'Fair call, but it's not deep country either.'

Fiona had a point. Newcastle had turned into a commuter hub for Sydney. Sarah didn't know what made her heart long for the wide, flat, open spaces of the Australian country like it did. Something about less people, noise and chaos perhaps.

'Okay, I think we're done.' Fiona sat back with a satisfied smile on her face. 'Shall I push go?' she asked. 'Or would you like to?'

'You're making it sound like this is serious.' Sarah's irritation arose as much from Fiona's bossiness as from some deeper truth she didn't want to examine.

Fiona shrugged. 'Whatever. You don't know if this is something serious until you see what's out there, now do you? Yes, or no?'

Sarah hesitated. There was no harm in looking. And yet, the very act of checking out single farmers online smacked of infidelity. 'I'm not sure.'

'I say yes.' Fiona clicked on the search button. 'Well, hello,' she purred as the screen flicked over to a series of profiles.

Despite her misgivings, Sarah scooted nearer. 'He looks nice.' She pointed at the screen.

'Let's take a closer look.' Fiona opened the profile. 'Nice and tall. Likes dogs. Looking for a relationship. Has kids.' She turned to Sarah. 'You ready to be someone's bonus mum?'

'I told you, this is not a serious search. We're being nosy. But for the record, no I don't think I'm ready for that

situation.' Sarah reached for her wine on the table and took
a big gulp. What was she doing? While curiosity might have
driven her to check out the dating site, she found herself
weighing up the candidates as if she was searching for love.

'Now this chap looks like a goer.' Fiona selected another
profile. 'Ah, damn it. Doesn't want kids. I'm guessing you
do, right?'

'Yep,' Sarah said. 'Not wanting kids is a deal breaker.'
The wine made her a little light-headed. 'How am I going to
raise kids with Greg? What on earth will I feed them?' She
blinked at Fiona, her mind blank for ideas.

'Tofu, veggies, coconut milk … I don't know. Greg will
be able to fill you in on all the nutritional info you need.
Better question is, what will your wedding cake be made
of?' She laughed as she watched Sarah's face change. 'See,
you hadn't thought of that.'

'I always wanted three tiers. One layer of chocolate, one
of vanilla and one red velvet,' said Sarah. 'I guess that's out.'

'The course of true love never runs smooth,' chuckled
Fiona. 'Hey, this one looks a bit delicious.'

She opened the profile of someone called Lonely in Longreach. 'Check out those blue eyes. Straight out of Hollywood.' She turned the laptop screen sideways a little more
so Sarah could get a good look. 'You have to admit, this guy
gives gluten-free Greg a run for his money.'

Sarah gave Fiona another nudge with her elbow. 'Greg is
a lovely, kind, considerate man,' she said. Then she looked
at Lonely in Longreach. 'Holy heck. He's straight out of
Central Casting. Send me one sexy farmer, stat.'

'Exactly,' said Fiona. '*This* is what I'm talking about.
Six feet tall, good. Loves dogs, even better. Good sense of

humour, a necessity. Fit from farming—yes, we can see that. Oh no.' Her shoulders slumped.

'What is it?' So far, he'd sounded as dreamy as he looked.

'He's got a kid. But oh, look—he's a widower.' Fiona sighed.

'How old is the kid?' Something about Lonely in Longreach's photo captivated Sarah. The way he smiled into the camera, as if he were looking straight at *her*. Every time she looked into his eyes her heart did a little leap.

'Fifteen, practically an adult. Might not be so bad. A boy, which might be easier than a teenage girl getting jealous because you're moving in on her dad.'

'Thank you, Dr Phil.'

Fiona snapped the laptop closed. 'Doesn't matter anyway. We're only window shopping.' She slipped the laptop onto the coffee table and curled her feet underneath her, settling in to watch the rest of the show. 'Want some more popcorn?'

'No, thanks.' Sarah longed to reach out and pick up the laptop. She wanted to read Lonely in Longreach's profile for herself, take another look at his photo. Fiona had been light on details. Sarah wanted more information but she didn't dare ask in case her flatmate mistook the question for interest. Which it wasn't. Not in the least. She was only curious.

Sarah had dreamed of becoming a farmer since she'd been a little girl. Her mother had been adamant this was not a career option for a lady and had steered Sarah towards journalism. Maybe all this fascination with working men of the land came down to a secret desire to live their life and had nothing to do with the fact her romantic life had stalled, tumbling into a free fall neither she nor Greg could save.

She sipped at her wine, feigning interest in *Farmer Goes a Courting*. But her thoughts kept coming back to Lonely in Longreach. Out there somewhere, deep in rural Australia, he went about his business, not knowing she existed at all.

What if he did?

CHAPTER FIVE

'Right, let's call this meeting to order.' Bella Brandon, Sarah's boss and editor-in-chief of *Seriously Sydney* flipped the lid off her coffee with perfectly manicured talons and took a sip without the slightest smudge to her cherry-red lipstick. 'What have we got for this week?'

Seriously Sydney held the position of number one weekend lifestyle magazine for women thirty to fifty-five. With fierce competition, Bella demanded new and exciting articles every week. She called it feeding the beast, giving Sarah the enduring image of Bella in a ringmaster's costume cracking a whip.

'Sarah, what does your razor-sharp team of journalists have for me this morning?' Bella flicked a piece of lint off her jacket in a bored manner, suggesting she'd rather be anywhere else than here. So would Sarah.

'Colin, please.' She turned to the more sparkly and annoying half of her two-person staff, being the type of chap who'd never met a boundary he couldn't ignore.

'I've got something on the wonders of ginseng, everything from helping to prevent dementia to curing adrenal fatigue. My naturopath swears by it.' Colin specialised in health articles linked to whatever his current hypochondrial complaint happened to be. Thin and rangy, he assumed a concave shape wherever he perched, looking rather like the old cartoon character Beaky Buzzard.

'Not bad,' said Bella, tapping her teeth with a pencil. 'It needs some pizzazz. Find out who's taking it—anyone famous and especially anyone infamous. I'm particularly interested in any connection to enhancement in sexual performance, got it?'

Colin nodded furiously, bright patches appearing on his cheeks as he stabbed at his electronic tablet with his forefinger. Sarah hated those things. Give her a notebook and pen any day; that way she could doodle and it looked like she was taking notes.

'What else? Arlene?'

Arlene, always nervous at the best of times, jumped at the sound of her name. 'Um … yes, I thought I'd do something like *The Truth About Fillers—How to avoid looking like a blow-up duck.*' She used her fingers to make air quotes, dislodging her glasses in the process.

'Been done,' said Bella, moving on.

'Not like this,' Arlene spoke quickly, before she lost her chance. 'Did you know fillers were invented over a hundred years ago and started out as mineral oil and paraffin?'

'Ew!' Colin screwed up his face with disgust.

'I thought I'd have a guide to how many syringes is enough for each age group, you know, if you're thirty or forty, and compare it to how many it takes to look over-stuffed, so our readers know when they're being misinformed by their cosmetic consultant.' She sat on the edge of her seat, becoming more animated as she seemed to recapture Bella's attention.

'I'm interested,' said Bella, pointing her pencil straight at Arlene. 'Write it up.'

'How many does it take, out of interest?' whispered Colin.

'More than ten,' Arlene whispered back, 'and you look like a Beverly Hills Housewife.'

'Sarah, hit me. What have you got?' Bella checked her watch while Sarah panicked. Her mind blanked as if thoughts of Lonely in Longreach had erased every idea she'd had ready to present. All she had was a pad full of doodles, swirls and little interconnecting boxes. As head of the Lifestyle section, she was expected to deliver the big, punchy ideas. If she couldn't get it together and remember her pitch, Bella might demote her in favour of Arlene ... or worse yet, Colin.

'I ... I was thinking about ...'

'Yes, hurry up, I've got a meeting with marketing to get to.' Bella pinned Sarah with her intense gaze, like a butterfly to a board, which only served to increase the level of complete blankness in her brain.

'Well ...' Sarah swallowed hard. What could she pitch? The horror of family get-togethers? Vegan bodybuilders? Bella wouldn't go for any of that. Then she had it.

'How about a piece on finding love in the country in the twenty-first century? It's hard enough getting a decent date

in the city where there's tons of people, right? What do people in the country do to find love?'

'I'm listening. You've got thirty seconds.'

Sarah hooked her hair behind her ears and wriggled to the front of her chair *a la* Arlene. 'There are these rural dating websites full of men and women who are looking for love. I want to investigate how successful they are. There are issues like isolation, distance, small communities. I think it will fit in well since *Farmer Goes a Courting* has been revived and I believe it's rating quite well.' She didn't have a clue how the show was doing but if Fiona's enthusiasm was anything to go by, then probably great. She crossed her fingers underneath the table.

'I like it, especially if you focus on those in their thirties to early forties. The young can go to their Bachelor and Spinster Balls. What do the older folk do? Excellent, Sarah. Make it a feature piece.' Bella stood up, sending her chair sliding across the floor. 'As you said, it's hard enough to find a decent date in a city full of men.' She sighed and for one spine-tingling moment, Sarah thought Bella might show a tiny bit of vulnerability.

Instead she straightened what looked like an original vintage Chanel tweed jacket and tossed back her perfectly ombré locks like a forties starlet. 'Sarah, tease that idea out into a four to six part series. I want to see pain, triumph, tears … you know the sort of thing. While you're working on that I want a piece on the trend towards vegan bodybuilders. You're dating one, aren't you?' Bella narrowed her eyes to something suspiciously approaching a squint.

'Um, yes.' Not for the first time, Sarah wondered if Bella possessed some kind of sixth sense which allowed her to read minds.

'You know the deadlines, I expect you all to have something to me on time. That means you, Colin.' She pointed her pencil at him like a gun.

'Yes, ma'am,' he said as she stalked out to her next meeting.

'God, she stresses me out,' said Arlene as she lay her forehead on the table. 'I don't know how much more of this I can take.'

Sarah spun slowly on her chair and looked out the window. The view of other office buildings did little to calm her nerves. Great concrete monoliths with shiny glass windows for eyes. She shuddered. Bella's hardnosed approach would unnerve a special forces commando. Now that would be an interesting story: see how the soldiers stood up to a week with Bella.

'Are you signing up to date a farmer, Miss Sarah?' Colin simpered, grating on her last nerve. 'I thought you were happy with that big lug of yours.'

'I am,' she said, her tone short and businesslike. 'The article has nothing to do with my love life.' She sounded defensive. Not the tone she'd been going for.

'Right,' said Colin, giving her a leering wink. 'I do love a good flanno shirt on a man. Heaven.'

Sarah stood up. 'I don't know about you, but I have a lot of work to do if I'm going to pull this off. Colin, I want the first draft of that ginseng thing on my desk by tomorrow morning.' Then she turned and walked out of the boardroom with as much self-righteous dignity as she could manage as Colin let out a dramatic groan.

Back at the safety of her desk, she threw her pad down and flopped in her chair. What had she done? Bella would expect an article on vegan bodybuilders on her desk by the end of the week. That bit was easy. The outback love series

she'd pitched had her tied up in knots. The minute Bella said yes, the switch had been thrown and the prospect of Lonely in Longreach became 3D and technicolour.

The prospect of meeting her internet crush aside, could she pull it off? There was more at stake than her heart; this was her career. She'd thrown her hat into the ring, now she'd have to fight.

Opening her laptop, she typed in OutbackSingles.com, guilt flooding her veins like an illicit drug as the home screen came into view.

She sat and stared at it.

She shouldn't be on here. There were bound to be other sites for rural singles. A Google search would take a second to find them. Her fingers crept towards the keyboard and found all the right letters to spell Lonely in Longreach and there wasn't a thing she could do to stop them.

Why should she feel guilty? Checking out the site constituted research for her article, nothing more. No harm to anyone, least of all Greg. She'd been faithful their entire relationship and had no interest in being anything else. They were planning on getting engaged after all. Serious stuff.

So what if her heart didn't leap at the sight of him, or her breath catch in her throat whenever she looked into his eyes. That kind of thing only happened in romance novels or movies. Not in real life. She didn't know one single person who had fallen in love at first sight. Not possible. Greg had his flaws, but he was a good, loving person who took care of her. He'd make a great dad someday.

'A great dad,' she said out loud as if the fact clinched the argument. 'Doesn't mean a thing,' she muttered as the profile popped up.

'Hello.' Her breath turned into a sigh at the sight of him. His gaze bored right into her soul. No one should be allowed to have eyes that blue. She lingered for a second before giving herself a little shake. 'Snap out of it, this is for research purposes only.'

What was she researching again? The trials and tribulations of dating for the rural lovelorn. That's right. The smart thing to do would be to get in touch with some people who might be willing to be interviewed.

'Good idea,' she coached herself. She'd pick two or three people and contact them about the effectiveness of online dating. No reason Lonely in Longreach couldn't be one of those people. Being super cute meant he might be quite successful, and it would be interesting to hear about his experiences.

'Keep it professional,' she muttered under her breath as she read his profile.

I'm a widower with a fifteen-year-old (completely independent) son. My wife died nearly seven years ago from breast cancer. I'm finally ready to date again and I'm looking for a pretty, kind, sweet, loyal woman who wouldn't mind moving to the country. Must love animals, no allergies, be able to cook and go without makeup if necessary. Dirt-bike riding skills considered a plus. If you think this sounds like you, send me a message.

'Oh, God.' Sarah put one hand on her chest and took a deep breath. She could picture Lonely in Longreach nursing his wife before she died, leaving him alone to raise their son. She could imagine him tucking his little boy in at night, reading him a story, sitting with him when he cried in his sleep because he missed his mummy. How he must have sat by his dying wife's bedside, holding her hand and promising her he'd take care of their boy no matter what.

Sarah's heart broke for him. She studied his picture again. Something about him spoke to her, something familiar and new all at once. Like she'd met him briefly somewhere before. Impossible of course, yet she couldn't shake the odd sense of connection she got every time she looked at him.

Her fingers were poised over the keyboard, waiting for words that would not come. What could she possibly write? She wanted to meet him, without a doubt. To talk about his dating experiences, though not necessarily for the reasons she'd stated.

'Why is this so hard?' She leaned back in her swivel chair and tipped her head back with her eyes closed. She pictured Greg and compared him to Lonely in Longreach. Greg was real while Lonely in Longreach was a projection of her romantic fantasy. She didn't even know his name. It might not even be his actual picture. He could be a Nigerian somewhere in West Africa, waiting to swoop on her fortune. She snorted at the idea. Slim pickings where her money was concerned.

Greg, despite his ailments and allergies, had a sweet and gentle quality about him. Who knew what qualities Lonely in Longreach had. He might have nursed his dying wife and raised his son alone. He might have hired people to do all that for him or shipped the son off to boarding school. His profile did say *independent* fifteen-year-old. What did that mean exactly?

She righted herself and picked up a pen. Opening her writing pad, she wrote the names of both men at the top and drew a line down the middle. Then she wrote down what she knew about each of them. Not much in the case of

Lonely in Longreach. Deducing facts from his profile could go either way.

Greg was handy in the kitchen. Didn't sound like Lonely in Longreach had mastered those skills if he wanted someone who could cook. Then again, maybe he wanted a break from doing all the cooking, someone to share the load.

Must love animals, something Greg struggled with due to his allergies. Sarah loved animals. Definitely a plus in Lonely in Longreach's column.

Must be able to go without makeup. Greg liked her to look polished, though he didn't push the issue. He was wiser than that. It sounded like Lonely in Longreach liked the natural look. Fine with her. Another tick in his column.

As for dirt bikes, she had no experience apart from the time she'd rented a scooter in Thailand. Not quite the same thing although some of those roads had given her a run for her money.

She looked at her list.

'What am I doing?' she groaned. She'd wandered off from writing a professional message inviting Lonely in Longreach to take part in her article and ended up comparing her almost-fiancé to a stranger. A stranger she could not stop thinking about. How could she have feelings for someone she hadn't even met yet? Was that even possible? She'd heard of people walking into a room and knowing the minute they set eyes on their future partner that *this* person was the one.

She didn't think it could ever happen to her.

Sarah picked up her mobile phone off her desk and dialled her mother.

'Sarah, darling, glad you called. I wanted to talk to you about your—our—wedding dress.' Her mother launched straight in, as was her habit.

'I need to ask you something,' Sarah interrupted, speaking quickly to head Eleanor off at the pass. 'Do you believe in love at first sight?'

'Of course I do, how do you think I ended up with your father?' Eleanor laughed as if it were the funniest irony of her life. Perhaps it was.

'Really?' Sarah had never heard her say anything about falling for her father the minute she laid eyes on him.

'I met him at a Bachelor and Spinster Ball in a little town near Maitland.' Eleanor sighed, and Sarah could imagine her becoming dreamy, her hand at her pearls, rolling them around with her fingertips. 'He wasn't the most handsome man there, or the most charming for that matter. But I took one look at him and I knew. Just like that. He felt the same. Like we didn't get a choice in the matter. We were made for each other.'

'I don't think you've ever told me that story,' said Sarah.

'Oh well, people think it's a lot of nonsense, so I keep it to myself. Some things must remain private.' Eleanor gave a little giggle, sounding a trifle embarrassed.

'How did it feel, the knowing?' Sarah swallowed as she jabbed her pen down hard on her writing pad.

'Let me remember.' Eleanor took her time, drawing her story out. 'I recall a sensation of dizziness, butterflies in my tummy and I couldn't breathe. It only happened when I looked at him, so I knew he had to be the one. Why are you asking me about love at first sight? You're quite happy with Graham, aren't you?'

'Greg, Mum, his name is Greg. I'm researching something about finding love in the country.' She was hardly going to tell her mother about Lonely in Longreach and the odd, niggling feeling that he was The One. Giving the thought voice might make it real.

'Sounds interesting. Keep me posted. Your father and I would love to be included if you think you can find a spot for us.' She'd forgotten her claim to privacy in the face of possible fame. 'Nice man, your Greg, even if he is a little odd.' They hadn't spoken since that fateful lunch. 'I'm glad he's thinking about asking you to marry him, but darling, are you considering it? Seriously, I mean?'

'Of course,' Sarah spluttered. 'Why wouldn't I be? He's a lovely, sweet, kind man with excellent knees.'

'As true as that is, are you sure there's enough … spark … to last a lifetime? I got the sense he's quite high maintenance. What on earth are you going to eat?' Eleanor's earrings clinked against the phone as she spoke. The sound irritated Sarah almost as much as the conversation.

'Look, Mother, love to chat about this later. I'm on a bit of a deadline right now. I should probably go.'

'I don't want to keep you from your work. Such a thrill having a journalist in the family.' Eleanor gave a deep, dramatic sigh and Sarah knew what came next. 'Shame your brother can't make something of himself.'

'I'll talk to him about it, I promise. Got to go. Bye … bye … love you.' She hung up while her mother was still talking and slumped in her chair.

Love at first sight. Her parents had it. She didn't. Not with Greg anyway. Maybe with Lonely in Longreach. Could that

even be possible? Who ever heard of falling in love with someone's photo?

'Ridiculous,' she said. If she did go and meet him, he'd surely turn out to be nothing special. And yet, as she stared at his profile her heart ratcheted up its beat, butterflies began zooming about her stomach, her breath became shallow. Something weird was happening to her.

'We'll have to go see, won't we?'

With trembling fingers, Sarah typed in the information required to set up a new dating profile completely separate from the one Fiona had created. She wanted privacy but the dating site was the only way she had of contacting Lonely in Longreach. She needed a profile photo. A quick flick through her phone showed nothing but head shots of Greg. She'd never been one for a selfie.

Sighing, Sarah bit the bullet and rolled her chair around the end of her desk until Arlene and Colin came into view.

'Would one of you two creative souls mind taking a photo for me?' She held her phone out with a sigh, bracing for the inevitable questions.

'Let me,' said Colin, jumping out of his chair as if it were electrified. 'I'm *extremely* good at taking profile pictures for dating sites.' He gave her a wink.

Sarah looked at Arlene who shrugged. 'No point asking me,' she said. 'I'll make you look like the kind of woman who has too many cats.'

Colin didn't hesitate a moment longer, taking the phone from her hand. 'Don't worry, boss, I'll make you look a million dollars. First, we have to do something with that hair. There's so much of it you're in danger of looking like Cousin Itt's little sister.'

'Don't call me boss,' Sarah muttered between clenched teeth as she pushed her hair back off her face. If he was looking for anything more glamorous, he wasn't going to get it. The whole situation was humiliating enough as it stood.

'Wheel over here by the window where the light can wash out those fine lines around your eyes. Now stick your chin out a bit; it's a great way to get rid of any double chin action. That's it.' He took his time fussing with angles, and all the while Sarah grew more uncomfortable and impatient.

'Would you take the damn photo.'

'Alright, keep your mascara on. We have to get your best side. You never know, true love may depend on it.' He winked lasciviously and snapped a shot.

From: Solitary_In_Sydney
To: Lonely_In_Longreach
Subject: Hello

Dear Lonely in Longreach,

I've sat here and thought about what I'd write to you. I've started my message several times and deleted every one. In the end, I think it's best to shoot straight so here goes: the truth.

I'm a journalist writing a story about love in the outback and I saw your profile on Outback Singles.

At first, I thought I'd contact you to see if you would be interested in an interview for my research. I'd be lying if I said that was the real reason for writing to you. The real reason is, I can't get you off my mind. I don't know why but your photo mesmerised me, and

I knew I had to get to know you. Maybe I'm guilty of having a bit of a fantasy about who you really are. I'm willing to take the risk. Would you be interested in talking some more?

Warmest regards,
Solitary in Sydney

PS I just want to reassure you that I'm not a serial killer or a general nutter but I do understand if you don't want to reply.

CHAPTER SIX

'I can't believe how many responses there's been.' Maddie undid her hair tie and Levi watched as her long blonde hair tumbled out of its ponytail. Three days had passed since they'd posted his dad's profile. Three days in which Levi had studiously avoided the subject.

He looked away, pretending a devoted interest in finding his house key in the deep, dark recesses of his backpack. 'What do we do?' He had no idea what came next. Maddie had masterminded the situation and now a dozen women wanted to date his dad. Things were out of control. She'd caught the bus home with him so they could go through the profiles together.

'We check out the responses and pick the ones we like best.' She said it matter-of-factly, like she did this every day.

Levi fished the key out of his bag and unlocked the door, to be met by the warm, slightly stale air of a house that had

been cooped up in the sun the whole day. He opened some windows in the lounge room, rewarded by the stirring of a cool afternoon breeze wafting into the house.

'Hungry?' His dad had left him a packet of assorted biscuits, supposed to last him all week. He tore it open where it lay on the kitchen bench and shoved a shortbread cream in his mouth.

'No, thanks.' Maddie sat on a kitchen stool, resting her elbows on the table and her chin in her hands. 'I'll have some water though.' The tips of Levi's ears burned hot as he felt her watch him get a glass from the cupboard and some cold water from a bottle in the fridge.

He got his laptop out of his school bag while she drank. Opening the screen, he navigated to Outback Singles and opened his dad's profile. 'I have no idea how to tell if someone is alright or a complete nutter.'

'We'll know by the photo. Slide it over.' She reached for the laptop, forcing Levi to come and sit next to her, something he'd been avoiding.

She tucked her hair behind her ears and squinted at the screen. He held his tongue. Nothing he said would convince her she needed her eyes tested; he had the bruises to prove it.

Maddie began to open and read the messages.

'Don't like the look of this one. Her eyes are too close together.'

Levi couldn't tell. The woman in question looked like a regular woman to him.

'Not sure this one would last out here in the country. She's as skinny as a stick insect and likes Vietnamese food. Good luck with that.' She laughed. The only takeaway places

in town were Chinese, pizza or the roadhouse. Every year rumours about a McDonald's opening up flew into town like a flock of migrating birds, but they always amounted to nothing.

'No. No. No.' Maddie deleted the messages with cruel vigour, amazing Levi with her cold-blooded, businesslike approach.

'This one I like,' she said, sliding the laptop around so he could get a better view.

The woman in the photo had hair the colour of dark chocolate falling in a soft wave across her face. Her dark brown eyes looked out of a face that even Levi had to admit was pretty. It was the sort of face that welcomed you in with its warmth. She looked nice, kind.

'I'm getting a good vibe off her and look what she wrote. It feels *authentic*.' Maddie said the word as if it were the holy grail of dating site requirements. Levi skimmed her message.

'Wow.' He sat back, blinking. 'Intense.'

'Love at first sight,' said Maddie, crossing her arms over her chest. '*This* is what we've been waiting for.'

'Really?' Levi had no idea about such things. He stared at the words on the screen, struggling to draw the same correlations.

'Of course. It's like in *Sleepless in Seattle*, when Meg Ryan hears Tom Hanks' voice and knows he's the one for her.'

'Can it work like that?' He had to get a handle on these things. Had it been like that for his parents?

'That's the whole point. You walk into a room and *boom*! There's your soulmate.'

Levi swallowed hard. What if Maddie walked into a room and found her soulmate? The thought sent a cold

shiver through him. If that happened, then they probably wouldn't be best friends anymore and he didn't think he was up for losing her yet. They had plans to move to the city and go to university and be something together.

'What if my mum was my dad's soulmate? Do you get more than one soulmate in a lifetime?'

'In *Sleepless in Seattle* Tom Hanks thought his wife was his soulmate and he was willing to settle for second best, until he met Meg Ryan—who, by the way, already knew they were destined to be together.' Maddie took control of the keyboard. 'I say we message her back.'

'I don't know.' Levi had begun to get a queasy sensation in his stomach. 'What if she's a psychopath or something?'

'Does she look like a psycho to you? She's a journalist. We can check her out online. There should be plenty of stuff.' Maddie had that lit-up thing going on, a pretty flush along her cheeks and a sparkle in her eye, making it hard for Levi to say no.

'What's her name?'

'Solitary in Sydney. Super cute, she named herself like your dad.'

'We're not going to be able to find her without a real name.' Finally, a way to end the madness.

'Watch.' Maddie gave him a Cheshire cat grin as she copied Solitary in Sydney's photo and dumped it into a Google search which returned an alarming number of matches. 'See,' she said, turning to him in triumph. 'All links to her articles.'

'Still could be a psycho,' he muttered. This was getting too real.

'Lighten up, Levi.' She punched him in the arm hard enough to make his teeth rattle. 'If your dad falls for this woman then you're off the hook and we can go away guilt free. Keep your eye on the endgame.'

The endgame.

If this crazy scheme meant he could go away with Maddie, then he didn't need to think twice. He was in. He just hoped his dad would understand when a strange woman turned up acting like she knew him. And that Solitary in Sydney would be understanding when she found out all her messages were to a couple of teenagers and not to a lonely farmer looking for love.

If the truth got out he'd be grounded until he turned thirty.

'Better hurry up,' he said. 'Dad will be home in a minute. We've got parent–teacher interviews, remember?'

'Dear Solitary in Sydney,' Maddie spoke as she wrote. 'I'm totally open to getting to know you better. I found your photo mesmerising too ...'

Levi rolled his eyes and put his head in his hands. What had he got himself into?

From: Lonely_In_Longreach
To: Solitary_In_Sydney
Subject: Hello back

Dear Solitary in Sydney,
I'm totally open to getting to know you better. I found your photo mesmerising too. To be truthful, I'm not

really experienced with finding love online. This is the first time I've done it and you're the first woman I've spoken with. I'm not sure I'd make great interview material. Like I said, I would like to get to know you better. Longreach feels like the middle of nowhere sometimes and there's not much chance to meet new people. Perhaps we could meet if you're willing to travel out to the country. Not a huge fan of big cities. What do you think?

Let me tell you a little bit about me.

Farming is in my blood. I was born and bred in Longreach, one of three generations to live on our farm. My son will hopefully be the fourth.

I farm merino sheep and a few years ago I started farming sunshine. Yes, I'm a solar farmer. Not always a popular decision for a farmer to make but it's been good to us.

I like cricket and rugby (no surprises there), fishing, the odd game of pool and, when I was younger, a bit of dirt-bike riding, something I've passed on to my son Levi. He's fifteen with big plans. He wants to go to university in a couple of years so it's time for me to think about my own future. I've learned the hard way that life is short, and you must take your chances where you find them.

I like good coffee, Mission Impossible movies, Italian food and hot chips. I'm not sure what else to tell you. I love wide, open spaces, and while the distances can get to you sometimes, our town is small and sweet. Everyone grew up together. Mostly that's a good thing. I can't imagine living anywhere else.

Tell me some more about yourself. Oh, before I forget. My name is Sam. What's yours?

Cheers,
Sam

✉

The P&C committee had set up a refreshment table in the school hall, offering tea, coffee and fruit punch. They also had a cake stall right next to the coffee cart, tempting parents in an effort to raise funds. Sam got himself a free coffee and forked out five dollars for a great looking carrot cake with its icing sticking firmly to the clear-wrap covering.

Levi sat in a plastic chair waiting for him, a jumble of too-long arms and legs.

'Here you go.' Sam passed him a cup of punch.

Levi took a sip. 'That is disgusting. I'd rather have a coffee.'

'You're fifteen years old. I am not caffeinating you at this time of night.'

'Geez, Dad, I'm not a baby anymore.' The sullen mask fell over Levi's face, something Sam recognised more and more. He made a note to call his mother and apologise for his own teenage years.

'I know.' Sam took a sip of his coffee to stem the flow of words threatening to trip off his tongue. One thing he'd learned was that a little space in a conversation with a hormonal teenager went a long way towards limiting the possible damage. 'How about you plug into that iPhone of yours and kick back while I go talk to your homeroom teacher?'

That earned him a grunt of acknowledgement. Levi had his earphones in before Sam had a chance to stand up. Steve Jobs had delivered both a curse and a blessing to parents across the world.

'Maddie coming tonight?' He'd come home to find the two of them hunched over the laptop on the kitchen bench. Some kind of assignment they'd said, before they'd scurried off to Levi's room. Sam had pondered the merits of leaving them alone and unsupervised at their age. At what point did he say no girls in the bedroom? Had they passed it when he wasn't looking?

Levi shrugged. He knew the answer alright, he simply didn't want to share the information. Sam sighed and placed the carrot cake on the seat he'd vacated.

'Make sure this is still here when I get back,' he said.

He ambled out of the hall, nodding to other parents he knew as he made his way across the courtyard towards the designated classroom.

The sun had begun to set, leaving streaks of vibrant orange and pink lingering in the sky. In a few moments the thick, velvety blanket of night would begin to draw up from the east, bringing with it a myriad of stars. Very little light pollution from the town meant the sky zinged with the brilliance of the Milky Way, something Sam never grew tired of despite the hardships and challenges of farming.

Climbing the handful of stairs, he made his way along the veranda looking for the right room. Each one he passed contained teachers and parents, some in serious discussion, others laughing and talking like old mates. Which would he be tonight?

Finding the right room, he took off his ever-present aku-bra and stepped over the threshold. The teacher sitting behind the desk at the front of the room stood up and came to meet him. Slim, pretty, and young. The teacher Big Mike had been talking about.

'Hello, I'm Kylie Kempton.' She held out her hand. The light gleamed on her blonde locks, piled on top of her head in a twisty style, and her smile carried an infectious qual-ity that drew him in. She wore a floral dress that made him think of the flowers his mother used to grow in pots on the front veranda when he'd been a kid.

'Miss Kempton.' He took her hand, so small in his that he was careful not to squeeze too hard. 'I'm Sam Costello, Levi's dad.'

'Lovely to meet you. Call me Kylie, please.' She sparkled like sun on water. 'Shall we sit?'

He followed her, taking a seat and stretching his long legs out. The chairs weren't built to take a full-grown man.

She watched him get settled, a smile on her face. 'Let's start with any concerns you might have about Levi's education.'

Sam didn't bother to hide his surprise. 'Should I have some?'

Kylie laughed. 'No, not necessarily. Sometimes parents worry their children aren't performing well in certain sub-jects. Do you have any of those concerns?'

Sam shook his head. 'He seems fine to me. Usual gripes about homework and assignments. Long sullen silences. Some smart-aleck remarks from time to time. I'd say he's typical for his age. What do you think?'

'I think you've summed up most of the student body, male and female,' she said. 'As for Levi, he's tracking well. While

he's not a stand-out student in the sports department, he has an above average performance across most of his subjects.'

'I'm reassured.' Having satisfied himself that Levi wasn't in any danger of going off the rails, Sam wondered if he ought to leap in and ask Kylie out for a drink. She looked like fun and a drink didn't mean anything more than a friendly interest.

'I understand you're a widower.'

Her statement took him by surprise. 'Seven years now.'

'I don't mean to pry, only sometimes kids can act out when they're missing one parent.'

'I hope that doesn't apply to Levi.' A tick of worry beat time in Sam's heart and he sat up a little straighter.

'Oh, no. Please don't get me wrong. I didn't mean to alarm you. Levi is great. Like you said, a sullen patch here and there, but on the whole he's a good kid.' She flushed pink along her cheekbones, lending her heart-shaped face a compelling appeal. It seemed that her interest in his marital status might not be connected to his son's welfare.

Sam smiled. 'Glad to hear it. If that ever changes, feel free to call me and let me know. Whatever I can do to support you from my end, I'm happy to do.'

'Glad to hear that.' She beamed with pleasure. 'Many parents are not that interested, to be frank.'

'Oh, I'm interested alright,' he said, hoping she'd pick up his double entendre. Her renewed blush told him she had.

'I'll be sure to make a note of that.' She recovered her equilibrium with grace.

'Right then,' he said into the eddy of silence building between them as they sat either side of the desk and looked at each other. It had been a long time since he'd flirted with

anyone. He'd forgotten how, unsure if this was the moment he ought to ask her out or not. 'I'll … um … go.'

He stood awkwardly, and she rose too. He nodded and put his hat back on. Kylie held out her hand.

'I hope to see you around town, Mr Costello.'

'I'm sure you will,' he said, grinning as he took her hand and held it for a moment longer than strictly necessary. 'And call me Sam.'

As he walked to the door, he argued the for and against of turning around and asking her out. Too soon versus the perfect time. Hell, he wished Big Mike or Craig were here to give him some advice.

Sam reached the door and paused, looking back over his shoulder to where Kylie stood looking super cute in her dress, those strappy sandals showing off shapely legs. He could be said to be too old for her. She could make up her own mind about that.

He cleared his throat. 'Miss Kempton … Kylie … If you're free Friday night, would you join me for a drink at the Royal Arms Hotel? It's not the flashiest place you've ever been to, but it's friendly and nearly the whole town passes through.'

Her face lit up. 'I'd love to.'

Sam felt his own smile stretch its way across his face in return. 'Great. Meet you there at seven.' He raised a hand in farewell and walked away as quickly as he could before she noticed the fine sweat that had broken out across his face.

He found Levi where he'd left him.

'Hey,' he said, nudging the boy's foot with his boot.

Startled, Levi surfaced from his reverie, pulling his earphones out. 'How'd it go?'

'You've got a clean slate as far as Miss Kempton is concerned but that comes as no news to me. You do much better at school than I ever did. Keep it up.'

Levi stood and stretched. Sam noted it wouldn't be long before he was eye to eye with him.

'Can we go home now?'

'Sure thing.'

Levi fell into line next to him as they made their way out of the hall, across the quadrangle and to the carpark where Sam's old battered farm ute waited for them.

Sam hooked his son into a friendly headlock. 'Think you should know I asked your teacher out for a drink.'

'What?' came the muffled response. 'Dad!' Levi wriggled free with surprising strength. 'You can't do that,' he said once he'd regained his breath. 'That is so embarrassing.'

Sam shrugged as he fished his car keys out of his pocket. 'Don't know why. Nothing to do with you. I'm only telling you so you hear it from me first and not someone at school.' He opened the door and slid in.

Levi wrenched his door open and threw himself inside the car. 'You *cannot* do this to me.'

'Why not? What do you care?' Sam backed out of the carpark and pointed the ute in the direction of home.

Levi looked out the window in broody silence for several kilometres, ignoring his father's question.

Finally, he spoke. 'Was it love at first sight?'

'What?' Levi's question rocketing out of the quiet caused him to swerve a little.

'Miss Kempton. When you walked in the room, was it love at first sight?'

'You don't believe in that stuff, do you?' He looked over at Levi, trying to get a read on his expression in the gloomy light.

'Was it like that with Mum?'

Sam returned his eyes to the road. 'Fair question.' He had to expect Levi to act out when faced with the prospect of a new woman in Sam's life. 'Yes, it was like that when I met your mother. We were thirteen when we met at high school. Her family moved here and took up the local haberdashery store.'

Levi frowned. 'We don't have a local haberdashery store in town. I don't even know what that is.'

'Material for sewing and stuff. Closed a long time ago. I can still remember the day your mum walked into class. She looked so scared that I wanted to take care of her then and forever. Silly, right?' He wound down the window a crack to let some fresh air in.

'Maddie says everyone has a true love, that one day you meet them and *boom*! You know right away it's them.'

'Maybe.' Sam nodded. 'Perhaps not for everyone though. Only the lucky ones.'

'About Miss Kempton then …'

'Miss Kempton seems like a really nice person. She's pretty and friendly and I haven't been on a date with a woman since your mother died. And besides, I think you only get one love at first sight in a lifetime.'

'Maddie says there's more than one person for you, more than one love at first sight.' Levi turned his face away, staring at the passing darkness.

Sam let the silence lengthen while he considered his response. He should have known he'd find Maddie McRae

at the bottom of this. Whether Levi realised it or not, he was in love with Maddie. His boy had grown up and there was nothing he could do to protect him from the inevitable heartache to come.

'You worried Maddie is going to fall in love with someone before she notices you?' he asked gently.

'Dad! Geez. What's wrong with you? You know we're best mates and nothing more. Focus on getting us home in one piece, would you.' Levi crossed his arms over his chest and pulled his ever-present baseball cap down low, signalling an end to this particular father–son conversation.

Sam smiled and shook his head. Love at first sight. He hadn't seen that coming. He returned his attention to watching the car lights slice up the night, wishing Michelle were here to help him navigate Levi's first big crush … and inevitable heartbreak.

CHAPTER SEVEN

'Did you put the chia pudding in the fridge to set?' Greg tucked the freshly laundered sheet around the corners of the mattress. He believed fresh linen every night helped with his allergies.

'Yep,' said Sarah from the ensuite where she diligently coated her face in expensive anti-ageing cream. She tended to sleep on her sheets for at least a week. Sometimes longer if she'd been feeling lazy.

'You know, you wouldn't need that if you gave up dairy and sugar,' he called to her, as he did every time she stayed over.

'My life is not worth living without cheese and chocolate,' she replied, as she always did. She set about cleaning her teeth using the special sonic wave electric toothbrush Greg kept in his bathroom especially for her. She used an ordinary manual toothbrush at home, a fact that horrified him.

'Did you read the blog I sent you? The one about the effects of sugar when combined with fats?' he called from the bedroom where she could hear him fiddling with his humidifier. 'There's real science behind this stuff.' Sarah was sorry she'd mentioned the vegan bodybuilding article to Greg. Since yesterday, he'd sent her seventeen emails with links to zealous plant-based overachievers. So far she'd read none of them.

Sarah rinsed out her mouth with water from a *Star Wars* cup she kept for the purpose. Another item causing Greg angst. He believed the cup, made from plastic, was slowly poisoning her, along with her cheese and chocolate and wine. 'Like the science behind the Paleo diet?'

'The benefits of the Paleo diet actually have scientific foundation,' he huffed, taking the bait like he always did.

'Because we can't really know what Paleo guy ate given we haven't found any with the contents of their stomachs conveniently intact.' She smiled as she rubbed her hand cream between her fingers and across the back of her hands, watching him put the last touches to his night routine which included taking St John's wort, a fresh set of earplugs, and a facial massage using some sort of special oil he got in a shop in Bondi. He believed in taking care of himself and it was wrong of her to tease him, but it was so much damn fun.

'You've got to admit, it's not hard to extrapolate what he might have eaten.' Greg's tone came across a little sulky and she felt bad for winding him up.

'Okay, I'll concede that.' She sat on the edge of the bed in her nighty, one made from organic cotton he'd bought her especially for the nights she stayed over.

'I've never felt better since I've been on this diet.' He stood and stretched, his pyjama bottoms riding low on his

hips. He really did possess an amazing physique, like one of those firemen from Fiona's calendar, the one her boss wouldn't let her hang in her office as it constituted a form of exploitation.

Sarah peeled back the doona and slid beneath it, the sheets cool against her bare legs. 'Paleo guy only lived to his mid-forties, didn't he?' She couldn't help herself.

What was wrong with her? Greg was a good man who wanted to take care of her. Why didn't she appreciate that? Why didn't she feel a zing in her blood whenever she looked at him the same way she got zapped when she looked at Lonely in Longreach's profile picture—a guy she didn't even know?

'To be fair, life could be harsh back then. No proper housing, medicine, or clothing, and food could be hard to come by.' Greg slid into bed beside her. 'Read or sleep?'

She took in the bedroom. Pale grey walls with soft blue curtains and bed linen. Clean lines, everything elegant and spare. It looked modern, yet the life lived in it could pass for old-fashioned. Their night routine, the same thing every single time, resembled that of an old married couple. Greg's insistence on nightwear when Sarah usually slept naked. The habit of reading themselves to sleep instead of making mad passionate love.

Suddenly she found herself looking down the barrel of the next fifty years of her life with Greg, the unchanging routine, the health obsessions and, if she were honest, the growing resentment that their life together had become boring and overly cautious. Thirty-five was the new twenty-five. She'd read that somewhere. Oh yes, on the pages of *Seriously Sydney*. Colin had written it. Possibly made it up.

She sighed and scooted down the bed, pulling the doona up to her chin. 'Sleep.'

'Okay.' Greg shrugged and turned out his bedside light. She felt him settle into his favourite sleeping position beside her. 'Good night, sweetie.'

'What about a goodnight kiss?' She tried to sound indignant to cover the fact she didn't really care. Kisses from Greg had lost their appeal and she couldn't pinpoint the moment that had happened.

He dutifully leaned over and gave her a peck on the cheek, staid and chaste. His lack of libido troubled her. She'd stopped taking it personally months ago and sometimes she wondered if his physique had truly been built naturally or if he'd hit up the steroids in secret.

'There, happy?' He didn't wait for an answer before rolling over. 'I'm beat,' he said. 'I'm going to put my earplugs in now.' He wore them as protection against the incessant hum of the humidifier.

'Okay,' she said. 'Sleep tight.'

Turning off her own bedside lamp, she lay in the darkness watching as the light of the city began to leak around the edges of the curtains. The rumble of Sydney accompanied the humidifier in a sort of industrial orchestral movement, added to by Greg's rhythmic breathing as he dropped into a deep sleep.

Sarah closed her eyes. She opened her eyes. She counted to one hundred, backwards and forwards. She daydreamed about shopping, about holidays she'd love to take and about shoes. Nothing made her sleepy. She thought about what life would be like when—if—she married Greg.

They'd live together in his flat. She'd have to make some modifications to the way she lived. He'd know if she hadn't been to yoga or out for a run like she told him she had in an attempt to stop him nagging. And there would be kale and quinoa. Lots of it. Kale was her nemesis; she hated its tough texture and its overly green taste. What was wrong with good old-fashioned spinach, anyway?

On the flip side, Greg was one of the last good men left in Sydney who wasn't gay. Compromises had to be made. A good man for kale could be seen as a fair exchange.

As she lay there in the darkness, listening to her biological clock ticking madly, she realised sleep had no intention of claiming her any time soon. The tug between loyalty and inexplicable attraction raged in her chest as a physical pain around her heart. Confusion bubbled up until the pressure became so great she couldn't stand to lie in bed a second longer.

Swinging her legs over the side, Sarah slid out of bed, careful not to disturb Greg who snuffled and rolled over. She hesitated while he settled then tiptoed out of the bedroom, closing the door behind her.

She padded to the kitchen and flicked on the light and the kettle, taking down a cup and a teabag from the cupboard while it boiled. The electric kettle sounded loud in the stillness of the night, its gentle roar filling the empty kitchen. Sarah made her tea and carried it to the table where her laptop sat. Earlier in the evening Greg had been showing her the health retreat he wanted them both to take. The website had shown a lush, green location with promises of Ayurvedic treatments, vegan meals and lots of

yoga. At least he hadn't suggested it as a potential honey-moon location even if Byron Bay itself had sounded rather nice.

Flipping the lid of her laptop, she absently scrolled through her social media, trying to ignore the urge to open the dating site and see if Lonely in Longreach had answered. She'd been hunting for other leads on the internet all week, yet Outback Singles remained her best source. Or that's what she told herself anyway. She sipped her tea, which scalded her tongue, a pain she took as punishment for her wavering heart.

Opening Pinterest, she scrolled through her collection of images of the countryside. They always managed to soothe her when restlessness struck. Tonight they only served to make her more curious about the kind of man who lived out in the middle of nowhere on a solar farm.

She sighed and closed her eyes. Greg had promised her nothing more than to consider asking her to marry him. To consider. What did that even mean? And when did she settle for so little? When her biological clock started ticking and there was not one single half-decent man in sight, that's when.

Her eyes snapped open. Greg cared for her, no doubt in her mind, yet he seemed as reluctant as she was to move forward even though they both clearly thought that's what they should do next. Maybe he thought she was the only half-decent girl he could find. The thought sent a shiver down her spine as if someone had tipped a bucket of ice down her back. Greg settling for her left her with the sense of not being good enough somehow. If he knew she was set-tling too, he'd feel the same.

Sarah leaned forward and tapped the keyboard with one hand. Outback Singles flashed up on the screen.

Whatever happened between her and Lonely in Longreach, one thing was suddenly clear: she couldn't stay with Greg out of love and respect for him. Weird paradox as that sounded, he deserved a better love than she had to offer him. And she deserved better too, someone who had no reservations about spending the rest of his life with her. Greg had struggled to get to the point where he could even *think* about the possibility of marriage. She wanted someone who couldn't live without her, not someone who, after two years, still scheduled their time together.

She logged into her account and a message notification flashed up. Lonely in Longreach had responded. Her heart beat painfully in her chest as if the blood flow had suddenly become restricted. Up until now, he'd only been a concept, an idea of a man. His message made him as real as if he sat opposite her.

Her finger hovered over the mouse pad. Once she opened the message nothing would be the same again. Regardless of what Lonely in Longreach had to say, she had to end her relationship with Greg. The message represented flag fall on the main event.

With a shuddering breath she put down her teacup. Carefully, as if the laptop might bite her, Sarah clicked on the message. It flickered to life and she held her breath while she read.

Sarah sat back in her chair, her heart still pounding. He found her photo mesmerising. Could it be possible he sensed the same connection she did? She took comfort in the fact he didn't have much experience online. He could be lying,

but she had no reason to think so. Benefit of the doubt, her mother would have said.

While she'd been the one to ask if they could meet, now he'd said yes, fear he'd find her lacking took hold. He might not find her attractive in real life. Or she might not find him attractive!

She'd heard stories of people showing up to dates only to find the person they'd been interacting with looked nothing like their profile photo. He could be years older, saggy and grumpy with his best behind him. The language he used seemed oddly youthful, although he did say he had a fifteen-year-old son.

The sound of the bedroom door opening gave her a start. She slammed down the lid of the laptop and picked up her now cold tea.

'Hey, babe, what are you doing?' Greg squinted sleepily at her as he rubbed his belly with one hand. While their emotional life might be on the wane there could be no denying he was a mighty fine-looking man.

'Couldn't sleep,' she said. 'I hope I didn't wake you.'

'I rolled over and you weren't there. Are you ready to come back to bed? Do you want some St John's wort?'

She sighed and stood up. 'You know what, I think I'll take you up on that offer. I need something to calm my mind. Too many thoughts about a work assignment.' Okay, so not entirely true but not a complete lie either.

'You work too hard,' he said as he unscrewed the bottle and shook out a capsule for her. 'You need to recharge your batteries. That retreat would be perfect for you.'

'I sure need something,' she muttered as she followed him back to bed.

She slid in next to him and he reached over to pat her hip in a comforting way, as if patting the head of a favourite dog. She wondered if Sam had a dog. Sam. She let the name roll around in her mind, savouring the simplicity of it. Sam from Longreach, farmer of sunshine, sports fan, dog lover, and hot chip eater.

Sarah sighed. What had she gotten herself into?

From: Solitary_In_Sydney
To: Lonely_In_Longreach
Subject: Urgent & Important Questions

Dear Sam,

I was excited to receive your response so quickly. You didn't even give me enough time to start obsessively checking my inbox. Thank you for allowing me to keep my sanity.

What can I tell you about myself? Here goes …

My name is Sarah. I am the eldest child and have one slightly disorderly brother. I'm from the suburbs of Newcastle and have been living in Sydney for many years. Too many. I came to study journalism and I stayed.

I too love wide open spaces. My flatmate is originally from the outback and she reckons we were switched at birth as I'm always longing for the country and she refuses to leave the city.

I find coffee essential to life. I hate traffic and crowds. I'm not fond of the beach or sand. I like pasta and cake and all the things everyone I know

has given up. Nothing a plate of pasta can't make right, especially if it's accompanied by a good red. If I were on death row my last meal would be pizza with the works. Thin crust. Extra cheese. What would your death row meal be?

I like watching rugby but only get serious about it when the State of Origin is on. I'd like to try fishing and horseback riding. I read like a fiend, and I slay at Monopoly. One day I hope to write a novel. I've been plotting it since I was nineteen years old. There never seems to be any time to sit down and start it.

I'm keen to come and visit Longreach but I disagree with you on one point: I think you'd make great interview material. I have a picture in my mind of you catching sunbeams in buckets. (I know that's not how it works but hey, I'm a writer.) I do agree with you on taking chances although, to be fair, I've not taken many in the past.

Before I do, I have two critical questions for you:

1. What is your opinion on kale?

2. How do you feel about yoga retreats?

Sorry this email is so long—I babble when I'm nervous.

Sarah

CHAPTER EIGHT

'How do I look?' Sam presented himself before Levi for inspection. His hair had been smoothed down and he wore a pale blue shirt Levi had never seen before.

Levi shrugged. 'Okay, I guess.' What he really wanted to say was his dad looked weird, like some alternate universe version of himself.

'Okay?' Sam looked at him as if expecting more, his large scarred hands placed flat on the kitchen bench, the only part of him still resembling himself.

'That's all I got.' Levi shrugged again. He didn't want to hurt his dad's feelings, but he didn't know how long he could hold his thoughts to himself. Words crowded his tongue, begging to be spoken.

Sam nodded as if he understood something Levi didn't. 'Right, I'll have to be happy with that then.' He pushed off

the kitchen bench and picked up his mobile phone. 'Call me if anything happens, not that anything will.'

'I'll be fine,' said Levi for what felt like the hundredth time. 'I'll sit here and study until you come home. Easy.'

Sam raised his eyebrows. 'If you say so.' He shoved his mobile phone into his back pocket as a set of headlights swung into the yard.

'That'll be Maddie,' said Levi, hopping off the kitchen stool. 'Shouldn't you be going?' If his dad insisted on going on this stupid date with Levi's teacher, then he should go. Levi wanted to discuss it all with Maddie and make a plan before Sam did something ridiculous like make Miss Kempton his new stepmother.

He opened the back door to usher Maddie in and Sam out.

Sam gave Maddie's mother a wave as she pulled away from the house and stepped aside to let Maddie enter.

'Miss Maddie,' he said by way of welcome.

'Not bad, Mr C,' Maddie said as she looked Sam up and down. 'You scrub up okay.'

'Just okay?'

'I mean, like, you're old and everything so we can't expect too much.' Maddie pulled her what-are-you-gonna-do face and shrugged one shoulder.

'Really?' Sam looked from Maddie to Levi and shook his head. 'And on that note, I'm leaving. Don't get into any trouble while I'm gone.'

'Studying,' said Maddie, raising the books she held in her arms.

'Yeah, right.' Sam grabbed his keys from the small occasion table beside the door and stepped out into the night.

'Don't worry, nothing will happen,' Maddie said as Levi shut and locked the door. 'They'll have a couple of drinks, a few laughs and a bite to eat. She's way too young for him and besides that, she's on country service so she'll be gone in about ten minutes anyway.' She dumped her books on the kitchen bench and shrugged out of her jacket, leaving it draped over a stool.

Maddie put her hand on Levi's shoulder and he nearly jumped about a foot into the air. She looked at him with those fathomless grey eyes of hers and he totally forgot what they'd been talking about. 'You've got nothing to worry about. You wanna take a look at our messages?'

'Okay,' he nodded, unsure if her gesture comforted him or confused him more.

She climbed onto the stool next to his and slid his laptop towards her. 'Okay.' She hooked her long blonde locks behind her ears. 'Let's log on and see what's happening.' She tapped the password, fingers flying. 'Whoa, check this out. He's got thirty-five incoming.'

The messages for Lonely in Longreach kept arriving. Dealing with them constituted a full-time job.

'I'm wondering if we should suspend his account for a bit.' Maddie turned to Levi. 'What do you think?'

Relief flooded Levi's body, making him light-headed. 'Great idea. Still leaves us with the problem of Miss Kempton.'

'We can take care of her,' Maddie waved away Levi's concerns. 'We've still got Solitary in Sydney.'

'I thought we were going to shut down Dad's account.' Panic started to bubble up in the bottom of Levi's stomach like bad indigestion.

'I never said that.' Maddie levelled him with her cool gaze. 'Solitary in Sydney looks like our best chance at success. Unless you're happy with your dad dating your teacher. On the bright side, you'd get bonus credit from your bonus mum.'

Levi wriggled on his stool, uncomfortable imagining his dad even remotely connected with sex. Maddie smiled at him like she knew every thought going through his head.

'Didn't think so,' she said.

'What do we do?' he asked miserably.

'We answer Solitary in Sydney's message.' Maddie swung her long legs back around to face the counter.

She proceeded to read out loud the latest email, sighing over the bits she liked. There were a lot of them.

'She gave us her real name.' Maddie's excitement left Levi cold.

'We already had that from the Google search,' he said, refusing to catch her enthusiasm.

'Yeah, did you read the stuff she wrote your dad? She's legit, the real deal. She's smart and pretty and I bet she's funny too.'

'How can you tell?' Levi slumped over the kitchen bench.

'By the way she writes.' Maddie had gone all dreamy. 'We need to write her back. What can we tell her about your dad?'

'I dunno.'

'Come on, Levi, keep your mind on our goal. You want the future to be about you and me at uni in Sydney and your dad happy here with someone *not* Miss Kempton, right?'

He nodded, mute in the face of her logic. His dream of leaving here and going to the city to have adventures with Maddie would only work if he knew he left his dad behind

in a happy situation. The thought of him wallowing in his grief and loneliness all by himself cut Levi to the quick.

He sighed. 'Fair enough.' He pushed himself upright and racked his brains for stuff about his dad. 'Dad grew up here in this house. He's always been a farmer, never wanted to be anything else. He went to agricultural college. I have no idea what he studied. He likes reading murder mystery novels and biographies.' Levi screwed up his face, trying to think of anything else interesting about his dad.

'Redundant,' Maddie said. 'We've already told her all of that. What else have you got?'

'I can't think of anything else,' he said, hanging his head.

Maddie's fingers flew over the keyboard in a nimble dance, the words flying up onto the screen in front of her. 'You've got to have more than that.'

'No, really, I don't.' Levi got up and went around the other side of the bench. 'You hungry?' He began to open cupboard doors, looking for something to eat.

'Got any old family photo albums or anything like that? We could go through them and take a good educated guess.' Maddie jumped off her stool and made a beeline for the bookcase in the lounge room.

'Dad keeps them under his bed.' Levi sighed and put down the packet of choc chip cookies he'd found. 'I'll get them.' He dragged his feet down the hallway to his father's bedroom. Getting down on his hands and knees, he reached under the bed for one of the dust-covered boxes.

Maddie followed, dropped to her knees beside him and together they pulled out the plastic tub containing several photo albums stretching back long before Levi had been born.

'Wow,' said Maddie as she settled herself on the floor next to the bed. She prised off the lid and reached for an album and opened it. 'Thank God old people don't go digital. This is a wealth of photographic evidence.'

'Yeah, yay for us.' Levi averted his eyes as she lost herself in his family's history. He didn't know if he wanted to see the photos of his mum and dad, so young and happy, oblivious to the grief the future held for them. Plus, he had an increasing sense of discomfort that they were squatting in his dad's room. 'We should move this stuff out into the lounge room or something.'

Maddie looked up at him, long lashes framing those mercurial eyes. 'Nervous your dad will come home and find us going through old photos?'

'It's not the photos that bother me,' Levi stood up, 'it's being in his room. I'd hate him to be in mine if I weren't home.' He held out his hand.

'Good point.' Maddie took his hand and let him pull her up. 'Let's eat cookies while we work.'

An hour later they had a decent list of things they thought interested Sam based on the photo collection. Levi had been surprised at how little looking at his mum had affected him. Rather than feeling sad, he'd been buoyed up by happiness, remembering all the fun they'd had before she'd got sick.

'I think we have everything we need,' said Maddie as she stacked the photo albums back into the plastic tub with care.

'What happens next?' Levi could sense all the good vibes of the last hour evaporating as he spoke.

'We write back of course.' Maddie stood up and brushed the dust from handling the albums off her jeans. 'And get a strategy together.'

'A strategy?' Levi swallowed hard. He didn't like the sound of that one bit.

'Don't worry, I've totally got a plan.'

From: Lonely_In_Longreach
To: Solitary_In_Sydney
Subject: RE: Urgent & Important Questions

Dear Sarah,
I'm happy to hear you're not a stalker (LOL) and you're welcome for the sanity. You're right about catching sunbeams in buckets—that's not how it's done but I like the idea a lot. I don't have to do much where the solar is concerned. We have contractors who do it all which makes sunshine the easiest thing in the world to farm.

My death row meal would be roast pork with crackling and the works. Good gravy of course. Goes without saying. I'm waiting for someone to invent a pizza with roast pork crackling. Perfection!

I've answered your questions below:

1. On kale: I can't stand it. It's way too expensive and what's wrong with good old-fashioned spinach anyway?
2. On yoga retreats: I can barely touch my toes.

I have a couple of questions for you:

1. Are you a cat person or a dog lover? (Spoiler—I love dogs. My old kelpie, Kevin, died last year and I haven't had the heart to replace him yet.)

2. What kind of novel do you want to write? Can I be in it?

Sorry this email is so short—I've got sunbeams to catch.

Sam

PS I've attached a photo of me when I was a kid.

Sixteen years, three months and eleven days. That's how long it had been since Sam had last been on a date. Not that he'd counted. The maths had come to him on his way to meet Kylie. Counting backwards through the years had been his way of calming his nerves. It had only served to increase them.

'What will it be?' Sharon asked.

'A glass of champagne and a beer.' Sam fished in his back pocket for his wallet. He'd thought a drink at the pub to break the ice might be a good idea. Why he hadn't counted on half the town coming out on a Friday night to do the same thing remained a mystery. He gave a nod to the father of one of Levi's mates. Overlooking *that* little fact was going to cost him dearly.

'Good to see you out and about at last.' Sharon slid the drinks across the bar and took the money he offered.

'I get out.' Sam couldn't help his grumpy tone. Three people had said the same thing to him since he walked in the door.

'Not like this you don't,' she said as she handed him his change. 'It's been a long time between drinks.' She winked before moving away to serve another customer.

'Ha, ha, very funny,' Sam muttered under his breath as he shoved his wallet back in his pocket and carried the drinks to where Kylie sat waiting.

A quick look around the room told him he had the prettiest date by far, which went a long way to mollifying his embarrassment at being the centre of attention.

'Thank you.' Kylie took her drink from him. 'I feel like a bit of a rock star tonight.'

'How's that?' He slid into his seat and took a sip of his beer. Cold and crisp, it slid down his throat like amber nectar from the gods.

She leaned forward, and he received a heady waft of her perfume along with a glimpse of generous cleavage. 'Everyone seems to be staring at us,' she whispered.

'That's because they are,' he whispered back, taking a moment to enjoy the closeness and warmth of a woman. He'd forgotten how it felt, to be mesmerised by feminine magic.

'I'm glad you said that because I thought I was imagining things.' She laughed and took a sip of her champagne, the bubbles dancing along the line of the glass as she tipped her head back. Her fair hair, artfully arranged in a twist which showed off the line of her throat, caught the light and reflected the golden tones of the champagne.

'As the new teacher in town, everyone knows you and …'

'As the town's most eligible bachelor, everyone knows you,' she finished, with a smile. 'I guess we're what passes for celebrities tonight.'

'Something like that.' He smiled back, enjoying her playfulness. Talking to women—who weren't family, the wives of friends or the mothers of Levi's friends—didn't happen very often. Unless you counted Sharon, the pub's landlady, or the woman who ran the bakery down the road. Otherwise, this town presented him no opportunity to practise his flirtation skills, which were pretty damn rusty.

Kylie didn't seem to notice.

'If you're hungry we can have dinner at The Woolshed Restaurant. They do a great mixed grill,' he said.

'I'd be happy to stay here and talk the night away with you,' she said as she shifted slightly closer. Her voice sent tingles up his spine. Her eyes, crystal blue up close, sparkled at him in a way that made him think going to a restaurant where almost everything had garlic in it might be a bad idea.

Before he could answer, his phone rang. Set on vibrate, it buzzed across the table like a thing alive. He grabbed it and, seeing Levi's number, answered.

'Yes, Levi,' he said in as measured a tone as he could muster.

'Dad, I need to talk to you about the races.'

'The races?' Sam shook his head, incredulous that his son would call him while he happened to be on his first date in over a decade to ask him about the Isisford Races.

'I thought we could go this year, you know, together. Like a family.'

'We *are* a family,' he growled, straightening one point out of the many things that needed sorting out with this conversation.

'Yeah, I know but I went with my friends last year.'

'Let me get this straight.' He stood up and walked away out of Kylie's earshot, stepping out the front door of the pub to stand on the street. He didn't want her to hear him tear strips off his son. 'You called me in the middle of a date to tell me you've changed your mind about going to the Isisford Races with your friends and, instead, think we should go together as a *family*.'

'Can Maddie come?'

'Can Maddie come?' Sam repeated each word slowly, with menace.

'Yeah, if that's okay and everything.' Levi sounded awkward, as if he'd only now picked up on his father's tone.

Sam closed his eyes and counted to ten. 'We will have this conversation when I get home,' he said between gritted teeth. 'Do not call again unless there's blood, the house is on fire, or a troop of foreign soldiers is staging a coup from our kitchen. Got it?'

'I'm just asking,' said Levi, as if it were Sam who was being unreasonable.

'Goodbye, Levi.' Sam hung up and ran his hand through his hair, frustration fizzing through his veins.

He got that Levi might feel out of sorts with his decision to go on a date with his teacher, especially as it was Sam's first date since Michelle's death. Trying to disrupt things with phone calls about dumb stuff wouldn't cut it. Levi would have to try harder than that. His tactics only made Sam more determined to walk back to the table and enjoy himself.

Sam took a deep breath and centred himself. Plastering a big smile on his face, he turned and walked back into the bar.

'Everything okay?' Kylie asked as he took his seat.

'Yep, fine. Teenagers.' He shrugged.

'Tell me about it,' she laughed. 'Teaching them makes me rethink having kids myself.'

'They say they're different when they're your own,' he said. 'I think the only difference is you can't give them back.'

They both laughed, and Sam felt a shift, an easing of the tension he'd carried in with him. Levi did him a favour. That phone call had riled him up and dissolved his nerves, shattering his reserve. He intended on having a good night tonight—no, make that a *great* night.

He raised his glass. 'To teenagers.'

'Are you sure I can't get you to change your mind?' Greg, shirtless in all his glory, had begun to pack for his yoga retreat. Even with the spectacular view of all those sculpted muscles, her body refused to stir in response to his obvious beauty.

They'd had dinner last night to celebrate the end of the work week and then she'd stayed overnight at his apartment. It's not that Greg didn't like Fiona, he said, just that her personality was super intense. Sarah suspected she scared him a little. Fiona could have that effect on people.

'I'm sorry, babe.' Sarah lay on the bed as he folded his clothes into the suitcase. 'I need to work on this piece for the magazine. There's no getting out of it.' The truth and nothing but the truth. Bella would have her head on a stick if she pulled out now. Regardless of what did or did not

happen on this trip, she had to go. 'And I get to go to the outback. Bella practically insisted. She doesn't think I can capture the feel of the place without being there so I don't really have a choice.'

'You'll be missing out on a great retreat,' he said, wrapping his electric toothbrush carefully in a towel. 'There'll be daily yoga and meditation sessions which I know you'll love, and there's Ayurvedic treatments. Totally vegan menu too, so that's a great opportunity for you to see what it's like.'

'All good points except for the fact I wouldn't have a job to return to.' She ignored the vegan comment. No point rehashing a conversation had too many times. 'You'll be fine on your own, won't you?'

She rolled back to lie flat on the bed, her hands behind her head. A gentle breeze wafted through the open window, billowing the blue curtains so that they briefly touched the bed before settling back against the window. The sounds of the street rose with the early spring heat. Summer would soon be here.

'Sure I will. I think there's about three or four other people going from the gym. Rachel is going. You remember her?'

Something about the way he said Rachel made her hesitate and steal a look at him. Greg kept his eyes trained on the suitcase and she couldn't read his expression.

'Blonde hair? Always wears those tiny workout shorts?' She tried to keep the cattiness out of her voice and failed. She'd met Rachel twice. Both times had left her feeling as if she were a faded wallflower by comparison to the dynamic and vivacious personal trainer.

He shot her a sideways glance. 'Is that a hint of jealousy I detect?'

'No,' she sniffed as she returned to contemplating the ceiling. 'I just think that kind of sportswear is only for the gym.'

Greg chuckled. 'She's got the legs for it.'

'That's true,' Sarah admitted reluctantly. 'She squats my body weight. She could crack walnuts with those thighs.'

'No reason why you can't have thighs like that if you wanted.'

'What man says that and expects to live?' She threw a rolled-up t-shirt at him. It landed on his head, covering his face.

He laughed. 'I'm saying that you too could wear tiny shorts if you really wanted to.' He pulled the t-shirt off and threw it back at her.

'Nice shot.' She picked it up and refolded it. Getting worked up about nut-cracking thighs seemed pointless when she intended on flying to Longreach to meet a man she may or may not be falling in love with based solely on his online profile picture. Something she tried not to think about, aware of how ridiculous it sounded.

'Will you miss me while I'm gone?' he asked.

'Of course I will,' she said with as much enthusiasm as she could muster. 'I'll be pining for you while I'm planning my feature on outback dating. I've got a lot of research to do.'

'Tell me the plan again.' He frowned as if the whole enterprise made no sense.

'I've been doing a lot of online work. Got a feel for the lie of the land, made some connections and have set up some interviews with people. Now I'm going out there to see for myself. I'll assess at the end of the week and work out where I need to go next and how long for.' She sounded dispassionate and professional to her own ears. 'Pretty dry and

desperate out there too. Kind of adds to the challenge of finding true love.'

'I think I get the better end of the deal,' he said. 'Byron is lush.'

'Yeah, the Queensland outback isn't exactly verdant. I read somewhere that in some places it hasn't rained in years.' She sat up, perching on the corner of the bed. 'Hard to imagine.' She crossed her fingers in the hope he wouldn't ask her why she would consider going up to country Queensland instead of out to the far reaches of New South Wales. Which would make more sense for someone from Sydney.

'That means there are kids who probably have never seen rain.' Greg's eyebrows shot up with surprise. 'Wow, I mean, imagine.'

'I can't.' She shook her head, relieved he'd passed over the Queensland location. 'I get drought conceptually, but I don't think I really understand what it means emotionally to the people who live through it.'

He turned to face her. 'You sure you won't change your mind? I'm planning to drive up with one or two of the others. It'll be fun.' He traced a finger along the inside of her arm. Once, such a gesture would have sent tiny electric thrills running to her heart. Now it merely tickled.

'And who might they be?' She cocked an eyebrow, knowing what he was going to say before he said it.

'Um ... Rachel and Mark. I don't know for sure yet.' He spoke quickly and had the good grace to look sheepish.

'That's okay.' She gave his leg a pat. 'You go and have fun. You deserve it.'

'I feel bad about you being stuck working while I'm getting pampered on retreat.'

Sarah nodded, while silently giving thanks to not having to get up at five am every morning to do endless rounds of sun salutations before a plant-based breakfast with no coffee. 'There's no need to feel sorry for me. I'm doing what I love, getting out in the field to chase up a story. You're getting to do what you love so I think we're about even in the happiness stakes.'

'I guess,' he said. 'Can't say I like the idea of you driving around in all that empty space by yourself. You're a city girl at heart.'

She stilled at his words. How little he knew her if he thought she belonged in the city. Hadn't he ever noticed all the rural romance books piled up on the bedside table, or the perennial CWA calendar she kept in the kitchen? She longed for the country like other women longed for chocolate or George Clooney.

'Greg,' she began after the silence between them had thickened noticeably. 'Do you ever wonder if we're properly suited?' She hadn't planned on having this conversation now, but something inside her compelled the words past her lips before she could edit the thought.

'To what? Our jobs?' He sounded genuinely confused.

'No, to each other.'

He hesitated, his eyes darting about the room. 'Look, I can't lie. It'd be great if you were a little more ...'

'A little more what?' Perched on the edge of the conversation, she wasn't sure she wanted to be here.

'You know, a little more fitness orientated. I feel as if I've got to drag you to it sometimes.'

She sighed. He had a point. 'I know. I can't change who I am. I'm not that interested in biomechanics and macrobiotic food.' She shrugged. 'I'm sorry.'

He sat down and took her hand. 'Don't be sorry. I don't want you to change who you are to fit in with my lifestyle. All I'm saying is it would be nice to share the same interests, that's all.'

She nodded. For two years they'd tried to mesh their lives as a couple, never quite making the fit. Couldn't he see that?

Sarah took a deep breath. 'I sometimes wonder if we should—'

His phone rang, a jaunty little tune from the eighties filled the room. 'Sorry,' he said as he fished it out of his pocket and looked at the screen. 'It's Rachel. I've got to take this. It'll be about the drive up to Bryon.' He jumped off the bed and, without a backward glance, walked out of the room.

She could hear him talking to the very fit, tiny shorts-wearing Rachel, his voice filled with animation. She'd be a good match for him—cute, athletic, vegan, enthusiastic about colonic irrigation. It could work.

As she sat on the corner of the bed and listened, a soft sadness enfolded her. Whether Greg realised it or not, whether anything ever happened between her and Sam, her relationship with Greg had come to the end of the road.

She watched him through the bedroom door as he moved about the lounge room, laughing at something Rachel said. All she felt for him now was a deep affection akin to friendship. No passion. No gut-wrenching, soul-searching, compelling vortex of emotion. Nothing like that, and she never had. A warm, safe, sweet friendship she'd mistaken for something deeper.

Sarah sighed and stood up. Greg would work out that his feelings for Rachel outweighed his feelings for her while he was away. She wanted him to be happy and Rachel would

make him far happier than she would. Now she had to work out what made *her* happy.

By the time Greg got back home, her whole life would have changed and she had no idea what that might look like. Whatever happened, the next chapter of her life would not be like the last. This one would be full of adventure and taking chances. She intended to live.

From: Solitary_In_Sydney
To: Lonely_In_Longreach
Subject: In praise of dogs and pork crackling pizzas

Dear Sam,
May I say I am impressed with your pizza vision. Now you've said it, the whole pork crackling topping thing makes perfect sense. What would you drink with it? A red or a good beer?

I am a dog lover but I've never had one of my own. My mother would never let us have a dog because, in her words, it would mess up the lawn. I live in an apartment so no chance there. Maybe one day I'll have a dog of my own. We'll wait and see.

About my novel, I want to write a sweeping family saga set deep in the outback. I'm not sure I'm even close to having a workable plot. Hey, it's only been a decade or so in the planning. I'll get there. Maybe you can give me a few pointers about life in the outback. And yes, you can be in it. I promise to be kind.

On the subject of visiting sometime, you know I'm working on an article about love in the outback. Well,

I'm coming out on a fact-finding mission, seeking the lovelorn and the romantics to add their stories to my series of articles the magazine will run. I know we've barely gotten to know one another and what we do know is via email BUT I'd like to meet you face-to-face. I've got a good feeling about you, Sam.

Cheers,
Sarah

PS You were a super cute kid. How old were you in the photo? I've attached a photo of me when I was about the same age. As you can see, it's me in a tutu at my annual ballet recital. Let's just say I'm a better writer than a dancer.

CHAPTER NINE

'You'll need to go and have a shower,' said Sam as he rifled in the cutlery drawer for the correct number of knives and forks. He had a casserole Veronica had made for the occasion in the oven. Something with a French name. It smelled delicious. She'd given him strict instructions on cooking temperature and timing. All he had to do was follow them.

'Why?' Levi stood at the kitchen bench; his shoulders looked too broad for him, or else his t-shirt had gotten too small. 'I can shower after dinner like normal.'

Sam dumped the cutlery on the table and began opening drawers looking for the placemats they only used on special occasions. Not having had a special event since Michelle died, he had no idea where they might be.

'You've got too many knives and forks out,' Levi pointed out in a tone that told Sam his son thought he might be going senile.

'I have the perfect number, thank you.' He wrenched open a drawer with a little too much force and it came flying off its runners, the contents spilling onto the floor. The elusive placemats lay in a crumpled heap at his feet. 'We have a guest coming for dinner.'

He pushed down the surge of annoyance which threatened to derail his calm and slid the drawer back where it belonged. 'Hence your need for a shower *before* dinner.'

Sam picked up the placemats, squares of green cloth with flowers embroidered in one corner, and smoothed them out on the bench. The damage didn't look too bad. Kylie wouldn't notice the wrinkles once he put a plate of food on them.

'A guest?' Levi screwed up his nose as if Sam had announced he'd invited a crocodile to dinner. 'Who?'

'Miss Kempton.' Sam didn't bother to look at the expression on his son's face, he knew what he'd see.

'You. Have. Got. To. Be. Kidding.'

'No, I am not,' Sam assured him. 'I need you to clear the dining-room table so we can eat there.'

'I'm doing my assignment.' Levi's tone had changed from contempt, to outrage, to whiny in the space of a two-minute conversation.

Sam shrugged. 'You can move it all back when we're done.'

'I cannot believe you're subjecting me to this kind of humiliation,' Levi said as he slouched to the table and began stacking his books by slamming them on top of each other.

'I'm not asking you to come to dinner naked so what's the big deal?' He had no intention of putting up with bad behaviour tonight.

'She's my *teacher*, Dad, in case you hadn't noticed. I mean, who dates their kid's teacher? Isn't there a rule about that or something?'

'Let me think about that for a minute.' Sam looked up at the ceiling, stroking his chin in a thoughtful manner. 'There's a rule about teachers dating students. I don't think we need to worry about that one in this situation. Nothing about parents dating teachers that I know of.'

'Very funny.' Levi picked up his books, staggering under the pile as they slipped about, while shooting Sam a dark look. 'At the very least this constitutes a conflict of interest. You could date some other teacher who doesn't teach me directly.'

'None of them are as pretty as Miss Kempton.'

'Oh, God! You're not going to have sex, are you? Not here in the house while I'm in the other room.' The blood drained out of Levi's face and Sam nearly laughed.

'I have no intention of having sex with Miss Kempton tonight,' he said as he struggled to keep a straight face. 'I hope that puts your mind at rest.'

'You are totally gross, Dad.' Levi stalked from the room with his nose in the air as if the conversation was beneath him.

'Shower,' Sam called after him.

A knock sounded on the door. He checked his watch. She was early.

He swung open the front door, letting the still warm air of the day into the cool house.

'Hello,' he said, wishing he possessed a snappier comeback.

'Hello, I hope I'm not too early. I didn't know how long it would take to drive out here.' She held a handbag in front of her like he imagined she carried folders at school. Dressed in

jeans and a shirt patterned with flowers, she looked younger than he remembered. Or he was feeling older these days.

'Not at all.' He stepped aside. 'Please come in.' He sensed the warmth radiating off her body as she brushed past him, causing him to wonder for the first time if he was out of his depth.

'Dinner smells delicious.' Kylie turned and gave him a dazzling smile. The knot in his stomach relaxed a little. 'You're cooking?'

'I put it in the oven if that counts.'

She laughed and put her handbag on the table. Shield down. She might need it again when Levi re-emerged. He could hear the shower running. The boy had already exceeded the four-minute shower limit. Drought conditions demanded showers be kept short. He got the sense he was being punished. They'd have to buy in more water before the end of the month.

'Would you like something to drink?' he asked. 'I have red or white.'

'White please.' She stood awkwardly, as if she didn't know what to do with herself.

'Have a seat,' he said with a nod to the partially set table. She did as asked while he poured the crisp, cold sauvignon blanc into two of their best crystal glasses.

'Coming up the road to your house is ... amazing,' she said as she accepted her wine. He pulled out a seat and sat opposite her. 'I had no idea what to expect of a solar farm. Rows and rows of panels all reflecting the sunset is breathtaking.'

Sam smiled. 'Sure beats looking at half-starved sheep. Here's to solar energy.' He raised his glass.

'Here's to solar-energy farmers,' she replied as she raised her glass in return.

'We are certainly a rare breed.' He circumnavigated the flirtation, not comfortable to engage in banter with Levi's brooding presence in the background. The shower had stopped which meant he'd be making an appearance soon.

'Did you give up sheep altogether?' Kylie asked.

'Nah, there are still a few head out the back,' said Sam. 'The difference is I can pay for additional feed with what I make from the solar.' He shrugged. 'Makes life a little easier.'

Kylie nodded. 'I had no idea what a drought looked like until I came here.' She laughed. 'I'm such a city girl.'

'I'm used to it now. I'm not sure how I'd handle it if it all greened up. We've spent half Levi's life without proper rain. Hard to imagine it now.'

'And yet you stay,' Kylie said softly, leaving him with the sense it was a question.

'Three generations of Costellos can't be wrong,' he joked. 'Where else would a man like me go? I'm not cut out for the city and I'd be lost in the suburban sprawl. What would I do? Farming sheep and sunshine is all I know.'

'The people out here are special,' she said. 'They're sort of open and reserved at the same time. Friendly and warm, yet blunt and practical. I'm not sure I'm entirely used to it yet.'

'Michelle, my wife, used to say real life was lived out here in the bush.'

'Interesting idea,' Kylie said. 'Is that her?' She stood and moved towards the wall where Michelle's photo hung.

'Yes,' he said, at a loss as to how to talk about his wife to someone who never knew her.

'She was beautiful.' Kylie turned and smiled at Sam. Her use of the past tense rankled him, and he didn't know why.

'Thank you,' he said, as if he had anything to do with Michelle's innate beauty. 'How's things at school?' He chose the most obvious change of subject as a haven from more conversation about his wife.

Kylie sighed. 'It's okay.' She resumed her seat opposite him. 'Most days are good, although the isolation gets to me from time to time. Don't get me wrong,' she held up a hand to ward off sympathy, 'the people of Longreach have been welcoming.'

'It doesn't take the place of your family and friends back home,' he finished for her.

'No, it doesn't.' She twirled her glass around, intent on watching the liquid move sinuously inside. 'Compounded by the fact my dad is ill.'

'I'm sorry to hear that.' He knew the pain of having a loved one suffer when there was nothing you could do about it.

'He had a massive heart attack about a year ago and we thought he'd recovered but then he had a stroke and, well …' she took in a shuddery breath, '… he's not doing so great now.'

Sam reached across the table and took Kylie's hand in his. 'If there is anything I can do,' he said, wondering what that could possibly be even as the words left his lips.

She offered him a wobbly smile. 'Actually there is something you could help me with, I mean, if it's not too much bother.'

He squeezed her hand. Such a sweet girl who deserved happiness, and he knew in that moment he wasn't the man who could give it to her. 'If I can, I will. Just name it.'

'I'm taking compassionate leave for the rest of the term.'

'You'll be gone for the rest of the year?' Kylie was fun, a bright spark in his world. He'd miss her.

She nodded. 'I need to be home in case ... you know.'

'Sure, I understand,' he said. 'You'd regret it if you didn't go. I know I would. Do you need a lift to the airport?'

'You read my mind.' She smiled, her spark back, at least temporarily. 'I'm leaving next Saturday.'

'No need to tell me the time. It's one flight in and one flight out per day.'

'That's what I like about the outback, you know exactly where you stand.' She raised her glass. 'To the outback.'

'To the outback.' He raised his in return.

'Hello, Levi.' Kylie's expression shifted to what he guessed was her professional teacher mask as she looked over Sam's shoulder and he knew his boy would be loitering in the doorway, possibly scowling.

'Come in, Levi, and pull up a seat,' he said without turning around.

'Dinner far off?' Levi slumped into the room, his hair still wet from his shower.

'You might like to greet our guest first.' Sam tried his best to sound lighthearted, fighting his parental instinct to pull Levi into line. Kylie didn't come here tonight to see him haul Levi over the coals.

'Hi, Miss.' Levi raised his chin in Kylie's direction. He didn't usually behave like this so Sam knew Levi intended to send a message. He didn't want Sam dating Kylie.

'Levi,' she acknowledged him. 'Good to see you outside school.'

'When's dinner?' Levi returned to his question.

'Why? Are you starving or something?' Sam's annoyance bubbled to the surface.

'I wanna call Maddie before we eat. Got something important to discuss with her. That's all.'

Sam could only imagine. 'Okay, you've got five minutes, make it snappy.'

Levi skulked out of the room. Sam watched him go before turning to Kylie.

'I have no idea how you manage to spend six hours a day with teenagers. Were we ever that bad?'

'I'm sure I was, and they're not so bad. He's miffed because his history teacher is sitting at the dining-room table with his dad for non-school reasons. I get it.'

Sam grunted. 'I get it too but I'd never tell him that. You hungry?'

'I could eat a horse.'

'Then I guess it's time to dish up.' Sam rose and headed for the open-plan kitchen.

'Can I give you a hand?' she asked.

'Nope. You can watch with genuine amazement while I serve you dinner with my questionable hospitality skills.' He got out three plates and placed them on the counter as the oven timer rang shrill announcing that the casserole had been heated through. 'It promises to be dinner and a show.'

'I can't talk for long,' Levi whispered down the phone. He loitered inside his bedroom door.

'Are you sick or something? You sound weird.' He imagined Maddie flopped back on her bed, crossing her long legs at the ankles and settling in for a chat. Probably in the

middle of watching season five hundred and ninety-seven of *The Kardashians.*

'No, I'm fine. I'm whispering.'

'Like, why would you do that?'

Levi sighed with exasperation. 'Because I'm hiding in my room while Dad makes cow eyes at Miss Kempton. He's making her *dinner.*'

'What the? You've got to be kidding. Having her over for dinner is serious.' Her tone of voice told him she'd sat up against her collection of kitten-princess cushions, all attention.

'I know, that's why I'm calling you.'

'Usually the home-cooked meal thing doesn't happen until much later in the relationship. It's only been a week since their first date.' He could practically hear her brain whirling in frantic overtime. Miss Kempton could derail all her plans.

'We've got to do something. This is getting out of hand.' Levi slouched against the doorframe, out of sight of his dad.

'Do you want me to come over?'

She'd be great at running interference. Not hard. When her parents fought about money or whatever, she'd be the one to sidle up to them, using all her charm to distract them by asking advice about school or some other dumb subject they cared about. She always said adults could not resist giving guidance using examples from their own sad lives. Worked every time.

'Nice idea but won't it look a bit suss if you suddenly show up? And Dad knows I'm calling you. He thinks it's about some assignment. God, I'm getting a stress headache.'

'Can I do anything else to help?'

'Nah, I can handle tonight by myself. What we need to do is make a plan so this never happens again.'

'And you've got to keep this quiet. What would happen if word got out your dad was getting down and dirty with Miss K?' Maddie dropped her voice to a whisper too. 'This information getting out is the last thing we need and Ariel can be counted on to spread the news far and wide given half a chance.'

'I can't even think about that right now,' Levi groaned. Maddie's little sister, Ariel, had an unerring instinct for drama. 'It's like Dad hates me or something.'

'We've got to ramp up project Lonely in Longreach. We have no choice. I'll think of something, I promise.'

'Great, but what are we supposed to do when this Sarah person actually gets here?' This was the part of the plan that worried him most. Levi reckoned Maddie's pride stopped her from agreeing he had a point. It was one thing to lure Sarah Lewis out to Longreach, it was another to get her face-to-face with his dad.

'Don't worry about that, it's all part of the master plan,' said Maddie confidently, the level of her voice returning to normal.

'That's what I'm worried about,' Levi groaned.

'I bet you're more worried that Miss K could end up your new bonus mum.'

A bolt of genuine fear pierced him as he watched life as he knew it implode.

'Okay, I trust you. Be nice to know what you're planning though.' He gave in. What else could he do in the circumstances? The reality of his dad and Miss K as a couple would

kill his social life, although no doubt Maddie had been hoping for a bit more rise out of him.

'She's a journalist, right? And she's doing a piece on love in the outback, so we make sure we're as helpful as possible in finding her people to speak to. We're with her and your dad, like, *all* the time. We can smooth out any speedbumps until they've hit it off for real.'

'People? I don't know any people. My life is in your hands and *this* was what you came up with?'

'But *I* do. I'm sufficiently connected. Leave it with me. I'll make sure we know where Sarah is staying and we'll make sure we catch up with her as soon as possible. This is totally going to work. I promise.' Maddie sounded convincing and Levi almost believed her. 'Besides,' she said, 'what else are you going to do?'

'Good point,' he sighed and felt the fight go out of him with it. 'Okay, I'm in. Anything is better than what's happening in my dining room right now.' The oven buzzer sounded in the background, signalling dinner and time for Levi to end this conversation. 'Do what you've got to do,' he said. 'Make this work.'

Maddie hung up her phone and threw it on the pale pink bedcover. She lay back on her pile of pillows and rubbed her eyes with the heels of her hands. She had to get this right. Despite sounding confident, she felt far from it. Only, she couldn't let Levi know that. He was counting on her to come through for him and she'd do anything not to let him down.

She stared up at her ceiling where the traces of a cobweb hung in the corner, unnoticed during the weekly clean.

It hung on by a thread, its owner having disappeared. She watched it waft in the breeze generated by the ceiling fan while she thought.

The situation might work if she could get to Sarah first and lead her to Mr C, find a way to introduce them. Then the trick would be keeping them busy and monitor them while they got to know each other. Sarah would know far more about Mr C than he'd know about her. Potential problem.

Maddie closed her eyes. Yes, this project constituted the biggest, most daring one of her life and she had the creativity and the confidence to pull it off. Mr C couldn't help but adore Sarah once he met her. She couldn't put her finger on what, but something about that woman seemed right for Levi's dad.

Once Mr C fell in love with Sarah, Levi would stop worrying and commit to leaving Longreach with her to go and live in Sydney. It had to be Sydney, more specifically, Bondi Beach. She'd never seen the ocean and if she could, she'd make sure the first time she did would be at the most glamorous beach in Australia.

One thing she knew, lying around *thinking* about her dreams would not make them happen. She needed action.

An hour later, Maddie sat with one leg folded up beneath her, wearing her favourite shorts and a t-shirt of Levi's, one he'd left behind last time they'd gone dirt-bike riding. She'd closed her bedroom door and hung a do not disturb sign on the handle. Privacy and peace were essential to come up with a plot strong enough to make her dreams come true.

She snapped the lid back on her coloured felt pen. Pushing her hair back behind her ears, she surveyed her handiwork.

An elaborate map filled a large piece of white card spread out across her bed. Lines traced their way from one thought bubble to the next. There were a lot of moving parts, even by her standards. She sighed. Could she pull this off?

She'd never done anything quite this grand before. She tapped the purple box marked Step One. This part seemed easy enough; she needed to find a way to introduce herself to Sarah. She'd talk to her history and social science teacher, who happened to be Miss Kempton, and ask if she could invite Sarah to speak on the importance of journalism in society. What teacher didn't love student initiative and this subject sat right in Miss Kempton's wheelhouse.

Step Two, written in fluoro orange, appeared much harder. She uncapped her pen and drew a little flower next to it as if to soften the challenge. In this step, she'd have to engineer a meeting between Mr C and Sarah. So much could go wrong. Her brain spun in circles like a spin cycle on a washing machine. Every idea that sprung up got cut down again with the sharp blades of logic. Perhaps Levi's gloomy pessimism wasn't as unfounded as she'd like to think.

She took a deep breath, she could do this. Her track record spoke for itself. Half her friends owed their personal happiness to her brilliant matchmaking skills. Slumping back against her pillows, she stared unseeing at Step Two.

Think, think …

Reaching for her iPod, she plugged into her favourite playlist, the one that always inspired her breakthroughs. As the music surged through her earphones she closed her eyes and let the music carry her thoughts on eddies of fantasy.

She could arrange for Mr C to be at Sarah's talk. She could introduce them and they wouldn't want to talk about

their connection in front of high school students and Miss Kempton. How would she get Mr C to attend the talk before he'd even met Sarah without raising suspicion? Not plausible. Scrap heap for this idea.

Okay, what next …

Maybe she could get Mr C to pick Sarah up from the airport? On the basis of helping out the school and all that. He'd be up for it. No, too risky. It would be obvious Mr C didn't have a clue who Sarah was. She needed a situation with more people around to distract him from asking too many personal questions straight up, questions he should technically know the answers to.

Her iPod shifted track and she hummed along, letting her thoughts drift once more.

Could they bump into each other at the pub? She could get Levi to go to dinner there with his dad and she could talk her parents into taking Sarah out for a welcome meal. Mr C could fall in love over a lamb roast and with all the extra people around, Sarah was bound to keep quiet about the whole internet dating thing. Wasn't she?

Maddie sat bolt upright. She had it. Once she got Miss Kempton to agree to having Sarah at the school, then it would be easy to get Mr C to come to a welcome dinner. Fate would take care of the spark between them.

Then what?

She studied her plan. Step Three, in hot pink, required a situation where Sarah and Mr C got to see each other in the best light. Preferably at their sexiest. Much harder. She tapped the pen against her teeth in time with the music.

This was the bit where she got them all to go to the Isisford Races. Only the biggest reason to dress up all year. Levi had

already broached the subject with Mr C, laying the ground-work. If she invited Sarah to come then it would be an easy thing to get them all there together, looking their finest. Even Mr C wouldn't object to making an effort, especially after he'd met Sarah. And, this was the kicker, Sarah could find people to interview for her series on finding love in the outback. Double bonus!

Her mind raced at a million miles an hour as she processed her plan, looking for flaws, of which there were many. Not that she intended on a few hazy details getting in the way. Too many people's happiness rode on her ability to pull this off. Mr C's broken heart would mend. Sarah would find the love she was looking for. Levi could happily go to university and she would get to be with the man of her dreams.

She sighed happily.

Convincing Levi would be her biggest challenge. He wobbled a bit from time to time. Every time she saw him she expected him to pull out of the plan. If he did that, then she might never get to go to Sydney. The thought of living in Bondi and attending university *by herself* terrified her. She wasn't brave enough to go through with it, even if she could afford it. If she didn't do her part she'd be stuck in Longreach for the rest of her life. Probably as some lame farmer's wife, complaining about the endless drought and worrying about the kids. She wanted more than that. She wanted a life.

Fired up, Maddie picked up her laptop from where it sat on the floor next to her bed. Opening the cover, she began to type a rough draft of what she'd say to Miss Kempton to get her to agree to have Sarah come and talk at the school.

Wouldn't be hard and Maddie wasn't star of the junior debating team for nothing.

As she typed, her fingers whizzing across the keyboard as if with a life of their own, a sensation of rightness settled over her. The only person she felt a little bad for was Miss Kempton. Having said that, anyone could see Miss Kempton was way too young for Mr C. He needed someone a little more worldly, not someone who worked at the school. Plus Miss Kempton would head back to wherever she came from once her country service finished and that's the last they'd see of her. It could be said Maddie might be saving Mr C from a potential broken heart.

Emboldened, Maddie finished her notes and began a rough draft of a message to Sarah. She'd be writing as herself so she had to be careful to make sure nothing even hinted at the fact she was also Lonely in Longreach. Sarah couldn't guess. It would blow the whole deal. Why would she suspect? Maddie shrugged and ploughed on, crafting what she believed to be an elegant invitation from a keen high school student. Once she got permission from school, she'd send it.

This was going to be *so* good.

From: Lonely_In_Longreach
To: Solitary_In_Sydney
Subject: Love in the outback

Dear Sarah,
A fact-finding mission sounds great. I'm sure I can help you find some people to talk to. There's a lot

of interesting stories out here and most people are
happy to tell them.

As to what to drink with the pork crackling pizza,
I'm thinking beer. Maybe we should try and make a
pizza when you come visit? Might be fun.

And let me just say, I've got a good feeling about
you too, Sarah.

Cheers,
Sam

CHAPTER TEN

'Seriously?' Fiona placed a steaming hot cup of tea down on the table in front of Sarah. 'Are you really going to go?' She sat down on the chair opposite and folded one leg under her. 'I mean, *you* taking a risk for love.'

'What's that supposed to mean?' Sarah picked up her tea. 'Thank you for this by the way.'

'Nothing and you're welcome.'

Sarah took a sip, the too-hot brew scalding her tongue.

'I take risks,' she said as she returned the tea to the table to let it cool. 'What makes you think I don't?'

'Are you kidding me? Two years of Greg? Plus, you look like a total townie.' Fiona, from the country herself, constituted the closest thing Sarah had to an expert on rural fashion.

'I could get a hat and some boots,' she suggested.

'That's exactly the kind of thing a townie would do,' Fiona scoffed. 'You don't need to dress up like it's Hallow-een. Regular jeans and a shirt are fine.'

'I've got jeans and shirts.'

'You've got designer jeans and fifty-dollar t-shirts.'

'What do I do? Go shopping at the charity shop?' Sarah threw up her hands in frustration.

'Now that is plain insulting,' said Fiona. 'Us country folk don't go around looking like we dressed out of a rag bag.'

'I never said you did, and you know it. Charity shops sell perfectly good, decent clothes. I'm confused as to how I'm supposed to dress is all. Jeans are jeans where I come from.' Sarah crossed her arms in frustration.

'Borrow some of my stuff. You're only going for a couple of weeks.'

'Thank you.' Sarah looked out the window at the tightly packed apartments and never-ending stream of cars passing by. She'd never been to the outback before despite dreaming about it for years and she found it hard to imagine what its reality would be like while she sat in suburbia drinking tea. Boots, there'd have to be boots which meant she'd have to get some new ones.

'You are going, right?' Fiona asked.

'Yes.' The question rattled her out of her daydream. 'It's a great opportunity to get out into the country and meet people. For my article, I mean.'

'Right, for your article.' Fiona nodded slowly. 'And what about Lonely in Longreach? Great to meet him too.'

'Of course.' A surge of irritation took her by surprise. 'I think it's important to interview as many people as I can about the challenges of finding love in the country, Lonely

in Longreach included,' she said primly. She really should tell Fiona she knew his name, yet something held her back. As if saying his real name had the power to conjure him up.

'Really.' It wasn't a question. They'd known each other since the first day of university and Fiona's straight-shooting personality refused to give quarter on Sarah's delusions.

'Alright then,' she snapped, more annoyed with herself than her friend. 'I do want to meet Sam. I want to find out if this … this thing I feel is real or all in my imagination before I go off and marry a man I have no right to marry in the first place.' She sunk down in her seat. 'There, happy?'

'Why, yes I am, thank you.' Fiona took a sip of her tea, smiling in an irritatingly satisfied way. 'Sam, hey? Not a bad name.'

Sarah rolled her eyes. 'I was totally *not* going to tell you his name.'

'You are a lousy liar and I wanted you to admit the truth about what you're doing, that's all. We both know you shouldn't marry Greg. The question is, does Greg know?'

Sarah sighed. 'God, I don't know.' She put her elbows on the scarred kitchen table and sunk her head in her hands. 'He's off on a retreat with some of the gang from the gym.'

Fiona's eyebrows ratcheted up a notch higher.

'No, I didn't want to go and I'm fine with him going,' Sarah answered Fiona's unasked question.

Fiona sipped her tea and regarded Sarah over the brim of her mug.

'And I'm fine with Rachel going too. I think it's possibly a good thing.' Sarah couldn't stop talking, goaded by her friend's silence.

'That's Rachel of the too-small shorts?' Fiona spoke at last.

'You know it.' Sarah mushed her face with her hands so her words were muffled. 'I bet she's taking those shorts too.'

'As if they'd agree to be left behind,' snorted Fiona. 'Those shorts want Greg, you mark my words.'

Sarah flopped back in her chair. 'Surely he must know on some level how different we are. He keeps hoping I'll change into a fitness-slash-health nut like him. And I have changed, a little, but I don't think I can change enough for a lifetime.'

'Honey,' Fiona's tone gentled and she reached out a hand across the table, 'you shouldn't have to change at all.' Sarah took her hand, comforted by her words. 'If you two were right for each other you'd click into place with no one having to completely re-scaffold themselves,' Fiona continued. 'Greg needs a girl who is as passionate as he is, and you need a man who is as crazy as you are.'

'Hey!' Sarah took her hand back, the tender moment evaporating under Fiona's acid wit.

'Just calling it like I see it.' Fiona chuckled.

'Yeah, good on you.' Sarah stood up.

'Where are you going?'

'To get my laptop and look up Longreach. I want to know what I'm in for.' Sarah padded the few feet into their tiny lounge room to collect her computer. 'And I want to look at photos to see what everyone is wearing.'

'And there I was hoping you were staging a flounce-out. Stop by the kitchen and bring me back some of those mini muffins while you're at it,' said Fiona.

'Are your legs painted on or something?'

'Fine, I'll get them myself.' Fiona sighed, stood up and grabbed the box of muffins as Sarah sat back down with her laptop.

'You want to read the latest message?'

'Love to.' Fiona sat back down and popped a muffin into her mouth.

'Here,' Sarah slid the laptop in front of Fiona, 'read this while I get more tea.'

She took the teapot with her to the kitchen, exactly four and a half steps from the dining area, and flipped the kettle on to boil water for a fresh pot. As she prepared the tea, Fiona read the message out loud.

'Wow.' Fiona sat back in her chair and stared at the screen. 'He's sounds like he might be the real deal.'

'Not a guy in Nigeria with a laptop.' Sarah bit into a double chocolate mini muffin, the kind the local supermarket baked on site. What Greg didn't know wouldn't stress him.

'This is all getting a bit real.' Fiona tucked into her strawberry muffin. 'These are okay, but I think I like the double choc ones better,' she said with her mouth full.

'I agree, on both topics. What have I got to lose? I go up to Queensland. I visit the man in question. I use the time to interview as many people as possible so I can write a killer series about love in the country. The weather is at its best out there and now is when the towns hold loads of events so there's a good chance I'll find some great stories in amongst that lot. I happen to be including Longreach on the agenda. Then I come home.' She stopped and took a deep breath. 'Worst case scenario, I get some great material for my story.'

'Best case scenario, you fall in love,' said Fiona.

'I can't even think about that right now,' said Sarah. 'My feelings are all tangled up like a ball of wool belonging to a rabid kitten.'

'Nice analogy. The rabid kitten of love. I think you should trademark that.'

Sarah offered up a weak smile. 'I guess I'll deal with the love stuff if it happens. One thing I know for sure is I have to go see for myself. The old woman I'm going to be one day would regret not going, not finding out when I had the chance. At least I'll have an awesome trip under my belt.'

'What are you going to do about Greg?' Fiona picked the muffin crumbs off her t-shirt.

Sarah shrugged. 'I'm hoping he'll ditch me for Rachel, I guess.'

Fiona snorted in an unladylike manner. 'Chicken.'

'Are you disapproving of me?'

'Actively. You should call off your relationship with Greg before you go.' She held up a hand as Sarah made to speak. 'Or at least confess to Lonely Sam that you're coming out of a long-term relationship. Keep it honest, kiddo.'

Sarah sighed. Why was the high road always the hardest? Fiona was right. She ought to end one relationship honestly and approach the next one from the same position.

'They don't call Longreach the heart of Queensland for nothing. Be a great angle for your series if you do fall in love. Might as well milk it for all it's worth.' Fiona closed the laptop with a click. 'Though take it from me, the outback might not be what you expect. There's nothing romantic about life out there. It's tough and the people are tempered by it.'

'You've gone soft, living in the city,' Sarah scoffed good-naturedly.

Fiona shrugged. 'Maybe, but I'd rather be soft here than hard out there. One thing I know for sure is that you're

going to need some wardrobe advice and I'm the girl to give it.'

From: Solitary_In_Sydney
To: Lonely_In_Longreach
Subject: True confession

Dear Sam,

I want to let you know I'm in the middle of the end of a long-term relationship. It's all friendly, as much as these things can be, I guess. We've run our course and are now more friends than we ever were lovers.

By the time I meet you we will be well and truly broken up. Why am I telling you this? Because I wanted to be honest and open with you. Start as I mean to go on, if you know what I mean.

The attraction I feel for you confuses me. I don't understand what's happening here but I know something is, so it's important to me not to have any secrets.

I hope you understand.

Warmest,
Sarah

Watching cricket on a lazy Sunday afternoon proved to be Sam's one true indulgence. He bought his favourite snacks, got the beer in, cranked up the air-conditioning and turned off his phone. Yes, he could watch it down the pub with his mates but there was something deliciously indulgent in

sprawling out on the couch and settling in for an afternoon of yelling at the telly.

And that's exactly what he was doing.

He shovelled a handful of peanuts into his mouth and chewed, enjoying the crunchy salty taste. He could do whatever he wanted. Put his feet up on the coffee table, have the telly up too loud, and balance the bowl of snacks on his belly Homer Simpson-style. Levi had gone out so there was no one to set an example for, no one to care.

Sam sighed happily. Before now, the thought of no one to tell him off might have left him depressed. It only served to highlight Michelle's absence. Since he'd gone out on a couple of dates with Kylie, he enjoyed his autonomy more. That part of him he thought had shrivelled and died with his wife's death, lived on. While he wasn't ready for any kind of commitment, he enjoyed the knowledge that he wasn't entirely dead yet.

He took a swig of beer and lost himself in the match, offering his opinion now and again to an umpire who couldn't hear him. Total immersion.

He didn't hear Levi come in until he stood right next to the couch.

'Hi, Dad.'

Sam started, nearly choking on a Cheezel.

'Geez, Levi,' he said between coughs. 'A little heads up would be nice.'

'Didn't realise you're so jumpy, old man.' Levi perched on the arm of the couch.

'Less of the old man thank you very much.' Sam brushed the crumbs off his t-shirt and sat up straight. He'd have to resume the responsible adult persona now.

'Who's winning?'

'Why don't you come and watch it with me?' Sam patted the empty space on the couch. Soon Levi would be too old to bother spending time watching sport with his dad. He'd have better things to do and more interesting people to do them with.

Levi slid sideways into the spot, his eyes glued to the screen. Sam smiled and offered him the peanut bowl. Levi took a handful without looking.

For some time the two of them watched the match, both offering their opinions whenever necessary, enjoying the simple pleasure of a good combative sport played well.

'Dad?'

'Yep.'

'Are you going to miss Miss Kempton?'

'What?' The question caught Sam on the hop. He'd been expecting Levi to say something about the quality of umpiring or debate the merits of a particular player. 'I guess. I mean I don't know her all that well. She seems nice.'

Could he be any lamer?

Levi nodded as if satisfied with the answer.

'Why? You worried she was going to move in or something?' Sam couldn't let it go.

Levi's head snapped around from the telly. He wore a frown. 'No, why would I worry about that? It's not like she could ever take Mum's place. She's not the right sort.'

'Right sort of what?' His curiosity had been peaked.

'You know, the right sort of woman.' Levi had turned his attention back to the match as if bored with the direction the conversation had taken.

'And you'd be an expert on that?' Sam shifted to face his son, the cricket match forgotten.

Levi shrugged without taking his eyes off the television. 'Wouldn't say that. From what I saw it's not love at first sight.'

'Not this again,' Sam sighed. 'Where do you get this crap from? No …' He held up his hand as Levi made to speak, '… don't tell me. Maddie McRae.'

'Speaking of Maddie,' Levi looked at Sam for the first time since he walked in. 'She wants to invite a journalist from Sydney to come speak at the school and she was thinking it might be nice to plan a welcome dinner. Maddie wondered if you'd like to come? I'd come with you of course and Maddie's mum and dad will be there.' His words became more rushed as he galloped to the finish line, no doubt worried Sam would give an automatic no.

He was tempted.

'When would this journalist arrive?' He'd play along.

'I'm not sure.' Levi returned his attention to the TV. 'Maddie hasn't emailed her yet.'

'Okay, this is a theoretical welcome dinner for a journalist who hasn't confirmed they're coming yet. Have I got that right?'

'Yep, that about covers it.'

Sam nodded. 'Then I agree to dinner. In theory, of course, pending their confirmation.'

'Thanks, Dad. Knew you wouldn't let us down.' Levi rose to leave.

'Can I ask why Maddie wants me there?' Not that it mattered, he was curious all the same.

'How would I know?' Levi looked at him as if he'd asked the dumbest question ever. 'I'm going to my room.' And he slunk off, leaving Sam to his cricket.

Sam slowly shook his head. Teenagers. How Kylie put up with thirty of them every day boggled his mind. He was flat out dealing with one.

He took a reviving sip of beer. Had to hand it to Miss Maddie, the girl had initiative. He had no doubt she was behind the plan to lure a poor unsuspecting journalist out to the sticks. Wouldn't have occurred to Levi. Maybe Maddie had her eye on a media career. Could do worse for herself. She might inspire Levi to some dream of his own. So far he'd shown little ambition for much more than dirt-bike riding and playing video games.

Sam sighed and returned his attention to the match. The kids would let him know when and where he was required. He considered it nice that Maddie wanted to stage some kind of welcome. Fair enough. He'd consider it his civic duty if the time came.

'That's definitely out!' Sam shouted at the television, his promise forgotten for the moment in the light of terrible injustices being carried out on the cricket pitch.

An hour later the cricket had finished and a kind of restless apathy descended upon Sam. Even though Levi was down the corridor in his room, loneliness wrapped itself around him, a bit like being caught in a spider's web. Every time he tried to shift the mood, it seemed to cling tighter until he despaired of ever untangling himself from its sticky grip.

He grabbed a cold beer from the fridge, screwing the top off and tossing it onto the kitchen sink where it landed with a tinny clatter. The bottle started sweating almost immediately despite the air-conditioning in the room.

Sam pushed open the back door, the eternal heat hitting him as he stepped out onto the veranda. He paused for a moment, letting the warmth of the late afternoon claim him, before he ambled over to the tree stump on the edge of the yard, kicking up dust plumes with his feet as he went.

The tree had been cut down generations before yet no one had ever thought to remove the stump, which provided a handy front row seat to the spectacular outback sunset. As he sat down upon the stump worn smooth from generations of Costello butts and silvered by weather, he absentmindedly traced the initials carved into its surface, a set for each Costello man who had come before him and one set made by his son. His fingers followed the curve of the crude carving, each letter like a message from the past and a talisman for the future. In moments like these, he missed his dog. Kevin used to sit on the stump next to him, tongue lolling, and watch the sunset as if he understood the significance of the event.

Sam settled in for the show, sipping his beer and allowing the great silence of the outback to recalibrate him. It never failed. He took a deep breath, exhaling slowly, the tension ebbing away as the sun began to dip below the horizon, its rays glinting off the solar panels as it took its leave.

The sky looked like a paintbox had exploded with vibrant pinks, electric orange, and deep violet tinged with gold. Beneath it, the land turned dark with shadow steeped in silence, that deep stillness only the desert brings. That was what he waited for; not the colours or even the quiet, but the stillness.

He couldn't remember when he'd first become aware of the presence contained within that peace, long ago perhaps,

when he was a little boy. The indigenous people of the region, the Iningai, knew it. They knew the stories and song lines which accompanied it. All he knew how to do was appreciate it, allow it to fill his soul. He did that now.

Sam stayed put until the riot of stars filling the night sky pushed all the colours off the edge of the earth. He sighed as the last of the light disappeared, leaving him and the unseen spirit of the land. This was what kept him here, these moments of deep communion with something greater than himself. People he met from the cities and the coast never understood why he stayed when life could be so hard. They didn't know how a land could claim your soul.

He sensed he'd somehow woken up from a sleep he hadn't known he'd been taking. Maybe his life was beginning to change but one thing would always remain the same—the outback's hold on his heart.

CHAPTER ELEVEN

Levi stood next to Maddie with a sense of doom invading every atom of his body. This was a very bad idea. Why he let her talk him into it confused him. He'd never been the kind to give in to peer pressure. When the other boys had set fire to a bunch of packing crates behind one of the hotels for a laugh he'd made sure he'd been as far from there as possible. He avoided trouble like other people avoided the dentist, deliberately and often.

Yet here he stood.

'So you see, Miss Kempton, having a bona fide journalist come and speak to us about her work and its impact on society can only benefit us in the context of social science.'

Maddie sounded like she'd swallowed a dictionary. He knew her well enough to know she'd probably been working on this speech for days, rewriting and editing it until she got

it perfect. He had to admit that pitching a changing-face-of-journalism-and-how-it-affects-society angle to a history and social sciences teacher had been a stroke of genius. How could Miss Kempton say no?

Maddie had her debate team captain persona on. Very impressive. The combined sensations of dread and awe made him a little queasy.

'I get where you're coming from,' said Miss Kempton as she packed up her notes from the day. They'd caught her at the end of the final class. She looked tired, dark rings circling her eyes. 'I don't think now is a good time.'

'Miss Kempton, this journalist will be in the area and it might be the only time we get someone from a respected Sydney publication out this way.' He could hear the panic edging Maddie's voice. She was losing and she knew it.

'Where did you say this journalist was from again?' Miss Kempton narrowed her eyes as if she could see right through their ruse. Levi swallowed hard and concentrated on looking normal instead of like someone whose life was about to explode.

'*Seriously Sydney,*' said Maddie, raising her chin an inch as if defying Miss Kempton to question the integrity of the publication. He'd looked it up online and it looked dodgy to him. Not exactly hard journalism, although the piece on unique glass tables designed to look like animals half-submerged underwater had been fascinating. He'd liked the hippo best.

'Mmm …' Miss Kempton cocked one elegant eyebrow that said everything that needed saying in his opinion. 'I still think the timing is not right. We have a lot on our

plate at the moment, not to mention exams are looming.'
She picked up her bag and stuffed her manila folders inside,
signalling an end to the conversation.

'But Miss ...' Maddie sounded whiny now, something
Levi would never tell her of course.

'Maddison McRae, that's the end of the discussion. I have
somewhere I need to be and I suggest you do too. We can
review your suggestion later in the year at a more appropriate time.' Miss Kempton held out her arm, herding them
towards the door.

Levi turned and dutifully made his way out of the classroom. He knew when they were beat. Maddie, on the other
hand, did not.

'Miss, we could do it afterhours in the hall and then it
wouldn't eat into school time. I'm sure there are heaps of
kids who would like to hear about a career in journalism.'
Maddie bounded alongside Miss Kempton like an overgrown puppy.

Miss Kempton ignored her, impressive when Maddie
towered over her by several inches.

'Please, please, please, Miss Kempton.'

Levi closed his eyes rather than bear witness to the incon-
gruous humiliation of Maddie McRae. Better for them both
if he didn't see it.

Miss Kempton stopped at the door to the classroom.
'Maddie, I said no.' Her tone brooked no argument and
Levi saw the fight go out of Maddie almost immediately.
She deflated like a week-old party balloon.

They all stepped out of the classroom and Miss Kempton
closed the door with a finality that sealed the deal. She left
them standing dejectedly in the corridor.

'What now?' Levi shoved his hands in his pockets and hunched his shoulders, braced for the firestorm.

Maddie sighed. 'I don't know. I have to rethink this.' She sounded like two things she absolutely never was, flat and defeated.

'Can I help?' He really didn't want to offer. Self-preservation told him to walk away and be grateful for the close call, but he hated to see Maddie like this.

'You can always help,' she said to his dismay. 'I don't know how right at this moment in time. Give me a couple of days. Like my nan says, there's always more ways than one to skin a cat.'

'What have cats got to do with it?'

'It's a saying, dummy.' She nudged him with her elbow. 'You know, for a really bright guy you sometimes don't have a clue.'

His inability to keep up seemed to cheer her up. They began to walk slowly along, silent in the golden glow of the afternoon.

'Does this mean the whole deal is off?' Levi asked hopefully. 'If Miss Kempton won't let us bring Sarah here to talk then how will we introduce her to Dad?'

'This is only a minor setback,' said Maddie as she hitched her school bag up on her shoulder. 'No way are we going back on the plan. Miss Kempton might say no now but I'm sure I can convince her. I just need to work out how.'

'Well, you'd better be quick because she's leaving soon.'

'What did you say?' Maddie stopped dead in her tracks and let her school bag drop to the floor with an ominous thud. He had no idea what she carried in that thing, it sounded like rocks.

'I said Miss Kempton is leaving. Her dad is sick and she's going back to the coast to be with him.' He blinked at her, understanding he was in trouble but not entirely sure as to why.

'And you didn't think to tell me this because …?' She crossed her arms and glared at him.

'Because … um … I don't see how it matters. We wanted Miss Kempton out of Dad's life and she will be. Problem solved.' He shrugged. What else was there to say?

'You've stood by and let me waste my time trying to convince a teacher who won't even be here to help us.'

'What does it matter?' He frowned at Maddie and pulled his who-cares face. 'You find out who the replacement is going to be and ask her. Tell the replacement Miss Kempton agreed to it.' As the words left his lips he could have kicked himself for being so stupid.

A grin lit up Maddie's face, the full wattage too much for Levi to look at straight on.

'Levi Costello, you are not as dumb as you look.' She stepped forward and hugged him, pinning his arms to his side. 'I could kiss you.'

Hot blood rushed to his face, sending his temperature soaring. His stomach squirmed like he'd swallowed worms, and something else he couldn't name overrode the lot as she planted a kiss on his cheek, her lips soft and warm.

He hadn't realised he'd stopped breathing until she stepped away and the oxygen rushed back into his lungs.

'You think I look dumb?' he mumbled, confused about what had happened.

'Some days,' she said, laughing at him. 'Mostly you're okay.' She bumped him with her shoulder and he staggered

under the unexpected force. 'Come on.' She picked up her
school bag and slung it over her shoulder. 'We're talking to
the wrong teacher. If Miss Kempton is not going to be here,
we need to get Principal Forsyth's permission instead. This
is not over until it's over.'

'That's what I'm worried about,' he muttered under his
breath as he followed her.

From: maddiemac@spacemail.com.au
To: sarah_lewis@seriouslysydney.com.au
Subject: Invitation to Longreach

Dear Ms Lewis,
My name is Maddison McRae. I am almost fifteen
years old and I live in Longreach, Queensland.

I am interested in a career as a journalist and have
been following your work in Seriously Sydney for
some time. While I don't live in Sydney (obviously) I
do hope to move there once I've finished school. I
want to go to university and study journalism.

To this end, I'd like to extend an invitation to you
to come to Longreach and speak to my school
about journalism in the twenty-first century, how it's
changed, where you see its future and its impact on
society.

I realise that coming all the way out here is a lot to
ask. We do have some wonderful events coming up
like the Isisford Races and there is a lot to do and see.
It might make a great article for your publication.

I've spoken to my principal and have attached her
email so you can see I am legit.

Hope to hear from you soon.

Your friend,

Maddie McRae

'You would not believe what happened today.' Sarah pulled
a bottle of chilled white wine out of her shopping bag and
plonked it down on the kitchen bench.

'Greg called and asked you to marry him for real?' Fiona
continued to chop up a red capsicum into long strips without missing a beat or losing a finger.

'As if.' Sarah squeezed past Fiona and retrieved two wine
glasses from the cupboard above her head.

'Okay, I'll play. Bella had an aneurism and you're now the
boss?'

'Fiona! That's an appalling thing to wish on someone.'
Sarah unscrewed the wine bottle and sloshed a good amount
into each glass.

'Technically I did not wish it upon your boss. I merely
suggested it as a possibility. No karma bounce back there.'
Fiona scooped up the capsicum and placed it in a bowl.

'Mmm … I'm not sure.' Sarah took a sip of her wine.

Fiona reached for her glass. 'Lonely Sam in Longreach
has declared his undying love based on an old photo of you
and that piece you did on tables that look like submerged
animals.'

'Hey! That was one of my most popular pieces. Everybody loved the hippo.'

Fiona began to top and tail some fresh beans, giving a little shrug. 'Then I give up.'

'You're partly right. It does involve Longreach.'

'Don't tease me. I have a knife and I know how to use it.' Fiona waved the offending blade in her direction.

'I got an email from a girl who goes to Longreach High. She's invited me to come and speak to the students about a career in journalism. How's that for timing?' Sarah stole a bean and bit into it, enjoying its crunchy greenness.

Fiona pulled her I'm-impressed face. 'That's one hell of a coincidence.'

'They say there's no such thing as coincidence.'

'Really? And who might *they* be?'

Sarah waved her bean around like a baton. 'They who know, of course.'

'Are you going to do it?' Fiona eyed her as she placed the beans in the bowl next to the capsicum.

'I guess. I can fly to Longreach, do the talk, interview some people, get a feel for the place ...'

'Meet Sam.' Fiona stopped preparing vegetables for another drink. 'You're not thinking this invitation has something to do with fate, are you?'

'Fate?' Sarah choked on her wine, spluttering her words. 'Only people who appeared in cheesy eighties movies believe in fate. The rest of us got over that long ago. This invitation merely adds additional weight to Project Outback.'

Who was she kidding? She totally thought the invitation indicated the hand of fate. Fiona mocking her about her delusional beliefs was the last thing she wanted.

'Project Outback?' Fiona laughed. 'Has a nice ring to it. When do you leave for Longreach?'

Sarah shrugged, relieved the subject of fate had been left behind. 'Bella wants me to leave this weekend. I need to talk to this student and find out what they had in mind. She did mention that the Isisford Races are on soon and I was thinking it might make for a great opportunity. You know, a bunch of people gathered in one place are bound to have some wonderful stories to tell.'

'Another brilliant coincidence.' Fiona raised her glass in a mock toast. 'Looks like all the signs are pointing to go. Do you want to consult my Magic 8-Ball and confirm your decision?'

'Why do you have to be like that?' Sarah groaned. 'All the romance has been trampled out of you.'

'Blame my mother. She made me sit through hours of awful romantic comedies when I was a kid. I'm totally inoculated against schmaltz of any kind.'

'Yet you watch *Farmer Goes a Courting* with religious zeal.'

'What can I say?' Fiona shrugged. 'I enjoy watching people tortured in a public arena. I keep hoping they'll have on someone I know. Speaking of which, grab that bottle and bring the hummus from the fridge. The show is about to start.'

Sarah did as she'd been bid, placing the items within easy reach on the coffee table in the lounge room. Fiona followed with her plate piled high with chopped vegetables.

They each curled up in a corner of the couch. Sarah crossed her legs and hugged a purple cushion appliqued with pink hearts.

Fiona turned the TV on, the show's familiar theme tune filling the room.

As she watched, Sarah let her mind drift. The offer to go to Longreach and speak couldn't have come at a better time. Definitely the Universe telling her she'd made the right decision. All she had to do was tee up a casual meeting with Sam. Being in Longreach for two reasons, research and the talk, took the pressure off. If things didn't work out with Sam—and she didn't even know what that meant—then she would come away with some great research, have done something meaningful for the students in the area and could chalk the whole thing up to experience.

And if things did work out …

Sarah veered away from that line of thought. If Sam liked her and she liked him *then* she'd worry about what came next. Right now, she couldn't be sure he looked anything like his profile picture. He could be years older, and boring. There could be no physical spark between them and the attraction she'd been feeling might be nothing more than a hormonally driven fantasy.

She'd need a new dress for the races.

Meanwhile, a farmer got his heart broken as the girl he'd chosen decided country life really wasn't for her. Fiona ran a commentary requiring no response from Sarah, who dipped a bean in the hummus and crunched thoughtfully.

She could contact the local paper and the local radio station, drum up a bit of support for her project. Also give her some contacts other than a teenage girl and a lovelorn farmer she didn't know. A bit of backup if things went pearshaped. Like if Sam turned out to be some kind of psycho.

Fiona refilled Sarah's glass and passed it to her without taking her eyes off the television. Sarah took it gratefully and sipped at the delicious chilled chardonnay. She lost herself

in the drama of the show, enjoying the moment with a sense that somehow, everything would work out as it should.

'Lonely Sam email you back yet?'

'Not yet. Might have been a bit much for him to take in.' She shrugged as her mobile phone buzzed on the kitchen table. She pondered fetching it to see who had messaged her. Decided against it and ate another bean covered in dip, followed by a capsicum strip.

The phone buzzed again. The little blue light flashed on the corner of the phone.

Read me. Now.

Sarah sighed. Lured by the siren song of the mobile phone, she unfolded herself from the couch and went and got it.

Hey babe! Having the best time. Wish you were here with us. Rachel says hi. Sending you some pictures. Don't be too jealous. See you soon x

'I bet she does,' muttered Sarah as she resumed her position on the couch.

'What's up?' Fiona asked.

'Message from Greg. Tiny-shorts Rachel says hi.'

'I knew she was the friendly type.'

The phone began to vibrate again, shuddering like crazy as a series of messages popped in.

'What now?' Fiona peered over Sarah's shoulder as she opened the files to reveal photos of Greg in workout gear in front of an array of beautiful lush backdrops.

'Looks lovely,' said Fiona. 'You should have gone along.'

Sarah shot her a sour look. 'You know I don't do well with all that chanting and kale.'

'Fair point,' said Fiona. 'Must say those tiny shorts really do suit Rachel quite well.' A photo showing Greg and Rachel

laughing popped up. 'You've got to give it to them, they're a good-looking couple.'

Sarah nudged Fiona with her elbow. 'Whose side are you on?'

'Didn't know we were picking sides?' She looked genuinely surprised. 'I thought you were considering breaking up with him.'

'I never said that.' True, she hadn't, although she'd thought it often enough.

'What's the whole Lonely in Longreach thing about then?' Fiona paused the live TV, crossed her arms and settled back.

Sarah swallowed hard. 'I told you, I'm doing an article,' she said in a small voice.

'I hope that convinced you because it didn't do anything for me. Look, Sarah, you know Greg isn't the right guy for you.' Fiona took Sarah's limp hand in hers. 'We've been friends for ages and if I can't tell you, who can? He's a nice guy but …' She shrugged as if it were self-evident what came next.

'I know but what if I'm wrong and Sam is a pipe dream? What if he's a stupid fantasy I'm having? Maybe I've got my city-girl-goes-country daydreams confused with real life. Then I've thrown away one perfectly good relationship for a ghost.' Sarah sniffed back the tears pressing for release.

'A perfectly good relationship? Honey, it's a great friendship but it's not marriage material, and you know it. It's okay to be scared. It's not okay to make do.' Fiona rubbed Sarah's cold hand between hers.

Fiona's words rang uncomfortably true. She'd already told Sam she intended to break up with Greg. Only right and proper the man himself know too.

She had to set Greg free.

'Do it now.' Fiona picked up her phone and handed it to her. 'Before you lose your nerve.'

'Can you read my thoughts or something?' Sarah wiped away one stray tear which had made a break for it.

'You think *really* loudly,' said Fiona. 'And you snore.'

Sarah laughed despite her leaden heart. She took the phone and dialled Greg's number. Somewhere up on the northern New South Wales coast, the phone rang.

She took a deep breath and braced herself.

'Good luck,' whispered Fiona as she made herself scarce.

'Hello.' Greg's voice sounded so familiar and dear that she nearly started crying again.

'Hello, there's something … I've got to tell you.' She took deep shuddering breaths as she tried to get the words out.

'Okay,' he said, sounding as subdued as she felt. 'There's something I've got to tell you first.'

From: sarah_lewis@seriouslysydney.com.au
To: maddiemac@spacemail.com.au
Subject: RE: Invitation to Longreach

Dear Maddison,
I can't tell you how excited I was to receive your email.
I would love to speak to you and your fellow students
about my career in journalism and how I see journal-
ism developing, particularly in the digital age.
 I am planning a trip out to the region in the next few
weeks to research a series about love in the outback.
The timing could not be better. I'll let you know once

I've booked my flight and we can sort out a date with your principal.

Kind regards,
Sarah Lewis

From: Solitary_In_Sydney
To: Lonely_In_Longreach
Subject: Here I come!

Dear Sam,

I hope I didn't scare you off with my last email because my flight is booked and I'm on my way! I arrive Saturday. I've hired a car so I can get about and interview people. I'm thinking I might drive out to Winton and some of the other towns and see if I can find some great love stories there.

How's this for a coincidence—I've been invited to speak about journalism at the local high school. The timing couldn't be more perfect, although I have no idea what to say to a bunch of teenagers. I've never done this sort of thing before.

In the meantime, I'll be staying at the Longreach Motel. Maybe we can catch up for a meal or something?

This is the only way I have to contact you so I'm including my phone number in this email. Feel free to contact me anytime.

I can't wait to meet you properly.

Sarah

I've booked my flight and we can sort out a date with your principal.

Kind regards,
Sarah Lewis.

From: Solitary_In_Sydney
To: Lonely_In_Longreach.
Subject: Here I come!

Dear Sam,

I hope I didn't scare you off with my first email because my flight is booked and I'm on my way! I arrive Saturday. I've hired a car so I can get about and interview people. I'm trying to
and some of the other low
some great love stories
How's this for a coincidence? I've been invited to speak about journalism at the local high

CHAPTER TWELVE

From: Lonely_In_Longreach
To: Solitary_In_Sydney
Subject: RE: Here I come!

Dear Sarah,
Sorry for the delay, it's been a busy week. You didn't scare me at all. I respect your honesty. As you know, I'm a widower and I've been out of the dating game for a long time. I'm ready to get back into it and see if I can find romance. Maybe with you. We'll see.

I'm excited that you're coming to Longreach. I can't wait to meet you either. I do know Maddie McRae, she's best friends with my son Levi. She told me she'd invited a journalist, but I had no idea it would be you. I couldn't believe the coincidence! What are the chances? I reckon it's down to fate if you ask me.

Maddie has invited me and Levi to your welcome dinner. She thinks it's a good idea for you to meet some locals. As I'm the local in question, I agree.

I haven't told Levi that I'm online with a view to finding a new relationship. I don't know how he'd go thinking I'm replacing his mother. So, if you don't mind playing things low-key at dinner, just until I can talk to Levi and he can get a chance to meet you. Hell, until I get a chance to meet you.

Can't wait,
Sam

Sarah had been all Maddie talked about for days. Sarah-this and Sarah-that. Her constant chatter was driving Levi nuts. He'd had a headache since Thursday and had solemnly considered whether or not underage drinking might help.

In the end, he'd given in. Or was that up? Either way, he did what he always did and Maddie got her way. It was too late to stop things, and he suspected he had no power to do so anyway. Not a pleasant thought. Maddie, a force of nature at the best of times, had successfully railroaded him. He knew the exact moment she'd done so.

They'd been in her bedroom on Wednesday, studying for a geography exam, of which Maddie could not see the point.

'I still don't get why the low life expectancy of babies has anything to do with the geography of Swaziland.' Maddie threw her pen down on the bed and leaned back into the mass of cushions. She rubbed her eyes with the heels of her hands.

'Maddie—' he'd begun.

'If you say one word about me needing glasses, Levi Costello, I will hurt you very badly,' she growled.

'Okay, okay.' He held up his hands in surrender. 'What I was going to say was the problem isn't with the geography, you know, like the *land* itself. Geography is also about stuff like urbanisation, services available to people, how far they have to travel, how the environment impacts them. Stuff like drought or floods.'

She crossed her arms over her chest and stared at him as if seeing him for the first time. 'I still don't get it,' she said after a little while.

He sighed. 'Okay, Mama Swazi lives in the countryside and can't get to the hospital because it's in the city and there's no health care service available to her.'

'That's the geography of urbanisation.' She squinted at him as if reading the answer off his forehead.

'Yes. And then let's say there's a flood and the roads get washed out so she can't get there anyway, even if she wanted to.'

'That's the geography of the land.'

'That'll do,' he said, exhausted from trying to explain the same thing to her for hours.

'I still don't get what the teacher wants us to do for our assignment.'

Levi put his head in his hands and groaned. He didn't think the assignment had been that complicated until he tried to work on it with Maddie. She could be bright about some things and then, sometimes … well …

'I'm going to do how the drought here in Longreach has impacted farming methods and changed the way some

people have lived for generations. Why don't you do something on how the drought has made young people look to the cities for their futures and how that impacts the town?'

She lit up, her smile like dynamite blasting through his frustration. 'Levi, you are a genius.'

She got excited then and started chattering a mile a minute. Made him wish he'd kept his mouth shut. He let her rabbit on while he scrolled through some pictures of solar farms he'd found online. Looked like they were farming on Mars but he knew he could go out the back of his farm and it would look exactly the same. He liked the idea of his dad being a solar farmer. Kind of cool.

'Oh my God!' Maddie sat bolt upright on her bed as if zapped by electricity.

'What is it?' He was all attention; the probability of disaster rated highly these days.

'I got an email from Sarah Lewis.' Maddie's eyes glowed as she hooked her hair back behind her ears.

'Really?' He inched closer from where he sat on the floor. 'What does she say?' he asked cautiously.

Maddie perused the email. 'Let me read it to you.'

When she was done Maddie clapped her hands together and squealed. 'See? I told you Fate would intervene.'

'How is that fate?' Levi said morosely.

'She's definitely coming out here and she wants to come and speak at our school. If that's not Fate, what is?'

A surge of annoyance rushed through Levi, making his skin prickle. 'All that has nothing to do with fate, and everything to do with you meddling in other people's lives. Like you always do.'

'I do not.' Maddie's voice rose an octave with indignation.

'Yes, you do.' Levi snapped shut the lid of his laptop, ready for an argument. 'You came up with the ridiculous scheme to find my dad a girlfriend so that I can go with you to university in Sydney. Not fate, you.' He punctuated his point with his index finger. 'And you were the one who put up the profile on Outback Losers or whatever it is.'

'Outback Singles,' she muttered.

'Whatever.' He dismissed the website with a flick of his wrist. 'Fate didn't do it. You did.'

'Yeah, but Fate brought us Sarah.' She closed the lid of her laptop and moved it aside, meeting him halfway on the battlefield.

Levi snorted in the way he knew always annoyed her. 'Right, fate was waiting for you to put up a fake profile of my dad so it could deliver him the girl of his dreams.'

'Woman, not girl.'

'Jesus, Maddie.' Levi threw up his hands. 'You can't be serious about going through with this.'

'Why are you always so budget, Levi?' she snapped. 'Always settling for second best. Why not take a chance on achieving your dream for once?'

'University in Sydney is your dream, not mine.' As soon as the words left his lips he wished he could take them back. Of course he wanted to go to Sydney with her. He couldn't imagine a life that didn't contain Maddie McRae.

'Is that so?' She narrowed her eyes at him, as if daring him to say it again. He was not that stupid.

He ran both hands through his hair. 'Look, I *do* want to go with you, only this plan of yours is asking for trouble. We still have a couple of years and maybe Dad will find

someone by then. He's started dating again and that's a good sign, right?'

This time Maddie snorted with unladylike zeal. 'You have got to be kidding me. When was the last time anyone date-worthy came through town? You can't leave these things ...'

'Up to fate?' He ducked as she threw a cushion at him.

'Can I remind you that I have a track record of successful matchmaking? You've witnessed every one of them.'

Levi threw the cushion back at her and she batted it away with her hands.

'Get over yourself, Maddie. All those people already liked each other. You hardly did anything to make it happen. Drop a few hints. Invite them both somewhere and then not show up so they're left together. Amateur stuff.' He could see her face getting redder and redder yet he couldn't stop. 'What you're doing now is outrageous. You're manipulating people, letting them believe something that's not true to get something you want.'

'I can't believe you said that.' She looked genuinely horrified and he waited for her to crown him with a pillow. Instead she slid off the bed to sit next to him. 'I cannot believe you really think that of me.'

He reddened in turn, not realising he'd thought about the situation in quite that way until the words were out of his mouth.

'Do you want me to stop? Do you want your dad to be lonely for the rest of his life? Do you want to stay here while I go to Sydney and have a fantastic life living by the beach?'

Levi wanted to say yes, they should stop before they got into trouble. That he didn't think his dad was *that* lonely, and explain that while he wanted to go to Sydney with her he hated the thought of his dad growing old alone. Missing his mum.

Like he did.

Instead he simply stared into her eyes, the colour of the sky at dawn, and said nothing at all.

'Well?' she said, giving him no quarter. 'I need to hear you say it.'

'No,' he said. 'I think the way we're going about things is wrong. I don't want to get into trouble. I don't want *you* to get into trouble. The parents are going to go spare when they find out what we've done.'

Maddie inched closer, invading his personal space and stealing all the oxygen. She shrugged one shoulder provocatively. 'What if they don't find out? What if we get away with it? By the time they find out they will have fallen in love. They won't care. They may even find it funny.'

'I don't think so,' Levi managed hoarsely.

'Love can do strange things to people,' she said.

He was feeling strange right at the moment.

Then she delivered the deathblow, one he had not yet recovered from and had doubts that recovering from this kind of death was even possible.

She kissed him.

Square on the lips for, like, the *longest* time.

Her lips were the kind of soft impossible to imagine without experiencing it. The scent of her—flowery shampoo, bubble gum, and Impulse body spray—overwhelmed his senses as his world narrowed down to the sensation of her

lips against his and her hands resting lightly on his leg. He was sure the imprint of her palms would be burned into his skin for eternity.

His universe began to spin counter clockwise and tip sideways. With eyes tightly closed, he had concentrated on staying upright, sure that once he opened his eyes again the world would have changed forever.

And he'd been right.

Three days had passed and he now found himself sitting in the Star Cinema watching an early session of some awful chick flick, way too close to Maddie for comfort, while his dad dropped Miss Kempton at the airport at the same time Sarah was due to arrive. Maddie hummed with excitement while he sank further and further inside himself, wanting desperately for something to happen to save him from the Armageddon he knew waited for him down the road.

Maddie's shoulder brushed his and all the muscles in his body bunched tight, as if trying instinctively to draw him away from her. He couldn't be near her without thinking about the kiss. Without his body betraying him in embarrassing ways. Levi didn't want things to be this way with Maddie. He rebelled against the change to their friendship, to the loss of the easygoing camaraderie they'd always shared.

He didn't have a name for what they were now, but he didn't like it. Mostly because she didn't seem to notice anything had changed at all.

Maddie watched the cinema screen with distracted interest. She could barely contain herself. In moments, her greatest

matchmaking enterprise would be well and truly under-way. Nerves clutched at her belly. The stakes were incredibly high. She'd done her homework, gone over her plan a zillion times looking for the flaws and the cracks. As long as she stayed on her toes, nothing should go wrong.

She'd worked her backside off finding potential inter-viewees for Sarah. Then Sarah would be grateful to her *and* stay longer in town. Her mum and dad had an extensive network of friends to draw from. Adults *always* liked talk-ing about the old days so everyone had agreed. She'd also drawn up an itinerary for Sarah's stay including a few out-ings with Mr C in case he needed a little prodding along. While she had absolute faith in Fate it didn't hurt to have a backup plan.

Right at this moment, Miss Kempton was getting ready to board the flight to Brisbane. She was pretty enough in her own way. Maddie could see what Levi's dad found attractive in her. But wait until Mr C got a look at Sarah. Miss Kemp-ton couldn't compare.

She sighed, happily perched on the edge of something momentous. She should consider a career as a professional matchmaker. Maddie made a mental note to Google career opportunities when she got home. No point having a natu-ral talent and not using it.

Levi shifted in the seat next to her, trying to fold him-self into a corner. An impossible feat given the lack of space a cinema seat offered. He'd been acting weird since she'd kissed him. Kissing him might not have been the smartest thing she could have done upon reflection, and she'd done a lot of that over the last few days.

Firstly, how could she get Levi to be normal again? Taking the kiss back couldn't be done. They could only move forward. If she could find a way to get him to move past the incident. He acted like she revolted him, pulling away from her every chance he got. The physical withdrawal wasn't the worst of it. He'd spoken in monosyllabic grunts ever since their argument. She missed their conversations, the banter and joking. She missed him.

Secondly, why had she kissed him? Big question without an answer. Her heart totally belonged to Liam Newson. He represented the magical future awaiting her in Sydney. Levi was her best friend. Or he used to be. Kissing him had crossed the line. She knew that. Up until that moment in her bedroom she'd never considered kissing Levi. Never. Why had she done it? No reason she could think of except the moment had demanded it. One minute she'd been arguing with him and the next she'd found her lips on his, a sweet tingly sensation moving seductively through her body like nothing she'd ever experienced before.

Would kissing Liam be like that too? Or better? Maddie indulged herself in her favourite fantasy, closing her eyes and conjuring Liam up. They stood on Bondi Beach—she'd looked up pictures of Bondi online so she could better imagine it—Liam slipped his arms around her waist and drew her towards him until their hips fused together. He brushed her hair back from her face, his eyes tender with love, and then he lowered his head. As their lips met Liam ... morphed into Levi! Maddie snapped her eyes open, pushing the disturbing image out of her mind. Since when did kissing Levi become a thing?

She crossed her arms and slid a little further down into her seat. The hands of her watch, barely visible in the half-light, told her Sarah's plane must have landed by now. After getting her hire car, Sarah would drive the short distance to town and book in at the motel.

Maddie intended to call in on her way home from the cinema and invite Sarah to dinner with her family, including Levi and Mr C. The trickiest part was the first proper meeting and everything hinged on Levi staying cool.

What if Levi betrayed her and didn't follow through on their plan? She studied him, his face partially illuminated by the flickering light of the movie screen. He might be angry enough. Try as she might she couldn't recall any time in their history when he'd been angry at her. Annoyed, yes. Frustrated, for sure. But angry? Never.

If he was willing to destroy their plan, then he wouldn't want to come to Sydney with her either. Suddenly a life without Levi in it loomed large in her imagination. The sensation of instability shook her. He wouldn't go that far, would he? He wouldn't abandon her like that. Not Levi.

Maddie worried her lip with her teeth while her thoughts tumbled around in her head. She'd always been good at two things, people and solutions. Levi was her people. She would find a solution to this. She had to.

CHAPTER THIRTEEN

Even though Kylie's leaving left him with genuine disappointment, Sam felt more like himself than he had since Michelle died. Human. Alive with possibilities of being human.

Kylie sat beside him now, trim in her jeans and t-shirt, the weekend alternative to the polished teacher version he'd first met. He liked all the versions she'd let him see. They hadn't had much time together, managing a few casual dates since the memorable dinner last week. *Note to self—do not invite potential girlfriends home before date number ten.*

Or until he had Levi's seal of approval. Whichever came first.

'I can't thank you enough for taking me to the airport,' said Kylie for the umpteenth time.

He smiled at her, one hand on the steering wheel, the other resting against the door. 'Like I said, it's no problem

at all.' And he meant it. Shame she had to go just as he was getting to know her. 'How is your dad?'

Kylie sighed. 'Not getting any better but not getting any worse either. I guess that's what they call stable, right?' She laughed unconvincingly.

'I'm sure he'll rally when he sees you.'

'I hope so. I want to spend as much quality time with him as possible.'

'When do you think you'll be back?' He'd avoided asking the question, not wanting to put any pressure on her.

She shook her head, blonde waves the colour of new wheat cascading around her shoulders. 'I really don't know. I've taken a leave of absence for the rest of the term. We'll see what happens.'

'Family first,' he said. 'No company or organisation is ever going to replace your family.'

'Never a truer word spoken. I'm not sure teaching is for me anyway.' She fiddled with a ring on her finger, spinning it round and round. 'I need to have a good think about what I want.'

'Teaching is not for you or the outback is not for you? There's a difference.'

'You're right. Being out here,' she gestured to the landscape flying past them, 'away from everything I know is hard. But I don't think it's that. I'm not sure I'm cut out for high school. Didn't like it all that much the first time around.'

He laughed. 'It's like being caught in *Groundhog Day*.'

'Never seen that film, but yes.'

'You're kidding me? Andie McDowell and Bill Murray. Classic.'

'I'm not much of a movie person. I struggle to sit still for that long,' said Kylie with a chuckle.

'We're here.' He turned into the airport carpark, easing the ute into a space as close to the departure lounge as he could.

Sam folded the tailgate down and retrieved Kylie's suitcase. If she decided not to return the school would arrange to have the rest of her stuff shipped to the coast. He put the case on the ground and extended the handle for her. She took it with a grateful smile. Right now they were pretending she'd be back soon when he knew in his bones she was as good as gone.

'Oh, look,' said Kylie, shielding her eyes from the sun. 'The plane is landing already. It seems too soon to be leaving.'

Longreach Airport prided itself on being the gateway to the outback. The Brisbane to Longreach run consisted of one plane in and out daily. Today, being Saturday, the flight arrived mid-morning. It would then turn around and go back the way it came shortly afterwards, and Kylie would be on it.

He fell into step with Kylie as they made their way across the carpark.

'I'm going to miss Longreach,' she said. 'I'm going to miss you.'

The confession made him blink with surprise. 'I'm going to miss you too,' he said. 'I'll be honest, I didn't expect to. We haven't known each other all that long.'

'It's been fun while we have.' She leaned in a little and he caught the scent of her perfume. It made him a little dizzy in a way that wasn't entirely unpleasant.

'Yes, it has. Makes me wonder what kind of fun we might have had if you'd been here a little longer.'

She let out a long breath as she surveyed the wide, flat open space surrounding her. This was hard country, anyone would attest to that, and Kylie had found that out.

'I'm glad I came,' she said. 'It's been one hell of an experience.'

He nodded, hearing the unspoken finality in her words. She wouldn't be back, even if she didn't know it herself right now.

Without thinking, he opened his arms and she stepped easily into them. They hugged, a warm friendly affair, a gentle goodbye to what might have been.

'Come on,' he said. 'Let's get you inside.'

A welcome chilled blast of air hit them as they stepped inside the airport.

'I'd better check in,' said Kylie.

He watched her walk to the counter with mixed feelings. While she was as sweet as pie there could be no denying they lacked the connection he'd felt with his wife. A man couldn't ask for that kind of love twice in a lifetime. Some might say that'd be selfish. He pushed his akubra back and rubbed his forehead. Either the band on his hat had got too tight or he was thinking too much.

From where he stood in the departure lounge he could see the first of the incoming passengers making their way out through the front doors to the carpark. Hadn't Maddie said something about her journalist arriving today? He scanned the faces of the passengers, trying to guess which one might be the journalist. A striking-looking woman smiled at the stewardess as she walked towards the car-rental desk. The

way she moved and how her thick, glossy hair swung against her shoulders caught his attention. Something innate in him responded to her, as if he had picked up on a signal she'd sent. She disappeared from view and Sam had the odd sense that he'd both found and lost something in the very same minute.

'All set.' Kylie reappeared, looking awkward and ever so young.

Sam nodded, snapping his attention back to where it needed to be. 'Got everything you need?' Of course she did. Why couldn't he say something meaningful or pithy?

'I think so,' she said. 'Look, Sam, it might be easier on me if you didn't wait with me.'

'Are you sure?' he asked.

She put her hands in the back pockets of her jeans and hunched her shoulders. 'Yeah, I'm bad at goodbyes and I'd rather get my head around leaving by myself. I guess I'm a bit of a coward.' She laughed and the sound came out wobbly.

'Okay.' He took off his hat and swept his hair back with one hand. 'I guess this is it then.'

She smiled then, stepping closer and wrapping her arms around his neck in a surprise move that caught him off balance. 'Goodbye, Sam,' she whispered in his ear before kissing him gently on his lips, a lingering kiss full of regret.

Kylie moved away first, putting space between them. A blush stole across her cheeks making her look prettier than ever.

'Okay, then. I'm going to …' She pointed over her shoulder towards the departure gate which hadn't opened yet but he got the gist.

'Yep, sure thing. Safe flight and all that.' He shoved his hat back on. 'Don't be a stranger.' Sam didn't want her to go thinking she wasn't wanted back here, that this door had closed, even though he knew deep in his heart she'd made her decision.

Kylie nodded, tears glistening on her lashes. She gave him a short wave and turned abruptly on her heel, giving him his cue to go.

He took a deep breath, hating goodbyes as much as she did. Kylie had done him a favour by helping him see the possibility of finding someone new, for which he'd be forever grateful. While they'd only had a handful of dates, it had been enough to wake him up from his long sleep. Securing his hat firmly to his head, Sam walked out of the airport without a backward glance. He caught himself searching the carpark for the woman he'd seen earlier. She'd gone. Probably a figment of his imagination in the first place.

Time he got back to his great big empty life.

The plane had been a great deal smaller than she'd bargained for. Never a fan of flying at the best of times, Sarah found the flight from Brisbane to Longreach trying. She should have hired a car and driven, even though it would have taken her the better part of two days. Twenty-twenty hindsight was a marvellous thing.

By the time the plane landed she'd had enough, grateful to unbuckle her seatbelt and step out on to *terra firma*. Someone once said, the more *firma* the ground, the less terror and she had to agree.

The airport looked smaller than it had in her imagination. Sydney Airport was so big it had its own postcode. The land surrounding Longreach Airport stretched out in a flat, brown expanse. The place had a different energy about it than the coastal region, making her wonder if she'd bitten off more than she could chew. Her Sydney game might not work as well here and she didn't have anything else. Newcastle, where she'd grown up, wasn't exactly deep country. Not like this.

She shaded her eyes from the punishing sun, even though her sunglasses were firmly in place. The walk across the tarmac didn't take long and she had already begun to sweat before she reached the terminal.

Stepping inside, she sagged with relief as the cool air enveloped her. Not for the first time since the journey began did she ponder the wisdom of this little adventure. The plane was refuelling and turning around for Brisbane within the hour. She could be on it before she made a fool out of herself.

Sam's response to her coming to Longreach had encouraged her. She'd almost forgotten he had a teenage son until he'd asked her to be low-key when they finally met at dinner tonight in case Levi took umbrage at his dad starting to date again.

She didn't have kids of her own and knew nothing about teenagers outside of surviving her own teenage years. Maybe it was a normal request. She didn't know.

Sarah's brother, Hayden, sprung to mind. If their parents had ever divorced and either of them had tried to date other people, Hayden would have given them hell. And that was as a grown-up; as a teenager he would have been even scarier. No reason to think Sam's son would be any different.

She'd agreed to the arrangement. Now she stood in the middle of the Longreach airport she had second thoughts. She couldn't handle a recalcitrant teenage boy. She could barely manage the grumpy adults in her life. Clutching her handbag tighter than necessary, Sarah looked for the baggage carousel. Not hard to spot in such a small place.

Retrieving her bag, she made her way to the car-rental desk. People milled about, waiting to board the return flight. She passed a man kissing a woman goodbye and wondered what it would be like to feel Sam's lips on hers. She turned away from the scene. It was too early to think about that sort of thing. She needed to meet him first and then decide if he was fantasy worthy. Sarah got the keys to her car and headed for the sunshine and heat.

The drive to the motel took less time than she'd thought it would. The cool of her room's air-conditioning was a welcome relief after the unfamiliar outback heat. She unpacked her case on one side of the bed and flopped down on the other, feet dangling over the side as she wondered why she'd embarked on this crazy adventure for the five hundred and fifty-fifth time. She'd had the thought so often it had become tedious. There could be no room for second thoughts or doubts. Sarah had leapt. It remained to be seen whether Sam would catch her or not.

A knock at the motel door roused her. Straightening her shirt and smoothing her hair, Sarah paused for a moment to look through the peephole and see who lurked outside. A cheerful looking blonde teenager bobbed up and down, chatting quietly to someone Sarah couldn't see. Curious, she opened the door.

'Hello, Miss Lewis,' said the blonde. 'I'm Maddie McRae and I wanted to drop by to welcome you to Longreach and to thank you for making the journey.' She spoke with practised maturity. Sarah guessed the kid probably competed on the local debate team.

'Hello, Maddie.' Sarah held out her hand. 'So nice to meet you.'

'This is my best friend, Levi.' Maddie yanked a lanky teenage boy into view. He darted a glance at Sarah before looking anywhere but at her face.

'Hello,' he mumbled.

Sam had said Maddie and Levi were besties, and here they were on her doorstep. She could see the resemblance to Sam in the shape of Levi's nose and the shock of dark hair he sported.

'It's very nice to meet you,' she said, hoping to make a decent impression. His awkward demeanour reminded her of Sam's concern the boy might overreact to someone wanting to replace his mother. She had no intentions of doing that. Maybe they could start by being friends. She held her hand out to him and he took it reluctantly.

Maddie glared at him before returning her megawatt smile in Sarah's direction. 'We wanted to make sure you're all good for dinner tonight?'

'Absolutely,' she said. 'Are you coming too, Levi?'

The boy shrugged then nodded as if unsure of the correct answer.

'Of course he is,' said Maddie. 'I wanted to introduce you to some Longreach locals so you can get a feel for the place. Wait until you meet Levi's dad. He's super cute and totally

single. We'll be having dinner at the pub across the road so come on over around seven pm and we'll all be there.'

'It's a date,' said Sarah. Levi's eyes shot up to hers and she regretted her lame response. 'I mean, I'd love to come.'

'Great, we'll see you then. Bye, Miss Lewis.' Maddie waved as she pulled Levi away.

Sarah waited until the kids were out of view before closing the door and allowing her nerves to get the better of her. This had become very real. If Levi was real then Sam was real too. A three-dimensional flesh and blood man who she'd meet tonight.

What if he took one look at her and decided he wasn't interested? God, how mortifying. She covered her face with her hands, trying to block out the scenario playing in her head.

She had hours before dinner, far too much time to kill with nothing to do. It wouldn't take her long to get ready. Maybe she could fit in her first interview? That would certainly help keep her nerves at bay. She reached for her phone and, taking a deep breath, she dialled her mother.

Notes for 'Finding Love in the Outback'
Interview #1
Adam (58) and Eleanor Lewis (less than 58). Met at a dance when they were eighteen.

Eleanor: It's not really a very interesting story.
Adam: Oh, I don't know. There I was, a strapping lad with my entire future before me. I was a football player, you know, had promise.

Eleanor: Yes, Adam. We've all heard the story before. The truth is you played reserves and you weren't good for much else.

Adam: Do you see what I have to put up with? Cruellest woman I've ever met.

Eleanor: And you wouldn't have it any other way.

Adam: I hate to say it but she's right. Any other woman would have bored me to death.

Interviewer: Mum, Dad, can we focus on the story of how you met?

Adam: Where did we meet? I can't remember for the life of me. I just remember you being there.

Eleanor: (*giggles*) Like a fairy queen.

Adam: I was going to say apparition.

Interviewer: Mum and Dad, please!

Eleanor: Alright, keep your hair on. Honestly, you've been so cranky since you've become almost engaged.

Interviewer: I need to talk to you about that later, Mum.

Adam: Is that a thing now?

Eleanor: Hush, Adam. Just tell the story.

Adam: I can't remember the bloody story.

Eleanor: Yes you do. We met at a Bachelor and Spinster Ball in some godforsaken little town. My cousin liked a boy there or I'd never have gone. You were there with the footy club.

Adam: I believe I was. Had a great game that day. We thrashed the other team ten to …

Eleanor: Anyway, I was loitering at the refreshments table when he walked in. To this day I cannot tell you what attracted me to him …

Adam: Thanks very much.

Eleanor: … but I knew the moment I laid eyes on him that he was the one. He wore this ill-fitting suit. He needed a haircut. I knew with a bit of polish he'd come up fine and dandy.

Adam: You make me sound like one of your bloody projects.

Eleanor: Yes, dear, you are. My very best one.

'That went *so* well.' Maddie stood with her hands on her hips as she looked back at the motel, a satisfied smile playing across her lips.

Levi wanted to burst her bubble so badly his skin itched with it.

'Do you think getting them together like this is the smart thing to do? It'll take less than a minute for her to work out Dad has no idea who she is.'

'Not worried.' Maddie waved her hand at him like he was some annoying bug. 'Your dad will be totally into her and she's already taken with him. We can help. We know all he needs to know about her for now, enough to get them through basic conversation. They'll flirt a bit. Talk about superficial things. Nothing deep or too personal.'

'How do you know all this?' She frustrated the hell out of him with her certainty.

'Because that's how women work and that's how love goes.' She put her hands on her hips and looked at him as if he lacked the required number of brain cells.

'Always an outlier.' *Thank you, statistics class.* Finally a reason to use something from it.

'Be that as it may,' she replied, sounding like she was fifty not fifteen, 'they will be so busy being dazzled by each other they will miss any clues that things aren't as they seem. Plus my parents will be there.'

'And you're good with that?' He hurried to catch up with her as she began to walk down the street.

'Of course, how else will true love find its course if I don't help it along? Are you hungry?'

He was always hungry. 'Yeah, but …'

'No buts, Levi Costello.' She stopped abruptly and faced him. 'I don't want to hear another negative word out of you. We're doing this. It is happening, and it's going well. Miss Kempton has left. Sarah has arrived. She likes your dad and your dad will like her, I promise. We're all having dinner tonight and from there I will arrange some more opportunities for Mr C and Sarah to hang out. All you have to do is keep your mouth shut and play along.'

Maddie stood so close to him he could feel her breath on his cheek. Close enough to kiss. All he had to do was lean forward …

'Got it?' She stepped back with her hands on her hips again, head cocked, waiting for an answer. He'd hardly registered a word she'd said. For some reason he couldn't think when she got that close.

'Okay?'

'Good.' She turned and marched on. He followed dutifully behind, happy his answer had turned out to be the right one.

As they approached the service station where they sold icy-cold slushies, Levi's heart sank. Standing outside in the shade were several seniors from their high school. Their

heads all turned as one and he braced himself for some smart-arse remark.

They all had the same haircuts, these nearly-men who made him feel as if everyone had got the handbook on how to be a man, and he hadn't. They were all on the same rugby team. They were a *they*, a collective he could not join—that he would not be asked to join. That was the worst bit.

Levi slouched out of habit, trying to fold in on himself and make himself so small no one would notice him. He needn't have bothered. The boys' attention had firmly fixed on Maddie.

'Maddison McRae.' The tallest of the boys sauntered forward with the kind of swagger that came naturally. Or so Levi thought because he'd totally been unable to replicate it after hours of practice in his bedroom.

'Well, hello there, Wayne.' Levi did a double take. Was he mistaken or did Maddie just *purr*?

She walked forward to meet Wayne, her whole demeanour changing right before his eyes. She swayed her hips as she lowered her lashes and peeked through her long golden tresses. He didn't know this Maddie, had never seen her before. The ground shifted beneath his feet and a sink hole opened up. Any minute now he was going to drop right into it and never be seen again.

'I thought if I waited here long enough you'd show up.'

'You were right.' Maddie shoved her hands in the back pockets of her shorts, causing her chest to thrust forward. A hot rush of blood suffused Levi's face followed by a gamut of emotions so thick and fast he barely had time to register them: embarrassment, indignation, resentment, sharp-edged longing and shame. Thank God for social invisibility.

'School dance is coming up,' said Wonder Wayne, rugby player extraordinaire.

'School formal,' Maddie corrected. Not any old dance. The end of year grand finale for the year twelve students, of which Wonder Wayne was one.

'Yeah, whatever. Anyways …' Wonder Wayne sucked in a gut full of air. Levi waited for his feet to leave the ground. '… Would you like to come with me?'

'To the formal?' Maddie's hands flew to her throat in a gesture that left a dent in Levi's heart. She actually wanted this. He couldn't take it in.

'Yeah, of course.' Wonder Wayne shrugged one shoulder and gave a little frown as if there really could be no mistaking the nature of his invitation. And he'd be right. Levi thought he might throw up a little in his mouth.

The other guys sniggered in the back, a clump of teenage testosterone, all of them supremely confident in the success of Wayne's invitation. Levi hated them in that moment. Every last one of them.

'I'd love to.'

'Awesome.' Levi wanted to wipe the smug look off Wayne's face. 'Right, then.' Wayne stepped back towards the group with a wave, clearly eager to share his triumph with his bros. If Maddie expected more then she'd be disappointed. Of this, Levi was glad.

As Wayne melted back into his homogenous pack, Maddie squealed and jumped up and down on the spot. Literally jumped up and down, like some demented four-year-old girl losing it over a unicorn birthday cake or something equally as stupid. Levi hated unicorns, and he wasn't feeling very fond of Maddie right now either. He took his pent-up aggression

out on a stone. Kicking it as hard as he could, there was a certain satisfaction to be had as it belted into the garage door on their right, causing a bang and a great deal of shuddering. People turned and stared, although no one connected him to the act. A win in an otherwise crappy afternoon.

'You can't be serious,' he said. After he'd told himself he wouldn't say anything at all.

'What do you mean?' Maddie stopped grinning inanely in the direction Wayne and his cronies had disappeared, fixing him with a WTF frown.

'Wayne is a dick.' Levi sat down on the ground and leaned back against the wall. 'Why would you want to even be *seen* with that guy?'

'Levi!' Maddie flounced over and sat down next to him. 'He's, like, the hottest guy in year twelve. Legit. Ask anyone.'

'Ask any girl, you mean.'

'Who else matters?' She held up her hands and looked around as if the lack of seriously cool people who might disagree with her in the carpark proved her point.

'I can't believe you like him.' He shook his head as he studied the ground between his feet. A black sugar ant reached one of his sneakers, got confused and ran back the way it'd come.

'He's okay when you get to know him.' She leaned her head back and closed her eyes, stretching those long legs out in front of her.

'You know him?' It was Levi's turn to give her the WTF frown. Wasted because she had her eyes closed.

'A little. I know he's a good kisser.' Maddie opened one eye and looked at him. He couldn't be sure if she'd cracked a joke or not.

'You've kissed him?' This came out a whole octave higher than he'd intended.

'At Veronica's party.' She closed her eye, blocking him out.

'Veronica had a party?' Why hadn't he been invited?

In the space of ten minutes the entire world as he knew it had revealed itself to be one big fat lie. He was clearly not as popular as he'd assumed. He'd never been full-on big league popular. More an everybody's friend, Mr nice guy popular. Now he'd been relegated to the don't-invite level. Total loser.

If only that were the worst of it.

Maddie not only had a crush on Wonder Wayne and intended on going to the formal with him, she'd *kissed* him at a party Levi had not even been invited to. He needed time to unpack this situation.

The fact she would go to a party without him was bad enough, but not even bothering to tell him there *was* a party—*then* kissing some senior dork on top of that— qualified as a betrayal in his eyes. Suddenly he was ten years old again. A little boy amongst the big kids. He hated appearing somehow less, not only in his own eyes but in everyone else's too.

Levi tipped his head back and scrunched up his eyes. For a moment there, he'd been convinced he was going to cry. Gripped by the need to be alone, he scrambled to his feet.

'I've just remembered, I've got to go,' he said. 'A maths thing I forgot about.' He was in a more advanced maths class than Maddie. She wouldn't question the lie.

'What do you mean?' Maddie came to life. 'We haven't had our slushy yet.'

'I'm good.' He needed to get away. 'I'll see you later, okay?'

His feet stumbled in their hurry to get him to safety.

'Okay, I guess.' Maddie got to her feet as he walked away.

As the distance between them grew, the constriction in Levi's throat eased. When had things become this complicated? When had being friends stopped being enough? He'd noticed changes, little ones, which he'd chosen to ignore. Like how Maddie seemed more interested in socialising than riding her trail bike lately. How he'd advanced to more academic levels in maths and science than Maddie. He didn't want to say he was smarter or anything but … Levi had thought he was maturing and leaving Maddie behind.

Turned out it was the other way around.

He turned the corner and expelled the breath he'd been holding in one long whistle. Deep weariness overtook him. He could lie down in the gutter and sleep for a week. What a mess. His best friend was leaving him behind. People didn't like him as much as they used to. He wasn't being invited to parties. What the fuck had happened?

He'd been perfectly happy in his little nerdy world.

Levi put one foot in front of the other. He could call Dad and his father would come and get him. Problem was, Dad would ask why he wasn't with Maddie. He didn't want to talk about it. He walked, and he'd keep walking until he felt ready to call Dad. Then, when he got home he'd have a hot shower and tell Dad he was too sick to go to dinner. Maddie could handle the lovebirds on her own. Seemed she handled everything on her own these days anyway.

As he began the long journey home, his thoughts tumbled about in his head. Sarah Lewis seemed nice, much prettier in real life than in her photo. Her palm had been soft in his when she'd shook his hand. He'd liked the way she'd

smiled at him, as if she saw him. Nerves clawed his stomach as his mind drifted to dinner tonight. So much could go wrong. What if the spark between Sarah and Dad didn't ignite? Worse still, what if their whole scheme got exposed? Even if things worked out, Levi could count on his world being turned upside down. Either way, he didn't think he was ready.

He calmed himself by running maths problems, eventually coming up with a maths theory to explain what had just happened with Maddie and Wayne.

A ratio is a comparison of any two people by hotness. A hot-o-meter is a special ratio that compares any guy to Wonder Wayne, with Wonder Wayne representing one whole hot human being. This representation makes comparisons simple.

And Levi didn't compare.

CHAPTER FOURTEEN

Going out for dinner at the Royal Arms with the McRaes and Maddie's journalist had seemed more like duty when Levi asked him. He'd said yes only because going was important to Maddie who was, in turn, important to Levi. Sam figured he'd get a good steak dinner out of it minimum. Maybe a laugh or two.

But he hadn't figured on Sarah Lewis.

He'd had his back turned towards the door when she'd entered. Maddie's face lit up at the sight of her, and she'd rushed to welcome the woman. Sam took his time turning around to take a look and as he did so, Ms Lewis used her secret super power to stop the space-time continuum. Or at least that's what he thought she'd done. Everything slowed down and complete silence fell across the pub. Like in one of those Marvel movies. He'd half expected to see Stan Lee wander past in a cameo role.

It was the woman from the airport.

Her eyes, like liquid amber, met his and the world had started up again, the noise crashing in on him like a wave at the beach. He'd needed a moment to gather himself. If Kylie had been like a fine spring day after a long winter, this woman brought the sun in all its fiery warmth. She wore a pale pink button-down shirt, her dark chocolate hair pulled up in a high ponytail. Her jeans hugged her obvious curves and she oozed sexual energy the like of which he'd never encountered before. Not even with Michelle.

All that in a minute.

He stood awkwardly by as Maddie made the introductions, leaving him until last. The moment arrived for him to hold out his hand and shake hers. Maddie sounded like she was speaking underwater. Amber eyes, a warm smile and the softness of her hand in his crowded out the entire pub. He said something inane about it being nice to meet her. She looked amused, which had to be a good thing, right?

They all sat down around the table and Sam let the small talk flow around him. He needed to recalibrate. His world had become oddly unsteady and he needed to find solid ground.

'What do you know about Longreach?' Joe McRae addressed Sarah from across the table.

She sat next to him at the too-crowded table and he was conscious of the warmth radiating off her. Even her perfume smelled warm and spicy, as if delivering an invitation to romance straight to his brain in case the rest of his body hadn't got the message.

How could two women be so different? Make that three. His thoughts leapt from Michelle to Kylie to Sarah. At least he could say quite truthfully that he didn't run to a type.

'I know only the basics,' she said. Her voice was pitched low and husky. He liked it, imagined listening to it while lying in the dark.

'Tell me what you know,' Sam said. He hadn't meant to speak up. What he really wanted to say was, tell me all about yourself.

She took a deep breath. 'Okay, I know this is Banjo Paterson country, although "Waltzing Matilda" was written outside Winton not Longreach.'

'Correct.' He nodded as he kept his eyes on the tabletop, longing to watch her mouth as she spoke.

'I know the name Longreach came about because of the length of the Thomson River. I know this is where Qantas started up and there's a Stockman's Hall of Fame out here too. After that,' she held her hands palm up before letting them drop to her lap.

'All good information,' said Joe. 'Let's add to it with some town trivia.'

'I'll go first,' said Maddie. 'All the streets are named after birds. Streets going east are named after water birds, streets heading north are named for land birds. No one knows why. It's always been that way.'

Sarah laughed. 'I guess they had to name them after something.' The heady scent of her perfume waylaid every reasonable thought in his brain, replacing them with deliciously unsuitable ones.

Like a fifteen-year-old school boy, he wanted her attention focused on him. 'The town of Blackall has streets named after flowers. Barcaldine's streets follow trees. Jericho's streets are all about scientists.'

She turned to look at him. 'I did not know that and it's weirdly intriguing.'

He smiled. 'I know, right?' Sarah smiled back and something shifted in his gut, something fundamental.

'You have to meet Tank while you're here,' said Charlene McRae, Maddie's mum.

'Tank is a bit of a legend in these parts. She drives the local cab and makes the best peach blossoms in town. She could tell you a story or two,' said Joe.

'We'll have to take you for one, won't we, Mr C?' Maddie piped up.

'Sure.' He met Sarah's eyes briefly. 'Providing Ms Lewis is up for it.'

'Call me Sarah, please,' she said and a little frisson of pleasure shot through him. 'And I'd love to try a peach blossom, whatever that is.' She laughed, a throaty sound that set off an arousal in him, one he'd been trying to keep in check from the moment he met her.

'It's like a cupcake and a lamington had a love child,' said Maddie.

The look of surprise on Sarah's face made Sam laugh.

'Great description, Maddie. You'll make a good journalist,' she said.

Sam caught Maddie's blush of pleasure. He could barely make Levi out, hunched over in the corner doing his best disappearing act. The boy seemed strangely disinterested in their guest, as if he'd rather be anywhere else but here.

'Can we go order now?' Levi said.

'Sure we can,' said Joe as he struggled to stand up. 'Dinner is on me, just tell me what you want.'

As might be expected, Joe couldn't remember everyone's orders and to give him his due, all of them speaking at once didn't help.

'I'll come with you,' sighed Charlene.

'We'll all come too and give you a hand, won't we? Levi? Ariel?' said Maddie, practically dragging her little sister out of her chair.

'Mum! Tell Maddie to stop,' said Ariel.

After a brief flurry of movement Sam found himself alone with Sarah. He could not screw this up. *Say something witty and charming!*

'Where are you staying?' *Total failure.*

She looked at him quizzically as if he should already know. 'At the Longreach Motor Inn,' she said. 'I'm guessing you know where that is.'

'Yep, sure do.' *Lame again. Try harder.*

Sarah didn't miss a beat. 'I bet farming out here is more challenging than I can imagine.'

'Try parenting a teenage boy,' he said, grateful for the small talk.

'I got the moody vibe. Were you like that when you were his age?'

'Of course not. I was the poster boy for perfection.'

'Maddie seems to be a firecracker.'

Sam chuckled. 'She certainly is. I can't help thinking that Levi might be a little in love with her.' Why did he go and tell her that? Levi would kill him if he'd heard.

'I can see why. She's beautiful and dynamic, a potent combination.'

'She likes to organise people.' By rights, he ought not to be sitting here dishing gossip about the kids with a journalist.

She was so damn easy to talk to that the words kept tumbling out of his mouth. Anything to keep her with him a moment longer.

'She's organised me,' Sarah said. 'I believe she's also lined up some people I can interview for my "Love In the Outback" article while I'm here.'

'Sounds like Maddie. She is nothing if not thorough. Helps she thinks of herself as the town's matchmaker.'

'She hasn't managed to matchmake you yet?'

He laughed at the thought. 'No, she has not. No one in town who is really my type.'

'Hence the need for internet romance.'

'I guess.' He shrugged. 'Folk have got to do what they've got to do. It's hard out here where the distance between neighbours and towns makes it tough to meet new people.' Not that it'd ever crossed his mind to find love online.

'Well I, for one, am glad of it otherwise I wouldn't get to meet you.'

'The world has certainly gotten smaller. Your newspaper is online, right?' Levi had mentioned something and he regretted not paying more attention at the time.

'Sure is,' she said.

'The internet has changed everything. I can't imagine what kind of world my grandkids will grow up in.' He sighed, not wanting to sound like some old fogey yet some days he struggled to keep up with technology and all the changes it brought.

'I think it'll be a while before you have to worry about that.'

'Can you imagine if Levi married Miss Maddie?' He looked at Sarah as the reality that thought presented sunk in.

'The look on your face!' She burst into laughter and his heart rose on the sound of it, like a bird catching a thermal updraft. She had a smattering of freckles across her nose and one right on the edge of her mouth. His eyes were drawn to it like a magnet. Kissable and very tempting.

The McRaes returned like a noisy flock of galahs, dragging Levi in their wake. With a flick of her ponytail, Sarah looked over her shoulder at them. He wanted to see her hair out in all its glory again, imagining the weight of it in his hands, inhale the warm spicy scent of her. Sam watched as she rose and made to help Levi with the drink tray he carried. He could not help but admire her derriere in those jeans, careful to quickly avert his eyes in case anyone caught him staring.

Sarah would be lying if she hadn't considered turning and going back to her motel room as she stood outside the Royal Arms. All she had to do was walk in that room and she'd know if Lonely Sam of Longreach might be the man for her. It took her a full minute to gather the courage to push the door open and step inside.

Maddie ran up to her, full of excitement and for a moment Sarah thought she might hug her. The girl restrained herself, barely, taking Sarah's hand instead and leading her into the room. She bobbed along in Maddie's wake, taking in the faces of the people assembled to greet her.

Levi gave her a shy nod of hello. Joe and Charlene McRae welcomed her warmly, clearly proud of their little girl. Maddie's sister, Ariel, was introduced next. Sarah barely registered anything they said due to the presence of a man

waiting quietly for his turn. She longed to get a proper look at him, but needing to give her full attention to her hosts meant she'd have to wait.

Finally, it was Sam's turn to be introduced. She turned very slowly. Time stretched like it does in that moment at the Oscars when they open the envelope and pull out the card with the name of the winner printed on it. Everyone holds their breath. *And the winner is …*

'Oh!' Her startled response popped out of her mouth before her brain had the chance to get past the fact that *the* sexiest man she'd ever seen stood right in front of her.

'Hello.' He held out his hand. 'I'm Sam Costello, Levi's dad.'

Sarah's hand disappeared inside his warm, firm handshake. His blue eyes twinkled at her as if he knew the effect he had on her and was enjoying every minute.

'I'm … I'm Sarah Lewis.' She'd nearly forgotten her own name.

'It's nice to meet you. Journalist extraordinaire, I hear.'

'Something like that.' She looked down at her shoes, already covered with a light layer of dust. She looked at the faces around her. She looked anywhere but at Sam Costello. He exuded male energy of the kind yet to be studied by quantum physics. The kind that could, without a doubt, be used to prove Entanglement Theory because she sure as hell wanted to get entangled with him. He had an aura that charged every particle in her body.

Sarah looked up to find four pairs of eyes trained on her, as if waiting for something. She blinked, at a loss as to what to say next. Sam's presence overwhelmed her. Was this what her mother had felt the night she'd met Dad? This weird

shift of gravity as if the whole universe had moved sideways when you weren't looking.

Thankfully they'd all sat down and Joe McRae had begun the kind of lighthearted banter she could deal with while her insides calmed the hell down.

She only half listened, caught up in Sam Costello. She wanted to study every inch of him. He looked like his profile picture, thank God, only the real-life version offered more than she could possibly have imagined.

So much more. She began to take mental notes to tell Fiona. His broad shoulders strained under his blue polo shirt which, by the way, matched the colour of his eyes perfectly. He was tall. Another point in his favour. And those arms. Wait until Fiona got a look at those guns. She'd have to find a way to take a photo of him. If what she felt wasn't love at first sight, it was definitely lust and that was a good start in her book.

The McRaes went to the bar to order food and drinks, leaving them alone. She wanted to say something pithy and clever, to let him know how excited she was about finally meeting him. He got in first with a standard question, warming up as they moved the topic to Levi. She sensed him relax a little, reminding herself that he'd be as nervous as she was, especially with Levi looking on.

They were only getting started when the McRaes returned to the table. Sarah took the opportunity to help Levi, mostly because the rising sexual tension she sensed between her and Sam made her feel vulnerable. She helped pass around the drinks and sat back down, every nerve in her body straining towards him.

Please God, don't let anyone notice. At least until she could be sure he felt it too.

'How's the heat treating you?' Joe asked, as he picked up his bottle of beer. Charlene slapped at his wrist.

'Glass please, Joe. You're in polite company,' she said.

Joe rolled his eyes and did as she bid.

'The heat feels different to the coast,' she said, instantly kicking herself mentally. Of course the heat had a different quality to it. They bordered the desert here while the coast was fringed with a lush green courtesy of the rain blowing in from the ocean.

'It's not the only thing you'll find different from home,' said Joe with a wink and Sarah wondered what he meant exactly.

'I'm taking it you've never been to the outback before,' said Sam, throwing her a lifeline she grabbed gratefully.

'No,' she said. 'I'm from Newcastle originally and I live in Sydney now. I haven't travelled Australia all that much. Frankly, if it's not been on the coast I haven't seen it.' Sam knew all that already but confessing her parochial travelling habits to the rest of the table sent a bolt of shame through her. This wide open country stretched for miles in every direction. The sky above arced in a brilliant blue dome. A stillness settled over the land in dramatic contrast to Sydney, a city that never slept.

He regarded her with those laughing blue eyes as if assessing her. 'You're here now and that's all that matters.'

Yes, it was.

Maddie nudged Levi under the table with her foot as their food arrived. He looked at her, confused, and she wiggled her eyebrows at him in a semaphore he clearly didn't

understand. She'd seen a bona fide spark arc between Mr C and Sarah. Surely, Levi had seen it too.

'Ms Lewis.' Maddie sat up a little taller and put on her brightest smile. The one that always got her what she wanted. 'How are you finding Longreach so far?'

Sarah laughed, her long dark hair so glossy it reflected light. Maddie made a mental note to ask her how she got it that way.

'I haven't had much time to really soak up the ambience,' she said. 'What I can say is the people are lovely.' Sarah cut a glance at Mr C as she spoke.

Maddie wanted to fist pump her victory. Sarah liked Mr C for real, not only on the internet. Now she had to gauge how Mr C felt. She watched him carefully, looking for romantic tells. Everyone had them. She speared a chip on her fork and chewed thoughtfully.

'Longreach is a very friendly place,' said her mum. 'We wouldn't live anywhere else.'

'I can see the charm,' said Sarah. 'Sydney is becoming so overcrowded and noisy that my ears are ringing with the silence out here.'

Mr C tucked into his steak without giving any indication he was interested in the conversation. She ought to have sat them opposite each other so she could watch them better. She searched Mr C's face for clues.

Nothing.

'It's great of you to come out and speak to the kids about a career in journalism. The local radio and newspaper are great support, although it's nice to get the broader perspective.' Maddie's dad used his best-behaviour voice, the one he saved for phone calls to the power company or the bank.

'I'd planned to make a trip out here for research any-way, so when I got Maddie's email it seemed like fate.' Sarah smiled at her with what Maddie liked to think of as grati-tude. Of course Fate led her here. Maddie was merely Fate's handmaiden.

'What are you researching?' Her mother picked up a cherry tomato with her fork and popped it delicately into her mouth. She knew exactly what Sarah was researching because Maddie had told her.

'I'm doing a series on love in the outback.' Sarah tucked her hair behind one ear as she spoke. 'I want to explore the challenges of dating in the country and how people get around them. If people use the internet and that sort of thing. If you know anyone who might be willing to tell me their story I'd be grateful.'

'Do we know anyone?' Mum looked at Dad with her squinty I'm-thinking look. Totally pointless because they'd done nothing but talk about who they might suggest as potential interviewees all the way over.

'Let me think.' Dad played on the charade like a seasoned actor. She wanted to scream. Helping Sarah find interview subjects was not the point here. Helping Sarah and Mr C fall in love was the main focus.

'There's Pete. He tried online dating.' Maddie's sister, Ariel, talked with her mouth full. Maddie wanted to kick her under the table, only she couldn't be sure which leg was hers.

Mum laughed. 'Poor Pete. The date turned out to be a total disaster.'

'The girl was a bit of a stalker, wasn't she?' said Dad.

'That's exactly the type of story I want to hear.' Sarah lit up with excitement.

'Pete's in Rockhampton,' Maddie said.

'I don't mind. Maybe he'll agree to talk to me over the phone or on Skype or something.'

'I'll give him a call and see if he'll be up for it,' said Dad. 'Might have to change his name to protect the innocent and all that.'

'Dad,' groaned Maddie. 'It's a story on dating, not murder or organised crime.'

'How about those friends of your parents? You know, Monica and Bruce.' Mum levelled her butter knife at Dad's chest like it had a target painted on it.

'Great memory,' said Dad. He seemed to be getting right into the spirit of things. 'They'd both been widowed and met recently. Things are really going well. Hard when you're older to find someone new to replace the person you lost.'

The table fell silent and all eyes swivelled to Mr C, who stopped mid-chew.

'I'm sorry, Sam,' said Dad, his cheeks turning red and a faint sheen of sweat appearing as if by magic on his forehead. Maddie cringed. 'I didn't mean any offence ...'

Mr C shook his head while he swallowed his bite. 'It's okay,' he said. 'None taken.' He turned to Sarah. 'My wife died of cancer a while back.'

Maddie held her breath.

'I'm sorry to hear that,' said Sarah softly.

Maddie blew her breath out and sagged in the middle. Thank God.

'It's okay,' said Mr C.

'He's officially back on the market, aren't you, mate?' Dad had to go and have a dig. 'Look out, Sarah. Not many

eligible ladies in town for Sam Costello. You might find yourself swept off your feet.'

Her dad could be *so* embarrassing.

'I am out here to experience the romance of the outback,' said Sarah, rising beautifully to the occasion.

'Not a great deal of romance out here,' said Mr C.

Why did he have to go and dampen the moment? She had to do something before things got off track.

'I beg to differ,' she said. 'There's the Thomson River. A boat ride on that is romantic, especially at night under the stars. There's even a paddle wheeler you can take.'

'What's more romantic than a paddle wheeler?' said Sarah.

'You should totally go on it while you're here,' said Maddie. 'Mr C can take you.' There, she'd said it. If he backed out now he'd look like a total dick. She waited with her fingers crossed beneath the table.

Come on, come on.

'Um … yeah, sure. Why not?' Mr C took the bait. Hard not to when the entire table stared him down.

'Thank you,' said Sarah in a tone of voice Maddie recognised. She'd used it herself on Wayne, and look where it had got her. A date to the senior formal. Score!

'There's the Cobb & Co Stagecoach ride,' she said, trying to push the advantage home.

'And the Qantas museum,' piped up Ariel. Typical. Who on earth thought the Qantas museum counted as a romantic date? Maddie rolled her eyes, making sure Ariel saw her.

'I'm up for it all.' Sarah laughed and Mr C got this peculiar look on his face for a second. Long enough for Maddie to see. She knew what that look meant. That kind of knowledge was her stock-in-trade as a matchmaker.

'Let me have your phone number and we'll organise something for early next week. Let you get settled in first,' said Mr C.

A shiver of excitement shot through her. Mr C liked Sarah. This was happening. It was all Maddie could do to stop from squealing with happiness.

Notes for 'Finding Love in the Outback'
Interview #2
Callum (45) and Jenna (42) both from Emerald, Queensland. Met during a taxi ride.

Jenna: I'd been divorced about a year when I decided to get back into dating. I figured if not now, when? Soon I'd be too old and saggy for anyone to find attractive. I'd set up a date at the local pub. Just a drink. Callum turns up at my house to pick me up and, well, the rest is history.

Callum: I picked her up in me taxi. I'd worked in mining originally. Got made redundant so took up taxi driving until I could figure out what to do next. The last thing I'd reckoned on was falling for a fare. I mean, what are the chances in a town like this?

Jenna: To be clear, he was not my date.

Callum: Nah, I was only the bloke driving her there.

Jenna: It's a pretty short drive from my place to the pub but that's all it took to know.

Callum: She got in the front seat and I dunno, something happened, like an electric shock. The whole situation was mad.

Jenna: I made him drive around town. I didn't want to get out of the car.

Callum: I ended up taking her to another pub for a drink meself.

Jenna: I felt awful about standing the other guy up. In my defence, how many times do you find a connection like that? I couldn't let him get away.

Callum: I ain't going nowhere, sweetheart. You've got me for good now.

Jenna: My perfect rough diamond.

CHAPTER FIFTEEN

'We are glad you could come and speak to us, Miss Lewis. Maddie McRae is one of our most promising students. I was delighted when she approached me with her proposal to invite you to speak.'

Lydia Forsyth represented everything Sarah imagined a high school principal might be. Neat appearance, no-nonsense manner, warm and friendly yet firm, of an indeterminate age, Lydia radiated confidence and a quiet power. Sarah felt herself respond to it, a sort of falling into line she vaguely remembered from her own high school days.

'No problem at all. It coincided nicely with my research trip and it's an honour,' she said. 'Please call me Sarah.'

They stood outside the school hall. Lydia wanted to show Sarah where she would be speaking. This was probably a bad time to mention that she'd never spoken in front of such a large group before. Public speaking wasn't exactly her

thing. She'd avoided it like the plague through university and no one had ever asked her to do it during her journalistic career. Leave that to those media tarts, the TV and radio journalists.

'We don't get many opportunities for the children to engage with professionals outside of town,' said Lydia. 'The local media are wonderfully supportive, of course.'

'Life as a journalist in Sydney is nowhere near as glamorous as it sounds,' said Sarah, sensing something in Lydia's tone she couldn't quite pin down. 'It's easy to get lost in all the noise. I imagine life as a journalist out here, living in a close community, would be quite rewarding.'

Lydia smiled. 'Perhaps. Small towns can be too small, if you get my drift.'

'Do you ever think of going back to the coast to teach?'

'Personally, I like living here. People know who I am and respect the position. Like you said, it's easy to get lost in the noise of the big city.' Lydia pushed open the hall door. 'Come in out of the heat and take a look around.'

The hall, which doubled as a basketball court, had a cosy vibe to it. She imagined homegrown theatre productions, assemblies and awards nights playing out inside these walls as they did all over the country.

'Many of our children will leave Longreach for further education. Some will return.' Lydia looked around as if seeing the ghosts of students past. 'Work can be hard to find out here.'

'So I gathered.' Sarah didn't have a clue about how a place like this worked. If you didn't want to follow your family into farming, what were your options? Mining? Maddie and Levi had plans to go to Sydney to study, but then what? She

had the sense young Miss McRae had no intention of being either a farmer's wife or a miner for that matter.

'Maddie is a very enterprising young woman,' said Lydia, as if reading her mind. 'How did you two cross paths?'

Good question. She never did get to the bottom of how Maddie came to know about her. Some garbled story about a piece she'd done on animal coffee tables. Seems as if everyone in the Southern Hemisphere had read that one.

'Apparently she's a fan of my work.' Sarah shrugged her shoulders at Lydia's surprised expression. 'Go figure.'

'That girl is a constant source of surprise,' Lydia said. 'I never know which direction she's going to go in next. Come and have a cup of tea. I'd like to hear about your research.' She turned and led Sarah out of the building, carefully locking it behind her.

Sarah noticed the force of the heat immediately as if someone had thrown a woolly blanket over her.

'I'm doing a series of articles on finding love in the outback.' Sarah wished she'd worn something a little more professional. Her khaki shorts and t-shirt were presentable, and with her bag slung across her body like a school girl's satchel she had the whole neat casual thing going on. Next to Lydia's trim, businesslike skirt and white blouse she looked like she might be on vacation.

'Really?' Lydia looked interested.

'I'm looking for people to interview about how they found love if you know anybody with a great story.' Sarah fell into step beside the principal.

'Everyone out here has an interesting story. The most fascinating people wash up in the outback.' Lydia held the

door open to the administration building. Another delightful blast of cool air enveloped Sarah. 'I have a dear friend over at the radio station who might be able to help you. Let me get in touch with her and, if you're open to it, see if I can set up a meeting for you.'

The familiar buzz of adrenaline kicked in, something that happened whenever a story started to come together. She loved this moment, like the spinning of a compass needle telling her she was headed in the right direction. This buzz was one of the things she loved most about her job.

'Thank you, that would be fantastic.'

For the moment, any guilt or unsureness she'd harboured about coming out here dissolved in the certainty she was about to uncover some really great material. Her phone vibrated in her pocket as they made their way to Lydia's office. Sarah snuck a quick look at the screen. Sam Costello, calling as he said he would.

A warm tingling sensation started in the pit of her stomach at the thought of spending time alone with him. Perhaps it hadn't been a mistake to come find a handsome stranger based only on a whim of her heart, and everything would fall into place after all. Maybe it *was* fate.

'I'm sorry,' she said to Lydia, 'I need to take this call.'

He walked out onto the front porch and back inside again for the third time in a row. Sam couldn't settle. All he could think about was Sarah Lewis and her effect on him. The marrow of his bones felt agitated as if something primeval had entered his bloodstream and wouldn't let him be. He hadn't felt this way about anyone since Michelle.

Monday morning dragged on with tormenting slowness made worse by the excitement fizzing in his veins.

He should call her.

No, too soon. He only met her on Saturday night.

Why was it too soon? He raked his hand through his hair. It had been such a long time since he dated that he no longer knew the rules. Might not be any rules now for all he knew.

Levi might know. He should ask him. Sam opened his mouth to call out to Levi who was home sick from school and abruptly closed it again.

How's his form, a grown man asking dating advice from a boy barely into puberty. He had to get a grip. She probably had a boyfriend back in Sydney, some handsome bloke with sophisticated habits. Someone who knew how to make a latte and cook with kale. Then again, she hadn't been wearing a ring.

He should call her. No harm in a friendly chat, see how she's settling in at the motel.

Only he'd never been any good at small talk. What would he say? Chances were he'd end up sounding like an idiot, some country bumpkin without a clue. He wanted her to like him, and that posed the problem. What if she didn't like him? She seemed to think he was alright at dinner Saturday night. Laughed and smiled at all his jokes. Good start. He'd got a friendly response to his follow-up text about showing her the sights. What if she wasn't attracted to him the way he was attracted to her? Maybe he could tell by her voice on the phone. You could tell a lot by the tone of someone's voice, especially when their looks weren't there to distract you.

He should call her.

Ask her out on a date. That's what he really wanted to do. Just her and him somewhere nice. He might as well borrow Maddie's suggestion and take her out on the Thomson River cruise, touristy but lovely all the same. The river looked beautiful at sunset and the stars filled the sky in such a way that took the breath of every city dweller who saw them. Still took his breath away and he'd grown up out here.

He should definitely call her.

Sam took a deep breath and let it out slow. He was getting nowhere fast. Wearing a new track in the carpet from all the pacing he'd been doing was all he'd managed to achieve. Nervous anticipation ballooned in his chest.

Just call her.

Get it over and done with. She'd either say yes or no. Yes, they'd go out and have a nice night. By the end of it he'd be sure if she liked him in a way that mattered. No, and he'd see her around town while she was here then that would be the end of it. Life would go on. He'd survive.

Call her.

He picked up his phone off the kitchen bench and opened the contact list. Press dial, that was all he had to do. His thumb hovered over the green call symbol. A sensation of being pushed up against some kind of invisible barrier overtook him, a barrier he didn't seem able to push through.

Make the call.

He wanted to scream with frustration. This was ridiculous. He was a grown man. So why did he feel like his seventeen-year-old self all over again?

Do it.

Sam scrunched up his eyes and shook his head. One … two … three …

He pushed the button and somewhere in town Sarah's phone rang.

'Hello?' She sounded as breathless as he felt.

'Hi.' He cleared his throat as his words caught. 'It's Sam here.'

She laughed softly. 'I know. Your name comes up on my phone.'

Good start.

'I thought I'd call and see how you're doing and if you're up to anything tonight.' He swallowed hard. Now he'd started he had to keep going.

'Tonight? I think my diary is pretty empty at the moment.'

'Miss Maddie made a great suggestion at dinner. They do this sunset drinks cruise down the Thomson River and I thought you might like to go on a paddle boat.' God, he sounded lame.

'Like the ones you see in movies about the Mississippi?'

'That's the one.' He tried to gauge the level of interest in the tone of her voice, suddenly deaf to everything but the pounding of his own heart.

'Sounds like fun.'

'That's a yes?' He was compelled to check in case his own enthusiasm caused him to misjudge the situation.

'That's a yes.'

Suddenly, the tightness in his chest which had been plaguing him for the last couple of hours dissipated to be replaced by the sensation that someone had pumped helium into his lungs. He could swear he floated above the ground. A Luna Park-sized grin plastered itself across his face.

She'd said yes.

'Okay, then.' While not the pithiest of responses, it was the best he could do under the current circumstances.

'I can't wait until tonight.'

That was the moment he knew. The space between her words carried all the meaning he needed to hear. She liked him. She wanted to see him and saw this as a proper date, not some kindness offered a stranger visiting town. This would be him and her getting to know each other.

Anyone watching might say there could be no future in it, with her from the city and him planted firmly in the country. They'd be right, or maybe not. He was happy to go along for the ride, see where it took them.

All he cared about right now was that she liked him. Sam hung up the phone and let out a whoop of sheer joy. Whoever Sarah Lewis might be, she was the first woman since his wife had died who made him feel alive. His body tingled with possibilities. Suddenly his day got a whole lot better.

✉️

Notes for 'Finding Love in the Outback'
Interview #3
Miria (25) and Dave (28). Met at the Mount Isa rodeo.

David: I've been on the circuit on and off for about ten years now, working my way up. Rodeo is a tough gig and the Isa Rodeo is the biggest in the Southern Hemisphere. I never miss it. Even if I'm injured, I'm there.

Miria: I've known Dave since I was a kid. He was best mates with my brother Jed when they were growing up. Dave went away to follow the rodeo circuit so I only really got to see him once a year and only if Jed let me tag along.

Dave: She'd always been as cute as a button but she was me mate's little sister, you know? Can't cross that line. There are rules about that stuff.

Miria: I always thought those rules were stupid. Jed doesn't though. Still not talking to us, is he, love?

Dave: Nah, but that's okay. He'll come around.

Interviewer: What changed? What happened to get you two together?

Dave: I got pretty badly injured and laid up in hospital. Broke my leg in three places. Not for the first time. They had to screw my leg back together with plates.

Miria: Jed suggested I visit him in hospital because he was bored. He needed the distraction. So I went.

Dave: We spent hours talking and watching TV. Nothin' special on the surface of things but she got under my skin.

Miria: I always had a crush on him so falling in love was pretty easy for me. I think it might have been harder for you, because of Jed, right?

Dave: Yeah, I didn't want to lose a good mate. The problem was, I'd never met anyone who got to me like she does. What's a bloke supposed to do?

Miria: Run away with me and get married.

Dave: Don't worry, honey, as soon as I can walk unaided, I'm planning to do just that.

CHAPTER SIXTEEN

'Are you sure you don't want to go over to Maddie's or have her come here?' Sam asked as he silently debated the merits of wearing a tie. He never wore ties. The one he held in his hand had to be twenty years old if it was a day.

'Absolutely not.' Levi slouched on the couch aimlessly flicking through television channels, his gaze never leaving the screen.

'You two had a falling out?' Sam watched his son in the mirror hanging by the front door, the one currently reflecting his less than polished image back at him. Something had been eating Levi for the last couple of days. He hadn't been himself.

'I'm still not feeling well. No big deal.'

'So you say.' Sam rejected the tie, hanging it up on the coat rack with the intention of putting it away later. Truth

be told, he could probably stick it in the bin. He was never going to wear it.

'I haven't seen you like this for years.' While he didn't want to pry, he did have a feeling Levi was having a hard time of it somewhere in his life. No one ever told you about how much your kid's pain would become your own. When to push and when to hold back? Seemed like a fine tightrope dance to Sam, especially during Levi's teenage years. Time was Levi would have told him straight away what bothered him. Now, he had little insight into his son's life.

Levi shrugged. 'Like I said, I'm fine. Go on your date. Have a good time. Don't worry about me. I'm a big boy now.'

'Mmm …' Sam sighed, unconvinced. 'I'll take your word for it.'

The way the kid acted and his avoidance of Miss Maddie suggested something was going on, and it wasn't the stomach flu. Possibly connected to Maddie's date to the senior dance. Sam wanted to jump in and give Levi some advice, tell him how to handle the situation. What would he say? Not like he knew anything useful about women and his own teenage years had been hell if he remembered rightly.

He grabbed his wallet and keys. 'No idea what time I'll be home. There's food in the freezer if you want to cook yourself something. You know the rules. Keep the doors locked and stay off your phone so I can call you if I need to, okay?'

'Yeah.'

When Levi had been younger Sam would make him repeat everything he'd said to make sure he'd heard. Most of the time he hadn't taken in a thing. He sensed now was not the time to re-enact that ritual.

'Right then, I'm off.' He waited for an acknowledgement and got none. If this went on much longer he'd have to sit the boy down and have a chat. Teenage suicide constituted his biggest fear as a father. Seventy percent of suicides were male and the rural suicide rate terrified him. Who knew what went on in teenage heads? He couldn't bear the thought of losing Levi. After Michelle, he didn't think he'd survive it.

He vowed to pay closer attention, even suss Maddie out and see if she knew what bothered Levi. Hormones, love, social disorder all topped Sam's list of possibilities.

'Goodnight, son,' he called as he shut the front door behind him.

Once outside he took a deep cleansing breath of fresh air. The sun had begun its evening routine, peeking up over the horizon winking goodnight to the moon who was busy rising in the east. Soon the stars would be out. A perfect night to take Sarah out on the Thomson River.

He threw his car keys up into the air and caught them again. Tonight was going to be a good night, he could feel it in his bones.

Whistling off-key, Sam slid in behind the wheel of his ute and started the engine. As he bumped down the long dirt driveway to the main gate of his property his phone rang. He didn't recognise the number.

'Hello?' Cautious in case someone tried to sell him something.

'Mr C? It's Maddie.' Like he'd conjured her up with his thoughts.

'How can I help you?'

'I wanted to check you were taking Sarah—Miss Lewis— out tonight.' She sounded nervous.

'Yes, I am.' He answered slowly, trying to figure out where the conversation might be heading.

'Good. I wanted to remind you she's speaking to the school tomorrow. Please don't tire her out or anything.'

'Okay, point taken. I promise not to wear her out and to get her back to her motel in time to get a good night's sleep. Anything else?' He smiled at the girl's over-eager organisational skills.

'Um … how's Levi? He wasn't at school today and he won't answer my texts.'

Ah, the real reason for her call.

'I might ask you the same thing. He's been down in the dumps for days. Says he's not feeling well. I wonder how true that is. Can't be the grub at the Royal Arms. Do you know any reason why he'd be flat?'

'Not really.' He didn't believe her. 'Has he said anything to you?'

'About anything specifically?' They were having a conversation constructed entirely from questions, both skirting the issue.

'Can't think of anything,' she said a little too brightly. 'I'll check on him tomorrow at school. He is coming, right?'

'I guess so,' said Sam. 'I don't think he'd miss Sarah's, I mean Miss Lewis's, talk.'

'Okay, good. Well, have a good night, Mr C, and say hello to Miss Lewis for me.'

Maddie rang off and Sam was left with the sensation of only having understood half of what had transpired. One thing had become clear, something was going on between Levi and Maddie. He'd bet his bottom dollar Maddie was

the reason for Levi's current mood. His son had fallen in love for the first time and he didn't know it yet.

How he wished Michelle could help him navigate the coming mess.

Sam shook his head and tried to reset his thoughts. He had a date tonight with a woman who electrified him in a way no one had since his wife. This was not the time to think about sad or worrying things. They could wait until tomorrow. Tonight he needed to be witty, intelligent and fun.

He took one hand off the steering wheel and wiped it on his trousers, repeating the action with the other one. Nerves.

What were they going to talk about? He wanted to have a few topics ready to avoid awkward pauses. Hopefully there wouldn't be too many. Maddie had told him all about Sarah and he'd looked up her work online. Curiously, Maddie knew a lot of trivial things about Sarah. Odd, although he couldn't pretend to understand women. The way they communicated with each other was far removed from how men talked to one another.

He remembered when Levi had been little and the kindergarten teacher had explained the way little girls played face-to-face, interacting with each other from a young age, while little boys tended to play side by side, often in parallel games which overlapped as they got to know each other better.

One thing he knew, he didn't have time to play side by side with Sarah until he got to know her better. He had to be on his sparkling best, charm her into wanting to see him again.

True, the long distance issue bugged him. If his heart's reaction had been any different he wouldn't bother pursuing things. But this woman defied any experience he'd had before. She'd hit him like a lightning bolt. Poor Kylie. She didn't stand a chance now, something he experienced mild guilt over. Mild because no one thought Kylie would be back.

He sighed.

When had his love life become complicated? A few weeks ago it had been non-existent, now he had dating experience. Okay, let's not get carried away. Still, he had only really ever dated Michelle. Here he was, about to take a third woman out in two decades. What a Casanova.

The town lights had begun to flicker on as the sun headed towards the horizon. In a moment he would arrive at the motel and there would be no going back. Excitement and nerves darted through him until he could no longer tell them apart as he navigated his way to the motel's parking lot.

Sam checked himself in the rear-view mirror. He looked passable, having done the best he could with what he had.

'Here we go,' he said to his reflection as he opened the car door and stepped out into what he hoped was a new future.

Levi toppled over sideways onto the couch as the door closed. Tonight marked the end of his life as he knew it. By the time his dad got home it would be all over.

He rolled over and clutched a cushion to his chest. Staring at the ceiling, he ran the most likely scenario through his head. Dad would pick up Miss Lewis, take her to sunset

drinks on the paddle boat (*so* touristy) and they'd talk, get to know each other. Which was the disastrous part, because Miss Lewis would work out quickly that Dad didn't know anything about her. Not in the way she knew things about him.

All that stuff about what foods she likes and what shows she likes to watch, stuff she'd put in her email, would trip Dad up. He'd know none of it and she wouldn't understand why. Then the truth would come out and Dad would storm home furious with Levi and Maddie for interfering in his life. He'd have a point.

Levi's anxiety ratcheted up a point. His heart began to beat too fast. Taking a deep breath, he tried to think of something calming and nice. The only thing coming to mind was Maddie in a ridiculously short formal dress leaning on the arm of that idiot, Wonder Wayne. *That* was a whole other crisis for another day.

His life was pretty well over no matter what happened.

Staying home from school was only a temporary solution. He could ask Dad if he could go to boarding school. Couldn't be worse than the social hell he'd somehow landed in. Dante had nothing on Longreach High after this. He struggled to sit up. Only one thing would restore his spirits. Ice cream.

He went to the kitchen and took out a bowl and spoon. The ice cream had set hard in the freezer, so hard he couldn't get the spoon in deep enough to get a decent scoop out. He set the ice cream on the draining board near the sink to soften a little. Neapolitan. His favourite. He'd eat all the chocolate first, then the strawberry, then make a spider with the vanilla and the little bit of cola left in the fridge.

While he planned his feast, his mobile phone rang.

The flashing screen told him Maddie wanted to speak to him. Too bad he didn't want to speak to her. He crossed his arms and leaned back against the kitchen bench, glaring malevolently at the phone while it buzzed away. Nothing could convince him to pick up the call. She only wanted to gossip about Dad. She didn't really want to talk to him. She had Wonder Wayne to talk to now.

The phone stopped and Levi dug his spoon into the ice cream with a viciousness it didn't deserve. The ice cream still wasn't soft enough to dig out. He didn't care. There was a pleasure to be found in stabbing at it.

His phone beeped. An incoming text message. No doubt from Maddie. He could read a text message as long as he didn't have to talk to her.

I know you're there. Answer your phone.

No, he wouldn't and she couldn't make him.

He took his bowl, filled with more chips of ice cream than scoops, and his phone back to the couch.

His phone buzzed again.

Are you shitty with me about something?

'You think?' he said through a mouthful of ice cream. 'What gives you that impression?'

He watched the cricket match without much interest. It was something to look at while he shovelled ice cream into his head.

If you don't answer the phone I will come over. I promise.

'Don't threaten me,' he said to the phone. 'You don't get to come over whenever you like anymore.'

I'll give you ten minutes to get over yourself then I'm coming around.

'So bossy,' he hissed on a long breath out. If he didn't want her to come over, he'd be forced to call her. No choice. However, he had no intention of calling before he'd finished his ice cream. She could wait.

It took him less than two minutes to finish the bowl and lick the spoon.

Taking a deep breath, he called her number. She picked up right away.

'What's wrong with you?' No hello, how are you.

'I'm perfectly fine, thank you,' he said in his haughtiest voice while he put his feet up on the coffee table.

'Really? Because you've been playing at being sick all weekend.'

'I'm better now.'

'It's a mental health thing then?'

'I'm not the insane one here.'

'What's that supposed to mean?'

'You and your crackpot schemes are going to get us both into trouble.'

'Not if you shut up and stick to the plan. Where are your balls?'

He hated it when she mocked him like this. Reminded him of how small he'd felt the other day at the service station.

'Where's your integrity?'

He heard a sharp intake of breath on the other end of the line.

'You did not just say that!' She sounded genuinely outraged. Good. She deserved to feel put out.

'What? You want me to say it again?'

'When did you get so mean, Levi Costello?'

'I learned from the best.'

'What's got into you? I rang to see if you're okay.' She sounded hurt. Levi knew better.

'No you didn't. You rang to make sure Dad's gone on a date with Miss Lewis.'

'You mean Sarah.'

'Whatever.'

'I already know he has.'

'He'll work out something fishy is going on within the first hour and we'll be goners.' The thought made him nauseous.

'You are such a negative person. They'll be fine. So what if it looks like your dad has forgotten some little detail of Sarah's life? It's not a job interview. It's drinks on the river watching the sunset and the stars come out. They'll have plenty to talk about.'

Levi closed his eyes and rested his head on the back of the couch. It wouldn't be fine. The whole thing was doomed to come apart at the seams.

His dad would ground him for the rest of his childhood and never trust him again. Maddie would be Wonder Wayne's girlfriend. No one would ever invite him to a party ever again and he'd enter the Social Wasteland at school. His life was officially over.

'Whatever you say.' Weariness overtook him. Let it all burn to the ground. He didn't care anymore. Let Maddie throw herself at that useless moron. If she couldn't see that their friendship was worth more than a stupid formal date then so be it.

'I've got to go,' he said and hung up on her. She wouldn't like that.

He stared at the television for a bit longer, having gone off the idea of an ice cream spider. Going to bed was out of the

question. Staying awake was proving impossible. His eyelids began to droop and his vision doubled. Finally, he gave in to the sweet, warm darkness of sleep, curled up on the couch with his head on a cushion and the TV announcing cricket scores like a modern day lullaby.

Notes for 'Finding Love in the Outback'
Interview #4
Pete (36) single, from Rockhampton. Active with online dating.

Pete: I'm still up on the dating site despite this incident, but it really made me think about a person's profile and to choose carefully.

I met this girl online. She seemed nice, good-looking, liked dogs, you know the sort of thing. So I arranged to meet her for a coffee at the shopping centre, nice and public so she wouldn't get nervous or anything. We have a good time. I think we're getting on well. I say I'd like to get together again if she's up for it. She reckons she is. So that's that. A nice time had by all and the prospect of a second date. Sweet.

I leave to go to my car and I notice she's following me. Not in a hey-wait-you've-left-something-behind kinda way. More a I'm-spying-on-you kinda way. Bit creepy if you ask me. She's ducking in and out of shops, hiding down behind rubbish bins. So, I decide to take a detour. I didn't want to get stuck in the carpark with her.

I go to the bus stop, out on the street, in the open with people around. I'm standing there, and I can still see her watching me. By this time, she's freaking me out, so I get on the bus. Figure I can do a lap of town. Won't hurt me.

I'm cruising along on this bus and next thing, I look out the window and there she is. I'm not kidding. She's in her car following the bus. Who does that?

I didn't know what to do. In the end, we pulled in behind another bus at some random stop and I switched buses real quick. Took me way out to the boondocks but anything is better than being stalked by that chick. Totally weird. I would have kept dating her too if she hadn't pulled that stunt. Can't help but feel I dodged a bullet.

CHAPTER SEVENTEEN

Every square inch of the sky seemed crammed with stars. She'd had no idea. Living in Sydney where the bright lights polluted the night sky, she could only see twenty or so. Here, they went on forever. Tipping her head back, Sarah let her eyes roam from horizon to horizon.

'Wow,' she said as her neck began to ache. 'This must never get old.'

'You're right,' said Sam. 'It doesn't.'

They'd spent the evening cruising along the Thomson River on the paddle wheeler, the only one west of the Great Divide so she'd been told. Birds flocked to roost along the riverbank as the sun set, their cries filling the night air with a strange melancholy for the day's end.

Sam had apologised for bringing her on a touristy first date. She sincerely didn't mind, finding a soothing old world beauty in the way the golden light from the boat reflected

on the river. The experience transported her to another time and place far out of her own, ordinary life and she was grateful for it.

The fact Sam had thoughtfully brought a bottle of wine helped with more than the atmosphere. The shiraz also took the edge off her nerves. Chatting to him over email had been easy. The keyboard and screen had acted like shields, protecting her from rejection. She knew that sense of safety had been an illusion, yet sitting close to him felt dangerous in a way that made her blood thrum with excitement.

The paddle boat ride had been a stroke of genius. Filled with other tourists, the guides had pointed out natural features and told stories about the area which made finding things to talk about much easier than if they'd been sitting alone in a restaurant. Sam had added to the guide's information with tales of his own, pointing out where he'd gone fishing as a kid or telling her about the time he and his friends had built a raft in a Huckleberry Finn moment that hadn't ended well.

He made her laugh.

Here, on the river, she'd been at ease in her own skin in a way that had eluded her in Sydney. As if the vast openness of the land was big enough to absorb all her doubts and anxieties, leaving her free of the burden of them. Having a handsome, charming man to look at didn't hurt either. It helped that he was as good-looking as his dating profile picture had promised. Those blue eyes of his had a way of looking right into her soul that was startling, like he saw her. He *really* saw her.

What she liked best were the lulls in conversation when the warm night air wrapped around them both, cocooning

them in their own little world and words weren't needed. Even the other guests disappeared. She'd never experienced anything quite like it before, and certainly never with Greg.

They'd gone ashore for dinner around a campfire while a barefoot bush poet recited entertaining rhymes. Sarah hadn't heard bush poetry since she'd been at high school where they'd studied Banjo Paterson and Henry Lawson. Listening to the poems while sitting beneath the canopy of stars gave her a sense of why those men had loved this land. Banjo Paterson had written his much-beloved Australian folksong 'Waltzing Matilda' at a Dagworth cattle station out near Winton. Suddenly the song had a layer of meaning she hadn't understood before.

How could you describe the majesty of this place? She couldn't find the words to capture the sense of timelessness surrounding her, as if something vast and ancient held them in the palm of its hands. Did Sam feel the same way about the land? She wanted to ask him as she watched his profile in the firelight. The right moment refused to present itself. Such a deep question for a night of light and laughter.

Before she knew it, they had moved on to a sound and light presentation showcasing the Kinnon family and other locals, along with the notorious Captain Starlight, a legendary cattle rustler.

The evening didn't offer much by way of chat time for the two of them. Sarah found she didn't mind. The easy companionship she'd found with Sam, along with the entertainment and other guests, allowed her to relax and enjoy his company. No intensity. No pressure. She knew the basics about him and he knew the basics about her. Now they could fill in the details at their leisure.

'Did you enjoy all that?' he asked as they ate their damper and drank their billy tea at the close of the evening's entertainment.

'You know, I did.' She turned to him. 'If you'd asked me before I'd left Sydney if I'd go for this sort of thing, I think I would have said no thank you. You know what? I've had a fantastic time.'

He smiled as if she'd told him he'd won the lottery and could pick up his cheque in the morning.

'Can I let you in on a little secret?' He leaned in close so their shoulders touched. A charge of electricity shot through her and her breath stopped with the shock of it. 'I've never done this before.'

'Dating or the sunset cruise?' She tried for a lightness she didn't possess. She longed for him to touch her again to see if she'd imagined the effect he had on her.

Sam laughed. 'Both I guess. I'm an amateur in the dating stakes and this is the first time I've taken the paddle boat. Always meant to but you know how it is when you live in a place.' He shrugged.

'I'm forever threatening to climb the Sydney Harbour Bridge. I never do. Everyone thinks because you live in Sydney you've done all that stuff, and it isn't true. I'm perpetually busy with something else and there's always tomorrow,' she said.

'Yep. Same here. I'd feel a bit of a pillock coming on this thing by myself.'

'I know, right? None of my friends want to climb the bridge with me. They think it's only for tourists.' She sighed. 'Now I've done this I'm motivated to go back and climb that bridge.'

'I hope you're not in a hurry to tick the climb off your bucket list,' he said. He didn't look at her as he spoke and she sensed a weight to his words.

She looked around at the other people who'd come on the boat journey with them and at the zillions of stars lighting up the night sky. She listened to the happy chatter, the laughter and the sound of insects, small animals and roosting birds rustling along the riverbank. Deep peace lived here, something she'd been looking for without realising it. In this wild, barren, flat, thirsty place she found she could breathe again.

Finally, Sarah looked at Sam. His ruffled dark hair, those incredible Hollywood-blue eyes complemented the part of him she found sexiest of all, the way he was comfortable in his own skin. He didn't seem to need to be anything other than what he was: a dad, a farmer and a man looking for love. He made her think about who she was, who she wanted to be.

She was Sarah: writer and woman looking for love. Simple.

'You know,' she said at last, half turning towards him, 'I don't think it would matter one way or the other to me. I think there might be more interesting things to do and to ... experience.'

She waited, hoping she hadn't been too obscure.

He nodded. With the half-light throwing his profile in relief, she could make out a smile.

She took a sip of her drink and smiled right back.

'Do you mind if I come along tomorrow and hear you speak?'

She shook her head. 'Not at all. I think it's an open invitation to parents and you're a parent.'

'That I am,' he nodded, 'of one hormonally-driven teen-age boy.'

'Problems?' She sensed his need to talk.

Sam shrugged. 'What is there to say? I suspect Levi has fallen in love with Maddie, a fact he's only coming to realise himself.'

'Ah,' she said, replicating his sage nod. 'The course of true love never runs smooth.'

'So they say.' He sighed. 'Turns out Miss Maddie has a date with an older boy. Levi tells me the star half-back is taking her to the school formal. For her, it's a big deal seeing as she's only in year ten.'

'And for Levi it's total devastation.'

'Something like that. I left him home on the couch sulking.'

'God, I remember my first high school crush. I thought my world ended when he hooked up with a girl from another school. She wasn't even pretty.'

Sam laughed. 'Still stings?'

'You better believe it. He didn't see me at all. Turns out this other girl had chops on a skateboard and that's what he was into. I could barely walk across the room without tripping over my own feet.'

'Ouch. He has no idea what he missed out on.' He raised his glass to her.

'What about you?'

'Mmm ... let's see. I guess I was about eleven when I first got a crush on a girl. I met her at the local rodeo. She looked at me across the bull pen and I was smitten.'

'Wow, did you speak to her?'

Sam shook his head. 'No, I sat in the stands and stared at her for two whole hours and then she left with her parents and I never saw her again.'

'Unrequited love is cruel, isn't it?'

'To unrequited love.' They both toasted their former heartbroken selves.

'I guess there's not much you can do for Levi.' Talking to her parents about her wild skater boy had never crossed her mind. They had seemed too old and too busy to really *get* what she'd been going through.

'Nah, I guess not. What would I say that would be of any benefit to him? What words of wisdom would he listen to? We wouldn't have taken any advice from our parents at the same age.'

'I was just thinking that,' she said. 'My folks seemed way too out of touch to be of any use. Mind you, I had a conversation with my mother before I came here that surprised me.'

'About relationships?' Sam's voice sounded tentative.

She nodded. 'She told me how she met my dad and knew straight away that he was the one for her. Love at first sight, she said.'

'And that surprised you?' Sam sounded like a man who knew about love at first sight. How come she didn't? How did she miss out on this stuff?

'Yeah, it did because Mum and Dad are two of the most conservative, straight-laced people you'll ever meet. I didn't think they'd do something as ...' she struggled to find the right word.

'Crazy?' he offered.

'Wild, imaginative, spontaneous and … trusting are the words I was going to use.'

He laughed. 'Plain old crazy works for me.'

'You don't believe in love at first sight?' She tensed, everything hung on his answer.

Sam took his time. He stared out into the inky night and disappeared into its depths right before her eyes. She had no idea where he'd gone. All she could do was wait for him to come back to her. Finally, he did.

He smiled, a sad slow gesture. 'Yes,' he said, 'I believe.'

She returned his smile, knowing he spoke of another woman and another time. Without thinking, she reached out and laid her hand on his arm. He looked down at her hand and then up at her. What she saw in his eyes left her in no doubt this was no ordinary date, the kind where you went home and used words like nice or lovely to describe the evening. No, this was not that kind of date.

The air was charged with an energy that sparked into the darkness while the stillness between them settled into a profound silence, as if they sat at the centre of the world while it spun around them.

Sarah swallowed hard, wanting to speak and reluctant to break the spell. Then he covered her hand with his. The warmth of his skin against hers, the realness of him, sealed the deal. She might never get an opportunity like this again, sitting out here under the Milky Way with cheerful strangers and the most enticing man she'd ever met.

The words rose from her heart, bringing an unbearable pressure with them. They wanted to be free, to be spoken. She couldn't leave here without knowing the answer to the question they held.

'Do you feel this too, or is it just me?'

He didn't take his eyes from hers, those impossibly-blue movie-star eyes that saw right through her defences.

'Yes,' he said quietly. She had to lean in to hear him. 'Yes, I do.'

The world began to spin with the possibilities unleashed by those three words. Giddiness overtook her.

'I thought I might be going mad.' She grinned, unable to help herself.

'No crazier than I am,' he said. 'I don't know about you, I've got nothing to lose here and this … whatever this is … doesn't come around every day. I know that for sure.'

She nodded. 'I've never experienced anything like this before.' She placed one hand over her heart to calm its hammering. 'I don't know what we're supposed to do next.'

'Neither do I.' He laughed. 'I don't think there's a play book for this sort of situation. Go home and get a good night's sleep, I guess.'

She raised her eyebrows. Was he suggesting what she hoped he was suggesting?

'I mean by ourselves.' He read her mind. 'Whatever we do we ought to take this slow. Or at least a little slower. How long are you planning on being in town?'

Loaded question.

'I have no idea. As long as it takes. I have interviews to get and I'm sure I can find other interesting stories to investigate.' The situation wasn't that straight forward. She had Bella to contend with. Sarah put work on the list of things that could wait until tomorrow.

She took in the lines around his eyes, the way his mouth quirked up to one side when he smiled, the broadness of

his shoulders, the way his thick dark hair had a mind of its own. The whole thing had a sense of unreality, like a dream. In a minute she'd wake up and find he was a figment of her imagination.

'Let's take it one day at a time and see what happens,' he said. 'I'm up for it if you are.'

'Yes,' she said. 'Please.'

Notes for 'Finding Love in the Outback'
Interview #5
Andy (53) and Cheryl (51). Met at a Bachelor and Spinster Ball in Yaraka twenty years ago.

Andy: We met at a B&S Ball by accident.

Cheryl: Well, if by meeting you mean you passed out drunk beneath my ute, then yes, we met at the B&S Ball.

Andy: You woke me up the next morning and offered me coffee from your thermos. Most beautiful thing I'd ever seen.

Cheryl: Me or the thermos? I was supposed to be chaperoning my niece and her friends and I came back to the car to find one of the tyres flat.

Andy: Yeah, that was me. See, I thought it was my brother's ute and I thought it'd be funny if he came back and had to change the tyre. Cheryl's ute looked the same as his to me and in my defence, I was pretty damn drunk.

Cheryl: Had more than a few beers I think.

Andy: And aren't you glad I did? If I hadn't I wouldn't have got lost and ended up letting down the tyre of the wrong car and we would never have met.

Cheryl: I have to give you that. Especially as you put the spare on for me.

Andy: Come on, you know it was love at first sight.

Cheryl: (*giggles*) There was something about you looking so sheepish … I just knew you were the one for me.

Andy: I woke up to your gorgeous face and thought, I want to do this every day for the rest of my life.

CHAPTER EIGHTEEN

Maddie craned her neck to see over the sea of students as they filed into the hall. Levi had managed to evade her all morning. She'd caught glimpses of him here and there. If she didn't know better, she'd think he was trying to avoid her.

Maddie stationed herself beside the main doors, tucked out of sight, and waited. Eventually Levi walked in, looking around nervously like a rabbit scenting a fox. She pounced.

'How did it go?' Never one for subtleties—she found them boring—Maddie launched into the topic that interested her the most. Mr C and Sarah. Having binge-watched *Getaway Bay* for six hours on Sunday night, she had recharged her belief in destiny, specifically hers and Liam's.

'What?' Levi hunched his shoulders up to his ears, hands shoved in his pockets.

'Your dad,' she hissed in his ear. He knew damn well what she was talking about. What had gotten into him lately?

'Dunno.' He shrugged as if the situation was of no concern to him whatsoever. He moved away from her, taken by
the shuffling tide of students trying to find a seat.

Maddie sighed. Ms Forsyth expected her to be up on the
stage with Sarah or she'd have followed Levi and *made* him
tell her what had happened. Boys. Utterly useless.

She'd have to rely on her specially honed senses to gauge
from Sarah how successful the date had been. Of course,
the location had been her idea, carefully planted in Mr
C's consciousness. He'd taken the bait as she'd known he
would. The tricky bit she worried about was whether or not
too much had been revealed and the whole plan had come
apart at the seams.

Levi's attitude this morning had her worried. He was acting like the world had ended.

'Maddie McRae.' Ms Forsyth called her from near the
stage. She stood with Sarah who looked every inch the
sophisticated Sydney journalist in a pair of fitted cropped
black pants, red suede ankle boots, and an asymmetrical
blood-red top that set off her colouring like nothing else on
earth.

Maddie sighed. Perfection.

She pushed through the crowd to where Sarah stood.

'Are you ready?' Ms Forsyth asked.

'Sure am.' Maddie had been born for this sort of thing.
She had her speech notes clutched in one hand, not that
she'd need them.

'I can't thank you enough for inviting me,' said Sarah.
'This trip has already been an eye-opener in many ways.'

'You're welcome,' said Maddie. What did she mean by
eye-opener? She seemed happy, so maybe the reference

didn't carry a negative connotation. She cocked her head to one side and surveyed Sarah. She looked fantastic. Glowing even.

If anyone were to ask her professional opinion as a match-maker she'd say Sarah looked like a woman in love.

A ripple of triumphant joy ran through Maddie. She loved the high she got from making a good match. There was nothing like it, except falling in love.

Movement at the doorway caught her attention. Parents had begun filing in, moving towards the seats reserved for them at the back of the hall. She noted Mr C looking dapper this morning. Another good sign. How come Levi was all bent out of shape? Things looked to be going well. Unless he knew something she didn't.

A cold wash of fear tumbled through her. Maybe she'd been exposed and they were waiting, rather cruelly, to confront her publicly. A sweat broke out on her brow as anxiety clutched at her heart.

She took a deep breath. *Slow down*. Her mother always told her she over-dramatised situations. Nothing was wrong. Everything would work out exactly as she planned. She hadn't failed at this yet. Matchmaking was her destiny.

'Are we ready to begin?' asked Ms Forsyth.

Maddie plastered her most dazzling smile on her face. 'I most certainly am.'

The event went without a hitch. Maddie had a seat of honour on the stage, being the person responsible for Sarah in the first place. She sat primly with her ankles crossed like she'd seen Kate Middleton do, her hands folded neatly on her lap. She'd worn her school jacket and braided her hair so she looked every inch the capable student.

From her place at the side of the stage she could see Wayne. He and his friends leered at her like the clowns they were until Mr Ozzie, the PE teacher, had words. Whatever he'd said shut them down immediately. She could see Mr C clearly. He had eyes only for Sarah, with a smile on his face and his body language nice and relaxed. It gave her a warm tingly feeling inside to see how happy he looked. She liked Mr C. He deserved to be happy after all the heartache he'd gone through.

She sat back in her seat and allowed herself to relax a little. Satisfied with her work, she counted her triumphs.

Sarah spoke with passion and she could see the other kids connected with stuff she said. Bringing her here might have served another purpose but the kudos from the talk was a total bonus. Ms Forsyth thought Maddie had initiative. No need to tell her Miss Kempton had nixed the project before she left.

Wayne had asked her to the year twelve formal. Given all the girls in the upper grades considered him a catch, this could be considered a coup, adding considerable weight to her social standing. Then there was the matter of the dress. She'd found the most divine gown online and it was winging its way to her right at this very moment.

Levi acting all weird constituted the only problem in her life.

She sought him out in the audience. He sat looking out the window, his arms crossed and slouching low in his seat as if he wanted to hide. What was his problem? A small crease formed between her brows. She tried not to frown, being too young for botox and everything, but sometimes a girl was driven to it.

He'd promised to help her organise some interviews for Sarah. They were supposed to work on the list this afternoon after school. As he wouldn't return her text messages, she didn't know if they were still on or not.

Levi turned his head and their eyes met. She smiled the warmest, most discreet smile she could. He gave her a look like a laser beam of ice, if laser beams could shoot ice. Maybe a ray of ice from an ice gun. Either way, she had no illusion his current mood had everything to do with her.

Maddie's previous high evaporated as if it had never been. Sarah sounded like she was speaking underwater and everyone's faces blurred together until they didn't look like people anymore. Her stomach suddenly appeared to be lined in stone.

For the first time in her life, Maddie McRae didn't know what to do. Her best friend of forever hated her, right in the middle of what had to be not only her most successful matchmaking scheme yet, but also her biggest social coup. What had she done to deserve this?

She racked her brains, combing over every interaction she'd had with Levi in the last week, looking for clues to her crime.

The only thing she could identify was the way he'd left suddenly after finding out about Veronica's party. Okay, he hadn't been invited. Big deal. Veronica had only invited the year eleven and twelve boys because she wanted to make out with an older man. Maddie hadn't had any control over that, and it wasn't like she could show up with Levi in tow. He would have been out of place. She didn't tell him about the party to protect him from feeling bad. She'd been doing him a favour so he had no right to be angry at her.

She smoothed her skirt down over her knees. Now she'd found the issue she could relax a little. After the talk had finished she'd find Levi and explain everything. He'd understand. That was the one catch when your bestie was a boy: there were certain things she could only do with other girls so there was always a risk of Levi feeling left out. Once they'd talked it through they could go back to being besties again. Sorted.

Settling back, she listened to the rest of Sarah's talk. Personally, she had no interest in journalism. Her job was to thank Sarah at the end of the speech. She had to start paying attention or she'd miss her cue.

She took a deep, happy breath. Things were going to work out fine, she could feel it in her bones.

The last thing he wanted was to get caught up with Maddie, so the minute Sarah Lewis finished her speech he'd slunk out on the pretext of needing the bathroom. The teachers didn't stop him. The main show had finished anyway.

His dad sat transfixed. Levi could set himself on fire and he'd bet his dad wouldn't notice. He rolled his eyes in disgust. He'd known the woman for three-point-two minutes and he acted like she was the love of his life or something.

Dad had come home from his date with her all buzzy in the most annoying way. Levi liked seeing him happy, and he didn't mind Sarah at all. He hated the way he felt right now and nothing he did seemed to make it go away. Everywhere he went he either ran into Wayne or saw Maddie. They mocked him with their presence. Leaving Longreach sounded great about now. He could leave everyone behind and start fresh somewhere no one knew him. He might be

able to convince his dad to send him to boarding school or something.

Anywhere was better than here.

He shoved his hands deep into his pockets and kept his eyes on the path in front of him. He'd go and get his school bag then wait in Dad's ute until it was time to go. Or he could get on the bus and avoid them all. Food for thought.

He was chewing on this when someone shoulder charged him from the side. He stumbled from the force of the impact and nearly fell.

'What the fuck?' He regained his balance and turned to face his attacker.

Maddie stood with her arms crossed and feet apart. He knew that stance. Her take-no-prisoners mode.

'I am not in the mood for your shit,' he said as he walked away. Never in the history of their friendship had he walked away from her before. He'd always been the faithful type. Not this time. Those days were done.

'Hey, I want to talk to you, Levi Costello.' He didn't bother to look around and she chased after him. Behind them, streams of students began to leave the hall, their chatter rolling over them like a wave.

'Well, I don't want to talk to you,' he shot over his shoulder as he picked up the pace.

'What is wrong with you?' She grabbed his arm, bringing him to a stop.

He shrugged like nothing bothered him. 'What do you mean?' He wasn't going to give her an inch.

'You know exactly what I mean. You're acting all moody and not returning my texts. What's going on? Has something happened?'

Yeah, something had happened alright. He'd finally seen the light. Maddison and her crazy schemes had gone too far. Sure, things might be working out right now but he knew her luck couldn't hold. None of this would last. And he'd end up paying for it with his dad. The price had already been too high.

'Look, I've got to get going.' He turned and began to walk away again. The less he had to do with her the better. Looking at her up close already made his chest hurt. He didn't want to have a D&M with her too.

'Levi! I thought we were going to hang out this afternoon.'

He shook his head without turning around. 'No thanks.'

Suddenly she stood in front of him, blocking his way. 'Not good enough. We're in this together and we're going to see our dreams through.'

He pulled back like she'd slapped him. 'Our dreams?'

'Yeah, all of this is part of the master plan.' Maddie swept her arms wide.

'*Your* master plan, not mine.' He couldn't believe he'd been so gullible to fall for her shit.

'You want to go to Sydney too. You said so. You and me together in Bondi.' She spoke to him like he'd had a sudden brain injury or something.

'*You* want to go live in Bondi because you've got a stupid crush on an actor who is never going to look at you twice.' He wanted to hurt her like she'd hurt him. Her eyes narrowed and her sharp intake of breath told him he'd hit his mark.

'Our fate lies in Sydney, *together*, and you know it.' She wasn't going to give up without a fight. What else could he expect?

'*Your* fate lies here with that wanker, Wayne. The two of you make a perfect couple. Now leave me alone.' He stepped around her. He had to leave before she noticed how badly he was shaking.

'What's Wayne got to do with any of this?' He didn't need to see her to know she'd be standing there with her hands on her hips.

'If you've got to ask, you don't deserve to know.'

At least he'd had the last word, and it had been a good one.

As he walked away he swore everyone stared at him like they knew he'd been played for a fool the whole time. They probably did. They could stay in this loser town. He intended to follow his destiny. As soon as he could work out what it was.

CHAPTER NINETEEN

Sarah sat in the reception room of Radio Longreach, a small space with two chairs and a framed aerial picture of the great expanse of the outback. Lydia Forsyth had been true to her word and contacted her friend, Ashley Reeves, to see if she had space to interview Sarah.

Ashley did.

She'd invited Sarah to come and chat on her afternoon radio show, hoping to generate the kind of conversation that would give her decent ratings and Sarah some great leads.

A short, powerhouse of a woman dressed in jeans and a t-shirt shot through the door. 'Hello,' she said, hand outstretched. 'I'm Ashley and you're Sarah.'

'Yes, I am.' Sarah stood and shook the proffered hand. 'Thank you so much for having me on.'

Ashley batted Sarah's gratitude away with one hand. 'I should be the one thanking you. I've been racking my brains

to come up with something fresh that isn't the same old gripes about what needs to be addressed out here like bad internet, wild dogs and mental health. We've got enough problems to tackle, we need some fun.'

'I hope I can help. Lead on.' Sarah smiled. Ashley appeared to be of a similar age to Sarah. She was compact and buzzing with energy. Sarah felt immediately drawn to her.

Ashley pushed open the glass door and ushered Sarah into the heart of the station. A small staff worked away in an open-plan office looking rather like any office anywhere in Australia with half-drunk coffee perched on the corners of desks and pictures of loved ones stuck on the walls.

'Everyone, this is Sarah Lewis. As you know, she's from *Seriously Sydney* so if any of you are planning a major career move you might want to talk to her before she leaves.' There were some polite chuckles and Sarah couldn't be sure if Ashley was serious or not.

She gave Sarah a wink, which confirmed nothing.

'Come on through to my office.'

Ashley's office turned out to be the studio itself. The engineer and producer, both sitting on one side of a glass partition, gave them a wave as Ashley indicated for Sarah to take a seat. 'That's Tom and John. They'll take care of all the technical stuff and keep us on track.'

'Are we starting now?' Sarah asked, startled. She'd been hoping for a few minutes to prepare herself, although she couldn't say how she intended to do that.

'Strike while the iron is hot,' said Ashley, handing her a set of headphones. 'You ever done this before?'

Sarah shook her head. 'I've been strictly a print woman.'

Ashley took her seat and placed her own headphones on her head.

'Nothing to it,' she said. 'You talk into that microphone. That light there,' she pointed to a red globe, 'shows us when we're live, although it will be pretty obvious what's going on. Follow my lead.'

Sarah nodded as she adjusted the headphones, which felt heavy and unfamiliar.

'Good to go?' Ashley gave her a thumbs up.

'I guess.' She returned the gesture, trying to catch up. She'd expected Ashley to want to chat a bit first, get the lie of the land. Maybe things turned out punchier this way.

'And we're live,' said a voice in her ear. The producer.

'Welcome to Radio Longreach: the voice of the West, your outback connection. I'm Ashley Reeves and this afternoon we have the delightful Sarah Lewis with us all the way from Sydney.'

Sarah stared at Ashley, mesmerised by her transformation from regular person to radio host. She nodded at Sarah, encouraging her to speak.

'Oh, hello, everyone.' Her voice sounded breathy, like she'd come in from a run.

'Sarah, you work as a journalist for *Seriously Sydney*, is that right?'

'Yes, Ashley. I've been with the magazine for several years now.' She leaned in close to the microphone, perching on the edge of her seat.

'Tell me, what brings you to Longreach?' By comparison Ashley sat back in her chair, arms crossed, looking relaxed and at ease. The complete polar opposite to Sarah.

'I'm researching love in the outback. Finding love in the city is so hard I wondered how people in the outback managed to find someone. I mean, you're all such a long way from each other and the towns are small.'

'Ah, yes, Sarah.' Ashley leaned in. 'We like to say that while the goods might be odd, the odds are good. You'd be surprised at how people fall in love out here. Not so many to choose from so less confusion.'

Sarah laughed and began to relax. 'I hadn't thought about it like that.'

'Tell you what,' Ashley became all business, 'how about we get some callers on who'd like to share their stories with our guest today. Let's show Sarah what love in the outback really looks like right after a word from our sponsor.'

Ashley pushed a button and let the ads roll. She slipped off her headphones. 'How are you doing over there?'

'I think I'm fine.' Sarah took a deep breath and let it out slow.

'You're doing great. You wait, in a minute or so you'll lose the nerves and it'll feel as if you've done this sort of thing forever.' Ashley shifted her attention to the booth behind Sarah. 'Okay,' she nodded and gave the producer a thumbs up. 'We've got a switchboard full of callers,' she said to Sarah. 'After we take the call, you let me know with a gesture if you want to ask them to interview. My producer will make sure we get their contact details for you if you do. Are you ready?'

'I have no idea but I guess we're going to find out.' Shaky nerves and a kind of bubbly excitement vied for the upper hand in her stomach.

'First caller is Monica, who is visiting her sister from Maryborough.' Ashley pushed another button and they were back on air. 'Do you have a story for us, Monica?'

'Hello and welcome, Sarah, to the outback,' said the voice of an older woman.

'Thank you,' said Sarah. 'Tell us how you found love out here. I'm struggling to find it in the city and I need some tips.'

Monica's laugh gave Sarah the impression of a light-hearted woman with a sense of humour. 'I'm a widow and I'll confess, I'd pretty well given up on meeting anyone. I wasn't even looking to be honest. I mean, what's the point when you're in your sixties and living in a small town where you know almost everyone. You know what I mean?'

Sarah didn't but she was happy to chat about it, and they did for the next few minutes. Monica proved to be as delightful as she first sounded and Sarah gave her the thumbs up for an interview.

Several callers later, Sarah had a great list of interviewees to go with the contacts the McRaes had given her. She'd always loved interviewing people and not all her articles for *Seriously Sydney* required this kind of research. The next week or so would be crammed with the work she loved best and the thought killed the last vestiges of nerves, replacing it with nothing but pure happiness.

Her allotted thirty minutes seemed to fly by.

'I'd like to thank Sarah Lewis for joining us today to chat about true love and how to find it. I hope we gave you a few pointers, Sarah.'

'I've had a wonderful time, thank you, Ashley. The people out here are super generous and warm. I'm only sorry we had such a short time to chat. I'm sure there are many more stories out there. Thank you, Longreach.' She'd begun to get the hang of this radio thing.

Ashley wrapped up the show with long-practised, polished flair. 'And we're done.' She took off her headphones and smiled at Sarah. 'How do you feel about a cuppa?'

'I'd love one.' Sarah slipped her headphones off and placed them gently on the desk in front of her. 'Did I do okay?'

'You did fine,' said Ashley.

'More than fine.' Tom stuck his head in the room. 'We had more calls for that piece than we've had for anything since we did the interview with the Simpson Desert ultra-marathon people.'

Sarah glowed with pleasure. 'I'm so pleased to hear that. I had a wonderful time and it generated some terrific leads for me. Thank you both for having me.'

Ashley regarded her, head cocked to one side and bright blue eyes sparkling with the intelligence that lay behind them. 'How long are you in town?'

Sarah shrugged. 'I've got a week's worth of work at least. Then, who knows?'

Things depended on the quality of the interviews she managed to get ... and Sam. While Bella had given her leave to go chase this story, she also had an expectation that Sarah would submit a weekly piece on other interesting things she'd found out here. That gave her enough time to explore ... everything. But she didn't have forever.

'Come get that drink. I've got an idea I'd like to run past you.' Ashley held the door open for her. 'You know

something, I've got a feeling you and I are going to be great friends.'

He didn't remember how to do this.

Sam lay on his back staring at the ceiling, his bed fast becoming his thinking place. Meditating on the lazy rotations of the ceiling fan calmed him. Things had moved very fast in the last few days. Way quicker than he was used to. Nothing at all happened around here most of the time. Then Sarah turned up.

Their date on the river had a dream-like quality about it. The way he'd known what she'd been thinking before she'd said it kind of spooked him out at the same time it thrilled him. He didn't know what to think.

One thing he knew for sure, he hadn't felt this way about anyone since his wife. Even then, this was different. With Michelle, he'd had a slow dawning that had begun when he'd met her. He'd been too young and wrapped up in his own world to realise what he'd been feeling was love. Bit like Levi.

He let his thoughts settle on his son for a moment. No one prepared you for how much you worried about your kid. Watching him get hurt wrenched at Sam's gut and there wasn't a damn thing he could do about it. He wondered if his dad had felt the same way about him.

Levi had to work this out on his own. Sam would let him know he could talk whenever he wanted to. In the meantime he'd stand by and keep an eye on the situation as best he could.

He had his own business to worry about.

Sarah couldn't stay in Longreach forever. She'd go back to Sydney and her job. He didn't want her getting caught up in the high octane excitement of romance in the country, only to get home and realise all the affair had amounted to was a bit of a distraction. She shared the same feelings, he knew that now. Didn't protect him from the possibility of getting hurt.

He sighed and closed his eyes. Images of Sarah standing behind the podium at the high school earlier today filled his vision. She'd looked amazing. To hear her speak about her life as a journalist made him realise Longreach might be too small for a girl like her. Most ambitious people made a beeline for the coast as soon as they could. Why would she want to swap the city for a country town on the edge of nowhere? Literally nowhere.

Opening his eyes again, he went back to watching the fan. Easier.

Did he give in to fear and stop seeing her before he got in so deep he couldn't get out again? Or did he carry on regardless of his reservations? It had been such a long time since he'd sat on a fence he'd forgotten how uncomfortable it could be.

'Dad?' Levi appeared in the doorway, slouching against the lintel like he'd grown there.

'Yeah, mate.' Here it comes, the big chat about girls and relationships. They'd had the sex talk. In some ways Sam thought that might be easier, all technical medical and physical stuff. Biology. Emotions, however, were a different kettle of fish.

'I was wondering if we could afford me going to boarding school on the coast.' He made his pitch so casually, Sam had to take a moment to make sure he'd understood what the boy had said.

'Boarding school?' He struggled to sit up, swinging his legs over the side of the bed.

'Yeah, I reckon they'd offer a higher level of educational standard which would help me get into a good uni when the time comes.'

Sounded reasonable enough on the surface, if only Sam wasn't aware of the trouble between Levi and Maddie.

'I see,' he said, rubbing the back of his neck. A tension headache threatened. He hadn't had this much to contend with for years. 'You've given this some thought then?'

'I think it's time to spread my wings, you know, grow up a bit.'

'You do, huh?' Blindsided, Sam stalled for time to think.

'Only if we can afford it of course. Hey, I could apply for a scholarship.' Levi lit up like the scholarship idea had just come to him. Sam didn't respond for a minute.

'Interesting idea.' He stood up. 'Want to discuss it over ice cream?'

'There's only vanilla left.'

'You're kidding me. I only bought the tub three days ago.'

Levi shrugged as if the ice cream must have eaten itself.

'Come on, vanilla will have to do.'

They moved to the kitchen and went about the automatic habit of taking out bowls and spoons. Sam made short work of the hard ice cream with a spoon he ran under hot water first.

'Cool idea,' said Levi, clearly impressed.

'Life skills, buddy. Now tell me what you're thinking with this whole boarding school deal.' He'd try to stay open to the idea even if his first instinct was to shut the proposal down.

Levi took a deep breath. 'I feel I need to grow up a little bit, you know, mature emotionally, and I think boarding

school would force me to do that. Being away from everything that's familiar, making new friends, living in a dorm, and being challenged would be good for me.' He stabbed at the ice cream with his spoon while he spoke, not meeting Sam's eyes.

Definitely trouble with Miss Maddie. 'Won't you miss your mates?' He'd ease around the subject. They had plenty of time.

Levi shrugged. 'They'd still be my mates. I need to grow and that's not going to happen here in Longreach.'

'It's not?' Sam scooped up a spoonful of ice cream and ate it.

Levi shook his head. 'I think I've maxed out my growth possibilities in this environment.'

'Right.' Sam couldn't remember ever being concerned about growth possibilities at the same age. 'What about Miss Maddie?'

Levi thrust his spoon into the ice cream with particularly vicious force. 'What about her?'

'Didn't the two of you have major plans of graduating high school and going to university in Sydney?'

'They're *her* plans, not mine.'

'I see. When did that change?'

'Nothing changed. I never said I wanted to do that. She assumed I'd be along for the ride. Well, I'm not her wingman. She wants to go to Sydney, she can go by herself. I've got my own future to look after.'

'Okay.' Sam nodded and concerned himself with the contents of his bowl. What had Maddie done to hurt Levi? Had to be the senior formal. How was Sam going to handle this? He ate his ice cream in silence while contemplating his next move.

'You two had a falling out?' Okay, not a brilliant response. He was completely out of ideas in the clever parenting department.

'We've grown apart, Dad. We want different things. I guess that happens, right?'

Who was this boy and what had he done with Levi? It was like having a conversation with a forty-two-year-old man instead of a fifteen-year-old boy.

'I get it,' he said. He got that his son had fallen in love with his best friend who did not love him back. Not that he'd point that out to Levi any time soon.

'So, boarding school?' Levi brightened up, clearly relieved Sam had no intention of pursuing the issue between him and Maddie.

'Let me think about it, work out the finances and stuff. Did you have somewhere in mind?' He'd let this notion of Levi's play out for a bit.

'I was thinking Brisbane Grammar. They take boarders and it's got a great academic reputation. It's not that far from Nan and Pop's. I can always visit them on the weekends.'

'Right. I see you've done your research. Leave it with me and we'll revisit the topic later.' What else could he say? He doubted very much he could afford to board Levi anywhere. The farm made enough money to keep afloat and ensure he had a tiny buffer in the bank. Not enough to stump five figure school fees.

'Are you sure this sudden desire to move to boarding school doesn't have anything to do with Maddie and her date to the formal?' He swore he never meant to say anything. The words slipped out before he could stop them. Prior to his mouth's rebellion, he'd been priding himself

on his restraint. Then, whammy! Out came the one thing guaranteed to drive Levi underground.

The boy scowled, his face a picture of hurt fury. Sam had hit a nerve.

'I told you, Dad. Maddie and I have grown apart. We want different things and besides, I think it's time I manned up. Can't have a girl as a best friend forever.'

'Really?' He struggled to suppress the smile threatening to unfold across his face. 'And what's wrong with having a girl for a friend?'

Levi shrugged. 'Nothing by itself. I think I need to spend more time with guys doing guy things instead of sitting on a kitten pillow watching dumb romantic movies.'

'Fair enough.' Sam couldn't argue with his logic. Not something he'd enjoy doing himself. 'The senior formal is tomorrow, isn't it?'

Levi's shoulders hunched to his ears. 'Whatever.'

'I'll take that as a yes.' It went a long way to explaining Levi's sudden desire to move to boarding school. Young Maddison would be dressed to the nines and out with her older boy. The thought must be killing Levi.

'Let's talk about you for a change.' Levi picked an apple out of the fruit bowl on the kitchen bench and took a bite. The crisp snap of the apple resounded in the small space. If Levi was voluntarily eating fruit then Sam was in big trouble.

'Nothing to tell.' Never a bigger lie spoken.

'I don't believe you.' Clearly, Sam was a very bad liar.

'What do you want to know?' Always best to be frank if he couldn't be anything else.

'What's going on with Sarah?'

'Miss Lewis to you.'

'Whatever. Don't avoid the question.'

'I wasn't avoiding the question, purely correcting your manners.' He stalled for time. Talking about Sarah, bringing the subject into the house, took her out of his romantic fantasy and into a reality he wasn't sure he was ready for yet.

'You went out on a date with her and ...' Another crunchy bite of the apple.

'And none of your business.'

'If she's going to be my stepmum I reckon it's plenty my business.'

'Who said anything about Sarah becoming your stepmother? We've been on one date.' A sweat broke out on the back of Sam's neck.

'Okay, let's start with some basic facts. Do you like her?'

'Yes, I do.'

'Does she like you?'

'I believe she does.' She'd said as much and he was confident about this statement. Levi nodded as he nibbled the last few bites surrounding the apple core.

'Are you going to see her again?'

'Yes.' He had every intention of seeing her as often as he could until she left or ... he had no idea what might come next.

'Have you made arrangements to see her?'

'Is there a limit on the number of questions you can ask me?' He ought to have put some parameters around this interview from the get-go.

'Nope. I get to ask as many as I need to until I feel a sense of safety about the issue.'

'Excuse me?' Sam shook his head in disbelief.

'Answer the question please.'

'I haven't made arrangements to see her. I'd been thinking about what we might do for our next date when you and
I started this conversation.'

'Sounds like you need some help.'

Sam doubted that. Levi's own emotional life appeared to
be a tangled hormonal mess. What guidance could he offer
his dad? 'Help away,' he said, curious to see what gems of
wisdom Levi had on hand.

Levi strolled to the pantry and opened the doors. He
retrieved the pack of assorted cream biscuits and returned
to sit on a stool at the kitchen bench.

'Right,' he said as he opened the pack and slid the plastic
tray all the way out. Sam knew the task of putting the wrap-
per back on the tray to be a near impossible one. He held
his tongue.

Levi selected an orange cream and bit into it with surprising delicacy. 'You could take her to the Stockman's Hall of
Fame,' he said through a mouthful of biscuit. 'She's here
to research the outback and they offer a dinner and a show
package.'

'We did the paddle boat thing. I want her to feel as if she's
on a date, not a cultural tour.'

'Fair enough.' Levi devoured the rest of his biscuit, selecting another flavour from the tray. 'Want one?'

'No thank you.'

'There's dinner at Harry's,' Levi said after giving his second biscuit a good chew.

'Good suggestion.' Harry's always delivered quality. Why
hadn't he thought of that? Possibly because he'd been off
the dating scene for decades and his imagination had only

ever stretched to the pub. 'Sarah heard all about Captain Starlight on the cruise which makes a restaurant named in honour of Harry Redford perfect.'

'See, and you thought I didn't know what I was talking about.' Sam didn't want to admit Levi had a point. 'The restaurant is nice and close to where Sarah is staying too.' Levi gave him a sly look. 'I'm old enough to stay by myself overnight. Good practice for boarding school.'

'Except at boarding school you're surrounded by responsible adults and a bunch of other boys.' Sam wanted to keep his distance from Levi's implications. Not because he didn't want Sarah, because he did. He wasn't interested in talking about his sex life with his fifteen-year-old son. The concept weirded him out.

Levi shrugged. 'The principle remains the same.' He slid off the stool and dusted biscuit crumbs off his shirt. 'Seriously, Dad, I want you to be happy. She seems like a decent person, but be careful okay?'

He sauntered out of the room before Sam could form a response, leaving the biscuits where they lay.

'Hey, Levi, come back and put the biscuits away,' he called after him, only to be answered with the sound of the bedroom door closing. 'Damn teenagers,' he muttered as he fished a plastic container out of the cupboard and put the biscuits into it.

How did Levi know if Sarah happened to be a decent person? He'd spent next to no time with her. Sam rearranged the top layer of biscuits, trying to fit the last one into the container.

Warning him to be careful rankled too. He was long past being careful. This woman had already breached his

defences. If this thing ended badly, he'd be crushed and there would be nothing he could do about it. He'd cast his lot whatever the outcome.

He gave up and ate the biscuit, jamming the lid on the container with unnecessary force.

If his fate was truly sealed, then what was he waiting for? He chewed the Monte Carlo thoughtfully. Best to make his move and see how Sarah felt about things. See how far they could take this, whatever it might become. Boots and all.

The revelation he had nothing to lose settled on him. Levi would leave at some point and he'd be on his own. Who knew when he'd feel this way about someone again? Maybe never. Longreach was a small town. The odds weren't good.

He picked up his phone to call Sarah and invite her to dinner. While Sam had no idea what the next step in their budding relationship should be, he did know he wanted Sarah in his life. All he had to do was go and get her.

Notes for 'Finding Love in the Outback'
Interview #6
Bruce (65) and Monica (63). Met six months ago at a CWA event in Maryborough.

Monica: My husband passed away ten years ago. Cancer. I didn't expect to meet anyone, not at my age, and not out here in the country. More likely to be abducted by aliens than meet a good man.
Bruce: You're only sixty-three! People from my planet are only considered middle-aged at sixty-three. Me,

I'd been alone for the last five years. My wife died of cancer too.

Monica: One thing we had in common (*she takes his hand and smiles into his eyes*).

Bruce: Not the only thing (*winks*).

Monica: We met when I entered a cake in the Country Women's Association district competition. I don't usually do that sort of thing, but a friend encouraged me, and I thought why not?

Bruce: I usually avoid those events like the plague, but my sister nominated me as a judge. Said getting out of the house would be good for me and there'd be cake. How could I resist?

Monica: He liked my cake the best.

Bruce: I couldn't award her the blue ribbon though. I was worried what people would say when we started dating. I didn't want them to gossip and say she only won because I fancied her. To be honest I don't even remember what kind of cake it was. I saw you and thought I'd like a slice of that to take home.

Monica: (*slapping his arm playfully*) I can't believe you just said that. Don't print that in the paper, whatever you do.

CHAPTER TWENTY

Sam had sounded different on the phone yesterday. Sarah couldn't put her finger on what it was, only that he'd sounded … definite. She liked the subtle shift in energy. They'd both been tentative and unsure on Monday night. Tonight already had a different quality, like a decision had been made. Certainly true for her.

She inspected the contents of her suitcase for something suitable to wear tonight. The trouble lay in her inability to make a single decision in the fashion department. Fiona would know what to do.

Moments later Fiona picked up.

'I was thinking about you,' Fiona said. 'Have you slept with him yet?'

'Steady on, and hello to you too.' Sarah laughed.

'So the answer is no.'

'I didn't say that,' protested Sarah.

'If you had slept with him you'd have said yes straight off the bat. What's taking so long?'

'We are connecting in the old-fashioned way, and it's only been a couple of days. Give me a chance to warm up.'

'You're in the desert. It's already warm enough.' Sarah had missed her flatmate's blunt humour. 'Bring me up to speed, what's going on?'

'We're going out to dinner tonight. Second date. For our first date we went on a cruise down the Thomson River, dinner under the stars, you know the sort of thing.' While she wanted to share details with her best friend, she also wanted to keep the tenderness of the special moments to herself. They were private and magical. Besides, she didn't want to hear Fiona's acerbic take right before date number two.

'He's a romantic, then?'

'Absolutely. And as handsome in the flesh as he is in his pictures.'

'How was the teenager talk?'

'Brilliant. Sam came to support me. It's like we've clicked on some fundamental level.'

Looking out from the podium yesterday and seeing his ridiculously handsome face smiling up at her with undisguised admiration had left her weak at the knees. She'd stumbled her words badly and prayed no one had noticed her distraction. Not super professional. She hadn't felt professional. She'd felt sexy, a sensation that had eluded her for a very long time.

There'd been no opportunity to speak with him after the assembly finished. She'd been pressed by students and parents with questions, all of which she'd been delighted to answer.

Maddie had been beaming with pride and had obviously won some points for her efforts. She'd introduced Sarah to people like a polished personal assistant. She'd also prepared a list of potential interviewees for which Sarah was enormously grateful. Made her job a great deal easier.

'Do we believe in love at first sight now?' Fiona chuckled.

Sarah sighed. 'I want to say no because it makes no sense, yet …' Here she was getting ready to see a man she couldn't stop thinking about since first seeing his photograph weeks ago. 'Did I tell you I did an interview on talkback radio? The school principal set it up and I've got some callers who will be happy to let me interview them for the series.'

'Total win,' said Fiona. 'Look at you go. Even if things don't work out with Lonely Sam you'll have a cracker of an article.'

'The woman who interviewed me also mentioned a potential job at the radio station, if I want one.'

'That's fantastic. Are you interested in moving into radio? Make a nice change from Bella the Beast,' said Fiona.

'You know, I think I am. I loved talking to people and hearing their stories. I felt much more connected to the Longreach community in one afternoon than I ever have in Sydney. There's so many people in the city and they kind of all blur together.' Sarah smiled to herself, knowing she probably didn't make much sense and yet feeling so right at the same time.

'I expect people in Longreach get blurry all the time.' Fiona laughed. 'No doubt you'll be a bit blurry yourself later on.'

'I do need your advice on something important,' Sarah said, ignoring the jab.

'You're on your second date so you can get away with sleeping with him, especially under the odd circumstances.'

'No, not that.' Sarah hoped she sounded outraged enough to be convincing. 'I have no idea what to wear.'

'Where is he taking you?'

'The best restaurant in town.'

They didn't have much time to waste. She wanted to be certain of him before she left here, willing to roll the dice on the burgeoning attraction between them. This meant spending as much time with him as she could. She needed to be a little more forward and see how he responded. She needed to look hot.

'Wear the blue dress, the retro one with the pleated skirt. Save the black dress for the races.'

The dress in question, a soft pale blue in colour, fitted her figure snugly, showing off every curve.

'Perfect choice.' She could have worked that out for herself if she hadn't been so nervous.

'Make sure your room is tidy so you can bring him back,' said Fiona. 'And don't drink too much because you're nervous.'

'How can you tell I'm nervous?'

'Why else would you ask me what to wear? You never ever did that for a date with Greg. Just saying.'

'Good point.' She sighed. Apart from a few texts, she hadn't spoken to Greg since they broke up. Being apart didn't seem to be upsetting either of them.

'How are the interviews coming along?'

'I officially start interviewing tomorrow. My schedule is full, which is brilliant and unexpected. I thought I'd have to work harder than this.'

'Serendipity. It's meant to be. Fate.' Fiona was quite capable of going on all night if Sarah didn't stop her.

'You should get a job with Hallmark. Now hop off the phone so I can finish getting ready. He'll be here shortly and I'll still be running around in my undies.'

'Can't see a problem with that,' said Fiona. 'Say hi from me.'

She hung up, leaving Sarah to contemplate the balance of makeup and what to do with her hair.

Half an hour later Sarah stood in front of the mirror in the bathroom trying to get her lipstick right. She'd changed shade three times. Why did she bother when the stuff would wear off over dinner? She persevered, settling on a soft pink very close to her natural lip colour.

A knock at the door startled her and she checked her watch. Sam was right on time. She raced out of the bathroom and picked up her clothes, discarded all over the room, and shoved them in the bottom of the wardrobe to give the illusion of tidiness. She grabbed her handbag and went to the door.

Her heart pounded painfully in her chest. After tonight she'd know where she stood. She swallowed hard and took a deep breath. *Here goes …*

She swung open the door to reveal a very debonair Sam, smelling better than a man had any right to, all leather and citrus. The smile he gave her lit up his eyes and turned her knees to jelly.

'Hello,' he said, his voice all gravelly and sexy.

'Hello, yourself,' she replied, feeling very Lauren Bacall as her hair fell over one eye.

'I like your hair out,' he said. 'Beautiful.'

A blush stole over her cheeks and she couldn't look him in the eye as the charge between them arced. The butterflies that had invaded her stomach earlier in the afternoon now moved to her chest. Her entire body buzzed with anticipation.

'Are you ready?' Sam held out a calloused hand, reminding her this man was of the land.

'I am.' She slipped her hand into his, the warmth of contact sending a little shiver of pleasure along her arm straight to her heart. 'And you're sure you don't like kale?' she asked as she closed the door to her room behind her.

'Kale? Hate the stuff. I find it tastes too green and it's chewy. I don't understand why people don't stick to baby spinach. Just as good in my book.'

She laughed and gave his hand a little squeeze. Everything was going to work out fine.

⊠

Maddie let her long, blonde hair tumble down her back, twisted in carefully formed curls she'd spent hours creating with her mother's curling iron. Her arms ached from the effort. It had been worth it.

Her mum had let her use her makeup to highlight her eyes and lips. Maddie had wanted to go full Kardashian with false lashes and enhanced eyebrows. Her dad had told her she could not leave the house looking like that. Like what, she'd wanted to know. He hadn't been able to explain himself properly, which seemed to be a challenge for old people.

Maddie didn't care. She had her perfect dress, pale pink lace with delicate spaghetti straps. The neckline plunged a little, just enough to get away with since her dad had suddenly become all protective. The skirt, layers of tulle, swished when she walked and fell to the floor so she had to wear high heels to make sure the hem didn't drag on the ground. The colour suited her perfectly, especially as she'd used some fake tan to give her skin a bit of colour.

Wayne's eyes had lit up at the sight of her. They'd met in front of the school, her dad insisting that he drop her off. He didn't trust Wayne, which was stupid because everyone knew him and he was the school's star rugby player. Wayne hadn't seemed insulted which was a relief. Maybe lots of dads acted like this. She wouldn't know as this marked the first time she'd ever been on an official date.

The school hall filled with chattering seniors, all determined to enjoy their very last dance before graduation. Maddie had been lucky to get an invitation and there were a lot of girls who obviously thought she shouldn't be there at all. A group of them stood over in the corner by the drinks table, whispering behind their hands and glaring at her.

She tossed her curls and showed them the perfect plunge of the back of her dress. What did that French chick say? Let them eat cake. Maddie was totally down with that.

Wayne stood with his mates, talking and laughing and ignoring her. He looked every inch the high school hero in his rented suit, his hair slicked back and his jacket stretching across broad shoulders. Every girl in the place wanted to be her, standing next to Wayne. The fact she was the only junior at the dance only rankled them more.

Getting glammed up and scoring some Insta likes had almost obscured the real reason she'd come tonight: to find a way to connect with Alexis, Liam's sister. Maddie craned her neck looking for Alexis but couldn't find her anywhere. Before long it became obvious she wasn't even at the dance. Crushed that Fate had sealed off an avenue to Liam, Maddie tried to enjoy the dance as best she could. After all she was here with the most popular guy at school. Social kudos.

She had to stick it out a little longer and then later they'd sneak off somewhere to make out. She'd text her dad and tell him they'd gone to someone's house for an after party. What could he do? It would be worth the grounding.

The music blared and she swayed side to side in time with the beat. Wayne wasn't really into dancing. She wished Levi could have been here. She'd have had someone to talk to and dance with. He'd have been blown away to see her all dressed up. In all the time they had spent together, she didn't think she'd worn a dress even once.

He was still pissed with her, more than she'd anticipated. If only she could pinpoint exactly where things had gone wrong between them. The Lonely in Longreach thing had gotten to him. At least he hadn't blown their cover, and you never know, things might work out happily ever after. Maddie still believed in Fate.

Wayne and his mates had spiked their drinks with whisky smuggled in hip flasks belonging to their dads. They'd gotten louder, shoving each other and laughing at jokes that made no sense. He'd totally ignored her the whole night. This dance had not turned out the way she'd imagined it.

What had Levi said? Her fate was to stay here in this town with Wayne. Why would he say something so mean? She'd thought he had been jealous of her social success. Standing here alone in her beautiful dress with no one to talk to she began to wonder if this was indeed success.

Her watch said there was at least an hour and a half to go. She should call her dad and get him to come fetch her earlier. He'd said he didn't mind. At the time, she thought him over-protective; now she understood what he'd been getting at.

'Hey, Wayne.' She didn't know why he'd asked anyone to the dance if he'd planned to hang out with the boys and act like morons all night. 'Wayne!'

'What?' He turned to her with glassy eyes and flushed cheeks, his bow tie askew.

'I want to go home.' She sounded like a petulant child and she hated herself for it.

'Home?' He frowned like he couldn't place the word. 'Whatcha wanna do that for?' he slurred. 'Party hasn't even started yet.'

'Well, I'm calling my dad to come get me because this is no party for me.' She crossed her arms and gave him her fiercest look, the one she used on Levi when she wanted to get her own way.

Wayne lurched towards her and threw his arm around her shoulders. She staggered under the sudden weight of him.

'C'mon, Madds.'

'Wayne, I want to get out of here.'

'Why didn't you say so?' He made no sense. How much whisky had he drunk? The stench of it rolled over her in waves as he spoke. 'Hey, boys! The lady wants to go.'

They all cheered as if she'd scored a point for the team. Their weird vibe started to creep her out. She shrugged out from under Wayne's grasp.

'It's okay. I'll call dad.' She reached into her clutch to get her phone when Wayne's meaty paw clasped her arm.

'The fun is only just getting started,' he said, his eyes suddenly startlingly clear in a way that sent a shiver down her spine.

'You stay and have a good time with your mates,' she said, starting to get nervous. 'I'll see you tomorrow.' She gave him her most dazzling smile in an effort to charm him.

He smiled back and for one blinding moment she thought he might let the issue drop. She was wrong.

The tricks she normally used had no power here.

'This dance sucks. Let's get out of here. Mark's folks have a fire pit. We can sit around and chill. Whatdya say?' He lifted her chin gently with his fingers and looked intently into her eyes. 'Have I told you how beautiful you look tonight?'

Maddie swallowed her doubts. Levi didn't call him Wonder Wayne for no reason. Captain of the rugby team, most popular boy in school and object of the female student population's fantasies, Wayne was the school's biggest catch and she, Maddison McRae, had caught him.

'Okay,' she agreed reluctantly. What could an hour hurt? She could text her dad the address and he could pick her up there.

'Fantastic.' He seemed genuinely delighted she'd said yes. Maddie relaxed a little. Once they got to Mark's house and settled down everything would be alright.

'I thought you might take me to an Italian restaurant,' Sarah said as they were seated at a table at Harry's Restaurant.

'I would if we had one.' Sam placed his napkin on his lap. 'Harry's has a lovely ravioli if you're craving.'

Sarah read the menu, tucking her hair behind one ear. 'The barramundi looks delicious. I think I'll have that and follow up with a dessert. What about you?' She loathed her inane chatter, like some high school kid out on a date. What she really wanted to say was, how about we skip dinner and head back to my room.

Possibly too soon.

'I always go the linguine, and I've never met a dessert I didn't like. Shall I order wine?'

'Go for it.' She watched him chat to the waiter with an open ease born of familiarity. In such a small town everyone must know everyone else, or their parents.

As she waited she let her eyes rove about the restaurant, which was conveniently attached to her motel. Cream and wood panelled walls hung with photos of Longreach life adding to the relaxed ambiance. She glanced at the food arriving at the tables of diners around her. It looked gorgeous, every bit as lovely as anything she'd get in Sydney. Her mouth watered as the scent of a freshly cooked steak caught her as it sailed past in the hands of a waiter. She should have ordered that.

Sarah came out of her reverie to find Sam watching her, a smile playing on his lips.

'What?' she asked as she smiled back.

'Taking in the view,' he said. 'I can't quite believe you're real.' He shook his head as if to test his theory.

'Oh, I'm real alright. Are you? You're like a dream. Has anyone ever told you that you have movie-star eyes?' She leaned forward, propping her chin on her hand.

He put his elbows on the table and moved closer. 'All the time,' he said. 'Made me wonder if I should have pursued a career in Hollywood instead of farming sunshine and sheep.'

'You would have made a great substitute for Tom Cruise in *Mission Impossible*.' She could see him now, in a sharply cut suit, raffish and chiselled. Those piercing blue eyes giving her the once over as she played the part of the enemy spy. She gave a little sigh as the image of Sam in her mind began to disrobe. Sarah couldn't help it. Every time she thought of Sam she imagined him without his clothes on.

'I love those movies,' he said. 'Never get old.'

'I know, right?' *Maybe you want to come back to my room and watch one later.*

'How are you finding Longreach now you've had the time to get to know us a little bit?' he asked as the waiter returned with their wine, pouring it deftly into two glasses.

'I think it's amazing. It's not what I thought it would be like.' She picked up her glass, the pinot gris lending her the scent of pear and apple.

'What did you think it would be like? Full of bushrangers and cow cockies?' He laughed as he spoke. She liked the sound.

She shook her head. 'I don't know what I thought. I didn't realise it would be so ... flat.'

'No mountain climbing to be had. Odd rock outcrop here and there, that's about it.'

'It has a kind of magic, a peacefulness, like the land is watching over us.'

'Very perceptive, Ms Lewis. The local aboriginals will tell you the same thing.' He took a sip of wine as if steadying himself. 'Do you think you could live in a place like this?'

'I think I might be able to. You know I hate crowds.'

'What sane person doesn't? What about the ocean, wouldn't you miss that? I guess it's right there in Sydney whenever you need it.'

'I never go. I think I mentioned I'm not fond of the beach.'

He looked blank. 'I must have forgotten,' he said. 'It's been a lot to take on board in a short time.'

She knew what he meant.

Dinner arrived, and they talked about Levi and Maddie, about Sarah's speech at the high school and Sam's farm. She learned more about him and shared information on herself. Being here with him was a sweet reprieve from pretending to be someone she was not. Sitting here having dinner with Sam highlighted how far from herself she'd strayed in the past few years. How hard she'd tried to be what others needed her to be, whether that was her family or Greg. Fiona could be counted in that lot too. When had she become the kind of woman who moulded herself to fit social situations instead of owning the room as herself?

He told her funny stories about his childhood, talking openly about his wife in a way she found endearing. He didn't seem to have her up on a pedestal, rather honouring her part in his life and the gift of his son. He talked about how hard dating was in the outback which led her to tell him her plans for her article. Sam had some ideas of his own and she longed for a pen to jot them down.

'I should have brought my notebook. I next to never go anywhere without it.' She stabbed her fork into the slice of mud cake she'd ordered for dessert, her sweet tooth running wild with her heart.

'I don't have anything on me either,' he said. 'Do you want me to ask the waiter to bring us a pen and paper?'

This was her cue to ask him back to her room under the pretence of capturing his ideas. What if he said no? She had to risk it. She'd come all this way to meet him and she couldn't go home without being certain. Without having tried.

'That's okay, I've got plenty back in my motel room if you don't mind coming back for a night cap.' She spoke lightly, focused on her cake, as if there was no import to what she said at all.

'Sure, as long as you have some whisky.' He answered in an equally breezy manner which meant he either didn't see the invitation for what it was, or he was as good an actor as Sarah.

'I do, as it happens.' She'd made sure she had a bottle and two glasses ready in the room for this occasion.

'Then I'm ready when you are.' Sam pushed his dessert plate to one side. 'Let me pay the bill and we can go.'

Oh my God! This is really happening.

She quickly ducked to the bathroom while Sam busied himself with the bill. After checking her makeup in the mirror, Sarah quickly cleaned her teeth with a miniature toothbrush kit she carried in her handbag in case of interviews. Or close encounters with hot farmers. Whichever came first.

She ran her fingers through her hair and took a good look at herself. Her eyes sparkled, dilated with desire, and her

cheeks looked flushed. Things between Sam and her had been magnetic and while she'd only known him a short time, she wanted to take things to the next level. Whatever that meant. Well, clearly she wanted to take him to bed.

Sarah's nerves fizzed with anticipation and a tiny bit of fear. What if he didn't fancy her? What if he rejected her outright?

She steadied herself, hands on the cool marble top of the wash stand and looked herself straight in the eye. She would not back out, get cold feet or otherwise lose her nerve. Sam was coming back to her motel room no matter what.

Swiping a lick of gloss across her lips, she flicked out her hair once more. Now or never.

Definitely now.

Squaring her shoulders back, Sarah grabbed her handbag and walked back into the restaurant with as much confidence as she could muster, which wasn't much but she made do.

'Shall we go?' she said, low and sexy, in case he hadn't picked up on her vibe.

He grinned and held out his arm to take. 'I thought you'd never ask.'

Wayne rounded up his mates and grabbed Maddie's hand with his sweaty paw. They left in a rowdy collective, tumbling out the door and into the school yard.

She trotted along as fast as she could in her high-heeled sandals.

'Slow down,' she tugged on Wayne's hand, 'I can't keep up. My legs aren't as long as yours.'

He laughed. 'Hey, guys, Maddie can't keep up.' Without warning he picked her up and threw her over his shoulder.

'Put me down!' She thumped his back with her fists to no avail. It was like he couldn't feel a thing. 'Wayne, put me down this instant.' His shoulder dug into her ribs and they throbbed with each bouncy step he took.

Her scalp prickled with unease. He'd stopped listening to her, caught up in his alcohol-fuelled fun. She became acutely aware of the fact she was the only girl in the group; the other boys had come stag. Up close, she could see why they were dateless. They reminded her of overgrown baboons in bow ties with all their hooting and jumping around.

They entered Mark's house through the side gate so as not to disturb his parents who had retreated inside to watch movies. This last fact was disappointing news to Maddie. She'd assumed there'd be adults around in some kind of remote supervisory capacity. She could see the flicker of the television around the edges of the tightly closed curtains.

Suddenly, Wayne put her down on her feet.

Maddie got her balance and smoothed her dress down. She took her sandals off and followed the boys into the back yard. The fire pit sat in one corner, the surrounding area neatly bricked in a herringbone pattern. A variety of chairs, all mismatched, circled the pit which had been piled with logs ready to burn.

Mark set about lighting the fire which sparked to life to a cheer from the lads. Everyone found a seat and one of the boys produced a joint, neatly rolled if not a little bent from being in his pocket. No one seemed to mind as they began to hand it around.

'No thank you,' said Maddie as Wayne passed it to her. The cold night air, seeping in from the desert, made her shiver despite the warmth of the fire. She had to get out of here.

'Come on, one puff won't hurt you.' Wayne shoved the joint in her face.

'No, Wayne,' she said as sternly as she could, turning her head away. 'I want to go home.'

'I'll get you home, but only if you take a toke on this.'

The other boys jeered and laughed at her, egging Wayne on. She had no friends here, no one to stand up for her. The curtains in the windows of the house remained resolutely shut and she could hear the TV had been turned up to drown out the noise in the yard.

'I said no.' She fumbled in her clutch for her phone, ready to call her dad to come and get her.

She made to rise but, quicker than she could blink, Wayne grabbed the phone from her hand and threw it to one of the others. He shoved her back down in her seat, his big hand covering one of her breasts.

'Hey!' she shouted, outrage simmering through her veins. 'How dare you.'

Wayne cackled like a hyena. 'Like I said, you can go home when you've had some of this.'

He stood over her, blocking any escape she might have.

'I'll scream for Mark's parents,' she said.

Mark scoffed from where he lay, sprawled in his chair. 'Right, like they'd care. They're in there getting stoned themselves. Where do you think we got the gear from?'

Cold despair doused her anger.

'Just do it, for chrissakes. What do you think is going to happen?' Wayne sounded annoyed.

'Just do it. Just do it.' Someone started the chant and the others joined in.

Maddie looked up at Wayne, wondering how she could have ever found him handsome. 'If I do, will you let me go home?' she said on a shuddering breath.

'Of course, you have my word.'

Somehow she didn't think his word counted for much.

Reluctantly, she took the joint between her fingers. She put it to her lips and inhaled like she'd seen the others do. Smoke filled her lungs in a rush and she doubled over, coughing violently.

Wayne snatched the joint from her. 'Jesus, Maddie. Don't smoke the whole bloody thing at once.'

Her eyes watered and her lungs burned. Otherwise she seemed alright. Perhaps the stuff didn't work on her.

Wayne passed the joint on to the next boy and sat back down, ignoring her as he had for the entire evening.

She sat too and stared at the flames as they danced in the fire pit. The way they changed colour from yellow to orange to red fascinated her. Why had she never noticed that before? They were the most beautiful thing she'd ever seen. Her arms and legs became heavy and all the thoughts flew from her mind. The boys' banter sounded as if it were coming from a long way away.

Suddenly, she could feel the heat coming off Wayne's body. He'd pulled his chair right up next to hers and had flung his arm around her shoulders. He smelled of alcohol and weed.

'Not bad, hey?' he asked. 'Do you still want to go home?'

She'd opened her mouth to say yes when he covered her lips with his own. One sweaty hand covering her breast and

squeezing it way too tight. She put her hands on his chest and pushed, unable to budge the enormous bulk of him. Much stronger than her, he pulled her closer and stuck his tongue in her mouth.

Fear and revulsion shot through her, making her struggle more furious. She had to get him off her. The whole world came down to the weight of him upon her, the heaviness of his arm around her neck, the slick wetness of his tongue in her mouth. Her mind reeled with terror at what might come next. As she pushed at him, she felt the outline of her mobile phone in his jacket pocket. She needed that phone. She needed her dad.

Instinct kicked in. The sense of survival outweighing everything as the adrenaline cleared her mind. Fumbling for the phone with her fingers, she waited until she had a grip on it before biting down on his lip as hard as she could. He leapt backwards with a yell, his hand to his mouth. She could see blood on his fingers.

'You ungrateful bitch,' he screamed at her.

She didn't wait to see what would happen next. She picked up her skirts and ran, leaving behind her clutch and her sandals.

She was out the gate and across the front yard before any of the boys realised what had happened.

Out of the corner of her eyes she saw a couple of them rise as if to give chase.

'Let her go,' she heard Wayne say. 'I'd never have brought the stupid bitch if I'd known she was frigid.' She heard the boys laugh at his bravado.

Her emotions swirled, threatening to engulf her as she ran towards town. Steaming rage, metallic fear, burning tears.

She found a place to hide behind a fence and scrolled through her phone. She couldn't call her dad looking like this. No telling how he would react and what he might do to Wayne. She didn't want to make things worse than they were already. She hesitated at Levi's number. Things were pretty bad between them right now. What if he didn't answer? Then their friendship would really be over. She couldn't face that right now. Mr C? No way. How embarrassing.

What was she going to do? Sitting out here in the middle of the night was not an option. What if Wayne came looking for her? She could walk to the police station but what would she say—Wayne tried to kiss her after she voluntarily went back to his place after the dance? It sounded silly even to her own ears. And if it ever got out, no one at school would ever talk to her again.

They'd call her a slut.

As she mindlessly scrolled through her contact list, backwards and forwards, she spotted Sarah's number. She seemed so nice and kind and smart. So she called the one person she figured might help her without judgement.

CHAPTER TWENTY-ONE

Closing the motel room door behind them had a kind of finality, as if an emotional threshold had been crossed to match the physical one. Sam took in the scent of Sarah's perfume lingering in the air and the makeup scattered on the vanity in the bathroom, so alien to his world and serving to remind him he was about to step off into uncharted territory.

Sarah placed her handbag down and slipped off her shoes. 'Drink?' she asked.

'Love one,' Sam said, faking a calm he didn't feel. 'Do you want to get those ideas of mine down before or after?'

Sarah unscrewed the whisky bottle and sloshed two fingers into a couple of water glasses.

'Before or after what?' She shot him a cheeky sideways glance. It had been a long time since he flirted with anyone and he'd never been very good at it. What was it Goethe said? Be bold and mighty forces will come to your aid.

Might as well take the gamble.

He came and stood beside her. 'Before or after I take you to bed, of course. Unless I've read this situation wrong and you have other ideas.' He picked up his whisky and took a sip, his gaze never wavering from hers.

Sarah took a gulp of her drink; a soft pink flush infused her face. No worries about his intentions being misunderstood.

'What would you suggest?' Her voice sounded husky thanks to the whisky and to the fact she was possibly as nervous as him.

Sam put his glass down and took one of her hands in his.

Here goes …

'Can I say, I've never met anyone like you before in my life. This thing between us …' he gestured back and forth between them, '… is unique. At least in my experience.' He traced a slow circle on the palm of her hand as he spoke. They both watched his thumb make a lazy arc. He longed to touch the fine skin of her inner wrist and trace a path with his fingers to hidden places. 'And I don't want to wait. I don't want to take things slow. I don't want to be cautious. I don't think you want to, either.' His awareness of her heightened to an almost unendurable tension. Every breath she took, the beat of her heart in the hollow of her throat, every inch of her called to him.

Their eyes met and he knew without a doubt that he was right. Life was too short to wait and see if this was a safe relationship, or things had a chance of working out. He'd done safe and still ended up alone. He'd been unhappy and lost. Now he'd found Sarah. Maybe she wasn't safe and things might go up in flames—Lord knows there'd be many people who'd tell him that, most of them currently

belly up to the bar at the pub—but tonight he intended to give in to the passion building deep within his soul and to hell with tomorrow.

The space between them became charged with an unbearable longing.

Sam couldn't take a moment more. He reached for her at the same time she hooked her fingers through his belt loops. He offered no resistance as she pulled him towards her until they were hip to hip. His hands slid along the contours of her waist as he kissed her, long and deep, causing her to tremble with what he hoped was need.

'I guess that's an after then?' he whispered against her throat as he kissed his way to her collarbone.

'Kiss me again,' she said and he pressed his mouth against hers. She had to feel the slam of his heart against the palms of her hands where they lay on his chest. He longed for the feel of her skin on his, wanted to peel the layers of her clothes away to reveal the sensuous warmth beneath.

He became lost in their kiss as his hands explored the outline of her body. His own hummed with spiralling desire. Soon, he would be unable to contain it.

Somewhere in the room, her phone started to ring. The jangly sound jarred Sam out of the moment. Sarah broke their kiss with a groan, echoing his own frustration at the intrusion.

Who could possibly be calling her this late at night? Something must have happened. Something bad. Or another man. The thought made him queasy.

'Do you want to get that?'

She scrunched up her face as she said, 'Do you mind?'

'Nah, it's late and it might be important.' He stepped back, keeping his hands lightly on her waist. He didn't want to break contact with her, to let her leave the circle of his arms now that she'd found her way into them.

'I'm so sorry,' she said as she began to hunt for her phone. It had fallen out of her handbag when she'd dumped it on the floor. Sarah got down on her hands and knees and retrieved it from under the table where it had slid. Sam took advantage of the moment to take in the curves of Sarah's very sexy butt.

'Hello,' she said, sweeping back the curtain of hair that had fallen across her face. She shot Sam a quick smile as he poured another glass of whisky while he waited.

The voice on the other end of the phone made Sarah frown and he paused to see what might follow. 'Maddie? Are you alright? Has something happened?' Sarah scrambled to her feet, fully alert.

Maddie McRae. Sam took a moment to process the fact, a dart of worry deflating his lust completely.

'Of course.' Sarah, all business now, waved Sam over. 'I've got Sam here with me and I'm going to put you on speaker, okay?' She didn't wait for a response.

Sam put his arm around her and moved close, a million awful scenarios running through his head.

'I'm not far from Mark's house, and I have no shoes and I don't know where my clutch is, and I want to go home.' The words tumbled down the phone in one long stream, Maddie not pausing for breath.

'It's okay,' said Sarah in her most soothing voice. 'We've got you. Can you give us Mark's address and we'll come find you?'

'I know where he lives,' said Sam, trying not to growl. 'Did Wayne lay a hand on you? Are you hurt?'

'I'm not hurt and I don't want to talk about it,' whispered Maddie. 'Can Sarah come get me, by herself?'

Sarah looked at Sam with raised eyebrows, silently asking his opinion. He hesitated, fighting his parental instincts to wade in and make sure Maddie was safe. While he didn't have a girl of his own, it wasn't a big stretch to guess why Maddie was embarrassed.

'How about Sarah comes and gets you while I go and get your things off that—get your things back?' That little bastard.

'Okay,' sniffed Maddie.

'Hold tight,' said Sarah, already grabbing her car keys. 'We'll be with you in a moment.' She hung up, and turned to Sam. 'Wow. Wasn't expecting that tonight.'

Sam shook his head. 'Never liked those kids. They get around here like they're the town's greatest hope, all because they play a little footy.' He grabbed the keys to his ute. 'Sorry about this,' he said, taking both her hands in his.

Sarah shook her head. 'Please don't. I'm only glad we're in the right place at the right time for Maddie.'

'You're right,' he sighed. 'I'll go get her things and head over to the McRaes' place. Joe is going to be livid.'

'And rightly so,' said Sarah. 'I hope those boys haven't done any lasting damage.'

'So do I. Thank God I don't have a daughter or I'd be in jail by now.'

Sarah gave a shaky laugh at his attempt to lighten the mood. 'Imagine if you had a son like Wayne.'

'Over my dead body,' Sam muttered darkly.

She picked up her handbag. 'Okay, let's do this. I'll find Maddie and bring her home.'

'Meet you there.' Sam leaned in and gave her the kind of kiss that he hoped would curl her toes. 'More where that came from,' he said as he headed out the door.

'I hope so,' he heard Sarah mutter as she followed him out.

Sarah had no trouble spotting Maddie sitting forlornly in the gutter, her pretty dress torn and her makeup streaked down her face by tears. She pulled over and Maddie climbed in.

'Thank you.' Seeing Maddie subdued, with her light dimmed, riled Sarah.

'Are you okay? Do you need to see a doctor … or the police?'

Maddie shook her head as a lone tear trickled down her cheek. She stared straight ahead, her fingers digging into the seat.

'Okay, if you're sure then I'll take you home.' Sarah put the car in gear and pulled away from the kerb.

'Wait,' said Maddie, the urgency in her voice causing Sarah to brake instinctively. 'I don't want to go home straight away. My mum and dad are going to go spare.' She turned her tear-stained face to Sarah. 'Can we just sit here for a little while?'

Sarah contemplated her request. 'I really think it's important we get you home.'

'I need a moment to pull myself together. Dad is going to go nuts and Mum is going to make a fuss. I cannot even

deal with that right now.' She sniffed and wiped her nose with the back of her hand.

Sarah sighed. The situation tore her in two. She should get Maddie home as quickly as possible. Once Sam let them know what had happened, they'd want their girl safe in their arms immediately. Having said that, if Maddie's mum had even a quarter of her own mother's fuss-ability then Maddie really did need to get herself together first.

'Sitting here for a minute or two probably won't hurt.' Sarah pulled back over to the kerb and cut the engine.

'Thank you.' Maddie offered a tremulous smile. 'I must look a mess.'

'I'm more concerned about how you feel.' Sarah killed the lights and lowered the windows a little to let in some fresh air.

Beside her Maddie shrugged. 'Wayne didn't hurt me if that's what you mean.'

'What did he do?' She glanced at Maddie. The silence inside the car seemed impossibly loud.

'He made me smoke a joint and I got all dizzy. Then he grabbed me and tried to kiss me. He said I was frigid and the other boys laughed. I think I was more scared of them than I was of him.' Maddie twisted the fabric of her dress in her fingers. 'I ran for it. Mum's going to kill me for leaving her shoes behind.' She looked at Sarah with tear-filled eyes.

'I don't think your mum is going to care about those shoes as long as you're safe.'

She rifled through her handbag for the wet wipes she always travelled with. 'You might want to use these,' said Sarah. 'That river of mascara is only going to make your mum and dad freak out more.'

Maddie accepted the proffered wipes with a grateful smile and scrubbed at her face. Sarah took the break in conversation to message Sam to let him know she had Maddie safe. She didn't want anyone to worry more than they should.

'That's better,' said Sarah as she held out her hand for the used wipe.

Maddie looked fresher, although dark rings shadowed her eyes. 'I don't suppose you have any face cream in your bag?'

'Sadly no,' said Sarah. 'Pop your seatbelt on and we'll get going.'

She waited until Maddie had made herself comfortable before turning the engine back on.

'Do you want to talk about how you're feeling?'

'Not really.' Maddie kept her head turned, looking out the window into the night.

'Okay, if you change your mind you know I'm here for you.' Sarah negotiated the unfamiliar streets of Longreach, made less complicated by the small number of them.

After a few moments, Maddie spoke.

'I made such a mistake going out with that loser.'

'You weren't to know what he was capable of,' said Sarah, as the lights of the town began to recede behind them.

'I shouldn't have gone to Mark's house with Wayne.'

'Yes, well that might have been a strategical error. But you know that doesn't mean you were to blame for Wayne's behaviour, right?' She flicked the headlights up to high beam as the road seemed to blend with the inky darkness.

'I wanted to be cool for one night, you know?' Maddie shook her head as if she couldn't believe she'd had the idea in the first place.

'Cool? And Wayne is considered cool?'

'Of course he is.' Maddie frowned, clearly telegraphing that Sarah was clueless. 'Everyone knows that. Me going to the formal with him was supposed to help me slay on my socials, instead the whole night was a total disaster.' She sniffed and wiped a stray tear away.

'Let me get this straight. You only went to the dance with Wayne to score some social points?'

'He's the hottest guy in school and he asked *me*. I mean, who wouldn't go? I had no idea he expected me to … you know.' She blushed and looked away.

'And being popular is important to you?' She couldn't help it, her inner journalist sat up and started taking notes.

'Isn't it to you?' Maddie fixed her with over-bright eyes.

'Not in the same way, I think.'

'If I'm not popular, then what am I? I disappear altogether.'

'That's not true,' said Sarah gently. 'If you show up as who you truly are, focus on what matters to you and let people see the real Maddie, then people will like you just fine.'

'Yeah, right.' Maddie was having none of it. 'I'd become one of those lame kids no one remembers.'

'What about Levi? I thought you two were tight. How does he fit into this story?'

'Levi is, like, my best friend and everything, but he's not cool.' She gave a hiccup-y little laugh. 'He's too smart to be cool. If I dated him I could kiss goodbye to being popular.'

'Would that be so bad?' Sarah reached over and squeezed her hand. The fact Wayne had acted so badly towards her was awful enough. The reason why Maddie felt she had to go out with such a boy in the first place broke Sarah's heart. She felt for Charlene McRae. Parenting a teenage daughter seemed like an impossible task.

'But I'd be nothing.' Maddie blinked at her as she contemplated the full horror of being ordinary.

'You wouldn't be *nothing*, you'd be you and I reckon that's pretty great all by itself.' Sarah smiled.

'You don't get it.' Maddie smiled back, pity in her eyes.

'Oh, I think I do. I was your age once. Girls haven't changed all that much. I imagine it's as cut throat now as it was then. Look,' she glanced over at Maddie, 'all I want you to do is consider who you would be if you didn't have to spend so much time pretending to be someone you're not. Imagine how happy you'd be if you were hanging out with girls who genuinely like you for who you are, not because of some made up social status.'

Maddie blinked, her face softly illuminated by the glow of the dashboard. Sarah couldn't tell if she was taking anything in or not.

'Imagine how happy you'd be if you could date someone you actually liked rather than a first-class wanker like Wayne,' she pressed on.

Maddie snorted with laughter. 'Wayne the Wanker. I like it. You know, I only went to the formal because I wanted to get to know Alexis Newson.'

Sarah frowned. 'And who's that?'

'She's Liam Newson's sister. I thought if I could get her to talk to me then we might become friends and then she could introduce me to Liam.'

'Sorry, but who's Liam Newson?' She'd lost Sarah entirely.

'He's only the hottest actor on the planet and my future husband. He comes from Longreach, you know.' Maddie gave her that look again, the one that told her she was bordering on nutty-old-woman status.

'Why do you think Liam is the one for you?'

Maddie slid her hands beneath her legs. 'Because being with Liam would make me somebody, not just a girl from the sticks.'

'Let me get this straight, you want to be with a guy from the sticks so no one thinks you're a girl from the sticks. I don't get it.'

'When you put it like that it does sound pretty dumb.' Maddie looked forlorn and Sarah realised she was witnessing the death of a dream. Bit of a crazy dream, but its death hurt anyway.

'I do like Levi, a lot,' Maddie said at last. 'But going out with him would be social suicide.'

'Going out with someone like Wayne leads to much worse.'

Maddie sighed. 'You're right I guess,' she conceded. 'I don't know if I can handle everyone gossiping behind my back.'

'They won't do it forever and it will show you who your true friends are. Right now, you're in a cage of your own creation. You think you have to impress people to get them to like you. Be yourself. Be authentic. You are good enough as you are, no improvement needed.' Sarah heard the words as they left her lips. Solitary in Sydney could have done with the same pep talk. Hadn't she tried to change herself to fit in?

'But what about everything I've worked for? I'd be chucking out my future with Liam. And I'd be … oh, God … I've made a mess of everything.' She buried her face in her hands and began to cry again.

'Oh, honey.' Sarah wished she could put her arms around the girl. 'Everything is going to work out okay. Sometimes

being yourself can be a hard path to walk but the destination will be better than you could ever imagine.' She hoped that was true for herself.

'Better than Liam Newson?' Maddie looked over and sniffed.

'Much better than Mr Newson. I know that might be hard to imagine right now but it's totally true. And I want you to know that nobody *ever* has the right to touch you without your permission. You did nothing wrong here, and you need to remember that.'

They drove in silence for a few minutes while Maddie cried. This had been a hard night with many home truths.

'We're nearly home.'

'Okay,' Maddie nodded and straightened up. 'Thank you for … this.'

'That's okay, sweetie.' Sarah rubbed Maddie's arm. 'Anytime you need to talk, you call me, okay?'

Maddie nodded. 'Turn here,' she said, indicating the entrance to a long dirt road leading to the McRae farmhouse.

They bumped along, letting the quiet of the vast outback night carry them in its silence.

'Sarah,' Maddie said at last, 'I'm going to think about what you said. You know, all that stuff about being authentic.'

Sarah smiled in the dark. 'Authentic people make a mark on the world and you, Miss Maddie, have a lot to give.'

Sarah brought the car to a stop in front of the farmhouse. All the lights were blazing and she could see the outline of people moving about inside.

'You're going to be okay,' she said, placing her hand on Maddie's arm.

Maddie nodded and took a deep breath. 'Yeah, eventually.'

Charlene McRae came out onto the veranda and hurried down the steps towards the car.

'Here goes,' said Maddie with a wobbly smile as she opened the door and climbed out, straight into her mother's embrace.

Charlene hugged her daughter tight, talking to her in a low voice as she stroked her hair. She looked over Maddie's shoulder and mouthed thank you to Sarah.

Sarah gave her a wave as the men appeared in the doorway. She could park up and join Sam but it felt wrong to encroach on the family's private moment. She didn't know them like he did.

Sam jumped down the steps and jogged over to her car. She wound the window down as he reached the vehicle.

'Thanks for this,' he said.

'No thanks needed.'

'I'm going to leave them to it. Follow me back to my house?' It was a question that didn't need an answer as far as she was concerned.

'Of course,' she said. 'Lead the way.'

Levi couldn't sleep. Not because the house creaked and groaned as its old bones settled for the night, nor because he was all alone in the middle of a field of solar panels and everybody knew that's when evil clowns bent on revenge were most likely to strike. Tonight both those fear-inducing scenarios ran second best to Maddie being at the school formal with Wonder Wayne. Then there was Dad and Sarah, who had probably worked out by now that something weird was going on.

Both those things impacted Levi in ways he didn't care to contemplate. Instead, he lost himself in a video game, letting it absorb him, leaving no room for worries of any kind.

How long he'd been at it, he didn't know. The mindlessness of it all had taken him a million miles from Longreach until the sound of his dad's ute crunching up the driveway to the house penetrated the noise of the game.

Unsure whether to go and greet him or stay hunkered down in his room, Levi switched off his game and listened. If he'd been sprung, Dad would probably come in roaring for blood. If he hadn't, Dad would most likely make himself a drink and go to bed.

Dad didn't come in at all.

Curious, Levi swung his legs over the side of his bed and tiptoed to the door. Silence. Maybe Dad had a good head of steam going and was trying to calm down before he grounded Levi for life. An uncomfortable tightness gripped his chest as he contemplated the shit storm about to break over his head.

The whole situation was Maddie's fault. Her with her crazy ideas about moving to Sydney to have some imaginary future with a lame actor who didn't even know she existed. How had he allowed himself to get mixed up in this crap? His role had been assigned to him. He'd gotten the part of Trusted Flatmate. What was he supposed to do? Sit by and watch while Maddie went off with some other guy? It would be like tonight all over again, and again, and again.

Nope. Levi was done. He'd ride this mess out as best he could but Maddie could find a new sidekick. It hurt too much.

Another set of wheels bumped up the drive. The engine turned off and he heard a car door slam, then voices. Dad and Sarah. Jesus, he was in real trouble if *both* of them had come to ream him out.

Dad's key in the lock. They entered the house. What should he do? Where could he hide? Pointless, of course. There was nowhere he could hide his father wouldn't find him, and fast. Nothing for it but to face his fate head on.

He threw on a t-shirt, something half decent he could be buried in if necessary. Despite his brave front, Levi's hands were shaking. He shoved them in his pockets, trying for a careless kind of cool he knew he had no hope of pulling off.

Dad and Sarah weren't in the kitchen where he'd expected them to be. They'd moved out to the front veranda, where they talked quietly. They didn't sound angry to him, they sounded worried. Confusion set in. If he hadn't been busted, then what was going on?

'Hey,' he said as he stepped out to join them, yawning a little to give the impression he'd been soundly sleeping like a boy without a care in the world.

'Hey there, kiddo. Sorry to wake you,' said Dad. So, he wasn't in trouble. Relief.

'Hey, Levi.' Sarah sat next to Dad, holding his hand. Clearly, things were going well in that department. Not that it would last.

He pushed aside the feeling of impending doom, a constant companion these days, and took a seat.

'What's going on? Have a good night?'

A look passed between Dad and Sarah, one he didn't like.

'What's wrong?' He sat up straighter. 'What's happened?' In his limited fifteen years of experience that look usually

meant someone had died horribly, was sick, or something had burned to the ground. The outback could be tough.

'No one's dead,' said Dad, reading his mind.

'Someone is certainly in trouble,' said Sarah.

'Not Maddie?' His heart started pounding heavily in his chest, like a bass beat from a serious sub-woofer.

The look passed between them again.

'Will someone please tell me what's going on?' he pleaded, his sense of dread multiplying exponentially with every passing second.

'Maddie got into strife with Wayne,' said Dad. 'She's not hurt, but she did get a bit of a fright.'

'What?' Levi fought a wave of nausea, then one of total rage, a very unpleasant combination. 'What did that bastard do to her?'

'Language, son,' warned Dad.

'How about you go get us a cold drink while I fill Levi in,' said Sarah, laying a hand on Dad's arm. He looked into her eyes for a moment and Levi got the sense a whole conversation had taken place between them. One he was not privy to.

'Sure,' said Dad, conceding in a way Levi had never seen him do before. 'I'll be back soon.'

The screen door banged behind him.

'You know Maddie went to the formal with Wayne the Wanker tonight, right?'

Levi nearly choked on his own spit.

'Um … yeah.'

'Wayne didn't respect some of Maddie's boundaries. She'll be okay, she's just a little rattled. Her parents will help her decide if she wants to take anything further.'

Levi slumped in his chair, shocked. He had so many questions and didn't want the answers to any of them.

'I should call her and see if she's okay,' he said, gripped by the need to hear Maddie's voice.

'I think she needs to rest right now. Give her a call in the morning. I think she'd appreciate that.'

'I knew going with Wayne to the dance was a bad idea.' He crossed his arms over his chest and scowled.

Sarah sighed. 'I reckon Maddie agrees with you. I understand things have been a little strained between the two of you lately. She needs you now. She needs a good friend who won't judge her for her mistakes.'

'She picked Wayne over me.' He hadn't meant to say that. Seems the truth had a way of getting out.

'I think Maddie was too scared to pick you.'

'Wayne is *way* more scary than I am.' How could Maddie ever be afraid of him? They'd been best friends forever. He'd never hurt her. Not in a million years.

'Not scared of you. She's got herself trapped between her feelings for you and wanting to be popular. I don't have to tell you how tough high school is, you're there,' said Sarah.

Maddie's chase for popularity had started at the end of primary school. Levi had always tagged along in her wake, not thinking much about the complicated world of girls. He frequently found himself confused in conversations with Maddie and her friends. He'd always thought it was because he was a guy. Now he wondered if he didn't get it because he wasn't cool enough. Disturbing thought.

'Did she tell you that?' Sarah mentioned Maddie had feelings. For him. He already knew she liked him as a friend.

Could she like him as something more? A spark of hope lit up deep inside him, so tiny he almost missed it.

'My advice to you, if you want it, is to spend some time with her and talk things through. Go gentle, she's trying to be herself but after so many years of being what she thought she ought to be, the process might take some time.'

Levi nodded. All that sounded okay to him. He could wait. He'd been waiting forever anyway, even if he'd only recently understood that himself.

Dad pushed open the screen door, carrying a tray filled with drinks. Beer for the adults and a cola for Levi. He took it gratefully and slugged it down. Sarah had given him a lot to think about and he wanted to be alone.

'If it's okay with you guys, I think I'll head back to bed.'

'Sure thing, kiddo. Sleep tight.'

'Goodnight, Levi,' said Sarah.

He paused before he entered the house. 'Sarah, thank you for … everything.'

'My pleasure,' she said as she raised her beer to him, as if wishing him luck.

Notes for 'Finding Love in the Outback'
Interview #7
Tony (45) and Bev (44) from Mundubbera. Found love online.

Bev: I'd tried online dating before. I hadn't had any success. Mostly full of nutters and lunatics. Total waste of time.

Tony: Then you found me.

Bev: Totally by accident. I thought I'd taken my pro-files down. I'd been on a few sites and I guess I'd lost track of which ones.

Tony: Her forgetfulness is one of the things I love about her best.

Bev: Next thing I know I get this message from him, and he's living near a town only three hours away.

Tony: Something about her photo said this is the one. I'd dated plenty when I was young yet somehow managed to end up single in my late thirties. Not sure how that happened. Too busy with the farm I guess. Not ready to commit. All that stuff.

Bev: Just hadn't met the right one yet.

Tony: Yeah, that too.

Bev: We've been married three years now.

Tony: Feels like five minutes and forever all at the same time.

Bev: I don't think I would have found you without online dating. You were so close yet so far away.

Tony: Fate, I reckon. Can't mess with that stuff.

CHAPTER TWENTY-TWO

'We promised you a peach blossom and here we are.' Sam held open the café door for Sarah and the kids. The cool of the air-conditioning made her skin sigh with relief as the door swung shut behind them.

Friday afternoon in Longreach was as sleepy as any other day since she'd been here. Today Sam had insisted on picking the kids up from school and taking her for afternoon tea. She'd been delighted at the thought of them all spending time together and, for the first time in a very long while, she felt like she was exactly where she ought to be.

Sarah took in her surroundings. A simple, homey café with a handful of tables and chairs scattered about the room, floral curtains framed the windows and the smell of fresh coffee and baked goods filled the air.

Maddie bounded to the closest table and dragged out a chair. While she appeared to be recovered from her scare

with Wayne, Sarah thought there was a new subdued air about her that hadn't been present before.

'Can I have a coke with my peach blossom?' Levi plonked himself down next to Maddie. It was good to see these two as thick as thieves again. Maybe there was a chance for a budding high school romance. They would have to wait and see. Sarah hoped she was around when it happened.

'Same for you, Maddie?' Sam asked as he pulled out a chair for Sarah. 'And for you, Sarah?'

The table, covered with a thick plastic cloth, had a drinks menu tucked between the salt and pepper shakers. She read it quickly. 'I'll have a cappuccino, please.'

'And peach blossoms for everyone.' Sam went to the counter to order.

'You're going to love these,' said Maddie, clearly excited by the prospect of sinking her teeth into the dessert. 'They make them with real cream here.'

'Personally, I like the fake stuff,' said Levi.

'I don't do fake,' said Maddie with a sniff and Sarah had to suppress a smile.

'Righto,' Sam returned and took a seat, rubbing his hands together in anticipation, 'who's ready for a sugar rush?'

'You know how much I love cake,' said Sarah.

'Second only to pasta,' said Levi.

'How did you know that?' Sarah asked, wondering if the boy had peeked at his father's emails.

Levi gave a little grunt and reached under the table. 'Just a wild guess,' he said in a strained voice as he glared at Maddie.

'Who doesn't love pasta, right? I mean it's, like, *the* ultimate comfort food,' Maddie chimed in.

'Yay, the Italians,' said Levi, shooting Maddie another dark look Sarah couldn't interpret. Those two were clearly still sorting things out.

'Gotta love the nation that gave us pizza,' said Sam with a wink. His buoyant mood lit up the whole place like a floodlight.

'Still waiting for that pizza with pork crackling, hey.' Sarah leaned over and gave him a little nudge.

He looked startled before a smile broke out. 'What a bloody good idea, Sarah Lewis. You're a genius. I'm going to spend the rest of the day trying to work out the best way to make that happen.' A little frown creased Sarah's brow. Hadn't the pork crackling pizza been Sam's idea? How could he forget?

'Oh look, our food is here,' said Maddie, knocking over the salt shaker in her enthusiasm. Salt cascaded across the table.

'Look out,' said Sam, leaping to his feet. 'Let me get some help to clean this up.'

The waitress, a teenage girl from the high school, deposited their peach blossoms. 'Enjoy. I'll be back with your drinks and a cloth for that mess.'

'Thanks, Tina,' Maddie called after her. 'I'm such a klutz.'

Sarah studied her peach blossom. She picked up a knife and cut it in two. A small vanilla cake, filled with cream, had been dipped in partly set raspberry jelly then rolled in desiccated coconut. 'I have never seen anything like this.'

'You don't know what you've been missing,' said Sam as he took a giant bite and closed his eyes to savour the flavours.

'Never a dull minute out here,' muttered Levi as he bit into his cake.

'You should definitely put these in your novel,' said Maddie, licking the cream off her fingers.

Levi stopped eating and stared at her. 'I can't believe you just said that.'

'What novel?' asked Sam with his mouth full.

Sarah looked at them all. How did Maddie know about her aspirations to be a novelist and Sam didn't? And what did Levi mean?

'Do you like your peach blossom?' Maddie asked quickly.

'It's like nothing I've ever tasted before,' she said.

'Is it a thriller?' asked Sam. 'Plenty of places to hide a body out here.'

'I think I mentioned it's supposed to be a big sweeping family saga set in the countryside.' Sam must have forgotten and who could blame him. Everything had moved so fast in the few weeks they'd known each other. Sarah didn't like talking about her novel because, after fifteen years, hardly any of it had been written. Embarrassing. She sipped her coffee and thought of ways to change the subject.

Sam nodded while he chewed. 'Of course. Be great if you could fit a murder in there too.'

'I'd like a car chase, if you don't mind,' said Levi.

'Give me a love story. Maybe two families who feud and their kids fall in love,' said Maddie.

'The boy is accused of sheep stealing,' said Sam, getting into the spirit of things.

'And the girl chooses him over the guy she's supposed to be with,' said Levi, studiously ignoring Maddie while he finished his peach blossom.

'I'm sure all that's happened, and more, out here at one time or another,' said Sam as he sat back and rubbed his belly. 'That was bloody good.'

'You should come and stay while you write your book,' said Maddie, 'you know, for authenticity.'

Sarah smiled. 'I might consider that advice.'

'Sounds like a good idea to me,' Sam winked, his blue eyes twinkling with mischief.

'We could turn the spare bedroom into an office for you,' said Levi. Sam and Maddie both looked at him with unmistakable exasperation. 'What?' he said.

Sarah laughed. 'Let's see how my article on love in the outback goes first. One thing at a time.'

'But even if you go, you will come back, right?' said Maddie and Sarah could hear a wistfulness in her tone.

She covered Maddie's hand with her own. 'Even if I'm not here, I'll be in easy reach,' she said. 'Always.'

'What say we call in at the butchers and see if he's got any pork belly? We can have a go at Sarah's pork crackling pizza,' said Sam.

'Sounds like a brilliant idea,' said Maddie, pushing her chair back, eager to get going.

'We'll need something to drink,' Sarah said to Sam. The three of them including her in their banter made her heart swell with happiness, the kind she'd been searching for all her life. The kind she hadn't been able to find in her old world. 'Beer, of course.'

'As if there'd be any other choice,' said Sam as he leaned in for a kiss and her thoughts dissolved into happy mush.

CHAPTER TWENTY-THREE

Sam couldn't stop grinning. From the time he got up in the morning until the time he went to bed, that's all he did. Something had switched on deep inside of him, lighting him up to the world in a way he hadn't thought possible anymore.

And it was all down to Sarah.

She had been in Longreach for three weeks and Sam had spent every spare minute he could with her. A little thing called life intervened from time to time. She had a job to do and he had the farm. Sometimes Sarah would be away for a couple of days working on her story series, which only made his heart grow fonder. Outside of duties, the two of them explored the area or simply hung out, either at his place or the motel.

The thing that amazed him most was the way they seemed to be in sync with each other, like Sarah had a *Sam Costello*

Manual somewhere and knew exactly how he operated. No explanations necessary.

His place could be a bit tricky with Levi, although the boy didn't seem to mind Sarah's presence in his life the same way he'd arced up about Kylie. A fact that made things easier. Sarah liked being at the farmhouse. She said she could feel the history of the place in its boards, like his family's stories were hidden in the timber of the walls. He'd never thought about the house that way before. It was just home. She made him see things in a different light.

He liked being at the motel for obvious reasons. They had privacy there. They could explore each other's bodies along with their minds. Being physical with a woman again after such a long time had intimidated him at first, to be honest. The only woman he'd slept with had been Michelle. They'd been together so young there hadn't been time for anyone else.

Now, Sam stood in front of the mirror in his bedroom and put his tie on. He wore his finest shirt, a crisp pale pink number, paired with a sky blue tie that matched his eyes perfectly, a gift from Sarah. He studied his reflection. The years and grief had left their mark in the fine lines etched around his eyes. The harsh environment he'd lived in all his life had shaped him into the man he was today, and he wouldn't have it any other way.

He sighed happily. Things weren't perfect and he still had more questions than answers about their relationship but he found himself filled with more hope than he ever thought he'd feel again.

'Dad, are you ready?' Levi called from the kitchen.

They were all going to the Isisford Races. Even Levi, who had reset himself back to his regular sunny persona, had

been keen to go. The races represented a big day on the calendar in these parts, a day when everyone dressed up in their best and bet on the horses. Kind of like their own version of the Melbourne Cup. Perhaps a bit less glamorous.

He whistled as he ran a comb through his unruly hair. His hat would hide the worst of it so he didn't spend too much time or worry on it. 'I'm ready,' he called out to his son. 'Are you?'

'Yep, better hurry or we'll be late.'

Today marked the first time he and Sarah would appear at a public event as a couple, because no matter how this thing ended he wanted everyone to know they were together now.

Sam walked into the kitchen. 'How do I look?'

'Great,' said Levi. High praise indeed.

'You don't look so bad yourself.' Levi had dressed in his best chinos for the event. His wrists stuck out the bottom of his button-down shirt, having grown a few inches when Sam wasn't looking. 'Are you sure you want to come? Maddie will be there.'

As far as he knew, the kids had ironed out their differences since the awful night of the school formal. Levi seemed happier and had withdrawn his request for boarding school on the pretence of maintaining the consistency of his education. Whatever that meant.

'Wouldn't miss it for the world. Let's pick Sarah up and get cracking.'

Levi's new found enthusiasm confused Sam a little, but who was he to question his teenager's upbeat mood? Might be a week before there'd be another one like it.

He grabbed his car keys, put his wallet in his back pocket and headed for the door. Sarah was waiting at her motel for them and he was keen for their day to begin.

A small town with a big heart was how Sam described the town of Isisford. A little over an hour from Longreach, the town hosted its annual big race event at the showgrounds, attracting visitors from all over the region. The ladies dressed up for Fashions on the Field and everyone enjoyed the bar and luncheon provided by the racing club.

They'd pulled up a little after eleven thirty when the gates opened at the race track. As the races didn't start until after lunch, everyone showed up to socialise and partake of the vintage wine and gourmet food. Some folk camped out trackside so as to not miss a thing.

The day promised to be warm. No surprise there. The heat never seemed to deter the punters, and if they could last out the day there would be entertainment after the final race. Everyone could let their hair down and have some fun. Outback life could be tough and people took their fun where they could find it and the Isisford Races always delivered.

Sam parked the ute and hustled around to the passenger side so he could open the door for Sarah. Levi had sat on the bench seat in the back, his head between their seats like a faithful dog, making small talk like he'd known Sarah for years.

'Why thank you, kind sir,' she said in a terrible Southern accent as Sam helped her from the car. 'Oh, look at those beautiful roses. My mother grows roses although not as nice

as these ones. I never expected to find a rose garden out here.'

Sam chuckled. 'I'm sure there's a lot of things out here to surprise you.'

'If my interviews are anything to go by, I think you're right. I don't know what I thought people in the outback got up to before. Finding out has been an eye-opener.'

'I'm sure you'll meet folk here today who will be happy to share their stories with you. Life out here can be hard on marriages and finding love in a small town can seem impossible.'

'It's the commitment to travel long distances to be with each other that blows me away. I'm put out if I have to go across Sydney for work, let alone love.' She laughed, exposing the long column of her throat, the same place he'd left a trail of kisses the night before.

'Are you going to compete in Fashions on the Field?' asked Levi. 'You could totally win, you know.'

Sarah blushed and smoothed down her skirt. 'I'm not sure about that.'

'Go on,' Sam gave her a nudge, 'Levi's right. You could win and what's the harm in finding out?'

Her form-fitted dress, black with a large red rose pattern, skimmed her curves in an eye-catching way. The neckline scooped low enough to cause a second glance while maintaining modesty. She'd pulled her hair back, letting the length of it cascade down her back in thick loopy ringlets. A black fascinator sat on a jaunty angle on top of her head. On top of all that, she smelled good.

'Come on,' said Levi. 'I'll take you over to sign up while Dad hunts down some champagne for you.' He took Sarah by the elbow. She glanced over her shoulder at Sam, a

startled look on her face as Levi propelled her towards the stage set up for the event.

He shrugged, laughing at his son's brazen manner. When had Levi become this certain of himself? Sarah let herself be led away and Sam looked about for the bar.

He hadn't gone very far before he encountered Maddie.

'Hello, Mr C. I was wondering if Levi was here.' She cut straight to the chase.

'Yes, he is. Try over at the Fashions on the Field stage. He's with Sarah.' He'd barely finished speaking before Maddie took off without a backward glance. He shook his head, glad his teenage years were behind him.

Reaching the bar, he found his mates already in position, one they'd likely stay in all afternoon unless their wives moved them.

'Look what the cat dragged in,' boomed Big Mike, who wore the loudest Hawaiian shirt Sam had ever seen.

'Maaaate.' Craig slapped him on the back and ushered him to the bar. 'What are you having?'

'On a mission to pick up a champagne,' he said, thrusting his hands in his pockets, suddenly awkward about Sarah.

'Of course, the new lady.' Craig leaned on the bar, settling in for a gossip like an old biddy. 'Word is you two are pretty tight.'

Sam shrugged. 'You could say that.' While he wanted people to know he was with Sarah, he also wanted to protect what they had from prying eyes and small town gossips. Sadly, his mate Craig fell into that last category.

'Leave the poor bloke alone,' said Big Mike. 'He has a right to be happy and she's a looker. Too good for you, if you ask me.'

'Thankfully, no one did,' said Sam.

Craig looked him up and down as if seeing him for the first time. 'Didn't think you had it in you.'

'Gee, thanks for the vote of confidence.'

'He did date that wee blonde creature,' said Big Mike. 'What was her name?'

'You mean Kylie, the high school teacher.' Sam took offence.

'Yeah, that's the one. Didn't muck about moving on.' Big Mike laughed, unaware of the effect of his words as Sam bristled.

'It wasn't like that with us,' he said. 'And Kylie left to take care of her dad.'

'Right, sure.' Craig nodded, his words dripping with sarcasm.

'We dated here and there, nothing more.' Sam began to regret having told the boys about dating Kylie, even if it had been their idea in the first place.

'And the journalist? What about her?' Craig took a sip of his beer. 'She here for a good time not a long time?'

Both Big Mike and Craig burst out laughing.

Sam gritted his teeth and took a deep breath. 'Can I have a beer and a champagne please?' He spoke to the bar staff and ignored his friends.

'Aw, come on, mate. We're just having a laugh,' said Craig. 'It's not like you're serious about her or anything.'

Sam turned and levelled a glare in Craig's direction.

'Oh, shit.' Craig shrunk an inch.

'Bloody hell, Sam. We didn't know you meant business with this chick. We'd never have taken the mick if we had.' Big Mike's belly quivered with the sincerity of his apology.

'Well, I am,' Sam said stiffly.

'You've only known her five minutes,' said Craig, surprised.

'Maybe,' Sam nodded. 'But you know when you know.'

'Know what?' Craig frowned.

'Know you're in love,' Big Mike said in a loud stage whisper. 'Keep up, mate.'

'Love?' Craig looked from Big Mike to Sam as if he'd woken from a coma.

'Yes, love.' The word felt good to say. He did love Sarah. They may have only known each other a short time. So what? For the first time in years his first emotion upon waking wasn't sadness, but joy. Why couldn't people be happy for him?

'I'm happy for you, mate,' said Big Mike, as if reading his mind.

'I'm worried for you, mate,' said Craig. 'It's all a bit sudden.'

'Maybe,' said Sam again. 'The whole thing might go up in flames tomorrow. She might leave me and go back to Sydney never to return. Who knows. What I do know is, I'm happy. The end.'

His two friends studied him in silence for such a long time he thought he'd have to repeat himself.

'Here's to Sam's happiness,' said Craig finally, as he raised his glass.

'I'll second that,' said Big Mike, taking a gulp of his beer.

'Okay, then. Thank you.' The bar staff returned with Sam's drinks. 'I'm going to go and find Sarah and Levi,' he said. 'Been good seeing you.' Not entirely true. They might be protective of him, but they had to trust he knew what he was doing.

'See you later,' they chorused as Sam picked up his drinks and made his way out of the bar area. Today might prove

more trying than he'd anticipated. People remembered Michelle. They remembered him with Michelle. Sarah's arrival in his life might take some getting used to.

'He's gonna get crushed,' he heard Craig say behind him.

'Totally devo'd,' Big Mike agreed.

'What the hell does that mean?'

'All the kids are saying it.'

'Right, and you're one of the kids now.'

Sam shook his head and continued on out of earshot. His mates meant well. His relationship with Sarah would be an adjustment for them all.

He skirted the groups of locals gathering ahead of the races, saying hello to those he knew, and trying not to spill any of the drinks he carried. As he came around a gathering of ladies in their finery he pulled up short.

Kylie.

Right in front of him.

Here in Isisford.

Sam swallowed hard and blinked.

'Hello, handsome,' she purred. 'I was hoping I'd see you here.'

'Um … hello,' he stumbled. His mind went blank and his feet jammed.

'I wondered if you'd heard I'm back.' She leaned in and took the glass of champagne out of his hand.

'I didn't think you were coming back.' His mind raced to catch up with reality.

'Dad recovered better than his doctors thought he would. I didn't see any reason to stay when things had started becoming interesting here.'

Sam didn't know what to do. In his mind, Kylie had been a lovely distraction which had ended when she left. In her mind, she'd obviously thought their dating had been building to something else. He must have been blind not to see that. He'd thought her leaving had tied up the loose string for him. Now she stood before him and his assumption was about to bite him on his backside.

He looked around for help, someone to throw him a lifeline only to find himself alone in a sea of familiar faces. This situation couldn't be got around. He'd have to go straight through it.

'Kylie,' he began, 'it's great to see you again. Ah, there's something you need to …'

She stepped up to him, slid one hand behind his head and kissed him like her life depended on it. All the blood pooled in Sam's feet and his head swam like he might pass out. He tried to refocus, shake off the shock, as he stepped back from her.

'Sam?' Sarah appeared with Levi, right behind Kylie. 'I've been looking for you.'

'Holy shit,' Levi hissed. He fumbled his mobile phone out of his pocket and turned his back. Sam hoped Levi was phoning a friend because he sure as hell needed one.

Suddenly Maddie was pushing her way through the crowd of spectators. 'Sorry. Excuse me.'

She took a deep breath as she reached them. Sam imagined the tension was palpable from three feet out. 'Hi, Sarah, can I introduce you to someone I think might have a great story for you?' Maddie placed her hand on Sarah's arm and spoke brightly.

Sam mentally said a prayer of gratitude for the interruption. Maddie's timing couldn't be better.

'Sorry, what?' Sarah looked confused, her eyes darting from Sam to Kylie and back again.

'Potential interviewee.' She gave Sarah's arm a gentle tug. 'Hey, there's Dad's mate Paul who works at the local ABC radio station. You *have* to meet him. He might even be able to get you on air. Publicity and all that.'

The words *ABC radio* seemed to catch Sarah's attention momentarily. 'That would be great, Maddie. Maybe later.' The look on her face was the kind he thought the people on the *Titanic* might have worn when they realised their ship was sinking.

'Let's go now, before we lose him,' Maddie said, trying to pull Sarah away. On Sam's other side, Kylie turned to take a good look at Sarah.

'Who's this?' she asked as she looked Sarah up and down.

Sam groaned internally. He could smell a cat-fight brewing.

'This is Sarah Lewis, a journalist who I asked to come and speak to the students about a career in journalism.' Maddie stepped in before Sam could draw breath.

Kylie narrowed her eyes and Sam noticed her champagne glass had been drained. 'Really? The one I forbade you from inviting?'

'Forbade is a really strong word,' mumbled Levi.

'Yes, that's the very one.' Maddie squared up, putting Sarah out of the firing line. Sam wanted to hug her.

'Maddison McRae, you disappoint me. I never thought you'd go behind my back like that.'

'I'm sorry,' she said, although her tone said something entirely different. 'You were leaving and Ms Forsyth

thought my idea was pretty great.' She shrugged as if to say fair game.

Kylie took a deep breath, as if preparing to blast Maddie, when Sam stepped in.

'It's okay, Kylie. Maddie wasn't hurting anyone. You know what teenagers are like, always going to take the advantage if they think they can get away with it.'

Maddie mouthed a silent thank you to him as Kylie turned her attention his way.

'Get me out of here,' he heard Maddie whisper to Sarah as she led her away. 'I am in *big* trouble.'

Sarah let herself be led, even though she dragged her feet and kept looking back over her shoulder at Sam. What a mess. This was not good. Not good at all.

Maddie needed to find her dad and get him to introduce Sarah to Paul. That ought to keep them busy until things settled down.

Maddie glanced behind her to see Levi giving her a surreptitious thumbs up and Mr C looking like he'd rather be boiled alive than stand there taking Miss Kempton's wrath.

'Who was that woman?' Sarah asked, following Maddie's gaze.

'Um ... no one. Well, she was my teacher actually. She told me I couldn't invite you and then she left the school so I went ahead and did it anyway because I thought it wouldn't matter and she'd never know.' Maddie spoke in one fast breath, her words like machine gun fire.

'I got that much,' said Sarah. 'Why is she kissing Sam?'

'No idea,' said Maddie, crossing her fingers behind her back against the lie. 'Maybe they're, like, really good friends or something.'

'Mmm ... doesn't look like the sort of kiss a friend gives.' Sarah's brows knitted together and Maddie knew she'd have to do better if she had a hope of convincing Sarah everything was okay.

'Or maybe she ...'

Sarah stopped walking. 'Or maybe she what, Maddie?'

'Nothing,' she said, changing her mind about telling the truth. Whoever said the truth will set you free had no idea what they were talking about.

'What do you know, Maddison McRae?' Sarah stood with her hands on her hips, her head cocked to one side, looking at Maddie as if she could read her mind.

'Jesus-on-a-cupcake.' Maddie sighed. She'd dug herself a hole now.

CHAPTER TWENTY-FOUR

'It really isn't what it looks like.' Sam struggled to keep up with her all the way to his ute. Finally he stopped trying. 'Sarah, if you'd stop for a moment and let me explain.'

Sweat trickled down Sarah's back and prickled her scalp. Despite the fact it was spring, the temperature had begun to climb to summer highs. The uncomfortable, sticky sensation only added fuel to her fury.

She stopped and spun around on her heel. 'I don't want to hear it.' Her voice rang out louder than she'd intended, and people turned to stare. Let them. She didn't care. Balling her fists at her side, she glared at Sam, daring him to fight her right here, right now.

He took advantage of her standing still and hurried to her, clutching his akubra in his hands, his blue eyes dark with worry. What exactly he was worried about hadn't been

made clear. She figured getting caught two-timing in a small town rated highly.

'I want you to hear it.' He stood in front of her, so close she could smell the earthy scent of him. Despite her best intentions, his close proximity made her giddy with desire. She tamped down her lust. Her body had no sense when it came to Sam.

She crossed her arms and rocked her weight back on one hip. Fiona called it her defensive stance, and she'd be right.

'What are you going to say? It's all a misunderstanding and that woman got the wrong idea about your relationship? Because from what Maddie told me, and from where I stood, it looked like she had a very clear idea about your relationship.'

Sam sighed and ran his hand through his hair. 'You turned up at the wrong time ...'

'Thank you, I got that.'

'What I mean to say is you rocked up in the middle of a misunderstanding. Kylie just got back and was saying hello. We were never doing anything more than dating, the odd dinner or a drink at the pub, that's all. Then she left to go back to the coast and I figured that was the end of things. No one thought she'd come back.' He threw his arms wide. 'Hell, not even she thought she'd come back.'

She considered his explanation for a nano-second. On the surface of things, it sounded plausible. Bored teacher and lonely farmer hook up for fun and dinner. Teacher hightails it back home and lonely farmer gets on with his life.

'Doesn't change a thing,' she said as she turned and stomped her way to the ute. She'd come so close to giving all of her heart away to Sam without knowing anything about

him. This woman turning up at the races only showed her what a dangerous game she'd been playing with her own emotions. She'd been so swept away by Sam that she hadn't stopped to consider what kind of a man he might really be. History had shown Sarah that she couldn't trust her own judgement.

'What do you mean it doesn't change a thing?' He jogged to catch up. 'Kylie is upset but she understands she made an assumption that we'd pick up where we'd left off. We haven't been in touch once since she got on that plane.'

Sarah reached the car and tried to reef open the door, only to find it locked.

'How long ago exactly did she leave?' She narrowed her eyes at him, her mind ticking away at a thousand revs per second, her journalist's instinct on high alert. There was more to the story here. She could smell it.

Sam paused. 'The same day as you arrived.' At least he had the good grace to blush.

'Right.' She held her hand out for the keys.

'You are not driving angry. Besides, you have no idea where you're going.'

'It's one road in and one road out. How hard can it be? Give me the keys. I want to sit in the air-conditioning out of this bloody heat.' By herself. Even have a little pity cry if no one was looking.

'I'll drive you back to town.'

'I'm fine, thank you. You stay with your friends. Levi can drive me back.'

'Levi is barely fifteen years old. He doesn't have a licence.' Sam spoke patiently with the kind of tone a person used with overwrought toddlers.

'I can drive myself and you can get a lift back with *Kylie*.' She spoke between gritted teeth.

Sam threw his hands up in the air. 'I honestly don't see what the problem is here. I feel completely differently about you than I do about Kylie. The two cannot be compared.'

'And you've had plenty of time to work this out, have you?'

'I didn't need time. I know.' He sounded frustrated and fed up. She knew how he felt.

'All that time you were chatting to me online, you were dating Kylie. I'd say that qualifies as cheating in anyone's book.' She watched the play of emotions across his face as he took in her words. 'Especially when you specifically told me that you hadn't dated anyone since your wife died. What does that make Kylie?'

'What the hell are you talking about?' It was his turn to narrow his eyes at her, as if suspecting a trap.

'You know exactly what I'm talking about, mister.' To her shame, her index finger sprang to life, driving her words home. 'You had plenty of opportunity to tell me about her. Especially after I told you about Greg! What does that make me? Another one of your short-term flings? What else have you lied about?'

'Shit, Sarah, if I had a clue as to what's going on in that head of yours we wouldn't be having this conversation. And who the hell is Greg?'

'Greg is my ex-boyfriend. And Lonely in Longreach doesn't ring a bell?'

He shook his head, frowning. 'Nope. The first time I laid eyes on you was at the pub the day you arrived. The rest is a mystery to me and I'd appreciate someone filling me in on what I've missed.'

'What you've missed? You have got to be kidding me. I knew this … us … was too good to be true. You are such a liar.' If she had anywhere to storm to, she would.

His face flushed with anger. 'Never call me a liar again,' he growled.

'Then don't tell lies,' she snapped. 'You had your profile up on Outback Singles fishing for new blood the whole time you were dating Kylie. I'm sure she'd like to hear about that. Are you still up on the site? Are you looking for fresh blood to replace me the minute I've gone back to Sydney?'

'What the fuck are you talking about?' Sam's confusion and hurt gave way to palpable anger. 'I don't use the internet for anything other than email, let alone have an online dating profile.'

'Right, and I'm expected to believe that.' The gall of the man to stand right in front of her, look her in the eye and blatantly lie.

'You can believe what you bloody well like, but that's the truth.' He looked angry, as if containing his fury cost him a lot.

'I have the emails from you. I have the Outback Singles link to your profile. I know the truth.' She held out her hand for the keys again. 'You've used me and played me for a fool. I want to go home,' she said, trembling. She had to get out of there fast before she started to cry.

He studied her, searching her eyes for something he didn't find because he handed the keys over without further argument. 'Fine,' he said. 'You believe what you want. I never sent you an email and I never had a dating profile. Someone has been impersonating me and I intend to find out who it is.' He took a deep breath. 'What I can't believe is that you

won't listen to me. When did I ever give you a reason to think I'm not genuine about us? You can walk away now but don't think for a minute this is over.'

'Whatever,' she said as she unlocked the car. All she wanted was to get back to the motel, have a shower and a good cry then get on the first plane out of this godforsaken place. She could finish her interviews by phone. Home was where she needed to be, as far away from Sam Costello as she could get.

She got into the car and slammed the door shut. He knocked on the window. Reluctantly, she lowered it.

'Aren't you even the slightest bit curious to find out what's really going on? How we ended up in this mess? Are you really willing to throw away what we've found without a fight?'

She stuck the keys in the ignition. 'What difference does it make? Everything we shared was based on a lie. A whopping great cheesy lie.' The car engine roared to life. 'I can't believe I fell for you. I can't believe I was so stupid as to not see you for what you are.'

'That is totally unfair,' he burred up. 'Everything I feel for you is one hundred percent genuine. I don't know what's gone on here but I am as much a victim of this as you are.'

'Really? That's what you're going with? I've *seen* you kiss another woman with my own eyes. What other evidence do I need?'

'I explained all that. What we have trumps any of this bullshit.' He took a deep breath. 'Sarah, please. I'm not sorry I met you or that you came out here.'

'Yeah, well I am. I was really falling for you but you don't even exist.' She revved the engine, the sound matching the roaring pain in her heart.

She drove off so quickly he had to jump back out of the way.

The ute bounced out of the carpark, dust kicking up behind. When she reached the end of the main street, she let the tears come with great racking sobs that shook her body. She had to grip on to the steering wheel to keep from veering off the road.

She'd been *so* sure Sam had been the one. Her heart had answered to his in a way she'd never experienced with anyone else. Her body responded to his touch as though no one else existed. How could she have got it so wrong?

Pain thrummed in her chest along with humiliation, shame, remorse and a double serving of anger. Her emotions shifted gear so quickly she couldn't keep up with them. Tears dripped from her chin and she didn't have a tissue. She sniffed mightily and pulled over on the side of the road.

Searching the unfamiliar car, she popped the glove box to find nothing useful. Resigning herself to remaining a mess until she reached the motel, Sarah pulled back onto the highway and tried to ignore the fact she'd done a runner in Sam's car which meant he'd come looking for it at some point. She'd not thought about that when she'd demanded the keys.

That was the least of her worries.

She pushed the power button for the radio. A country tune about love lost filled the car. Exactly what she needed. The words spoke of hearts betrayed and broken, like hers. She had an hour to drive so she cranked up the volume and let the tears fall freely as she drove down the highway.

She'd go back to Sydney, write the best article she'd ever written and swear off men forever. Maybe even look for a new job somewhere as a reporter on a news service. Or get a

job at a TV station. Or give it all up and run away overseas
to work in an orphanage for a few years.

Anything to be as far away as possible from here.

What the hell had just happened? One minute everything
was fine, a little hiccup with Kylie, but fundamentally fine.
Next minute Sarah was yelling at him about some internet
profile and all the lies he'd supposedly told. It was like falling down the proverbial rabbit hole.

He watched Sarah drive off in his ute, at a loss as to what
had happened and what he was going to do about it. The bottom had fallen out of his world in minutes for a crime he didn't
even know he'd committed. Anger, confusion, loss—hard to
know which emotion to deal with first and none of them he
wanted to feel in the public carpark of the Isisford Races.

Sam slapped his akubra against his thigh to dislodge the
dust Sarah had kicked up when she'd spun the wheels, and
pushed it down firmly on his head. He needed to find Levi
and organise a lift home. Once there he might be able to
piece together the disaster of the day and make some sense
of what Sarah had said. Once he had the facts straight, he
would talk with her. She'd have calmed down a bit by then
and might be willing to listen.

He turned to go back to the festivities, aware of people politely turning away to gossip about him. Let them.
Wouldn't be the first time and probably not the last.

Levi appeared with Maddie in tow.

'Are you okay, Dad?' He put one hand on Sam's shoulder
and for a blinding second, Sam thought he might cry at the
gesture.

'I'm right, son,' he said gruffly. 'We need to find a lift home since …'

'We saw,' said Maddie in a small voice.

Sam nodded and bowed his head, keeping his eyes on the ground. Everyone saw. He took a deep, stabilising breath. Time to get out of here, which meant explaining why he needed a lift. Not looking forward to that and the inevitable told-you-sos to follow.

'I've got an idea,' said Maddie. 'Wait here.' She darted off through the crowd, giving Sam some much needed time to gather himself.

'Can I get you anything?' Levi asked, worry written all over his face.

'I don't think so.' Sam shook his head, looking at the festivities around him and wanting to disappear. 'I don't know what happened. One minute we were fine, better than fine, and the next we're breaking apart at the seams.'

Sam crouched down behind the other cars parked in untidy rows, seeking privacy while they waited for Maddie.

Levi ducked down next to him. 'Was Miss Kempton the problem? She seemed mad to find out you'd moved on.'

'How was I to know she intended on coming back and picking up where we left off?' Sam held his hands out, palms up. 'I get Sarah might be angry at the thought I could have a girlfriend, but I got the sense she had a whole lot more mad in her than I can reckon for.'

'What was the, um … the problem then?' Levi sounded nervous. He didn't blame the poor kid. No boy should be comforting his father this way. Sam hadn't meant to burden Levi with his raw emotions. It was sure to be overwhelming.

'Sarah kept going on about a dating profile and emails. I had no idea what she was talking about.' He ran their fight through his mind, looking for clues to explain her behaviour. She had been so hurt, angry and upset. But why?

He fished his phone out of his back pocket.

'What are you doing, Dad?' Levi asked.

'Sarah said something about a dating site and I thought I'd look it up while we wait for Maddie.' He tapped the name in. What was it? Outback romance or something. Google took a micro second to find the site. Outback Singles.

Now what? How did he find out if he was on here or not?

'She mentioned a profile. If only I could remember the name.' He tipped his head back and stared at the blue cloudless sky as if the answer might fall from there at any second.

'Come on, Dad. What would you be doing on a dating site? Sarah's spent too much time looking at that stuff for research. She's confused.'

Sam looked at Levi. 'Sarah is the least confused person I've ever met. Why would she say something that isn't true? She must have had a reason to think I'd been emailing her. Like emails for example.'

Levi shrugged and stood up. 'Where's Maddie gone?' He looked around then typed a quick text on his phone. 'Hurry up, Maddie,' he muttered.

'What's the rush?' Sam stood up. Something was off. He could sense it. 'What's going on with you two? One minute you're not talking to each other and you're asking to go to boarding school. The next you're thick as thieves.'

'Oh, it's nothing.' Levi waved away Sam's concerns. 'A minor disagreement. All sorted.'

'Mmm …' Sam studied his son. The boy wouldn't meet his eyes and he couldn't stand still. Something was definitely up.

'Hopefully Maddie can get us a lift back to Longreach. That'd be good, huh?' Levi forced a smile.

'Yeah, great.' Sam's mind ticked over at a thousand miles an hour. The memory of what Sarah said sat there, on the edge of his mind. He almost had it.

'Here comes Maddie now.' The relief in Levi's voice was more than evident. 'Over here!'

Maddie spotted them and navigated her way to where they stood.

'I've sorted a lift for us. My dad says we can borrow his car. Mum and Dad will go home with some friends so we're all good.' She puffed a little as she caught her breath, a big smile of triumph on her face as she dangled the car keys from her fingers.

'Thank you,' said Sam, taking the keys from her outstretched hand. He'd thank her parents later when he got home and got a handle on his situation.

'You coming with us?' Levi's question sounded more like a plea, his expression all puppy-dog.

'Sure,' said Maddie, looking from Levi to Sam, her previously cheerful demeanour dimming. 'Everything okay?'

'No,' said Sam. 'It's not okay.'

'Oh.' She looked at her shoes as if they'd become the most interesting things on Earth.

Then it hit him. Lonely in Longreach. He punched the name into the website.

He stared at his profile in disbelief. The picture was him alright. It looked like the one the kids had taken weeks ago

for some project they reckoned they were doing. Profiles on multigenerational farming families or something. He couldn't remember and it hardly mattered now.

Oh, God. No.

The penny dropped. Surely they couldn't have. Maddie maybe, not Levi. Sam scrolled through 'his' profile. No wonder Sarah seemed to know him so well.

He shook his head in an effort to make all the pieces fit together properly.

'I thought you took that down,' Levi hissed at Maddie.

'I thought I did,' she whispered back.

'I'm right here,' said Sam, a slow fury beginning to burn in his gut. 'If either of you have something you need to tell me, now would be a really good time.'

'Sorry, Dad.' Levi looked as guilty as Maddie did.

'What's going on here? What have you two done?'

'I … we …' Maddie looked at Levi for help.

He looked scared, shrugged and shook his head. She'd get no help there.

'We set up a dating profile for you to help you find a girl-friend so you wouldn't be so lonely anymore.'

'Lonely?'

'We'll be finished high school in a couple of years and then we'll be gone. What are you going to do here all by yourself? You don't even have a dog, Dad.'

'Right, the two of you in the car, now. We'll talk about this when we get home.' His anger surged like a firestorm inside him. Anything he said now would be destructive.

'We were only trying to help, Mr C,' said Maddie timidly.

He could barely breathe.

The drive would give him some time to calm down enough to get to the bottom of this. Whatever the two of them had done—and they'd obviously been meddling in his life without his permission—would reverberate through their small community whether they liked it or not. Because if they'd done what he thought they had, then everyone would be gossiping about it for years. The story would be too good not to.

'Where is the car?'

Maddie pointed to her father's four-wheel drive.

'You have exactly thirty seconds to get in and buckle up and then I don't want a single word spoken on the way home. Got it?'

Levi and Maddie nodded in unison and bolted for the car. No need to ask them twice. He followed more sedately, self-control in every step. His mind tumbled around the facts, refusing to examine one for more than a moment before moving on to the next horrifying piece of the story. He figured it would take the better part of a bottle of whisky and several hours before he'd get to grips with the mess that his life had become.

Who knew what the state of affairs would be by this time tomorrow. First he had to understand the situation so he could explain it to Sarah. He *had* to sort it out before she had a chance to fly home. Once she left, she might never come back.

Notes for 'Finding Love in the Outback'
Interview #8
Christina (44) single, from Gympie. Tried online dating without much success.

Christina: I'd moved to Gympie after my divorce. I thought a bigger town than the one I was from might yield more luck in love and life in general. I signed up to online dating because I was struggling to find blokes my age to date. I found a profile of what I thought was a great guy. He looked kind. We chatted for a bit, then we decided to meet.

He lived in a small community outside Gympie— I don't want to say where in case he reads this—and we agreed we'd meet up in town for a coffee, you know … see what happens.

Anyway, he arrives, and he seems lovely. We have a nice time. We both agree we're attracted to each other and I think, right I'm in. Then he says he needs to pop to the loo. Fair enough. Then he returns with a woman in tow. Turns out she's his girlfriend. He asks me if I'd be up for a threesome. A threesome! Me! I didn't know what to say, so I said goodbye and left. Let him pay the bill. Went home and deleted my dating profile. Never bothered again.

CHAPTER TWENTY-FIVE

When Maddie heard herself tell Mr C what she'd done in all the technicolour detail, the explanation sounded crazy. She'd admit that.

'Let me get this straight.' Mr C paced back and forth across his kitchen while she sat with Levi on stools at the kitchen bench. 'You put my profile up on some country dating site in the hope you could find me a girlfriend so that, one day when you graduate high school, you can go to Sydney without feeling guilty about leaving me behind.' He stopped and looked at them both. 'Have I got that right?'

'Pretty well.' Levi kept his eyes on the counter top.

'Why didn't you just talk to me about your concerns? Graduation is still a couple of years away and who knows if you'll get into a university in Sydney or somewhere else.' He threw up his hands, exasperation outlined in his expression.

Maddie knew that look well, her mum wore it almost all the time.

Levi snorted. 'And how was that conversation supposed to go? I want to leave home and I feel guilty about that so how about you get a girlfriend and then I won't feel so bad.'

'If that's how you feel. Is it?'

Levi crossed his arms and slouched forward. 'Maybe,' he muttered.

'Then we need to talk about that, not have you run off and do something I'm sure is illegal.'

'It is?' Maddie couldn't keep the squeak out of her voice.

'It breaches the Privacy Act at the very least and maybe even constitutes fraud. I don't know.'

Maddie swallowed hard and joined Levi in staring at the counter top. She hadn't given any thought to those issues when she'd signed Mr C up to Outback Singles. Sure, they'd pretended to be him, but they'd represented him one hundred percent as himself. Surely that counted for something.

'Are you going to press charges?' she asked in a small voice. Wait until her dad heard about this. He'd take away her trail bike, and probably send her to boarding school like her cousin Karen, who'd been caught having sex with her boyfriend in her bedroom. Maddie figured her crime would probably rival Karen's, if not eclipse it.

'What? No.' Mr C frowned. 'Having said that, it will be up to Sarah if she wants to take any action.' He stood with his hands on his hips, the sunlight pouring in through the kitchen window setting his hair alight like a halo. The avenging angel like the one in her hand-me-down copy of *Bible Stories for Children*.

'I know you didn't like me dating your teacher, but going behind my back to find me someone online is a bit rich.'

'Oh, we'd started the online profile long before you began dating Kylie … I mean, Miss Kempton.' The minute she opened her mouth to speak she realised her mistake. Too late. The words had spilled out before she could stop them.

Levi turned his head to glare at her as if she'd lost her mind.

The expression on Mr C's face was no better.

'I'm sorry.' Maddie held her hands up as she shrugged. 'I am totally sorry. I really thought we were doing the right thing. We'd already got a message from Sarah and she sounded fantastic. She *is* fantastic.'

'I know,' said Mr C darkly. 'That's the problem. She's hurt and angry. I'll be lucky if she ever talks to me again.'

'I can call her and tell her it was all mine and Levi's idea, that you had nothing to do with it.' She knew she could fix this. Mr C and Sarah didn't understand about Fate. They were meant to be. The fake profile had got them together because sometimes Fate needed a hand, and she was Fate's handmaiden. Everyone knew that.

'I don't think that's going to work,' said Mr C.

'We won't know until we try,' she said, determined to turn this situation around.

'Maddie, leave it,' said Levi. 'This whole thing has gone far enough. You only wanted to go to Sydney to meet that actor you're in love with.'

'I am not,' she said automatically, catching herself in the lie. Funny thing was, when she thought of Liam Newson, imagined them together on Bondi Beach, she felt …

Nothing.

All the sweet fizzy energy thinking about him used to invoke in her had disappeared.

She blinked at Levi, stunned silent with the shock of realisation.

'Yeah, right,' he said. 'You've got this big idea that you two are made for each other and that you're some kind of match-maker, when you're not. You may not talk to me about that stuff, but don't think I don't know.'

She watched Levi's mouth as he spoke. The words passed over and around her. Yes, he was telling her off. She didn't care. His spiky hair, so like his dad's, his lanky frame, his annoying way of knowing everything about everything—she loved it all.

'I don't think I want to go to Bondi Beach after all,' she said.

He paused, as though taking the time to read her mind. 'Really?' She could see the hope in his eyes.

'Really,' she said, a smile breaking loose even though now was *not* the time.

An answering grin spread slowly across Levi's face.

'Hate to break this up, lovebirds. Can I bring your atten-tion back to the fact that while you've been sorting out your complicated emotional life, my own life has blown up in my face. Largely thanks to the bomb you two planted there.'

Mr C's voice snapped Maddie back to the present.

'Like we're some kind of love terrorists?' Maddie asked.

Levi snorted, before quickly covering up the sound with a cough.

'What? No.' Mr C shook his head. 'I want you two to take ownership of the fact that you've meddled in my life

in a way you had no right to, and you've hurt a number of people along the way.'

'We didn't mean to,' said Maddie as Levi's hand sought hers under the counter top. Their fingers entwined and she took strength from the warmth of his palm against hers. 'We only wanted to make you and Sarah happy. I really thought you'd fall in love and none of this would matter.'

'Well, I did and it does.' Mr C sighed and ran his hand through his hair. He looked sad and deflated. She realised she hadn't made his life better at all. She'd made it worse than it had been. Now he'd be more lonely because he knew what he was missing. Sarah.

'What are we going to do now?' she asked.

'I don't know.' Mr C looked out the window as if he could see the answer out there on the horizon. 'Nothing for now until I figure things out.'

'Are we in trouble?' She already knew the answer but the compulsion to ask drove the question from her lips.

'Damn straight you are,' said Mr C. 'I will be talking to your parents about this. There will be consequences.' He placed both his hands flat on the bench. 'I'm disappointed in both of you. You're old enough to know better than to get carried away with some fantasy. What were you thinking?'

'We saw it in a movie,' said Levi.

'Levi!' Maddie nudged him to be quiet. Whatever he had to say would only get them in more trouble.

'Which movie?'

'I dunno, ask Maddie.'

'Thanks, Levi,' she muttered. 'Way to drop me in it.'

'What? Like you're not already in trouble up to your neck.'

'Maddie, focus.' Mr C sounded like a teacher. 'What movie?'

'*Sleepless in Seattle.*' She sighed. Her mother would never let her borrow a DVD again.

To her surprise, Mr C burst out laughing.

'That's rich,' he said. 'This gets better and better.'

'So, everything's okay?' He didn't sound as mad anymore.

'No, Maddie, it's not okay. You're still grounded for the rest of your teenage years.'

'Oh.' Genuinely disappointed, she put her hands in her lap and picked at her cuticles. This had turned out to be one weird day.

'Come on.' Mr C grabbed her dad's car keys. 'Let's get you home and we'll work this out.'

Maddie and Levi slid off their stools.

'What about Sarah?' she asked. Maddie could take Mr C and her parents being angry with her. They'd punish her and she'd take it because it would be a way of making things up. Sort of. She'd really hurt Sarah and she'd never meant for that to happen. She wanted to say sorry and let Sarah know she truly believed she was supposed to be with Mr C.

'Leave Sarah to me,' said Mr C, grabbing his hat off a peg near the front door.

'Make sure you mention that you're fated to be together. It's no accident that she saw your profile and came here.' Maddie had to make Mr C understand how important Fate was, that he had to fight for Sarah if he wanted her. He couldn't give up.

'You're right,' said Mr C as he opened the front door. 'This whole thing has been no accident. It has been a cunningly executed plan with one major flaw.' He ushered them out into the yard.

'You think our plan was cunning?' Maddie perked up at the thought.

'Out of curiosity,' said Levi, 'what was our major flaw?'

'You forgot the truth would be waiting at the end of it all.'

'I will do anything to make it up to you.' Maddie sat cross-legged on a chair in the school library, her long blonde hair forming a curtain around her face. They'd skipped Wednesday afternoon sports at school in favour of a so-called study period. So far they'd studied exactly nothing.

Levi rocked back in his chair, hands behind his head, feeling like he finally had some influence on his life. 'Anything?'

'There might be a couple of things I won't do,' said Maddie.

'For example?' He liked teasing Maddie. Half the time she didn't even know he was doing it.

'Umm … I won't rob a bank or murder someone for you.'

'Good to know where we stand.' He had something much better in mind. Something he'd been thinking about ever since Saturday when Sarah had stormed off, leaving his dad devastated. Then angry. Really, really angry.

All that had happened just under a week ago. It had taken that long for the heat to die down. Maddie's parents had been ropeable and for a minute there he'd thought they were going to ship her off to boarding school. Or worse still, ban her from seeing him as if *he* were the bad influence in the relationship.

In the end, they hadn't done either. They'd ranted and yelled before grounding Maddie for the rest of the year.

She hadn't cared. After the horror of the year twelve formal and the dating site debacle, she said she was more than
happy to hang out at home. Grounding became a gift, not
a punishment.

He'd been grounded too. Like Maddie, he didn't mind.
What hurt him most was how his dad had been super disappointed in him. He wondered what his mother would have
thought, but only for a minute as the potential answer to
that question proved to be deeply unpleasant. He knew she'd
be even more disappointed in him than his dad had been.

Which is why he had to fix things.

'I want you to hide me in your barn for a few days.'

'What are you talking about? Why would you want to
do something like that?' She frowned at him as if he'd suggested setting himself on fire in the middle of Eagle Street
on a Monday morning.

'I have a plan to get Sarah and Dad back together again.'

'Oh, no.' Maddie held her hands up. 'I'm not touching
that. Are you mad?'

'A little,' Levi grinned. 'I feel compelled to try and fix
this. We got them into this mess, only we can get them out.'

'I don't know.' Maddie had a bruised ego from her epic
matchmaking fail. He got that. She owed his dad as much
as he did. Her ego would heal. Levi wasn't sure his dad's
heart would. 'I'm not agreeing to anything until I hear the
full plan. I mean, wouldn't your dad fix this by himself if
he wanted to?'

'Dad has been trying but Sarah won't talk to him. He
keeps leaving messages and she never calls back. Never
answers her phone. No one expected her to run out of here
so fast. I thought she'd at least stay long enough to hear

Dad's side of the story but he said we'd done too much damage, that he'd be lucky if she ever spoke to him again. And you said you'd do anything to make up for the way you treated me,' he reminded her.

'Don't take the mick,' she said. 'There is a limit. Self-preservation and all that.'

'I'm not asking for much. All I want is a little camp in a corner of your barn where no one will look for me for about forty-eight hours.'

'What do I tell people when they ask where you are?'

'You'll tell them I got on a plane for Sydney.'

'They'll just check and know that you didn't.'

'Privacy Act. You can't just ask, the airline won't tell you. Much more complicated than that. I'm counting on it.'

Maddie cocked one eyebrow and regarded him. 'And what happens next?'

'If Dad thinks I'm in Sydney looking for Sarah, he'll jump on a plane to chase after me.'

'And get back together with Sarah.'

'Something like that.'

Maddie grinned. 'Levi Costello, you are amazing.' She launched herself at him, knocking all the air out of him in the process.

Laughing, he steadied her as he looked around furtively for the librarian. He liked being amazing.

'You'll do it?'

'Of course I'll do it.' Her hair fell around his face as she looked down at him. 'Then we're even, okay?'

'Okay,' he reluctantly agreed. This new arrangement of theirs suited him very well and he didn't want anything to change.

'We're going to have to find a new life plan,' she said. 'After this we'll be grounded until we're forty. Goodbye, Sydney.'

Levi shrugged. 'Never much liked the idea of the big smoke anyway.'

Notes for 'Finding Love in the Outback'
Personal notes
Sam (38) from Longreach and Sarah (38) from Sydney. Found love online.

I didn't set out to look for love online. It happened accidentally. I stumbled across Sam's profile and I couldn't get him out of my mind.

We connected, at least I thought we did. Emails sailed back and forth. I began to think I knew this man well enough to take the risk to meet him.

I was working on this story, 'Finding Love in the Outback', and shamelessly used a research trip to bring me into Sam's orbit. It helped that a student from the local high school asked me to speak to the student assembly about a career in journalism. I found out later that had been arranged deliberately to lure me to Longreach.

I met Sam and I knew instantly he was the guy for me. I can't describe to you exactly how I knew. The feeling wasn't logical or rational. It didn't appear in the form of a list or a well thought out argument. Instead, the certainty came from deep in the marrow

of my bones. As mad as that sounds, he was made for me and I for him.

We had a wonderful time cruising on the Thomson River, dining out, getting to know each other. He became caught up in the same whirlwind of emotion I had. The sense of togetherness and rightness was something I'd never experienced before, not even with the man I had planned to marry. This fact made me realise what we had found might be the real deal, the love movies are made about, the stuff of novels.

I was cruelly mistaken.

As events transpired, Sam's fifteen-year-old son, Levi, and his best friend, Maddie, had concocted the online profile to attract possible candidates for Sam. They shared dreams of moving to Sydney to go to university in a couple of years. Levi didn't want to leave Sam on his own. Sam lost his wife, Michelle, when Levi was young. The boy harbours a sense of responsibility towards his father which, while touching, tangled us all up in an elaborate web of lies.

Yeats put it perfectly: 'Things fall apart; the centre cannot hold.' And fall apart they did.

I got hurt. Sam got hurt. The kids got hurt, despite their best intentions. Anger, humiliation, pain and yes, a sense of loss, all gripped me over the following days. They still assault me when I least expect them.

In the aftermath I learned a valuable lesson about love and online dating. Profiles are not true representations of the individual. They are aspirational, how the person would like to be seen or how they would

like to see themselves. Perhaps this closely shadows reality, perhaps it's a dire departure. You cannot tell until you are in the mix, until you are face-to-face with the individual.

Until then, the internet can draw a veil across reality, letting you see what you want to see and what the other person wants you to believe.

Be warned. Be careful. But also be brave.

Will I try online dating again? No. I think I'll leave that for others with more resilient hearts. I shall try and find my love the old-fashioned way.

*Note to self: change the names of the people and the town.

CHAPTER TWENTY-SIX

Bella Brandon leaned back in her chair and tapped the manila folder in front of her with her fountain pen.

'I have to say, this is very good work, Sarah. I love the personal angle. It makes the whole story zing. Our readers are going to love it.'

'Well, you know what Tolstoy always said.' Sarah sat opposite Bella on a seat so low her chin barely cleared the top of the desk. She tried to maintain as much dignity as possible when her knees were up around her earlobes.

'Tolstoy?'

Sarah guessed Bella was probably trying to frown, because her eyebrow twitched. She clearly hadn't taken Arlene's advice on botox.

'If you want to write well, write in blood. Or words to that effect.'

'Sounds more like a quote from Anne Rice,' Bella grunted. 'Has Lonely in Longreach seen it?'

Sarah sighed, deflating further into the designer chair clearly created with toddlers in mind.

'I haven't spoken to him since …'

Bella nodded, words not necessary. 'Do you think you should?'

'Maybe,' she conceded. Getting in touch with Sam and telling him she'd used part of their story in her article series would be the right thing to do ethically. She wasn't feeling like doing the right thing at the moment. Her anger had abated, leaving humiliation to sizzle away in the pit of her stomach.

'There might be a chance you can save this relationship. Turn things around.'

Sarah had told Bella the full story during a long lunch involving too much champagne and a whisky chaser. Bella, being much better at that sort of thing than Sarah, had easily wheedled the story out of her. To her surprise, her boss had proved to be a sympathetic confidante, having experienced her own online love disasters.

Sarah shook her head. 'Nope. No way. I'm done. I spent time with a guy pretending to be someone I'm not. Now I've got a guy pretending to be someone he's not. I want something authentic and real.'

'Technically, the boy was pretending to be his father. Did he say anything about his dad that wasn't true?'

She hated it when Bella had a point.

'No, he did not.'

Bella leaned back in her luxurious leather desk chair and threw her hands in the air. 'Well, there you go then. Call

him. Talk to him. Get the truth from his perspective. You're a journalist, you know there's always two sides to a story.'

'I hate it when you're right,' she muttered.

'Darling, I'm *always* right. Now scuttle off and do something. I'm not paying you to sit here and chat about your love life. If you want counselling, I'll send you my hourly rate.' Bella dismissed her with a wave of her hand.

Sarah rose with as much dignity as she could muster, clutching her pad to her chest.

'Right, thank you. I'll go and ...' she pointed over her shoulder at the work spaces beyond the glass partition of Bella's office.

Bella didn't answer. She studied the screen of her laptop with her glasses pulled halfway down her nose, her head tipped back as she tried to focus.

Sarah waited a heartbeat, then turned and left.

Once back at her desk she put her forehead down on the table and groaned. Her life sucked.

Should she call Sam? She could text him. Would that be considered poor form? She could email him. Except according to him, that wasn't his email address. Who knew if her message would ever get to him. She hadn't contacted him because, aside from the fact he'd broken her heart, she hadn't used his real name in the article. She also hadn't mentioned which site she'd found him on, and the profile had been removed anyway, so there would be no way for readers to trace him there. So what did it matter if he knew or not before publication. She had no intention of sticking around anyway.

The afternoon of the Isisford Races, Sarah had driven back to the motel, thrown her belongings together and

driven straight to the airport in time to catch the flight to Brisbane. Her phone had rung hot with calls from Sam and Maddie. She'd ignored them all and, after listening to the first one from Sam explaining what happened, deleted their messages too. Mostly because she felt like an enormous first-class fool. How did she, an intelligent and educated woman, a journalist at that, get sucked into the whole love-at-first-sight rubbish? She ought to know better.

Sitting up, she pushed her hair back and opened her desk drawer. She took out a folder with the jobs she'd applied for, carefully catalogued so she could keep track of them. Spending time in the outback had shown her where her true heart lay. She couldn't go back to being the girl she was before. She'd applied for all sorts of rural positions, some overseas, some more serious than others. They all had one thing in common: there were as far away from Sydney as she could get.

Time for a change. Time to really start living instead of waiting for something that was never going to happen. True love and a family might not be in her destiny. She didn't know. The best thing to do was to get out there and have an adventure so she didn't waste away on the treadmill of daily city life in the vain hope something would change.

Besides that, she wanted to avoid running into Greg. Done that once. Awkward as all hell with Rachel in her short shorts being gracious and bubbly. Greg looked happy and to her mortification, she was shot through with jealousy at the thought.

Still, on some level she was happy for him. Genuinely. He deserved someone like Rachel who would appreciate him for who he was and who got a kick out of being with him. If only she could find someone like that for herself.

Her phone buzzed on her desk, vibrating itself across the surface as if on a mission to get to the edge. She grabbed it and checked the number.

Sam.

Sam was calling her again. He'd called every day for the last week and a half.

Should she answer?

She stared at the screen while the number flashed. Yes. No. Yes. No.

This was *so* hard.

Taking a deep breath, she accepted the call.

'Hello?'

The plan had seemed simple when they'd been hanging out in the library last week. All Maddie had to do was hold her nerve, repeat the words Levi made her memorise and stay calm.

'When did you last see Levi?' Her mother stood in front, the leader of the adults. Behind her stood her dad and Mr C. Maddie sat at the kitchen table. The whole thing was like a scene out of one of those old Hollywood war movies where they interrogate people under harsh lights.

'Yesterday. He said he was going to Sydney and no one could stop him.' She could be an actress, she was that convincing. She'd even managed to fool Ms Forsyth when she'd asked why Levi wasn't at school today. Maddie had shrugged and said something about him having a case of Mondayitis. She'd acted so cool, no one would have guessed how nervous she'd been about them getting caught out.

'Yes, and how was he going to get there?' Mr C sounded super anxious.

'I have no idea. Plane?'

'We could check with the airport, see if he got on a plane or if there's film footage of him at the airport,' said her dad.

Shit. Had Levi thought of that?

'Won't that take ages?' she asked and all the adults turned their attention back to her. 'I mean, you know, the Privacy Act and all.' She crossed her fingers beneath the table. This had better work. She had no idea about the Privacy Act or what it was even meant to do. Her performance had moved into the impromptu space.

'She has a point,' said her mum.

Mr C sighed and ran both hands through his hair.

'Do you have any idea where he was going?' Dad asked her.

'I do,' said Mr C. 'I've got a good idea of where he might be headed. Am I right?' he asked Maddie.

She nodded, not trusting her tongue. So far, Levi's plan was working. She did not want to be the one to stuff it up. She didn't want to get into trouble with nothing to show for her efforts.

'Then I have to get to Sydney and find him.'

'Hang on a minute, if you know where he's going why not call and give them the heads up in case he turns up there before you can find him?' Her dad was always the reasonable one and today, she loved him for it.

Mr C stopped and gave her dad a look she couldn't interpret, which was annoying because she was usually good at this sort of thing.

'Ah, I get it.' Her dad coughed to cover his embarrassment. 'Well, calling would be the smart thing to do. All

things aside, Sydney is a big city for a boy from the bush. Does he know where she lives?'

'No,' said Mr C, 'although he knows where she works.'

'If we leave now we can get you on a flight. Otherwise you'll have to wait until tomorrow's plane,' said her ever practical mother. 'Let's drive your ute and then we can keep an eye on it here while you're gone. Least we can do.'

'Thank you, for everything,' said Mr C. Her mum and dad nodded and said nothing. The subject of Sarah was like this great big elephant in the room no one wanted to discuss.

'I'm sure Maddie will keep us updated if she hears from Levi,' said Mum, giving Maddie a sideways glare which, she had to admit, was impressive.

'Of course I will,' Maddie said, trying for concern and the right amount of enthusiasm.

'Do you need anything from home?' asked her dad.

'No,' said Mr C. 'I can manage with what I'm standing in. I don't plan to be in Sydney long. Let's go. I don't want to waste another minute.'

The adults hustled out of the room without a backward glance, which suited Maddie fine. She waited until she heard the front door slam and the car start up before she got up from the table and began to make some food for Levi.

He'd be keen to hear how things were going. He'd turned off his mobile phone so he wouldn't be tempted to check Facebook or anything. She didn't know how he managed to cope with no phone. She couldn't do it.

Quickly, she made Levi a ham sandwich and grabbed him a bottle of cola from her dad's stash. Her parents would be ages yet and she wanted to spend as much time as she

could with Levi before they got home. Who knew if they'd let her see him once this was over.

'Hey, Levi.' She kept her voice down because her sister had hearing like a bat. Ariel was all the way across the yard in the house with her bedroom door closed and her headphones on, but Maddie wasn't taking any chances.

'Here,' he called. She found him sitting up on a pile of bedding, surrounded by empty chip packets, playing on his iPad. She sighed and her heart gave a little flutter at the thought of their very first love nest together.

'Brought you food,' she said, holding out her offerings.

'Thank you, I'm starving.' He took the sandwich off the plate with both hands and sunk his teeth into the soft, white bread. 'How'd it go?' he asked through a mouthful of sandwich.

'Just as you planned.' She sat down next to him. 'My parents were majestic. They totally supported the whole you-have-to-go-to-Sydney thing. Your dad is on his way to the airport now.'

'Do you think he'll call Sarah first?'

'My dad told him to so who knows?' she shrugged.

'You want a bite?' Levi offered her his sandwich.

'No thanks.' She shook her head. 'Are you going to contact Sarah yourself? You know, like you're really going to visit her or something?'

Levi swallowed hard. 'Nope,' he said. 'I'm going to let it play out. Dad will find Sarah and then we let them know I'm safe here. There they are, both in Sydney, both worried about me. Perfect, I say.' He took another bite of sandwich and chewed contentedly.

'I have to say, it's a great plan. I'm almost jealous I didn't come up with it.'

'Almost?'

'My boyfriend came up with it so, close enough.' She smiled at him shyly. They'd known each other all their lives yet this new situation had a weirdness about it she hadn't come to grips with yet.

Levi grinned. 'Your boyfriend?'

'Yeah, you might know him. Annoying, self-obsessed smart-arse who tells terrible jokes.' She threw one of his pillows at him.

'Can't say I know anyone like that.' He abandoned his sandwich and returned the pillow with force.

'Hey!' she cried as it knocked her sideways. 'You'll pay for that.' She picked up another one and swung it at him.

A pillow fight got underway with full gusto, the blows a substitute for the kisses they longed to give each other.

'I know I'm the last person you want to hear from,' Sam said. She didn't answer right away and he could hear her breathing on the other end of the line.

'I wouldn't be calling if it wasn't important.'

Still nothing.

'It's about Levi.' He needed her to say something, anything. 'He's gone missing.'

'What do you mean he's gone missing?'

Sam sighed with relief. For a moment there, he'd worried she might hang up.

'He left for school early this morning but the school says he never turned up and he's not come home. He's reportedly heading to Sydney to find you.'

'Me? Whatever for?' She sounded shocked.

'That's something you'll have to ask him when he gets there. I'd say it's probably got something to do with the mess Levi and Maddie have made.'

'You're kidding me.' He couldn't tell if she believed him or not. 'What is he thinking?'

'I have no idea. That'll be the first question I ask him once I know he's safe.' At least they were talking. So far so good.

'You've tried to call him, right?'

'Of course.' If one more person asked Sam if he'd tried to call or text his son, he'd scream. 'He has his phone turned off or he's lost it or it's run out of batteries. Either way, he's not answering.'

'How will he know where to find me?'

'I don't know. I figure he knows where you work and he'll make his way there. The police are requesting the security camera footage and passenger manifest from yesterday to see if he was on the flight. No one remembers seeing him, which is worrying.' Sam could not keep the concern out of his voice. The fear he worked harder at controlling. He didn't want anyone to know how scared he was that Levi might have gotten a lift to the coast with a stranger, that he didn't get on a plane at all. Every passing second scoured his soul as one more missed opportunity to find Levi.

'If his phone is turned off then there is a good chance he got on a flight. Does he have any money?'

Sam blinked at the question. He didn't know the answer. 'I presume so.'

'He would have gotten an afternoon flight from Long-reach to Brisbane …' He could hear her tapping on a keyboard in the background, no doubt looking up the flight information. 'Then he'd have to change planes to Sydney.'

'Yep.' He waited for her to work the route through. He already knew it off by heart. If his son didn't stay overnight in Brisbane, and let's face it which hotel would put a fifteen-year-old boy up without his parents' permission, then he must have gotten on a night flight for Sydney.

'Which means he could have arrived last night and spent a night sleeping rough.'

She had to go and say it, put words to the very fear that held a dagger to his heart.

'Thanks for making me feel better about this.'

'You're welcome,' she said, her tone dripping with honey-eyed sarcasm. 'What's the plan?'

He blew out a breath, all out of fresh ideas. 'I don't know. I guess I catch a flight to Sydney and try to find him.'

'And what do I do?' she asked.

'Wait for him, I guess. He'll turn up sooner or later.' He wanted to keep her talking on the phone. He missed her voice and the smart sassy way she talked. He missed the sharpness of her thinking and the way she had of being one step ahead of him all the time. He missed her.

'What else can I do?' she asked.

Her words took him by surprise. He thought she'd hang up and the next time he'd hear from her was to tell him Levi had arrived. The fact she wanted to do more did funny things to his heart. 'I'm not sure there is anything else you can do.'

'If you think of anything …'

'I'll text you what time I'm due in Sydney in case Levi does turn up.' He could imagine her sitting at her desk in some flash office wondering how she ever managed to get caught up with a bunch of country bumpkins. 'I know it's probably

not the right time to say this but I am truly and deeply sorry you got caught up in Levi and Maddie's scheme. They really did have everyone's best interests at heart, although it might not feel that way.'

'Let's focus on finding Levi,' she said. 'He's our main priority.'

He liked the word *our*. Hearing it from her lips filled him with hope, even while his fear grew and spread through his body like some dark disease of the soul. 'I'll let you know if I hear anything from him, okay?'

'Okay.' He swallowed the lump forming in his throat. He wished Michelle was here. None of this would be happening if she'd lived. He wished he was with Sarah and none of this stupid internet stuff had ever happened. Neither of those two wishes would ever come true.

He had to man up and face the prospect of Sarah being lost to him forever. He could understand why she might not want to be with him after all that had happened. What was incomprehensible to him was the prospect of never seeing his son again. Nausea rippled through him. He had to get to Sydney and find his boy.

CHAPTER TWENTY-SEVEN

Sarah turned off her laptop and grabbed her handbag.

'I'm heading out,' she said to the receptionist. 'Can you call me if a boy called Levi turns up looking for me?'

None of her other work colleagues paid her the slightest mind as she almost ran to the elevator. She punched the button far too many times, aware the repeated action didn't make the lift come faster, but enjoying the release of tension button pushing gave her.

It seemed to take her train ages to get to Sydney Airport. She had a novel stuffed in the bottom of her oversized handbag, which proved to be a useless distraction in the face of her building anxiety for Levi.

He was terribly young. Yes, he was tall for his age and had a certain self-possession. As far as she knew, he'd never been to Sydney before, let alone navigated its network of public transport and bustling urban natives. She contemplated

all the terrible things that could happen to a young boy all alone and clueless in the big city. It was not a pleasant journey.

Finally, the train pulled into the airport station and Sarah flew off it in search of the arrivals terminal. Pushing her way through crowds of travellers and business commuters, she found a café where everyone seemed to merge together before spitting out to baggage claim and exit gates. She took a seat and ordered a coffee. Not that she needed the caffeine when her blood buzzed with adrenaline. A wine was out of the question right now. She needed her wits about her.

Her eyes scanned the people as they came and went. Under ordinary circumstances, people watching would be fun. Today, she worried she might miss him in the crowd, the whole affair feeling like a giant reality *Where's Wally*.

As she sipped her coffee she let her thoughts wander to Sam. Hearing his voice had felt good. She realised she missed him underneath all that anger and pain. He'd said Levi and Maddie had set up the dating profile with good intentions. Some kind of catfish they turned out to be. She could imagine them scheming together. Maddie taking the lead, of course. Levi probably didn't have much say in the matter. She allowed herself a little smile at the thought.

The big question was why did they do it? Obviously they wanted Sam to find a partner. Surely there were easier ways to do that. Ways that didn't unravel in spectacular fashion.

She wanted to stay angry at Sam. He might have been a victim of Maddie and Levi's scheming as much as she was, but there was still the issue of Kylie. Seeing them kiss had made her feel rejected and angry. And worse, the sense she'd

been conned, taken for a fool. Sarah had fuelled herself on a steady flow of anger, white-hot justified anger. Even now she knew the truth, she didn't know how to back down and accept Sam's apology.

Bet Sam had a mess to clean up at home. Everyone would be talking about it. Everyone heard the argument, after all. If they hadn't caught the argument between Kylie and Sam then they would have caught the second act with Sarah and Sam. Either way, Sam got to be the star of the show.

Two and a half hours into her wait, Sarah ordered a toasted cheese and ham sandwich to keep her occupied. She'd love a magazine to read but the whole point of her being there was to watch the arrivals concourse for a sign of Levi. As she munched on her snack she thought about everything that had happened. Nothing new there. She'd done this every day since the Isisford Races, taking a little piece of the puzzle and examining it in an effort to get the situation to make sense. Now, she looked at things in a different way, through the lens of a teenage boy desperate to find a partner for his lonely father.

Maddie must know what was happening with Levi. Those two were as thick as thieves. He wouldn't run off without telling her the plan. She had to know where he was going and how he intended to get there.

She picked up her phone and typed a quick text.

Hello Maddie! Sarah Lewis here. We're looking for Levi. His dad is sick with worry. I'm staking out Sydney airport arrivals terminal in the hope he's coming in by plane. Tell me everything you know, and don't leave a single thing out.

She waited, checking her phone every ten seconds to see if Maddie had responded. Sam would be on his connecting

flight to Sydney by now. Regardless of how quickly he'd responded, he was still at least an hour away.

She'd already been at the airport for hours herself. Her bottom was numb from sitting so long.

Sarah scanned the crowd back and forth like an automaton, searching for a fifteen-year-old boy on the run. How did he book the tickets? He must have done it online with someone's credit card. Maybe Sam's, might be someone else's. She wondered if Sam had checked with his bank.

Her phone pinged with an incoming message. Finally.

Hi Sarah! Levi is on a plane to Sydney. He bought a ticket with his savings. He's going to go to your work to find you. You might see him first at the airport. Love, Maddie xx

Sarah read the message with mixed feelings. All the people surging past her only served to remind her how easily a young boy could become lost, disappear never to be seen again. She pushed her rising tension down and dialled the office to see if Levi had slipped through and turned up there.

She checked her watch. 'Come on, Levi, where are you?' she muttered as she waited for someone at *Seriously Sydney* to pick up the phone.

Then she caught a glimpse of a familiar face in the crowd, walking down the concourse towards her. Her heart pounded with the surge of adrenaline that had her up out of her seat waving like a maniac, her telephone call forgotten.

'Does that sound okay?' Maddie let Levi read the message before she sent it to Sarah. They had to let the adults believe Levi really had done a runner to Sydney if they had any chance of getting Mr C face-to-face with Sarah.

'Sounds good,' said Levi through a mouthful of potato chips as he played a game on his iPad. 'What time did your mum say Dad was getting to Sydney?'

'He should be landing shortly,' said Maddie, preoccupied with her text to Sarah.

'Unless he missed his connecting flight to Sydney.'

'I'm not worried.' Although neither of them had ever flown in a plane before, Maddie had faith in the online flight schedules. Those people knew what they were doing. 'Do you think we should send your dad a text to let him know you're okay? He'll be worried sick. He *was* worried sick when he left here and that can only have got worse.'

Levi shrugged. 'Sure, why not. Can't hurt.' He didn't take his eyes off the screen.

'Do you want me to do it for you?' Her fingers itched to pick up the phone and text Mr C. She couldn't sit here and do nothing when all this drama was being played out a thousand miles away.

'If you want to.' He shot her a brilliant smile before disappearing back into his game again.

She sighed and reached for his phone.

Hi Dad. I wanted you to know that I'm in Sydney and I'm okay. I'm going to find Sarah and apologise for everything. She wasn't at her work but I've got her address and I'm heading there. Love, Levi. PS Don't try and call, I'm nearly out of battery.

'Hey, I never said I'd apologise,' said Levi when she read the text out to him. 'I'm not sure about that bit.'

'Sounds convincing to me,' said Maddie, 'and it will ease your dad's mind. If he knows you're definitely looking

for Sarah then he'll go to Sarah too. Genius. Once they're together they'll remember why they love each other.'

'Because they do,' said Levi.

'Yes,' agreed Maddie, 'they do.'

She pressed send and picked up the packet of potato chips. 'Hey, you've eaten them all.'

He leaned over and kissed her, his lips all salty, and she forgot she had ever been hungry.

Sam's head pounded. The plane hadn't flown fast enough for him. He walked quickly along the concourse looking for the exit. People surged around him, too many people. Everything pushed in on him, the noise, the activity, the fact he had no idea where Levi could be.

Suddenly someone stepped in front of him, stopping him dead. Thoughts of his son raged like a storm in his head, forcing him to blink as he tried to refocus.

'Hello,' he said as the tempest cleared and the sun came out.

'Hello,' said Sarah shyly.

The airport bustle around them disappeared to leave the two of them, as if they'd been caught in a time bubble, suspended from the rest of reality.

Sam wanted to take her in his arms and never let go. An awkward barrier of unspoken words prevented him from doing so. Instead, he stood perfectly still and hoped for a miracle.

Sarah hesitated for a second before throwing her arms around him. The pressure of her body against his, the gardenia scent of her and the warmth of her arms around his neck released something in him, as if he'd been holding his

breath this whole time. He sagged against her and she tightened her hug.

'It's going to be okay,' she said softly. 'We'll find Levi.'

He nodded, mute with suppressed tears. In that moment, Sam realised how alone he'd felt. Now Sarah was here, that loneliness faded away. They would weather this together even if they parted afterwards. He had her now and that was all that mattered.

She pushed away, holding his shoulders and searching his face.

'You want a stiff drink?'

He cracked a smile. 'Might help,' he said.

'Come on.' She took him by the hand and led him to a nearby bar.

Depositing him at a table, she organised two whiskies and returned carrying the liquid amber as carefully as if it were gold.

'Here you go.' She deposited a glass in front of him. 'How are you holding up?' Sarah sat opposite him and he sighed, suddenly tired.

He scrubbed at his face with both hands. 'I have no bloody idea,' he said. 'A part of me thinks everything will work out and the other part of me is imagining all sorts of horror.'

She nodded, taking a sip of her drink and pulling a face as the whisky hit the back of her throat.

'Same here,' she said at last. 'I figure Levi is a smart kid. He's shown us he's clever. We need to have faith in that. On the other hand, he's not street smart.'

'Not by a country mile.' Sam put up a mental barrier against all the images of the terrible things that could happen to his son. Panicking wouldn't help.

'Kind of puts things in perspective, though.' Sarah's long fingers turned her glass around in a slow circle, her eyes fixed on the tawney liquid within.

He thought he knew what she meant. The gravity of the situation made the recent past look like a picnic. Funny how Levi had managed to get himself at the centre of both events. 'I guess you're talking about the dating profile?'

She nodded. 'I guess I am. Look, Sam,' she placed her hand on his arm, 'I'm sorry I went off like that. I got triggered and I felt vulnerable and, well …'

'No one likes feeling like that,' he finished for her. 'I get it. I didn't feel real great myself. Those kids did a number on us.'

She laughed. 'I'll say they did. Have you heard from Levi?'

'Not yet.' His worry gnawed at him, creating a hollow feeling in the pit of his stomach. All the terrible possibilities crowded on the edge of his mind and it took all his strength to keep them at bay as his phone vibrated in his pocket. Taking it out, he read the text that had arrived. Relief swamped him, making his knees weak. Levi was safe and sound. He read the message aloud.

'You're kidding,' Sarah said. 'How did he get my address? Doesn't matter. Let's head there and wait.'

He sent a quick text back saying he was in Sydney too and would meet Levi at Sarah's. While he wouldn't be at ease until he had Levi with him, he sank into the sweetness of knowing he got to spend time with Sarah while they waited.

He followed her through the airport, amazed at how easily she negotiated the people and the landscape. You could turn him around twice and he'd be lost.

The train came as a surprise. He couldn't remember the last time he'd been on one. Sometime back in high school

when they'd gone on a camp to the coast. They'd ridden an old steam train in Gympie. Not quite the same thing as the sleek, modern electric version he rode in now.

They hadn't spoken on the train. What could they possibly say in front of all these people when everything he wanted to talk about was for her ears only. He'd been content to simply sit next to her, to feel the warmth of her body next to his, as the train gently rocked them closer to the city. He sensed the words he needed to say circling him, waiting for an opportunity to emerge from his lips. They'd walked from the train station to her flat talking about inconsequential things like the ridiculous cost of Sydney property and which local cafés did the best coffee.

As she walked, Sarah flipped her hair, glorious in the spring sunshine. She moved with ease, at home in this urban environment so alien to him. He could see what she meant about parking when she had complained about living in Sydney. Too many cars. Too many people.

He listened to her talk, enjoying the sound of her voice, something he hadn't thought he'd ever hear again. He could listen to her read the telephone book every day for the rest of his life.

And that was the problem.

Sam wanted more. He wanted Sarah in his life. Not part time with flying visits here and there, but on a full-time, live-in basis. How the hell he was going to achieve that was beyond him right now. He couldn't come out and say what he wanted. Too much, too soon. Especially after what she saw as a betrayal, and it was, although not by him. Didn't seem to matter. Her hurt and pain had spread over to him and he had to take some responsibility for it.

'Here we are.' She indicated a red-brick apartment block, unforgivingly square and squat in appearance. 'It's not the Taj Mahal, but it's home.'

Sam followed her upstairs to her apartment. She unlocked the door and ushered him inside.

The space appeared much smaller than how he'd visualised it. He'd seen her in a glass and steel edifice with views of the Harbour Bridge. She lived in a shoebox instead. Somehow, that fact was a relief.

'Make yourself at home,' she said as she stepped into the kitchen. 'Would you like a cup of tea? We have every sort of tea available to mankind.'

'A regular tea would be fine, thank you.' He sat on a purple overstuffed couch, sinking into the cushions immediately. Luckily he had no plan to go anywhere soon. It would take him fifteen minutes to find his way out of the couch.

He contemplated the room. Modern prints on the walls alongside posters for long-passed rock concerts. Mismatched cushions surrounded him, effectively corralling him. The kitchen and dining room were through an arch, so close he figured he could lean over and touch the kitchen table if he wanted to.

Sarah placed two cups on the coffee table and sat next to Sam. He felt the couch sag a little with her weight.

'So,' she said.

'So,' he echoed. This was the time. Right now. He had to say what he'd wanted to say since the day at the races. The silence in the room hung heavily. The tension mounted. Something had to give.

'I really am sorry,' he said at last.

'Please don't say that. You've said it enough.'

Okay, not off to a great start. Not that he'd expected the conversation to be easy or even friendly. Now he was here in the moment things seemed more challenging than he'd accounted for.

'I don't know what else to say,' he said, putting his truth out there. 'I'm sorry you're hurt. I'm sorry you got caught up in Levi and Maddie's machinations. I'm not sorry I met you. I'm not sorry we were together. And I'm not sorry I fell in love with you.'

Sarah gave a little gasp and sat up straighter. 'What did you say?'

'The bit about how sorry I am?'

'No, the other bit.'

'The bit when I say I'm not sorry.'

'That's the one.'

He chuckled, knowing exactly the bit she meant. 'I'm not sorry I fell in love with you. And I'm not, Sarah Lewis. Not one bit.'

She held his gaze, looking at him for the longest time as if trying to outstare him. He'd never been good at that game as a kid. He'd always been first to blink.

'Do you really?' she asked, a stillness about her like a deer deciding whether to run or not.

'Yes, I do.' He said the words with such certainty, surely she couldn't fail to believe him.

She nodded as if assessing his claim, calculating the balance sheet and seeing if he was worth the investment.

Now what? He ought to say something, anything. He was losing her, he could *feel* it. This whole situation was proving too much for him. Between Levi and Sarah, the two people he loved most in the world, the possibility of loss hung over

him like a looming tsunami. He wanted to run, driven by a primitive need for self-preservation. He wanted to hide from the potential pain. Right now, nothing had been decided. His fate hung in the balance and he could do nothing to prevent catastrophe from coming his way.

His phone vibrated with a new message. Levi.

He felt around for his back pocket with as much dignity as he could muster, trying to keep his desperation to a minimum.

Sam read the message once, twice, three times. He could not believe his eyes. 'What. The. Fuck.'

Sarah grabbed the phone out of Sam's hands.

Surprise! I'm not in Sydney. I'm in Longreach. I never left. Happy reunion.

Love, Levi xxx

She read the message, her disbelief interfering with her ability to process the text. 'Is he serious?'

'As a heart attack.' Sam slumped further into the couch.

'Are you okay?'

'I don't know. Part of me wants to kill him and the other part is overwhelmed with relief. I think there might be a few other parts unaccounted for yet.'

'He's safe and sound which is a good thing.'

'For now,' Sam growled. 'Wait until I get home.'

'Okay, tiger.' She laid one hand on his sleeve. 'Take it easy. Plenty of time to skin him alive.' As he struggled to sit up, her hand slipped down his arm. Her fingers encountered the hard, corded muscle of his forearm and she froze. Her

eyes widened and she willed her hand to remove itself. It refused.

Sam's bluer-than-blue eyes found hers. She'd always been a sucker for that stare, diving right in without a care for her own heart. This time was different. She knew he loved her. He'd said so twice. They teetered on the cusp of something wonderful. All she had to do was tell him she loved him too. Forgive him all the pain and confusion, and comfort him for his.

Her heart beat in time with the clock on the kitchen wall as the seconds crawled past. He said nothing, simply looked into her soul and waited.

Her move to make.

If she moved forward she would begin a new life she had no reference for. A farmer's wife living deep in the country on the edge of the outback. Or she could remove her hand, say nothing and remain here, looking for a job to fulfil her and living in a city which suffocated her. What would it be?

As she hovered over her decision, unwilling to expose herself yet, Sam made as if to stand up. Had he had enough? Withdrawn his affections? Where was he going? She looked at him questioningly, her eyebrows raised, silently willing him to stay.

He turned, inching closer as he cupped the back of her head with one calloused hand, slipping the other around her waist and pulling her closer to him until his lips met hers. Warm, soft and insistent; she gave way to his kisses, offering no resistance to the very thing she'd wanted since she'd first seen him at the airport.

She melded against his chest, revelling in his hard, familiar contours. Even though her bruised heart hadn't healed, she belonged here in his arms.

'I should have stayed,' she said. She snuggled into him, resting her head on his shoulder.

'Might have been easier if you had,' he chuckled.

'I had fallen for you so hard and then to discover I'd been tricked …' she sighed, 'I guess I got scared. I was so mad, letting myself be exposed like that. I wanted to get as far away from my embarrassment as possible.'

'You don't have to explain anything to me,' he said as he gently tucked a strand of hair behind her ear with a tender gesture. 'I had all the same feelings on the other side of the fence. I was set up and no one likes to be duped. Left me feeling like a whole lot of stuff had gone on behind my back and I only had half the story. I was worried you were falling in love with Lonely in Longreach instead of me.'

Sarah took his face in her hands and kissed him as if her life depended upon it. Because it did. While the two of them had been duped by the kids, they might never have found each other without them. And the thought of life without Sam in it was intolerable.

She had to choose and she chose him.

'Do you think I should let Levi know I'll be coming home on the next possible flight?' he asked her, his face flushed in the early evening light.

'Tell him tomorrow,' she said, her voice husky with desire. 'Tell him we'll both be home to kick his arse.'

He laid his forehead against hers and chuckled. 'Let him wait. Let him wonder if his plan worked.'

'Did it work?' She knew the answer as she moved her hips closer to his, lust burning her to the core. She needed him now.

'I like to think so,' he said, pulling her onto his lap where she could feel the full extent of his certainty. 'I knew that night on the Thomson River that you were the one I'd been waiting for. And you?' He cupped her cheek with his palm and she nuzzled his hand like a kitten.

'I knew you were the one the day I saw your profile picture,' she said. 'You might have at least known the first time you saw me.' She pretended outrage when the only thing raging out of control was the heat between her thighs.

'You know, I think I did. The first night at the pub, I got such a charge out of you. I don't think I understood what it was until later, but it was there the whole time.' His eyes had darkened to a shade of blue she had no name for.

'I guess I need to show you all the emails you sent me,' she said. 'That way you can fill in any blanks. I'm sure there's a few.'

'I've read them. I made Maddie show me. For the record, my dirt-bike riding days are way behind me. And I really, truly do not like kale.'

'But you do like Italian food.' She gave him a nudge. 'And Kevin the Kelpie was real.'

'I miss that dog,' Sam sighed.

He stood suddenly, swinging her up into his arms. 'Enough small talk. Where's the bedroom?'

She laughed as he hitched her higher and strode towards the nearest room without waiting for direction.

'No, not that one,' she cried. 'The other one.'

He deposited her on the bed and joined her, brushing the hair from her eyes with a gentle gesture that made her stomach flip.

'You never told me your profile name,' he said.

'I'm Solitary in Sydney,' she said as her fingers found the buttons on his shirt.

'Not anymore, you're not,' he growled, pulling her towards him.

Notes for 'Finding Love in the Outback'
Footnote
The Sam and Sarah story.

My story didn't end the way I thought it would. It surprised me in the way stories sometimes do.

Levi ran away from home. He said he was coming to Sydney to find me and apologise. Really, he planned to lure his dad to Sydney to be with me. Another cunning and elaborate teenage plan based, apparently, on *Sleepless in Seattle*. The kids thought they could make the plotline work twenty-first century style.

Clever children.

Levi's plan worked. Sam and I are together and I am moving to Longreach. I'm planning on writing that novel I always said I would write. If not now, when, right? My friends at the local radio station have invited me to have my own talkback show which I'm excited about. Getting to know the com-

munity in this way has made me feel like I belong in this wild place on the edge of the outback.

We've bought a kelpie puppy. His name is Dave. I've never had a dog before and I already love him to bits.

Have I changed my mind about online dating? Yes and no. Yes, it clearly has positive outcomes for some people. And no, there remain pitfalls, both emotional and physical. Predators lurk about online, but so do the good guys.

I found one. Maybe you will too.

ACKNOWLEDGMENTS

Writing a book is an all-consuming occupation that makes me a little eccentric. To my friends and family who have weathered my wide-eyed distraction as I've emerged from my writing cave, blinking, into the real world, thank you for your patience.

To my son, Xavier, thank you for putting up with having to share a computer. We must fix that. Heartfelt thanks to my wonderful husband, Guy, who can spend hours listening to me prattle on about a plot line, is a dab hand at grammar and often comes up with an idea or two that makes the story richer.

Special thanks to Rebekka Napper, my doppelganger sister-in-arms, who always comes through.

A big thank you to the crew of the Old Corner Shop who provide the best coffee on the peninsula, without which I would procrastinate my day away.

Thank you to my cousin, Vicky, for sharing stories of Longreach and reminding me about the flies.

Thank you to the handful of people who shared their online dating stories with me. All identities are kept private to protect the innocent. You know who you are.

A big, heartfelt thank you to Alli Sinclair, one of the sweetest, most generous authors I've met on my writing journey. A happenstance conversation turned this story around in a different direction to the one I had originally mapped for it, and the story turned out all the better for it.

Thank you to Johanna Baker and the Escape crew for their impeccable taste in everything and being so damn easy to work with. And thank you to Sarana Behan, for helping me navigate the rocky shoals of publicity and marketing.

To the people of Longreach, who have created a warm, generous and welcoming community on the edge of the outback. I apologise for any parts of my story which may not hold true to Longreach, the town. Some things I've altered to fit the story the better. For example, there is no such place as the Longreach Royal Arms Hotel. Rather than try and pick one of the many hotels in Longreach and risk the possibility of offending someone, I decided to make up one of my own. The Royal Arms is an amalgamation of several different pubs.

The dating website Outback Singles is entirely fictional.

The magazine, Seriously Sydney, is a figment of my imagination.

For more information about Longreach and the surrounding country please go to: www.outbackqueensland.com.au

COMING SOON

Don't miss …

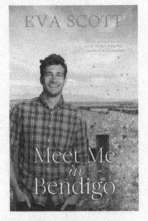

Meet Me
in
Bendigo

by

EVA SCOTT

Available August 2021